THE DRIVER'S WIFE

Also by S.K. Keogh

The Prodigal
The Alliance
The Fortune

The Driver's Wife

A Novel

By
S.K. Keogh

The Driver's Wife
S.K. Keogh

Copyright 2018 S.K. Keogh
Leighlin House Publishing

ISBN: 978-0-9906774-8-2 (Paperback)
ISBN: 978-0-9906774-9-9 (e-book)

Connect with S.K. Keogh at

www.skkeogh.com
www.facebook.com/S.K.Keogh
www.twitter.com/JackMallory

This book is also available in paperback at most online
retailers.

Cover design by Jennifer Quinlan, Historical Fiction
Book Covers

"One sees unbelievable graces which penetrate the evil soul, and even the depraved soul. Even that, which seemed to be lost, is saved."

---- Charles Péguy

PART I:

Unus

CHAPTER 1

Charles Town, Carolina
1693

Ketch had endured a great many things in his thirty-odd years, and those sufferings he could bear again if he had to, but a woman's tears he could never endure.

He suspected that the two slave women before him in the bustling Charles Town street were mother and daughter, which made the tears on their cheeks even more poignant. The daughter, perhaps eighteen years of age, had caught his eye first, for her skin tone was lighter than that of the eleven other female Africans in the group, including her mother. Yet the rest of her features reflected the older woman to whom she stayed close, apparently attempting to soothe her parent with quiet words.

Ketch knew the power of his own gaze—over the years he had perfected to great effect a wide range of influence from malevolence to unreadable vacuity—so he was not surprised when the mulatto girl looked his way, as if wanting to locate the source of the weighty attention. The moment their eyes met, she turned away, but whether from alarm or simply from a practice of not directly meeting a white man's gaze, Ketch was unsure. Whatever the cause, she never looked his way again and stepped even closer to her mother, a hand upon the woman's arm, the Carolina sun beating down upon her colorful headscarf. Neither did she acknowledge the sharp scrutiny of Hiram Willis, her new overseer, as he moved among the slaves, eying them and poking and prodding for any physical weakness that would keep them from field work.

Although Ketch stood in the shade of an awning in front of Malachi Waterston's brokerage, the harsh, humid heat found him. Beneath his rumpled shirt, perspiration trickled down the furrow of his backbone to further dampen the waistband of his breeches. His brown hair hung limp and damp to his shoulders. His beard—cultivated to hide pockmarks—itched as much as the cursed stump of his amputated right arm.

The brokerage door opened, and the slaves' current overseer emerged with Waterston's young apprentice. Neither paid Ketch any heed, instead stepping into the street where the overseer unchained the mulatto's mother from the others. The older woman clutched her daughter's hands as if to deny the inevitable but said nothing, all her words instead crowding her eyes. The girl's grasp did not appear to have the same strength. She would know that to resist would only lead to punishment and further sorrow. When the overseer growled a curse and lifted his hand to strike the mother, the girl gave her a helpful shove beyond his range. There was no wailing, no great display as the two were separated; it was as if once their physical bond had been broken, they both allowed themselves to succumb to the hopelessness of the situation. As the apprentice led the older woman away down the busy street, she continued to look over her shoulder, but the daughter lowered her eyes, the last of her tears falling into the dust.

Willis's order broke through Ketch's reverie: "Look alive there, Ketch; let's get 'em aboard the *Nymph*."

***

As sometimes happened when Ketch left Charles Town's large harbor and the adjoining Atlantic Ocean behind, he felt a twinge of desire for his former life as a sailor. Serving as a pirate under James Logan for two years had brought him to the pinnacle of wickedness, and though he did not mourn the absence of those past practices, he did miss the sea and the freedom and security it had offered him then and during his previous years in the Royal Navy. Once Logan had followed his beloved wife, Ella, in death, Ketch had no alternative but to forsake the sea to live at Leighlin Plantation, to uphold a promise made long ago to Ella Logan that he would always see to the safety of her daughter, Helen.

The tubby *Nymph* left the harbor and entered the mouth of the broad, marsh-bordered Ashley River. The rivers of the region, large and small, were the highways to the interior plantations, for no roads had been carved through the thick wilderness. Ketch wondered if such things would exist in his lifetime.

Ketch isolated himself near the *Nymph*'s bowsprit. Behind him the four slaves who made up the crew went about their duties, quick to obey commands from Jean Latiffe, the Frenchman who was the *Nymph*'s master. Latiffe and Willis gossiped aft beneath an awning rigged for protection against the merciless sun. Ketch, never a conversationalist, kept his attention on the sails or the tortuous river ahead, but he found himself also observing the mulatto girl.

The slave women had been herded into the waist where they now sat in an anxious knot. After the *Nymph* had gotten underway, they had moved away from the mulatto, as far as their chains allowed. Ketch wondered why the others ignored her. And why had they inched away? Did she have some concealed disease? He had no understanding of the Mende the slaves spoke, but their furtive eyes revealed that they sometimes discussed the girl. She appeared to know she was the subject, though he wondered if she spoke their language—Ketch knew the various regions of Africa had different dialects. Whether she comprehended or not, she shrank ever so slightly within herself.

After a time, Willis called forward to Ketch, "Unchain 'em now. This sun'll make them irons powerful hot. Our young master would be vexed if we delivered damaged goods, eh?"

Ketch moved among the slaves, freeing them of their weighty burdens. He came to the mulatto last, and she held out her hands and pushed forth her bare feet from beneath her worn gray dress; perhaps the fabric had once been a different color but the elements and time had faded it. Accustomed to paying little heed to slaves other than those under his direct authority, Ketch had not bothered to look any of these in the face, but when he crouched to unbind the girl's ankles, he felt her eyes upon him. When he glanced up, she quickly looked away from the burn scar on his left cheek. Then her attention bounced from the manacle scar on his wrist to the small gray scars at the base of his neck left by a Spaniard's heretic fork. Shifting her weight, she stared at the deck as if afraid he would be angry with her visual exploration.

She murmured, "Thank you, sir."

It surprised him to hear her speak. A soft voice. Up close, her pale brown eyes were intriguing and unique, bearing a hint of mossy green. He wished she would look up again. She rubbed her wrists. Small-boned she was, too delicate to be a field hand. And from whom did she get her lighter skin tone? A previous master of her mother perhaps?

Ketch stood, disturbed by his unexpected curiosity. True, duties in his past had required close observation of others, but those subjects had all been men. He was not by practice an observer of women. In fact, he went out of his way to avoid them. The sea had been a convenient, safe

11

place; being on land was dangerous.

For the rest of the four-hour journey, he tried to avoid watching the mulatto, but several times his attention wandered back. Still the other women said nothing to her. Ketch knew what that social wall was like.

The hottest part of the day bore down upon the *Nymph*. Hours of boredom as the ketch-rigged vessel labored upstream on the rising tide, her crew attentive to trimming sail whenever the river changed direction, which was often. Ketch tried not to watch Latiffe's boatmen or think of how his nautical skills had been rendered useless with the loss of his arm. Without the damn arm, he was worth less than a slave, truth be told.

Finally, a sharp left-hand bend of the Ashley ahead indicated their nearness to Leighlin's landing. They had been abreast Leighlin land these past several minutes. The south rice field lay to the left, separated from the brackish river by a long earthen dyke, some four feet high. Just yesterday the sprout flow had been drained from the field into the river through trunk gates in the dyke, gates that were now hidden from view by the rising tide. The pale green of early plant growth—pips—could just barely be seen from this distance. Since this was late Saturday, no slaves were in the field, for their master required them to work only in the forenoon on Saturdays and not at all on the Sabbath.

Around the bend they sailed, and now the breeze was too far forward for the sails to draw, so the crew lowered them. The *Nymph* rode the tide for the landing dead ahead where the river again changed direction, this time back to the north, away a few narrowing miles more to its origin in the Black Swamp.

"Here he comes," Willis said in a rueful tone.

Ketch looked beyond the landing, past a bordering row of birch trees, further beyond a matching pair of man-made ornamental ponds then up manicured grass terraces to see Jack Mallory striding downward along a well-worn path. His young wife, Maria, was with him, trailed by his seven-year-old half-sister, Helen. Behind them rose the low bluff upon which Leighlin House sat, there beyond the broad front greensward and flanking gardens.

Leighlin House had been nearly demolished by a fire a year ago, but months of hard labor by the plantation's Negro workforce and small white population, as well as slaves charitably loaned by other plantations, had brought the Georgian-Palladian manor back to its original glory. Well, Ketch considered in his usual critical way, not completely. True enough, the three-story brick structure was just as grand on the outside as the original, but the inside was a different matter. The rich furnishings, rugs, and paintings had not been—nay, could not be—replaced with the same level of value, not with so much capital put into the rebuilding process. Leighlin's current master, while not as enterprising as his stepfather had been, tried to maintain an illusion of palatial grandeur out of respect for his dead mother and his very-much-alive half-sister. Ketch would give Jack Mallory that much credit at least.

When the sails had been furled, the new slaves got to their feet. They clustered about the mainmast and stared at the distant stateliness of Leighlin House, the reddish roof shining in the sun, the windows sparkling, the front portico's white colonnade dazzling. They talked to each other in hushed tones, pointing at various things, including another rice field to the north, alongside the river. The mulatto girl's eyes were large with wonder, but she said nothing. Leighlin would be a startling contrast to Tom Clark's woebegone plantation whence she had come.

The Mallorys passed through the birches, Maria's hand light upon her husband's arm. Jack Mallory was dressed formally to meet his new charges, something unusual for the twenty-two-year-old Englishman; he was more commonly seen about the plantation in workaday breeches, loose shirt, and perhaps a jerkin. His white cravat accentuated his complexion, a darkness that came naturally, not just from the brutal Carolina summer sun. His hair was even darker, almost as black as his wife's, and his eyes to match. A striking youth with high cheekbones and well-defined nose and mouth. Ketch did not begrudge his master's good looks; Jack Mallory was Ella Logan's firstborn and for any offspring of hers to be anything less than remarkable would be impossible.

Maria, three years younger than her husband, was certainly no less attractive than her mate. Her father's Spanish blood as well as perhaps her mother's French heritage had bestowed upon Maria a dusky, almost olive hue, unseen among the Englishwomen of the region, giving her a somewhat exotic look, a characteristic that some of Charles Town's higher-bred gentlemen found unappealing. Her small, fine-boned frame belied her inner strength.

As the Mallorys stepped onto the dock, Maria spoke close to her husband's ear and came away smiling, as did he. They had been exceedingly happy these past weeks since discovering she was with child. Ella Logan's first grandchild.

"Ahoy, Mr. Ketch!" Helen cried as the *Nymph* arrived at the dock.

Grinning, she waved as if he had been gone a year.

Ketch returned the wave with a brief, self-conscious smile. Never in his adult life had anyone but Helen showed joy at seeing him. He did not deserve the child's love, so it was often painful to accept her affections, especially in front of those who knew it was he who had killed her father.

Once the *Nymph* had been secured, Willis stepped down to the dock to report to Mallory. Ketch paid no attention to what was said. Willis lacked any deep love for his master, but the overseer was a man of duty—the Royal Navy had instilled that attribute—so he did what he was told. He was not shy, however, about voicing displeasure to his mates over what he considered the new master's faults and shortcomings compared to his predecessor.

As Ketch shepherded the slaves ashore, the women took in the land and their new master, perhaps shocked by his youthfulness and his wife's dark skin. Once the women stood upon the dock, huddled together, Mallory stepped closer and offered them a reassuring smile.

"Do you understand English?"

Most of the women nodded.

He introduced himself as Captain John Logan, a name all but a select few people knew him by, a name adopted after his stepfather's death to conceal Jack's true identity and piratical past. James Logan had been known in the region only as a planter, his nautical persona also concealed.

"I am the master of Leighlin Plantation. And this is your new mistress, Mrs. Maria Logan."

The slaves offered shallow curtseys.

"And I'm John's sister," Helen piped with her irresistible smile from next to Maria, who restrained her from jumping forward in her enthusiasm. The child's friendliness seemed to ease some of the women's tension. Ketch wondered if Mallory had brought Helen down here for the very purpose of distracting the women from their fears.

Maria took a step forward and spoke with her slight Spanish accent, "Have any of you experience as a house servant?"

No one responded. The mulatto glanced to either side then stared down. Some of the women exchanged glances until one spoke up, "Isabelle do."

The mulatto's head snapped up, and she gaped at the smirking young woman who had spoken.

Maria seemed to consider the undertones. "And which of you is Isabelle?"

The mulatto hesitated then curtseyed again. "I am, ma'am."

Patiently, Maria asked, "Why didn't you speak up directly?"

Isabelle gave the slave next to her a glare. "Because it's not true."

The other slave scowled. "Is too!"

Ketch detected a tiny tremble upon Isabelle's chin. Perhaps Maria saw that anxiety, too, for she refrained from pointing out the fact that someone was lying.

"Perhaps you just didn't like housework, Isabelle?"

"I was a field hand, ma'am."

Maria glanced pointedly at her husband, who allowed the argument to drop by asking Willis, "Did they have something to eat on the journey?"

Now Willis's broad, bewhiskered face colored, and he stammered and stuttered the start of excuses. Mallory's brow lowered, and Ketch suspected an oath lay upon his tongue, but he chose to refrain from verbally thrashing his overseer in front of the slaves. Instead, he turned back to the newcomers.

"These gentlemen will take you to the kitchen house for something to eat. There my man Samuel will show you to your quarters in the settlement."

Willis led the way from the landing, taking the nearby lane that skirted the base of the bluff's north side. Ketch brought up the rear. Isabelle trod just in front of him, and he could see tension in her shoulders and back as if she anticipated a blow from him. He offered her no reassuring words, for such a skill he lacked, never having been given any himself.

As a distraction, he reflected upon her voice—virtually no African flavor. This made him tend to believe the other woman's story that Isabelle had indeed been a house servant, someone who had spent more time with whites than with her own people. But why would the girl lie about it? Working in a house should be highly preferred over field work with its exposure to Carolina's crippling heat, drenching rains, poisonous snakes and clouds of insects.

Once beyond the bluff, the lane curved to the west beneath the shade of ancient live oaks. Shrouds of gray moss hung from the oaks' branches, moving with a ghostly swing in the breeze coming off the Ashley, the narrow leaves barely putting up a whisper. Once clear of the trees, the lane took them to the kitchen house just north of Leighlin House, a safe distance away should a fire ever start. The five African women who made up the kitchen staff sat in the shade of the front porch, enjoying the relaxation they took at that time of day just before

15

dinner preparations. Their chatter and gossip stopped the instant they saw the group shuffling up the lane. It resumed in a quiet, guarded way, especially from the younger pair. One of them—Iris, Leighlin's biggest gossip—hid her mouth behind a hand, eyes flitting between her companion and the approaching ragamuffins. She and the others looked none too pleased when Willis ordered them back into the kitchen to provide food for the group.

"Stay with 'em until Samuel gets here," Willis directed Ketch then headed toward Leighlin House.

The women ate ravenously. Ketch figured their former master had not wanted to waste victuals on property he was sending away that morning.

In time, Samuel arrived, a tall, formidable black man with shoulders like a topgallant yard; a former slave, freed from bondage in Barbados by James Logan years ago. He had been Ketch's shipmate, as well as something of a friend.

As the women looked Samuel's way, a spark blossomed in Isabelle's eyes, and Ketch abstractly wondered if the girl thought Samuel handsome; most of Leighlin's slave women did, according to plantation gossip. But Samuel had yet to take a wife, perhaps due to the memory of the spouse from whom he had been separated in Africa long ago or because of his unique standing here at Leighlin. Besides advising Mallory on crop growing, Samuel's duties also included slave relations, keeping Mallory informed of the inside world of the bondsmen, acting as intermediary between the two cultures. He was not intrusive, and whatever he imparted to the master was ultimately for the slaves' benefit, so the Africans accepted Samuel's role.

Samuel paused on the first porch step, his intelligent gaze taking in each newcomer. "My name is Samuel. I am to take you to the settlement."

Isabelle got to her feet with the others as they quickly stuffed the last of their meal into their mouths.

"No need to choke yourselves," Samuel cautioned in his smooth, deep, deliberate voice, a man who always thought about what he said before saying it. "You won't go wanting for food here."

Samuel did not smile often, but when he did, as he did now to reassure the women, it came with an ease Ketch envied.

Ketch lingered until Samuel led his charges away. Isabelle was the last to round the corner of the kitchen house and disappear from sight. He wondered what would become of her but then berated himself for his curiosity over a woman, especially a slave who apparently had a penchant for lying.

***

Isabelle, savoring the sensation of a belly full of warm food, followed the others along the dusty lane that led westward from the kitchen house. Tom Clark had never been very free with his victuals, and so she hoped Samuel had been truthful when he had spoken of an abundance here at this plantation. And what a grand place it was. If it were not a place of enslavement, a place of unknown distance from her mother, she could have admired the carefully tended grounds and gardens as well as the regal manor home. Other slaves in the region—those fortunate enough to be able to move about the countryside in their duties or with their master's written permission—had told her about Leighlin's grandeur, but never in her wildest dreams had she pictured such opulence.

When she thought of her mother, even the magnificence around her failed to lighten her heart. Where had that man taken her? Was she somewhere in Charles Town or was she being taken from the province? Having been born a slave, Isabelle had seen many families torn asunder, but she and her mother had been fortunate to remain together, brought from Barbados to Carolina where they had been with Tom Clark for the past five years. But now would they ever see one another again? What type of master would her mother have? She could bear whatever was to come here if only she knew her mother's fate.

As they left the open stretch of lane and entered the blessed shade of a thin forest, the other women, perhaps in hopes of engaging Samuel, gossiped in broken English about all they had thus seen, including their master and his dark-skinned wife and fair sister.

Hannah, the snappish thing who had called her out in front of their new mistress, said to her friend Ester, "The Master seem to like 'em dark. Maybe Izzy will end up in the Big House after all."

Isabelle held her tongue, for she knew her words would only lead to more hurtful ones from the others. To distract herself, she reflected upon her new mistress and master as they had appeared upon the dock, standing there close together, looking very comfortable in each other's presence. She feared she had displeased her master and given her mistress a reason to suspect her falseness. Sometimes, safety required lying, though she hated doing such a thing. Perhaps they already knew the truth. No, if that were so, her new mistress would not have inquired. She hoped they would never discover the details of her life at Clark's.

"What about that li'l yellow-haired child?" Ester asked Samuel. "Where her parents?"

"Dead." The starkness of Samuel's reply unsettled Isabelle. "Just about a twelve-month ago now."

Ester clucked her tongue. "What from?"

"Murdered."

This drew interested stares.

"Who murder 'em?" Hannah asked.

"'Who' don't matter no more." Samuel's stern tone closed the subject. "All you need to know is that Miss Helen is deserving of nothing but kindness. I won't hear none of you speak disrespectful of her."

Isabelle considered Samuel and his manner of speaking. Still a hint of Africa in his speech but so minimal that she knew he had been closely associated with white men for some time. A man with authority—she sensed that from the silent respect the other white man had shown back at the kitchen house. Was Samuel merely a driver or something more? How had he come to be at Leighlin?

Through the trees ahead, Isabelle began to make out the dark, squat shapes of cabins. The smell of cook fires tickled her nose.

Hannah continued, "What 'bout that horrible-lookin' man? The one missin' his arm? Is he the overseer?"

"No," Samuel replied. "The overseer is Hiram Willis, the other man who brought you. The one missing his arm—that's Ketch. He's a driver, but none of you will be assigned to him. Half of you will be going to another white fella by the name of Gabriel, the other half will be going to Amos or Baruch."

Hannah scoffed. "Never heard of no white man bein' a driver."

"Well, Ketch and Gabriel are. Not physically fit to be much else."

Isabelle asked, "What happened to his arm?"

"Got took off after a water snake bit him."

Isabelle marveled at this, unsure whether Samuel was being truthful or not, for she had never known anyone to survive a poisonous snake bite. She remembered how Ketch had watched her in town. She was worldly enough to be surprised not by what she saw in his gaze but by what she had not seen. All white men seemed to leer at her in only one way, but this man had not. Her curiosity had been strengthened aboard the river vessel when he had unchained her. With him so near and somehow almost intimate, they had shared some sort of communication; a sense perhaps of something in common. Maybe she was being foolish—her mother often cautioned against her keen curiosity—but Isabelle thought she had read a deep, hidden sadness in his dark gaze, a sadness similar to what reflected in the looking glass in Tom Clark's bedchamber when she chanced a glance at herself. She had noticed how the other men aboard the *Nymph*—white and black—avoided Ketch, just as the other women avoided her. Perhaps his peers considered him repugnant because of his physical defects: the amputation, the burn scar, the pockmarks, the manacle scar on his wrist, and that odd scar at the base of his neck. When she thought of the scars upon her back where the lash had struck her, she wondered if he also bore unseen scars.

The slave settlement was in a protective wood of towering conifers, oaks, and hickories. The soft, loamy ground silenced the fall of Isabelle's bare feet as the group entered the community. She was shocked to see Leighlin's field hands relaxing amidst the neat rows of clapboard cabins. Many of the cabins had small truck gardens near them, carefully tended. The inhabitants all turned as the group came down the main street, those inside creeping out of their dwellings to stare. Most seemed cautious and unfriendly, perhaps a hundred slaves, most under the age of thirty. Their lack of surprise revealed that they had been told to expect the newcomers. Isabelle noted their clothes—most in good order—and their physical well-being. All appeared healthy and in good flesh. The men had particularly interested stares for the group, those expressions so familiar to Isabelle. Most turned away at the sight of her light skin. One actually kept his attention on her for a long moment and even smiled, giving her a brief moment of hope that this place would allow her a new start, a place where she could forget what had come before.

The Leighlin slaves closed in around them, forming a loose circle in the center of the settlement where a large, cold fire pit gaped like a black scar. Children of various ages stared, remaining close to their parents. Several adults began asking questions of the newcomers, inquiring of their previous servitude, among other things. Isabelle felt increasingly uneasy, wishing more than ever that her mother were here with her. To find some solace, she searched for the young man who had smiled at her. He was not far, standing on the inside of the group, arms crossed in confidence, sleeves rolled up, muscles defined. He swiped one hand across the top of his shaved head to ward off a deer fly. This time his smile was small and sly, making her feel sheepish.

Two men approached, bearing the air of elders in the community, though both were perhaps only thirty summers old. Samuel spoke their names—Amos and Baruch. The two slaves sized up the women with critical eyes.

"These men," Samuel told the women, "will take you to your cabins. You will find clothes and victuals there. You may take your ease today and tomorrow. The next day report to the rear of Leighlin House at daybreak with Amos and Baruch, and Mr. Willis will assign your tasks." He turned to the observing crowd. "These women are to be welcomed into this community. They are part of Leighlin now."

The forcefulness of his words invited neither debate nor comment, nor did his glance around the circle. Samuel gave Amos and Baruch a meaningful nod then left them, the ring of slaves opening to let him pass. Isabelle could not tell if the people remained silent out of resentment or respect, but once Samuel was out of their midst most drifted off. A handful of young men lingered as Amos invited the women to follow him. Isabelle heard comments among the onlookers but discerned nothing, especially since some spoke in languages foreign to her. Instead, she tossed one final glance toward the muscular young man who had smiled at her. He winked at her then said something to a companion, his teeth flashing white. Despite herself, she returned the smile before turning away.

CHAPTER 2

Over the next few days, Ketch banished Isabelle from his mind with a dismissive skill well honed. His focus returned to whatever was directly in front of him. And at this moment it was Zeke and the others of his small work gang, wrestling into place a new cypress trunk gate in the north rice field.

Rice was Leighlin's newest endeavor, adding to the plantation's variety of produce that ranged from peaches to corn, the latter being the majority; the Carolina lowcountry's soil scorned wheat, so corn provided bread for the population as well as fodder for the animals. Leighlin, like many area plantations, owned beef cattle as well as dairy cows, hogs, sheep, chickens, and goats.

From atop the riverside dyke, Ketch supervised while to his right Baruch's field hands moved among the green rows of pips, hoeing and weeding. The sprout flow had allowed the tender plants to germinate and grow, protected from weeds below and from hungry birds above. To Ketch's left, the languid Ashley River moved along with current and tide. Now and then a vessel passed by, and usually someone hailed or waved, then one of the field hands would try to recognize a friend among the slave boatmen, but most were wise enough to keep to their task. Across the river, red-winged blackbirds chirred and clicked from the broad reach of marsh that stretched to the distant, green-forested shore, answered by others from reeds along the near shore. A pair of wood ducks flew past, headed for Leighlin's ornamental ponds.

Leighlin Plantation functioned on a task labor system, and the plantation's most arduous tasks were assigned to Ketch's gang, for his six young men boasted Leighlin's strongest backs. Within this unique labor system, slaves worked each day until their assigned tasks were completed, meaning if they were industrious and skilled they could finish with enough time left for leisure or for hiring themselves out to other plantations to earn wages. Ketch's Africans—bachelors all— were hard horses, the disgruntled of Leighlin Plantation's slave population, with Ezekiel—known as Zeke—being the worst malcontent, and they were rarely interested in working beyond their daily tasks, regardless of any money to be made.

With unblinking eyes, Ketch watched the young men sweat and grunt in the late morning sun. The trunk gates were unwieldy contraptions, and after each flow was drained from the fields, there were always faulty trunks to be replaced. This meant foraging in the swamps for appropriate cypress trees, cutting them down, hollowing them out. The old trunk gate had to be excavated from the dyke, a task made odious by the muck and smell of rot. Then the new trunk replaced it, which in turn had to be covered again with earth, one end facing the river, the other the field. Then plugs had to be precisely fitted.

Ketch removed his hat, set it next to him so he could drag his fingers through his unkempt hair in an attempt to reorganize it and keep it from his eyes. No matter how hot and uncomfortable its sweaty curtain made him, he never solicited anyone to tie his hair back into a queue, though Helen often offered and obliged him. Perhaps he would ask Maria to cut it for him. She was the only person of whom he would ask a favor, and even with Maria, he found it difficult. He looked down at the murky river water sliding past the dyke. Even that water would be too warm to offer any relief, and with but one arm he could no longer swim.

When the Leighlin House bell clanged at eleven o'clock for the midday meal, Ketch led his gang away from the scorching field, followed by Baruch's hands, all in search of shade among the nearby live oaks. Ketch chose a tree on the low bluff above the field. There Zeke and the others sprawled to eat the chicken and corn biscuits provided by the kitchen house.

Ketch leaned back against the massive, gnarled trunk as he ate and watched the lazy sway of moss dangling like crepe from the oak's limbs, tangled amidst the leaves. Then his attention swept over the beauty within view—the river, the landing, the languid creek that lay hidden beyond the southern edge of the bluff, the ornamental ponds where white egrets and blue herons hunted, the green terraces above, upward to the gardens that flanked the sward then to the majestic house. Ketch never shared his appreciation of this place's splendor with anyone. They would think such things lost upon someone of his ilk.

Leighlin was a contrasting paradise to his boyhood Southwark, England. The quiet routine brought peace, a peace he had never had in his life. The violence, the crimes he had committed in the past had taken a toll on him. Having Helen around him every day, learning to accept her love…it provided hope—hope that he could somehow atone for the evil he had done; hope that he could leave the nightmares behind him and become someone Ella Logan would be proud to have living on her land, worthy of his role as her daughter's protector.

A burst of laughter from Zeke intruded upon his thoughts, shredded them. The young man rested on his side, his back to Ketch, facing the five other members of his gang as they ate, the center of attention as usual, just the way he liked it. Zeke, slim but powerfully built, was taller than many of his people and kept his head shaved or close-cropped. He had narrow eyes and a mouth often harsh yet also capable of a broad, winning smile when his companions amused him or when he amused himself. He had been born on a Barbados sugar plantation, and if he knew any of his mother's native tongue, he had never revealed as much to his driver. Ketch suspected Zeke felt superior to his comrades for his grasp of the English language.

"I already has mines picked out," Zeke proclaimed.

"Which one?" Jacob, Zeke's closest friend, squinted. "Best not be the one *I's* gettin'."

"You not gettin' nothin' with that stick of your'n," Zeke sniped, drawing more laughter from the others.

Jacob scowled. "You jus' wait. You seen how she look at me last night when we walk past her porch."

"She was lookin' at me, fool. But I didn't pay her no mind; she has the face of a horse. She not the one I gonna have."

Spider, the youngest of the lot, grinned admiringly. "Zeke lookin' for trouble, he is."

"He don't need to look," Jacob said. "It find him on its own."

Asa, the oldest, looked closer at Zeke. "You not talkin' 'bout that mulatto, is you?"

"I is. And I'll bet you half the truck in your garden that I's married afore any of you."

"You best pick someone else," Asa cautioned. "Besides bein' a mulatto, I hear tell she trouble."

"So long as she can spread her legs, that's all I care about," Zeke replied.

"They say she don' have no trouble wit' that," Spider said. "But you may be the wrong color, Zeke."

Zeke fondled himself. "She get a look at this and color won't matter no more."

The others laughed, and Zeke tipped up his tin cup of water to drink. Their mirth, however, vanished when they saw Ketch marching toward them. Zeke did not turn, but he nearly dropped his cup when Ketch gave him a swift kick in the ribs.

"Quit gossipin' like old women and get back to work."

The others scrambled to their feet. Zeke rolled his angry eyes up at Ketch, his attention pausing at Ketch's crotch, then he scoffed and started to rise. Ketch's next kick caught him in the belly, drove the air from him. The others backed away.

"Mind yerself, boy," Ketch growled. "If yer not careful, you might come up missin' that prick you value so highly."

Zeke wisely stayed down until Ketch took a step back. Then, slowly, he got to his feet. Careful not to turn his back on Ketch, Zeke shuffled over to the others. Ketch gave them a dark look and shepherded them back toward the rice field.

Another hot hour passed alongside the river. Bugs bit and sweat ran down Ketch's body in an uninterrupted flow. The sultry weather and his sour expression kept the gang on task. They finished burying the new trunk gate and fit the plugs on either end then restored the dyke before the rising tide could encroach upon the field. They would be unable to place the other new trunk until the next low tide. In the meantime, work needed to be done on the canal that brought water to the field from the inland creek.

As Ketch led the gang along the series of dykes to reach the far canal, distant, alarmed shouts drew his attention. One of the slaves who tended the gardens was running down the terraces to the landing. There the *Nymph* awaited the turn of the tide to take deer hides and wood downriver to Charles Town.

"Mr. Willis! Mr. Willis!" Frantically, the gardener waved, tripped, and nearly fell in his haste. All the way to the landing he called Willis's name. Willis stepped from the *Nymph* to the dock where he listened to a brief explanation before rushing toward the house as fast as his persistent limp allowed.

Ketch watched until Willis disappeared through the front door. He frowned, thought first of Helen. Had the child hurt herself? She was always too reckless on her pony. Or perhaps it was only one of the servants that Willis—once a surgeon's mate and now Leighlin's physician—needed to treat for one careless injury or another. But there was no time for further thought on the matter; he had work to do.

As Zeke and the others began the mucky, smelly task of shoring up the damaged canal, a messenger from the house appeared at the landing, and soon the *Nymph* cast off without Willis. Normally disinterested, Ketch found himself uneasy. He was relieved when

Leighlin's bell rang in the early afternoon to call a halt to all field work until the cooler part of the day.

He dragged himself to the manor house, having almost forgotten about the earlier alarm. Once in the house's lower level, a wave of moderate coolness wafted over his skin. The hard-packed dirt floor was slightly lower than the sward outside and thus retained a bit of the earth's chilled dampness. Crates, barrels, and bags of provisions filled this common room, neatly organized and catalogued. On one side of the room, doors opened upon two chambers shared by the house servants, while chambers for Leighlin's white workers—Ketch and four other ex-sailors—were on the opposite side. Three of those ex-sailors, Willis among them, had arrived in the common room just before him. They removed their hats from sweat-darkened hair and their wet shirts from their backs then settled at the table in the center of the room.

Gabriel, the youngest at twenty and also an Englishman, dove upon the tankard of beer awaiting him and downed it in nearly one long guzzle before coming up for air to ask Willis, "So, how is she?"

"She'll be fine in a day or two." Willis dragged a weary hand down his face. "But she lost the babe."

Ketch quickly looked up from his drink but then hid his reaction by lifting the mug back to his lips.

Silas McBain asked, "How's the young master taking it?"

"Bearin' up, of course. Put on a brave face for Maria, but the lad is crushed."

Ketch downed the beer in long gulps and poured more from the flagon that the servants had left.

Gabriel asked, "Does Miss Helen know?"

"Aye."

"Poor thing must be disappointed," McBain said. "She needs another young 'un to play with beside the Negroes. It's not natural."

Ketch finished his beer and left them to their gossip and speculation. He retreated to his bedchamber off the common room—a chamber no one was willing to share with him—and shut the door. The small space was cool, for he had closed the west shutters that morning to keep out the inevitable sun. The chamber was sparsely furnished: a bed, a crude nightstand, and a chair.

The chair he had crafted himself. Since his days as a carpenter's mate in the Royal Navy, he had always been skilled with wood, and he had taken up the challenge of constructing the chair with just his secondary arm. It had been a struggle, but with a series of clamps holding the pieces, he managed. He had labored on it in the carpenter's shop, away from his white counterparts so they could not see his frustration and diminished skills. He had worked on it during this time of day between the morning and evening tasks, as well as on his days off. Helen often stopped by to help and to chatter, the type of conversation he preferred—nonsensical, one-sided, the kind where his presence was appreciated but his active participation was unnecessary. If he smiled during the day, it was Helen's doing. He liked to imagine Ella Logan had been as cheerful and angelic at that age. Often, he remembered Helen's sadness following her parents' deaths, and he feared that one day she would learn the truth about what he had done and loathe him, as he loathed himself.

He lay upon his bed and stared up at the stout beams. Commonly he would fall asleep at this time of day, alone in his quiet chamber, but now when he closed his eyes, he wondered what was taking place two floors above him in the master bedchamber. Maria was strong, but this loss would be a blow to her. He admired her spirit over this past year as he had come to know her, though she often proved to be unbearably stubborn like her husband. Her love for Ella Logan's child had earned Ketch's respect, as well as her efforts to treat him as a human being, as Ella Logan had, compared to the begrudging tolerance of the rest of Leighlin's population.

When Maria's pregnancy had become known, Helen had asked, "How come you aren't married, Mr. Ketch? Don't you want babies?"

The questions had thrown him off balance, for such had certainly never been asked of him before, nor had he even entertained such specious concepts. "Well, Miss Helen," he had managed to say. "I don't need a parcel of me own children when I have you."

Children of his own? He gave a wry scoff and rolled onto his side to stare at the wall. Nay, the world would never want nor ever see the fruits of his loins, for he durst not lie with a woman ever again.

***

The bright Sunday morning sun sent a long shadow behind Ella Logan's headstone. As if out of respect for the woman, the world lay quiet before Ketch, save for the birds—a variety of waterfowl and songbirds that dwelled in tree, river, and swamp, ranging from tiny to formidable; Leighlin even boasted a pair of peafowl that had now ventured out to the front sward—he heard the peacock's strange cry from the opposite side of the north garden. Ketch gazed across the bluff and beyond the landing, down the stretch of river to the bend where the sparkling Ashley vanished behind trees.

He knew this place well, this small quiet spot upon the bluff, for he came here every Sabbath and often during the week. As always, he reflected upon how different Leighlin was since Ella Logan's death. Even after these many months, her memory still left a certain sadness upon the plantation. Slaves and whites alike still spoke of her. How he missed seeing her drifting about her beloved gardens, straw hat shading her exquisite face, a face he still remembered floating above his hammock aboard the *Medora* after Logan's men had freed him from the Spanish. For days, he had lain near death until she alone brought him back from the brink.

When Ketch had emerged from unconsciousness that long-ago day, Ella Logan was the first thing he saw. The lantern that hung from the deckhead threw a glow about her golden hair like a halo, worry darkening her eyes to indigo. He stared at her for some time, unsure if he was alive or dead, his body still wracked by the tortures of his former captors. Somehow, looking at her flawless skin soothed the agony.

She offered him a smile. "What is your name?"

His name. A simple question but a puzzle right then, calling for great concentration. His mother...she had called him Ned. His stepfather had called him Edward. Aye, that had been it—Edward Inman. But he had forsaken that name long ago. To Ella, he had hoarsely uttered his name simply as Ketch, his mother's maiden name.

"Rest easy now, Mr. Ketch. You are safe here."

Her smile came again, and he closed his eyes, feeling indeed safer than he had felt in many, many years.

Now his attention rested upon her elaborate marker. Cut roses adorned the grave. Helen brought them every day, often with her brother. The red petals would curl and dry under the day's driving sun, but as the orb passed the zenith, the headstone would then shade the flowers. Roses had been Ella Logan's favorite. The house had always been filled with them when in bloom, arranged with an artist's hand in vases large and small. Now, whenever he smelled them, he thought of her, both a comforting and an unendurable sensation.

The grave was a solitary one, for James Logan was not buried next to his wife. That day at sea, when Ketch had shot him to avenge his half-brother's murder, the big man had fallen overboard, the crimson blood upon his chest a bright contrast to his paling face. The blue of the Atlantic had swallowed him and claimed his body forever. To Ketch, it was a relief that Logan was not buried here, for he could not have borne the sight of Helen mourning the man.

Ketch never stayed long at Ella Logan's grave; it pained him too deeply. On his way back to Leighlin House, he trekked through the north garden, his thoughts far away. Helen's bright voice from near at hand brought him back to the present.

"Mr. Ketch!"

He halted, startled by her sudden appearance from where she had been crouching at her task among the rose bushes. She stood before him as a smaller version of her mother, while behind her a black gardener hovered, shears in hand, at her beck and call.

"I'm almost done cutting flowers," said the child. "Would you like to take them to Maria with me?" She pointed to a growing bouquet in a sweetgrass basket at her feet. As usual, she had pricked her fingers on the thorns and snagged her dress several times.

"No, child."

"Why not? She's very sad. We can cheer her up."

"I don't reckon I'm of much account when it comes to cheerin' folks up, Miss Helen."

"Please," she drew out the word, stepping closer to ply her effective trade of persuasion with those large blue eyes of hers. She had learned the art from her mother. "I know she wants to see you."

"Do ye now? And how be that?" he teased. "Has she told you?"

Not one to lie, Helen frowned and scuffed her bare toes on the dirt path. "She told me she likes visitors. John can't stay with her all the time." Helen's habit of using her brother's Christian name still jarred Ketch after all this time. She, after her mother's practice, was the only person close to Mallory who used the name.

Studying her somber form, he realized Helen, wounded by the loss of the baby, was not quite sure how to make things better for herself and her sister-in-law. She was hoping some adult would help her with that burden.

"Very well," he said and received an instant, gratifying grin from the girl.

On their way upstairs, Helen held his hand as if to keep him from bolting. Whenever she placed her tiny hand in his, the sensation pleased him like nothing else. Her touch had provided him with the will to survive the snake bite and, even more lasting, had given him the resolve to leave behind the violence of his past.

When Helen opened Maria's chamber door, she put her finger to her lips. Maria, seemingly asleep, looked particularly small in the large, canopied bed with its mound of white pillows, her dark hair spilling from beneath a lace-fringed cap. A slave girl, Pip, stood on the far side, cooling the young woman with a palmetto fan. Helen tiptoed across the pine floorboards undetected, but Ketch's fourteen-stone weight creaked the boards and drew Maria's attention. Her gaze widened upon him, and she drew the bedclothes higher. Helen smiled and no longer bothered with stealth, freeing Ketch and bounding forward. She restrained herself from jumping onto the bed and instead stiff-armed the bouquet of thorn-free roses out in front of her.

"Look what me and Mr. Ketch brought you, Maria!"

"How lovely. Thank you."

Her reserved voice, such a contrast to her normal bright tone, disturbed Ketch. At the servant, he growled, "Fetch a vase for Miss Maria's flowers."

Pip dropped the fan and hurried from the chamber.

"Are you feeling better today, Maria?" Helen chirped hopefully.

"Yes, I am."

Ketch could tell there was the taste of a lie in Maria's words. Perhaps physically she felt better, but it was obvious by the loss of color in her cheeks and the dullness of her brown eyes that she was grieving. She also clutched at the gold locket around her neck, a familiar piece of jewelry never far from her in which she kept a lock of her father's hair. Ketch hated seeing her this way—vulnerable—and he wished he had not come, though he had admitted to himself on the way up the stairs that he did feel a certain obligation, indeed a desire to show his concern for her. As Helen chattered on in a stream of cheerful, benign, one-sided conversation, Ketch shifted his weight. Maria noticed his unrest and glanced at a nearby chair, but he looked down and pretended he had not understood her invitation.

"Mr. Ketch and I have been making something for you." Helen's words sharply drew Ketch's attention, but before he could dissuade her, she blurted, "A crib for the baby. We worked on it a little bit each day, didn't we, Mr. Ketch? I help hold things for him. He says I'm his right arm." Her proud grin melted away when she saw Maria's tears.

Quickly, the young woman smiled and sheepishly brushed at the moisture that had gathered in her eyes. Then she touched Helen's golden hair. "That's very sweet of you and Mr. Ketch. Thank you."

Her caress seemed to ease Helen's conscience, returning the light to her expression. "We haven't finished, but we can keep making the crib for the next baby."

"Of course, sweetie. But perhaps not right away. Losing the baby has troubled your brother very much."

"I know," Helen murmured.

"He's afraid the same thing will keep happening. He's being silly, isn't he?"

As the two delved deeper into Jack Mallory's behavior, Ketch scoffed to himself. That boy would not be able to keep away from his wife any more than a rutting stag could keep itself from a doe.

As Ketch listened to Maria, he realized Mallory was not the only one. Maria would look for her own flaws before another's, so if she could not conceive again, she would think it due to some cruel defect in her own body before ever thinking the fault could lie with her husband. So, the sooner she was able to conceive, the better she would feel.

Ketch was eternally glad to be a man.

Pip returned to the bedchamber and busied herself arranging the flowers in a vase on the nightstand.

Maria asked, "How are the new slaves working out, Ketch?"

Helen chimed in, "I heard Iris talking about them. She said Isabelle is trouble."

"And how many times have your brother and I told you not to listen to gossip?" Maria chided.

"I couldn't help it. I was sitting on the kitchen porch playing with Rose's baby, and they was all talking." Her fingers toyed with the edge of Maria's pillow. "They called her a funny name I've never heard before."

"Well, you must not listen to them. And I'll speak with Rose about allowing such idle talk around a child."

"I'm not a child; I'm going to be eight soon." She turned a wily smile upon Ketch.

"What of the new slaves, Ketch?"

"I don't see 'em much, but they've stirred the interest of me bucks. That much I can tell you."

Maria frowned. "Well, hopefully, wives will settle them down. Jack hopes so, too."

"Cheaper to breed 'em than buy 'em, that's for certain sure."

He could see his comment perturbed the young woman on more than one level, so he entreated Helen to retire.

"She can stay, Ketch. I'd like the company."

Ketch frowned, unsure if such busy company was what the woman needed, but he knew better than to debate his quick-tempered mistress. He made a slight, awkward bow and turned for the door.

"Ketch."

Struck with fear that he would be asked to stay, he held his breath.

"Thank you for coming." Her smile told him that she understood what an uncomfortable task it had been, that she would not hold his hasty retreat against him. "And thank you for the crib."

Her tears were again not far away, and though he felt cowardly for fleeing, there was no help for it.

***

The blaze from the settlement's fire pit bronzed the faces of the encircling slaves. Above, the night sky was a gray velvet canvas, the clouds covering the stars and moon. Isabelle stared up through the trees and welcomed the air's relative coolness after a long, hot evening in the south rice field. The work left her back aching, her hands blistered, and her feet sore. In Tom Clark's house, she had worn shoes every day, so trudging about barefoot now was a trial for her tender soles. They would toughen, she assured herself, as would her hands upon the hoe. She hated the work; no scrap of shade in the field, the sun oppressive, especially to someone used to being inside all day, the work dull and repetitive. Again, she told herself she would grow accustomed to it.

A lazy buzz of varied conversations, interspersed with children's sleepy chatter, hummed about Isabelle but excluded her. No one had included her in anything since her arrival here a week ago except for a short visit from Baruch's wife, Selah. Their prejudice against her half-white heritage, coupled with Hannah's gossip about her life at their previous plantation, had effectively isolated her. Regardless, Isabelle came every night with the others to the center of the settlement where the fire circle served as a social gathering point. They would talk, sing, tell stories, or sometimes dance if someone had the energy for such, an energy at which Isabelle marveled. The first few nights she had tried to join in the discourse but received a lukewarm response except from Baruch and Selah. The only other one who spoke to her for any length was Ezekiel, though he never lingered long. But often she saw him watching her from somewhere else among the circle, and his almost-private smile made her feel hopeful that someday she would be accepted into this community.

"Things will be better for you," her mother had tried to sound optimistic the night before leaving Clark's plantation. "You will make new friends."

She pulled from her thoughts as the discussions slowly turned into a central subject—their mistress's miscarriage.

31

Baruch sagely offered, "Miss Ella couldn't have no mo' babies after Miss Helen. Mebbe Miss Maria can't neither. Mebbe it the swamp air."

"Swamp air didn't stop us," Selah said with a tired laugh, holding their six-month-old son in her arms.

"Mebbe it affect white folk diff'rent," Baruch insisted.

"Or maybe it just the mistress," Ester spoke up. "Maybe somethin' wrong wit' her, like Mrs. Clark. She couldn't have no babies neither."

Hannah laughed darkly. "Only thing wrong with Mrs. Clark was Mr. Clark. He too busy lying with that mulatto to visit his wife's bed."

Isabelle glared across the fire at the young woman, heat rising to her cheeks. She could tell by the lack of reaction from the others that this was not the first time Hannah had revealed her shame.

"That's why Isabelle here. Mrs. Clark had 'nough." Hannah addressed the now-attentive group. "Maybe our new master could have a baby outta Isabelle like Mr. Tom did."

Isabelle leapt to her feet. "He never!" She started toward Hannah. "That's a lie, and you know it!"

Baruch intercepted her. "Put yo' claws away, girl. I won't stand for no cat fights here."

Isabelle countered, "She's just sour 'cause no man'll lie with her, white or black."

Now Hannah stood, though she lacked the nerve to advance. "You nothin' but a half-caste whore, gettin' favors from the white man 'cause you spread your legs for 'em!"

"Another lie!" Isabelle shouted back at her from around Baruch. "You make up things about others just to look better yourself."

"She not lyin'!" Ester shot. "I was there at Mr. Tom's, too, don't you forget. I knows what I saw."

"Enough!" Baruch took hold of Isabelle and led her outside of the circle. Lowering his voice, he cautioned, "Go back to your cabin, girl. It'd be best for everyone if you do."

Furious, Isabelle stared from Baruch to the smirk on Hannah's round face. How she wanted to slap away that expression. How she wanted to erase what the wicked creature had said in front of everyone. She knew once she left, Hannah would expound upon her lies.

"Go on," Baruch ordered, showing no inclination to free her unless she agreed to obey him. Selah's gaze urged her to do so. A couple of the children whispered and giggled.

Isabelle's lips pressed tight together. Most were looking her way, including Ezekiel, and he was no longer smiling. With a jerk, she pulled from Baruch's grasp and hurried away. Immediately swallowed by the dark, she could allow the tears some leeway. They sprang into her eyes, but she refused to let them fall down her cheeks. She blinked and wiped them away, cursing them. They always came too easily. She hated their display of weakness.

Her cabin was second to last in the row, newly built for the arrival of Clark's slaves, one she shared with Ester and two other women. An insufferable place where she could not escape her past. She had asked Amos and Baruch if she could perhaps live with women not from her old home, but Amos pointed out that all the Leighlin women were married, that there was no room for her elsewhere. Now her cabin was dark, empty, for everyone was at the fire circle. She stumbled to the porch and sank down upon the top step, sniffed and wiped her nose with the back of her hand. There she remained, staring off toward the distant glow of the fire circle, occasionally hearing a burst of laughter, wondered if it was at her expense.

Who was she fooling? She would fit in here no better than she had at Clark's, field hand or not. Her home could change but her color could not.

For some time, she sat there, missing her mother terribly. At least at Clark's plantation she had had her mother to talk to, to laugh with and feel loved. She re-directed her self-pity to hoping that her mother was safe, that she was in a better situation, that one day they would see each other again. Desperately, she clung to her mother's words, her urgings to forget what Clark had done to her, to start anew and allow herself to trust. But who was there to trust here? They would all be poisoned against her.

A shadow moved against the faraway glow of the fire. Isabelle squinted then blinked, thinking her eyes were playing a trick upon her. Then she realized the shadow was close, coming toward her. A man's shape, alone. She wondered if he could see her.

Ezekiel's voice came boldly through the night: "That you, Is'belle?"

Surprised, she hesitated before replying, "Yes."

He drew closer; she could hear his steps now. She held her breath, afraid he had come to say something cruel.

"Can I set with you?"

Relieved to detect no animosity in his tone, she swallowed and breathed again. "If you'd like."

When he sat inappropriately close, she blamed his miscalculation on the darkness and inched slightly away. Isabelle searched for something to say to stave off her uncomfortable feeling and drown out the hammering of her heart.

"It's not true," she murmured. "All the things Hannah said, I mean. And it was Mr. Tom who couldn't have children, not his wife, so I sure never gave him one."

He shifted his weight, turned toward her. His finger touched her forearm, briefly, moved a couple of inches downward then retreated. When he spoke, that now-familiar smile was in his voice. "I don't give much account to a magpie like Hannah."

"Everyone else seems to."

"We're not used to new folk; some don't know what to think. So, they talk."

"How long have you been here?"

"'Bout three summers."

"Where was you before?"

"Barbados."

"So was I. I mean, before Mr. Tom's."

Ezekiel fell silent, and Isabelle regretted mentioning Clark.

"So, was you really in Mr. Tom's house? You wasn't no field hand there, was you?"

She hesitated.

"I seen your blisters."

She frowned and self-consciously curled her fingers, though it was a pointless concealment, considering the night. "That part is true. I did work in the house."

"Why don't you tell Samuel? Mebbe the white folk take you for a house servant. Better'n workin' in the fields."

"No."

"Why not?"

He slid closer, and his nearness made her feel as if he were touching her again. She found herself leaning slightly toward him.

"I didn't like being a house servant."

"'Cause of that Tom?"

"Maybe."

"Did he hurt you?"

Isabelle started to stand, but Ezekiel's hand upon her arm halted her. For an instant, she feared what he would do, wished she could see his face to read his expression.

"Don't run away," he said without hostility but with enough authority that she obeyed out of habit. The persistent pressure he applied finally brought her back down to the step. "I's sorry, Is'belle. I won't ask you nothin' like that no more."

She tried to determine if true compassion lay in his voice. "What I did," she quietly said, "I did to protect my mother. I'm not..." Emotion unexpectedly welled up in her, but she fought it down. "I'm not...like that."

The surprising warmth of his hand enveloped hers. "I knows you're not. I could tell jes' lookin' at you that first day."

Again, she desired light to see his face, to read his eyes. Was he just playing a heartless game with her? Before she could withdraw her hand from his, he released her.

"You don't have to be afeared of me, Is'belle. In fact, if folks pester you, you jes' tell me, and I'll make 'em quiet."

His kindness nearly choked her. All she could manage was a whispered, "Thank you, Ezekiel."

"You can call me Zeke, if you'd like." The smile was back in his words, and she caught a pale glimpse of his teeth. "Now, I'd best get to my cabin afore someone gets the wrong idea 'bout us."

Isabelle wished he would stay, for she had no desire to retreat inside alone to await the return of her cabinmates. Yet she knew she could not keep him here forever; they needed to rest for tomorrow's long day.

"Can I come set with you here tomorrow night?"

She smiled. "Yes, that would be nice."

The porch boards protested as he stood. He hesitated as if considering something then wished her good night and drifted away up the row of cabins.

She listened to his footsteps, his form gone as if he had never been there at all.

Isabelle was no fool; she had heard the reasons why her new master had acquired her and the other women. The climate and the brutal work claimed the lives of slaves quickly in this land, and those who could produce offspring helped defray the cost of such losses in the future. No doubt Ezekiel was as interested as any man would be in acquiring a wife. It was obvious during the past few days that he was popular among most of the people. Perhaps if he continued to pursue her, the others would eventually accept her. But she was uncertain how to handle the situation. Since being at Clark's, she had often wondered if she could have a relationship with any man, if she could trust one, if one would want to lie with her.

"You can't let what happened to you here close your heart, child," her mother had warned. "Remember, the same thing happened to me, and if I had closed my heart, I never would have met William. And you know how happy he made me. That's how it can be for you. Once you're away from here, you'll have the chance to make the choice on your own."

And Isabelle had vowed that she would try. In fact, she was eager to do so, to prove to herself and others that she was not tainted, that she could rise above her past and be just like any other man's wife.

CHAPTER 3

The evening rain fell in a mundanely vertical, unceasing pattern, turning the south rice field to sticky mud and drenching the two dozen field hands who toiled there, too miserable to sing work songs. Inland from the field, Gabriel—their driver—rested beneath the relative protection of trees near the storage barn. The soaking at least alleviated some of the day's heat, and Ketch welcomed it for the cleansing it gave his body. Crouched upon the riverside dyke where his gang worked, he had removed his shirt and hat long ago to allow the wet to run down him. Inwardly, he smiled in satisfaction whenever any of the slaves glanced at the ugly stump of his right arm or the broad burn scars on his chest and left arm from last year's house fire. He knew the value of keeping them unnerved simply with the aversion to his body's past torments and the invincibility they projected.

As Zeke and the others of his gang muscled a new trunk gate into place, Ketch stood to stretch his legs and relieve himself into the river. Once finished, he turned back as he buttoned his soggy breeches and found Isabelle's eyes upon him from two rods away. She stood ankle-deep in the field's muck, rain dripping from the brim of her straw hat. Abruptly, she returned her attention to her hoeing. Oddly self-conscious, Ketch looked away, felt his mood shift to peevishness. No doubt among the slaves his cock had taken on the same mythical qualities as the rest of him. Is that why she had been looking at him, thinking of all the stories told by others? Or was it the flogging scars upon his back that had piqued her curiosity? She probably had never imagined a white man would suffer such. Did she also bear marks of punishment upon her body? He glanced at her willowy form in the drab dress, her face now hidden by the broad brim of her hat, which kept away most of the rain. He imagined her skin through the coarse fabric—smooth or marred? While his eyes roamed over her, his unheralded arousal both surprised and irritated him. To distract himself, he forced his attention back to his gang and saw Zeke staring lustfully at Isabelle.

"Keep yer eyes on yer work, boy," Ketch growled, "or I'll take that girl's hoe to yer thick, ugly head."

Spider snickered. "Might break the hoe."

"Shut up, you cur, and mind yer business," Ketch ordered.

The evening dragged onward, and the rain finally began to slacken. The rows between the rice pips overflowed one into the next. The slaves moved like sodden ragamuffins, bare feet covered by water and slowed by mud. The monotony of the rain dulled Ketch's senses, and he drifted into blank reverie—an old defense—growing tired and thinking only of his dry bed. But then, sharp voices drew him back to clarity, women's shrill calls, men's laughter, including from his gang.

"Look at your li'l mulatto, Zeke." Jacob pointed. "A sight more muddy now."

At the opposite end of the field, two brown forms wrestled, feet kicking, fingers reaching for hair. The other slaves had stopped work to watch, the women shouting at the combatants, the men leaning on implements and laughing. Gabriel emerged from the tree line with little urgency. When the slaves saw him, they quickly went back to work, still attentive to the fight which continued unabated as the two female combatants screeched and howled at each other. When Gabriel arrived near the fight, he merely stood by, hands on his hips, grinning from beneath his sagging hat. Ketch jumped from the dyke and slogged down the field.

When Gabriel saw his approach, his grin broadened. "I have odds on the bigger wench, mate. What say you? Two to one?"

"They're smashin' the fucking plants."

Ketch grabbed the arm of the woman who was on top of the struggling mass of legs and arms. She came away with a fistful of her adversary's hair and a bloody lower lip, grappling to reach the other woman with hands and feet, teeth bared amidst the slime.

"Avast, damn you," he demanded, yanking her farther away from the one on the ground. Through his captive's thick veil of mud, he recognized Isabelle.

"Now, Ketch," Gabriel said, "why do you always have to ruin things?"

When Ketch freed Isabelle from his grip, she instantly lost her fire, perhaps realizing the physical consequences that might occur. She snatched up her hoe and went back to work as if the confrontation had never happened.

"Filthy little whore," the other woman snapped. "Just wait."

Ketch took a step toward her, and his menacing, half-naked bulk set her back on her heels. She scrabbled for her hoe.

He turned back to Gabriel and jabbed a finger into the young man's chest. "You'd have seen this a-comin' if you hadn't been asleep, you lazy bastard. Mebbe I should tell yer master you let his slaves damage each other and ruin his crops."

Gabriel scowled through his patchy blond stubble. "These are mine to do with what I please. You should mind your own, eh? Look at 'em yonder—jumpin' about like monkeys, not doin' a lick of work without you standing right over 'em."

When Ketch looked back toward the far trunk gate, Zeke and the others hastily resumed their duties.

Considering the two sodden, mud-caked women, he asked Gabriel, "What're you goin' to do with 'em?"

"Reckon they enjoy the muck so much, they can stay out here all night in it. But I'll have to clap 'em in irons, else they might murder each other, and then what'll I say to the Captain?" He winked and grinned then moved back toward the trees.

Ketch turned to Isabelle. She kept her head bowed. With her headscarf lost somewhere in the quagmire, the rain sloughed filth from her short hair and streaked the mess on her face. Lips tight together, she worked her hoe with an energy driven by anger and frustration. Ketch retrieved her straw hat, now mud-stained, and held it out to her. She stopped her brisk movements and looked up at him then at the hat. When he said nothing, she tentatively took it from him, murmured, "Thank you, sir." She slung it around her neck from its rawhide cord so that it hung against her back.

"Why was you a-fightin'?"

When Isabelle's glance reached to her former opponent, her gaze hardened. "Hannah was using me something fierce with her tongue. Saying false things as usual."

He noted that the other slave had also come from Clark's plantation.

"You should learn not to listen to fools."

"Yes, sir. I'll try to remember that. I'm much obliged." She gave a shallow curtsey.

Ketch figured residual anger caused her trembling more than fear of him. He considered sending her to the river to wash, but it was not his place to order one of Gabriel's hands about; it would diminish Gabriel's authority in their eyes, and that was not a safe course. Then an unheralded image of Isabelle naked in the river took him by surprise, shook him, brought back his churlishness.

Gruffly, he said, "Get back to work," as much to himself as to the girl before trudging back across the field.

As he climbed up the slippery dyke, the easing rain hissed upon the river.

"Wipe that grin off yer face, boy, afore I knock it off."

Zeke begrudgingly obeyed. "I knows why Is'belle was a-fightin'."

Jacob groaned and rolled his eyes at Spider, shook his dripping head.

"That's none o' yer affair," Ketch grumbled. "Buryin' this trunk gate is all you need to think about."

Zeke grinned. "They's fightin' over me. I bedded the one but I 'spects to marry t'other, and the one I bedded don't much like that."

"You don't get back to work and quit talkin'," Ketch said, "all yer goin' to be concerned about is yer funeral, not yer wedding."

Through the slate-gray curtain of rain, Zeke stole one last triumphant glance toward the distant women then returned to his task.

***

A crack of thunder awakened Ketch in the blackness of his bedchamber. Rain drove with a racket against the closed shutters of the west window. A flash of lightning illuminated the room, and another crescendo shook the house. He sat up and listened to the violence of the storm, cursed it for disturbing him; sleep had not come easily. He had lain awake for some time, wondering if rest would ever arrive. And now, awake again, the subject responsible for his earlier insomnia leapt back to the forefront to torment him once more.

Since Isabelle's arrival at Leighlin, he had been aware of her presence even when he did not see her, for Zeke spoke of her daily. Hearing the slave's bawdy talk was nothing new, but having it pertain to Isabelle agitated him. And being privy to the young man's designs upon her troubled him even more. Occasionally, when he could no longer tolerate Zeke's bragging, he ordered him into silence, but because he hated the knowing, almost superior look this brought to Zeke's face, he usually pretended to ignore the talk. Seeing the way Zeke had looked at the girl earlier in the south field contributed to Ketch's difficulty sleeping. Hopefully, Isabelle had no interest in Zeke. Yet, what did it matter to him? Isabelle had been acquired for the very purpose of placating a rogue like Zeke and producing more slaves. He had no more business in what slave fornicated with another as he did in the breeding of Leighlin's sheep.

The very thought of Isabelle in Zeke's bed made him leave his own bed, as wide awake as he had been just a short while ago. The old familiar stirring in his blood concerned him deeply. The peace of this past year had settled him, shelved those urgings that used to arise whenever something harassed him. He did not want to again fall victim to the violence inherent in his breeding. To return to that realm could lead to banishment from Leighlin. But could he continue to deny his very nature now that the unrest had reawakened in him?

Naked, he paced the small chamber, listened to the driving storm, thought again of Isabelle exposed to its wrath, alone in the blackness of the rice field. When he had left the field, he had looked back to see her chained to one of the new trunk gates Zeke and the others had placed that day. The forlorn sight had haunted him since. Now, with a curse, he crossed to the nightstand near the bed and stuffed the remains of his supper into a small bag. He pulled on his breeches and shirt. He would do this one kindness, then he would avoid the girl at all costs.

To decrease the chances of being detected by anyone in Leighlin House, he carried no lantern. The tempest's white flashes were problematic enough, so he moved quickly away from the house, down the lane that trailed between the south edge of the bluff and the broad, sluggish creek that fed the rice fields. He crossed a narrow bridge into the trees, bent from the wind's force, creating a roar of branches and leaves above the lane. He was already drenched, his hair plastered and streaming. The lane led to the river then curved right to parallel the shore until it reached the south rice field. Once there, he took refuge beneath an oak to catch his breath.

Again, he questioned his motives, marveled at the very fact he was here. A compulsion; that was all it was. Foolishness, especially considering his physical reaction to Isabelle hours ago, that terrible, unexpected rush. He blamed his being here on Gabriel. If the fool had been attentive, Hannah and Isabelle would never have come to blows. Then to punish Isabelle for his own dereliction of duty had been unjust. While Ketch cared for no man living, he had always tried to protect women from men's cruelties, for he had seen the evils his gender wrought upon the fairer sex, beginning with his stepfather's wife-beating and the drowning of Ketch's sister, Sophia, to shipmates who often used their superior physical strength against women. It all sickened and angered him, for he could not understand how anyone could take pleasure in such criminal odds.

Slowly, the storm rumbled away to the northeast, dragging behind it cooler air and a moderating breeze. As the lightning weakened and moved onward with the body of the storm, Ketch emerged from his sanctuary tree.

***

Isabelle pressed as tightly as she could against the trunk gate, huddled into as small a shape as possible, trembling. She kept her sobs muffled for fear that Hannah would hear her weakness. A silly concern, for the rain and thunder drowned out all other sounds in the world, and Hannah was chained far down the field at another trunk gate. Although the storm was slackening, its fury still terrified Isabelle. The deep booms of thunder and ear-piercing cracks reminded her of the hurricane long ago when she, only a child at the time, had gotten separated from her mother by the violent wind and torrents of rain. To this day, a storm of any kind frightened her witless. Adding to her fear was Ezekiel's story two nights ago of how three slaves had been killed in this very field by lightning during last summer's stretch flow when water lay protectively over the field. He claimed their ghosts still haunted the field, though she could not tell if that part of the story were true or not; Ezekiel did love to tell yarns. All the same, his tale, true or false, did nothing to alleviate her suffering as she sat soaked, starving, and thirsty.

She wished Ezekiel were here with her. He had been visiting her every night before she retired to bed. They would walk together, talking until the mosquitoes finally drove them back to the light. They had shared but two or three walks before he progressed to taking her in his arms and kissing her. At first, she had been hesitant but soon welcomed the protective strength of his muscular arms and looked forward to his displays. He had even mentioned something about marriage just yesterday. Although Isabelle did not believe him to be serious, she did allow herself to entertain the thought. That was why she discredited Hannah's claim that Ezekiel had come to her bed. After all, Hannah was plain, almost ugly, and because she was coy at stealing food, she had an unappealing softness to her figure, and Ezekiel said he would never lie with someone who had the shape of a farrow sow.

A foreign sound in the night caught Isabelle's ears. She held her breath and listened. A faint squishing... Footsteps? Had Hannah somehow gotten free? No, this sound came from the opposite direction. She thought of Ezekiel's ghost story and cowered even tighter against the dyke, pulled against the ring bolt that tethered her to the trunk gate,

42

suppressed a small murmur of fear. The tears welled up again, but she dared not dash them from her eyes lest the manacles clank and give her away. She waited, heart pounding. The footsteps halted close…above her…on the dyke… She forced herself to breathe. Maybe it was Ezekiel…

A large, dark shape dropped in front of her with a splash. Before she could scream, a rough hand clapped over her mouth. Instinctively, she tried to push away but had nowhere to go, the man's weight restraining her against the dyke.

Sharply, he hushed her, close to her ear; definitely not Ezekiel. "I'm not goin' to hurt you. Be quiet."

But her terror made her struggle more. Her cries against his hand continued until the force of his body nearly crushed the breath from her. She closed her eyes and steeled herself against whatever was to come.

"I'm not goin' to hurt you," he rasped more stridently. "Hush yer noise afore yer heard."

Through her fear she recognized the white man's voice. Dumbfounded, she unwittingly surrendered ever so slowly, her trembling body loath to relax and trust.

Before Ketch removed his hand from her mouth, he said, "I brung you victuals."

This revelation won the day, and she stopped all resistance, sniffed back her tears, her famished stomach growling. A weak flash from the storm confirmed his identity.

Ketch reached for a bag secured at his waist and offered it to her. "There's a small bladder of water in there, too."

Tentatively, she took it from him, her shackles rattling, and set it against the side of the dyke, above the standing water. Her teeth chattered in the cooling breeze. Although she wondered why he was here, her interest lay in the provisions. Keeping one eye on him, she pulled a corn biscuit from the sack, faltered then said, "Thank you, sir," before she fell to devouring the food and greedily gulping the water. She had never tasted better.

"You must eat and drink it all now," he said needlessly. "If I leave the poke here, someone'll know you was fed."

Enthusiastically, she obliged, so much so that she nearly forgot his presence until she finished. Then she settled, swallowed the last, and handed the sack over, suddenly sheepish over her ravenous display.

"Thank you, sir," she said clearer this time.

He shifted his weight in the muck. "Yer welcome."

With her hunger now sated, her inquisitiveness took over. "But, sir…why?"

Her question apparently flummoxed him, but eventually he stammered, "Gabriel should've given you somethin' to eat." He paused. "Tell no one I was here, d'ye hear?"

"No, sir. I…I won't." Gabriel would certainly punish her further instead of persecuting Ketch for his indiscretion. If her tongue slipped, she would not know which man to fear more. Her wonderment over Ketch's presence grew. "Did you give Hannah victuals, too?"

"No."

"Why not?"

"You ask too many questions, girl. If there's to be questions, I'll do the askin'."

"Yes, sir."

"Why did you light into that wench? What was it she said to get you in this fix?"

Isabelle hesitated, surprised he should even take an interest in what had happened. "She was speaking false about Ezekiel."

"And why should you concern yerself with that?"

"Well…Ezekiel is my friend."

He scoffed. "You should choose yer friends more wisely."

The chains rattled as she settled her weight slightly away from him against the gate.

"That boy is nothin' but trouble. I've been his driver for a twelve-month now; I know a sight more about 'im than you."

How could he truly know anything about Ezekiel other than the value of his brute strength? What did it gain him to speak badly about Ezekial?

Lightning stabbed the sky again, and she shrank tighter against the trunk gate.

"Does the storm affrighten you?"

"Yes. Very much."

"Well, 'tis nigh over, I should wager." His eyes felt strong upon her, making her even more uncertain and puzzled. "When this rain and breeze dies, the mosquitoes'll pick yer bones clean. Smear more mud on yerself. It'll help protect yer skin."

"Yes, sir."

He stood from his crouch and started to climb the dyke.

Afraid of being left alone, she called out impetuously, "They say you've done evil things."

He paused, remained with his back to her.

Afraid she had angered him, she continued, "But it wasn't an evil thing to bring me food."

"Some might say it was."

She hesitated, surprised that he lingered. "Sir…why is your back scarred like a slave's?"

Roughly, he said, "You wouldn't be chained out here in the dark if you learnt to mind yer tongue better." He climbed the dyke, slipped on the greasy slope, nearly slid back down, but managed to regain his footing. He cursed and left her to the darkness.

***

Ketch dreaded returning to the south rice field the next day. But his gang had a canal to repair and another trunk gate to replace, and Ketch knew he could not avoid the job or Isabelle forever.

His gang arrived at the field shortly after Gabriel's gang had started the early morning work, which was more difficult than the day before because the mud was now calf deep and great care needed to be taken not to damage the tender pips. Unintentionally, Ketch's attention went to Isabelle midway down the field, almost in the very center. She already looked as if she had worked most of the day, her body bent, shoulders rounded, hat gone, hair a massive mess of tangle and mud.

"Izzy's lookin' poorly this mornin', Zeke," Spider taunted. "That sun go up high, she fallin' face first in that there mud, what I reckon."

Zeke grinned. "Looks like she could use a good duckin' in the river. Mebbe I could see to that." He glanced mischievously at his driver. "Mr. Ketch wouldn't mind."

For a stark moment, Ketch wondered if Zeke somehow knew what he had done last night, but then he dismissed the ludicrous thought.

He avoided looking at Isabelle the rest of the morning. When the distant bell sounded for the midday meal, he went away from the slaves and Gabriel, who had already made one too many comments about the welcomed effect of his punishment upon the two women. Ketch took his bowl of beans and rice scooped from the cauldron and retreated upriver to a quiet spot among the trees below where the river lane met the creek. He found solace under an ancient live oak. With the gentle flow of the river before him and the tranquility of two white swans with their young near the marsh opposite, Ketch ate in peace then lay down and hoped to sleep.

But his mind would not rest. All day he had been berating himself for his foolishness last night. True, he had eased Isabelle's sufferings, but the encounter had increased his own, for being close to the girl, touching her had only stirred his interest even more. What would such attraction produce except frustration? Even if it was not imprudent and scandalous to be drawn to her, she would never return his feelings. Besides the color of his skin and his many physical flaws, there were the things she had heard about his past, stories which no doubt magnified even the least of his crimes. She must believe them. Or did she? Judging from her question last night, perhaps she nurtured a kernel of doubt. It irritated him that her opinion mattered, for he was normally unmoved by others' judgment; life was easier that way. Yet he wished she knew the truth—he had not always been the monster others portrayed him to be, and he desired to be something better, as he had been this past year.

When he returned to where the slaves were finishing their meal near the storage barn, his steps slowed. In the shade of the barn's lee, Zeke reclined next to Isabelle, who sat with her bowl in hand. Zeke said something that made her laugh through the gray, dried mud on her face. It was the first time Ketch had seen her happy. The brightness of her smile and the ludic quality of her laughter transformed her, banished the fatigue and disarray of her outer appearance. Zeke used the back of one finger to scrape some of the dirt from her cheek. Umbrage brought heat to Ketch's face, and he marched toward Zeke, who had his back to him. Isabelle saw his advance. Her smile vanished, and she looked down at her bowl. Before Zeke could turn to see what concerned her, Ketch swatted the young man's ear.

"Back to work, you lazy dog."

"You heard the man," Gabriel added, coming out of the barn. "Back to work, the lot of you."

Zeke shot Ketch an angry glance, but not before he gave Isabelle a rakish grin to show that his driver did not cow him. Ketch kicked him soundly in the ribs. With a frown, Isabelle started back to the field. She chanced a glance over her shoulder at Ketch, as if wondering if he was the same man who had come to her the night before.

When the afternoon bell tolled, suspending work, Ketch trailed off to the stables, shuffling along the edge of the lane that led past the south side of the house, the mud deeply cut by wagon wheels. The sweet scent of the last magnolias in the trees to his left seemed particularly strong in the breeze made fresher by the previous night's rain. To his right, the rear sward opened before him, the grass of the flat sweep shining in the sun like polished emeralds, the sheep mowing the tender pasture that appeared to have grown an inch overnight. A peahen, perched upon a fence post near the entrance to the stable-yard, twisted its neck to turn a glistening, wary eye upon him.

The stable-yard was quiet save for a couple of slave children racing about the barn, voices high and ceaseless, chasing one another, laughing. The yard was a quadrangle with the barn at one end and a small carriage house opposite. On the far side from the entranceway, a row of slave cabins for the skilled workers formed the third side of the yard, and the shops of the blacksmith, cooper, and carpenter on the near side completed the shape.

Ketch's feet made no sound upon the soft earth and thus went undetected by Jack Mallory, who stood near the half-finished crib at one end of the carpenter's shed, his back toward Ketch. His hand rested upon the railing, caressing the cypress wood. His rolled-up sleeve exposed a simple leather bracelet bearing two sapphire beads that he wore always on his right wrist, a creation he had crafted as a boy and presented to his mother.

"I plan on finishin' the crib."

Mallory started at the sound of Ketch's voice but turned only partway. His hand came away from the wood, and a small frown twitched the new growth of his mustache. "Maria told me you and Helen were making this."

Ketch said nothing, allowed the boy to be uncomfortable.

Mallory looked at him at last. "'Twas kind of you to visit her, to think of her with this." He nodded to the crib.

Warily, Ketch eyed him. While usually focused and active, Mallory seemed distracted and almost lethargic since the death of his unborn child. Normally in the evenings, master and mistress sat upon the rear portico, watching the sun set over the western wood after putting Helen to bed, but since the miscarriage, some evenings Mallory was absent from the portico. Was the grief for himself as much as for Maria and the child? Ketch knew the boy was prone to brooding.

A foreign sensation prodded Ketch until he recognized the sensation as pity for his master. The realization disconcerted him. Over the past year of serving Mallory, Ketch had felt anything but pity, for he could not forgive him for Ella Logan's death. After all, the young man's search for his long-lost mother had ultimately led to her end. Mallory bore him the same ill will for killing Helen's father, and no matter Ketch's reformation, the boy mistrusted him; if Ketch could betray one master, he could betray a second.

Mallory studied him as if he, too, revisited their turbulent past. "Since we came to Leighlin, Maria's had faith in you. As you know, I

47

have not. But I admit you've surprised me over this past twelve-month."

Cynicism twisted Ketch's thin lips. "Well, that makes two of us."

Mallory considered him, nodded then started past him.

Emboldened, Ketch said, "She's not afeared to bear another child."

Mallory halted.

"She's strong, like yer mother."

The boy turned back to him, mahogany eyes now black with anguish. "Aye. And I don't want to lose her like my mother." He gave a look of significance to remind Ketch of their shared grief before briskly leaving the stable-yard.

***

"I think Mr. Ketch fancies you, Izzy," Ezekiel said with a roguish smile flashing through the night. "My bruised ribs tell me so."

Isabelle gave his arm a playful swat. "You've been teasing me all night, Ezekiel. Stop."

They sat close together upon a log at the edge of the woods where the lane to the settlement emerged and trailed in a gray line toward the kitchen house. The kitchen house was dark, its occupants asleep like most of Leighlin. One light, however, faintly shone in Samuel's cabin across the lane.

Samuel, who lived there alone, was fodder for Isabelle's ever-insatiable curiosity about all things. She admired him, though his austere manner intimidated her a bit. She could tell from what she had seen and heard so far that he was a man of integrity and honor. Hannah and Ester often pined over him, but he paid them no heed, which made Isabelle like him even more. Sometimes, when she and Ezekiel sat here, she saw one or more of Leighlin's white men come calling on Samuel. In fact, Ketch and two others had left just a few minutes ago and had disappeared into the lower level of the Big House, bringing about Ezekiel's comment.

"I'm not teasin' you, Izzy." He put his arm around her in the sticky warm night. "Didn't you see Mr. Ketch look over at us jus' now? He jealous. Why else would he cuff me in front of you today for nothin'?"

She almost mentioned Ketch's opinion of him, just as she had several times considered telling him about Ketch's visit to the field. But her promise and the concern over the consequences should she break it kept her tongue silent.

"Why would he be jealous? Everyone says he don't desire women."

"Mebbe not most womenfolk, but he desire you." Ezekiel kissed her neck. "And I's glad he do."

"Why?"

"'Cause for once I has somethin' more than he do."

"But what would stop him from doing whatever he wants with me? You couldn't stop him."

"The Cap'n; he don't let no white man lie with no slave. That's one of his rules."

"But…the Captain…does *he* lie with his slaves like Mr. Tom does?"

"Never heard tell of it. But give 'im time, Izzy. If'n his wife can't give him no babies, he jus' might take someone who can. So, you take care he don't notice you. That is, if he hasn't already. You said they asked if you been a house slave before."

His words worried her. "Yes, but I told 'em I hadn't."

"That was smart of you. That's what I like about you, Izzy. You a smart one. Not thick like those other goats what come with you from Clark."

She smiled to herself, delighted whenever he put her above the others who so maligned her.

They fell into silence, his arm still holding her close. Isabelle lowered her head against his shoulder and closed her eyes, barely able to stay awake after Gabriel's punishment and today's unending hours. She had fallen asleep over her supper plate, and that was where Ezekiel had found her before taking her hand and leading her off to enjoy the sight of the Big House with its windows alight. But first, Ezekiel had taken her to the side of his own cabin, pressed her up against it and kissed her in his urgent, hungry way. She had allowed it, even enjoyed it, which pleased and relieved her. His advances had grown bolder, and she had feared he would force himself upon her right there, but when she resisted more strongly, he sighed impatiently and stepped back from her.

Almost angrily, he had asked, "Is it 'cause of that Mr. Tom?"

"I want to be married next time I do it. They say all those bad things about me; I won't make 'em right."

He chuckled and said, "Married, eh?" then took her hand and started back toward the lane.

"Why Hannah hate you so much, Izzy?"

"We grew up together. She had no parents, and she was jealous of

49

how close me and Mama were, how happy we were. She was always getting in trouble and getting whipped. I stayed out of trouble, so I wouldn't get whipped, but she figured because I was half white that was why I didn't get beat like her. And she thinks Tom Clark gave me privileges because I'm half white, too. Didn't matter how much I told her about how horrible he was to me. She didn't believe me."

Now she looked toward the manor house, dark save for a light in the two lower chambers on the north side—those belonging to Ketch and the other white men. She wondered about the one-armed man and his behavior last night, a far cry from Tom Clark. Whatever had driven him to do such a thing? Was Ezekiel right about him being interested in her?

"Maybe," she said aloud, almost to herself, "Mr. Ketch hasn't done all the things people say, just like the cruel things people say about me aren't true."

Ezekiel laughed. "Now you bein' a foolish thing, Izzy. Everything they say about that devil Ketch be true. You go ask Jemmy."

Isabelle frowned at the thought of the mulatto stable-boy, a shy, kind young man. She murmured, "Maybe I will ask him."

Ezekiel laughed even harder, squeezed her against him. "You is a funny one, Izzy."

"Why would he do that to Jemmy? Why Jemmy?"

"'Cause Jemmy was our first master's favorite; he treated that boy almost like he was Miss Helen's brother. Ketch was mad at Cap'n Logan, so he done that nastiness to Jemmy to make the Cap'n mad, to spit in his eye, so to say."

"Why was Ketch mad?"

"'Cause Cap'n Logan let our young master come here. Ketch hate him, somethin' to do with Miss Ella dyin'. No one know for sure. But Ketch didn't want our new master nowhere abouts here."

"But, if Mr. Ketch hates the Captain so, why is he here?"

"'Cause of that li'l girl—Miss Helen. They say he made a promise to Miss Ella that he would keep her safe."

"But she has her brother for that."

"Well, like I said, Ketch and the Cap'n, they not 'zactly friends. Ketch prolly don't put much store in the Cap'n when it come to that child."

"But if Mr. Ketch cares so much for that child…well, he can't be all bad. A bad man wouldn't care an owl's hoot for a child, especially one what's not his own."

Ezekiel laughed again, buried his nose against her ear. "You of all folk should know there nothin' good 'bout no white man."

"My mama says there's good in everyone, black and white."

Ezekiel snorted skeptically. "Was there good in Mr. Tom?"

Isabelle frowned. "Maybe…before I knew him."

"Well, think what you want 'bout Ketch. I has to put up with him every day, and I's here to tell you, your mama wrong. Now," his hands moved over her, his lips sought hers, "enough about that one-armed devil. Let's talk 'bout us."

She smiled and kissed him back. "What about us?"

"When you gonna marry me, Izzy?"

"You haven't asked me."

"Well, I's askin' now." His touch grew bolder.

"What if I say no?"

"And why would you go and do that?" One of his hands worked its way beneath her skirt and up her leg. "Don't you want to see the look on everyone's face when we tell 'em?" He chuckled roguishly and kissed her neck. "That Ketch just might turn purple and bust."

"Ezekiel…"

"Don't you reckon I's a good man, too? Remember what your mama said."

Quietly, she laughed and half-heartedly fended off his upward creeping hand, rearranging her skirt, tucking it between her thighs. The gesture made him moan with disappointment.

"C'mon now, Izzy. Don't be cruel to me. I want an answer, right now. Hasn't I been good to you?"

"Yes," she murmured, infinitely happy to have someone to think fondly of when she lay in bed at night.

"Then say yes." He kissed her and grinned. "Say yes right now."

She closed her eyes and softly giggled, knew this was the new beginning for which she had hoped, a way to start her own family and join the larger family around her, to be accepted. She just needed to say one simple word.

She slipped her arms around him, kissed him, and whispered, "Yes."

CHAPTER 4

Once a month, Jack Mallory and his wife invited two of Leighlin's hired hands to Sunday dinner. Ketch often wished—as he did today—that they did not, for he was no hand at trivial conversation, nor did he fancy being social with Jack Mallory. True, his rancor had eased over the past year, but it displeased him to see the pup ensconced at the head of the table like a prince, as he was this blistering July afternoon upon the shaded front portico.

Thus far, Ketch had been spared from conversation as Samuel and Mallory discussed crops and slaves, and Helen kept Maria occupied, though often Maria's attention drifted downriver. Wishing she were somewhere else perhaps. Maybe that was what she needed right now—a distraction, something to take her mind off her loss. Perhaps a sail aboard the *Adventuress* would set her up once Leighlin's merchant brig returned from New York. Ketch, however, knew it was not his place to suggest such a thing.

"Mr. Ketch," Helen chirped, her fingers deep in a sweet potato, "are you coming to the wedding today?"

Her question stirred a sourness in Ketch's belly, and he felt the eyes of everyone at the table turn to him. But he refused to look up from his meal. "No, Miss Helen."

"Why not?" came the inevitable, dreaded inquiry. "You're Zeke's master."

"No, child; yer brother is Zeke's master." He put new effort into eating his mutton and keeping his mouth full.

"Maria and I picked flowers, and I have a basket of rose petals that I'm going to throw at the wedding. That's what Mamma used to have me do. Remember, Mr. Ketch?"

He grunted.

"Helen," Maria said, rescuing him, "if you don't quit chattering like a squirrel and finish your dinner, we'll miss the wedding. You wanted me to do your hair, remember?"

This tactic shushed the girl for a bit, and Ketch was left to the safety of his food. He had no desire to think of Zeke's impending marriage or to think of the bride. Last month when Zeke announced his good fortune, Ketch kept his own counsel but grew ever more perturbed as the event drew closer. Yet he scoffed at himself for having any sort of interest in the matter. After all, it had no effect on his life, his waking and eating, working and sleeping. It did not affect those whom he safeguarded. The whole thing was nothing but the meaningless passage of time and events for slaves, beings whose "marriages" held no more lawful validity than if Mallory officiated the union between the plantation's stallion and one of its mares.

When he looked down the rectangular table at Jack Mallory, who was finishing the last of his wine, he experienced a wild moment in which he considered voicing his opinion in the hopes that the boy would intervene and forbid the wedding. But Ketch held his tongue, for Mallory would not like to hear that anyone wanted to stand in the way of what he viewed as the success and validation of his prescience. And he and Maria could both question Ketch's motivation for meddling in such affairs, and for that he could give no answers, nor did he wish to search for any.

"When are you going to get married, Mr. Ketch?" Helen's onslaught continued with her usual bright expression of innocent inquiry.

"Helen," Maria scolded. "That's not a polite thing to ask of someone. What are you thinking, child?"

"I was just wondering."

"Well, you must keep your wondering to yourself. Now, come along. If these gentlemen will excuse us, we'll go to your chamber and get you ready."

Shortly thereafter, Jack Mallory apologized for his hasty departure in order to prepare for the ceremony. Ketch listened to the young man's footsteps as they receded into the house. Like James Logan had done before him, Mallory presided over all slave weddings at Leighlin and gave his blessing, a tradition that for some reason pleased the slaves.

Ketch felt Samuel's attention upon him from across the table. He scowled at the black man. "What?"

Samuel took a swallow of wine, all the while studying his former shipmate with his almond-shaped eyes. Once the servants had removed the deserted settings and gone into the house, Samuel set his glass down and said, "This wedding vexes you."

Ketch scoffed. "What vexes me is that infernal bugger Zeke. He's not fit to marry anything, not even a dog. You know how he is." He tossed his linen onto the table. "This is just another way to get attention. That girl's nothin' but a prize to him, a prize won in a contest to get married afore his mates do. That's all she's ever been to him since she got here. I hear his braggin', and I seen his struttin' about like a cock with a new hen. But that girl don't have enough sense to see it."

"She's an outcast, Ketch. She's lucky even Zeke will marry her. *He* damn sure won't be an outcast, so I doubt he'll let his wife continue to be treated like one."

Ketch had failed to see the situation in this light. Perhaps Samuel was right and Zeke was better than nothing for the girl. Perhaps Isabelle had confided in Samuel, told him things that Ketch could never conceive.

Yet no matter the logic, Ketch still felt ill at ease about the wedding when he left the table. From there he armed himself and headed into the west wood, traveling deep into the swampy forest to a favored deer blind. There, with musket balanced patiently upon a rest he had cleverly fashioned, he remained into the evening, far from the sounds of celebration, waiting for something to kill.

***

"I wish Mama was here," Isabelle murmured, more to herself than to Selah, who stood behind her, trying to tame Isabelle's hair. Realizing how her comment might be misconstrued as unappreciative, she added, "Thank you for helping me, Selah."

The older woman gave a quiet grunt, intent on weaving flowers into Isabelle's small, frizzled curls. Isabelle was glad to have someone near, someone who listened to her nervous, excited prattle about her mother and about Ezekiel and sometimes even offered comments.

The sweet scent of roasting pork infiltrated her cabin, drifting over from the central fire pit where a pig was slowly turning on a spit, attended by one of the few slaves remaining in the settlement. Earlier, Isabelle had seen the tables at the center of the settlement, tables provided by the master, which would bear the wedding feast brought by the women of the kitchen house. These preparations, however, were not unique to her wedding; as Selah had told her, the Captain and the master before him had always provided such things for a slave's marriage. Just the same, Isabelle felt special for one day, proudly singled out among the people. Her optimism about the future rose.

Anxiously, Isabelle smoothed the front of her new dress. A pale brown thing, nothing fancy, but it pleased her all the same. The mistress had also provided a new apron, its white almost dazzling to Isabelle.

The jangle of a horse and carriage reached her ears, then a mild voice from outside said, "Whoa, Curly."

Just then Selah finished with her hair and touched her shoulder. "Are you ready?" Selah gave her a small smile, like someone who knew a secret.

Isabelle hurried to the open doorway. Her breath caught. Leighlin's polished gig waited at the foot of the porch steps, Jemmy grinning at her from the driver's seat. Greenery and wildflowers wreathed the gig. The bay gelding nodded in irritation at the flowers woven into forelock and braided mane. When he shook his great body, the harness trembled but shed only a few of its daisies.

Isabelle managed to strangle out, "This is for me?" as Selah stepped onto the porch behind her.

"It be," Jemmy said as he hopped down to assist her navigation of the steps, as if she had never walked before. "Miss Maria…she say the bride would be all dirty and melted by the time she walk to the Big House, so she sent me and Curly to fetch you. I'm afeared Curly's not too pleased 'bout the flowers an' all, him being a boy. And Sunday's normally his day off."

"How kind of Miss Maria." Isabelle glanced uneasily at the fussing bay horse as she gathered the folds of her dress. Jemmy and Selah helped her climb into the gig without her dress disturbing the decorations. Jemmy sprang aboard and reclaimed the lines.

"But, Jemmy, there isn't enough room for Selah."

"No need," the woman answered. "I'll follow along behind. Don't look like that hawse can move no faster than me no how."

Curly let out a displeased snort, and Isabelle laughed.

Shyly, Jemmy said to her, "You look purty," and clucked to the horse and tickled the hindquarters with a short whip.

Isabelle blushed and thanked him. She felt a moment of fellowship with the boy, considering he was a mulatto, too, and, from what she had heard, he often suffered some of the same prejudice she did, perhaps even more so because of what Ketch was said to have done to him. The very thought made her look away from Jemmy, though she felt ashamed for doing so. After all, who was to say those stories were true? She of all people should know to ignore gossip.

By the time they left the settlement, Jemmy had managed to prod Curly into a slow trot. Isabelle put her hands to her hair to keep the flowers in place. Soon they emerged from the shade of the trees near the sward where afternoon sun flashed against the sweaty horse and sparkled on the well-oiled harness. A fresh smile captured Isabelle's lips when she saw most of Leighlin's people across the sward near the Big House. Soon all faces turned her way, and she laughed nervously at being the center of attention. At the top of the rear portico steps stood master, mistress, and Helen, colorful beacons above the drab cluster of Africans. Flowers in vases and hanging baskets decorated the portico. She searched for Ezekiel and at last saw him near the steps. Joy swelled in her bosom. If only her mother were here... She must remember every last detail, so she could relate all of it should they one day reunite.

The crowd parted as the gig drew near and halted at the portico steps. Voices around her, mostly those of the men from Ezekiel's gang, called out encouragement and witticisms. Isabelle glanced up at the Mallorys, who waited patiently. Helen's bright smile gave Isabelle courage. Ezekiel looked oddly unsettled, dressed in new breeches and a clean shirt whose collar had been tied closed for a change; he even wore shoes. Isabelle had never thought it possible that he would be unnerved by anything, but his apprehension was quite plain now. He did his best to hide it, offering her a wayward grin as Jemmy helped her from the gig.

Helen bounced down the steps, sweetgrass basket in hand.

"You look so pretty, Isabelle!"

Surprised Helen knew her name, Isabelle felt her cheeks redden from all the attention. She tried to ignore the fact that few in the crowd appeared truly joyful over the event. She suspected many were there just to see the spectacle and partake in the feast afterwards. Hannah was not among them.

"Are you ready?" Helen asked both of them.

Isabelle could only nod. She looked to Ezekiel, and he offered her a strained smile and took her hand. She squeezed it in return.

Helen reached into her basket and preceded them with a rain of red rose petals as they slowly ascended the steps. Some of the petals landed on Ezekiel's shaved head, and Isabelle stifled a giggle as he wiped them away while she ignored the ones that alighted in her hair. Helen's enthusiasm eased the tension and made Isabelle realize how tightly she was holding Ezekiel's hand.

Once they reached the sandstone tiles of the portico, Isabelle looked to her master. This was the first time she had seen him up close since the day of her arrival at Leighlin. He had seemed a bit stiff and stern that day, but now he offered a small smile to the couple. Perhaps he was remembering his own wedding day.

Maria came to stand at Isabelle's side, giving her a heartening nod and smile. When Maria had offered to be her witness, Isabelle had been surprised. Perhaps her mistress had feared that no one in the settlement would volunteer for such a position and so had offered her services out of pity. Or maybe it was simply a tradition for her to stand up for any female slave married at Leighlin. Isabelle had lacked the courage to ask the reason, but she had expressed her appreciation all the same.

From the direction of the settlement, Asa came racing across the sward, drawing some laughter among the audience, especially the youngsters. Soon he darted up the steps two at a time to stand next to Ezekiel, breathing hard. Ezekiel tossed him a wry look, and Asa grinned sheepishly and whispered, "Sorry, Zeke," bowed to their master and apologized again for his tardiness.

With Helen beaming from slightly behind her brother, the Captain began to read from a worn book. From her days with Tom Clark, Isabelle knew it was the Bible by the words on the cover. She wondered if the Captain thought she were a Christian. Some of the slaves were, those who had never known Africa, while others clung to the religions of their home countries. Isabelle's mother had little belief in either side of the subject. Because Tom Clark claimed to be a Christian, Isabelle had discounted the religion some time ago.

Isabelle forced herself to pay attention to the story the Captain was reading. He spoke of many things, and though she tried to listen attentively, her heart pounding loudly in her ears distracted her. The birds seemed overly strident in their songs, the cicadas particularly shrill in the rise and fall of their unearthly sounds. The Captain said something about a man leaving his parents and clinging to his wife. Isabelle focused hard upon the book. Surely the words were important, otherwise the Captain would not be reading them.

"What therefore God hath joined together, let not man separate."

For a moment, Isabelle expected him to continue, but he closed the book with a gentle but significant thump and held it to his breast. Isabelle looked to Ezekiel, unsure.

"I now pronounce you man and wife."

Helen burst forth with a cheer and tossed the rest of the rose petals into the air. Laughter escaped mistress and master and a few of the watching slaves. Isabelle started to laugh as well, a nervous titter, but then Ezekiel took her face in his hands and kissed her, stealing her breath. From below came a few shouts and a smattering of applause. When Ezekiel freed her, they turned together to face their people, but it was Asa whom Ezekiel addressed first.

"See here, Asa," the young man grinned at his friend. "I done told you I'd be the first one married. When is I ever wrong?"

***

"The Cap'n wants to see you in the library, suh." Thomas, Leighlin's oldest house servant—tall, reed-like, and dutiful—stood in the doorway of Ketch's bedchamber only long enough to make his announcement.

Ketch grumbled as he struggled out of bed. Rarely was he summoned thus. If Mallory required something of him, orders were simply relayed through Willis. He had planned an early night of it. The July days seemed hotter as one passed into the next, each draining him a little bit more than the one before. The fact that his sleep was often disturbed by unpleasant dreams of Isabelle's wedding only heightened his need for true rest. What could the boy possibly want from him at this hour?

Still complaining to himself, Ketch marched past the other men playing cards at the table in the common room. Only for a second did he consider using the servants' spiral staircase that led to the upper floors, but then he decided against the tight passage and went outside to the portico steps to access the main floor.

As was his habit, he glanced up to the windows of Helen's chamber. Already dark. The girl was abed, tucked in and read a story by her brother as usual. She had probably been asleep before the story advanced very far, for her day had been a busy one. Young David Archer and his wife, Elizabeth, had spent much of today at Leighlin, having come downriver from their neighboring plantation, Wildwood. They were particular friends of the Mallorys, and Helen adored both of them, especially David. She had known him since her first days at Leighlin and had looked upon him as a brother until the genuine article showed up.

Thomas was there at the front door to admit Ketch into the spacious, high-ceilinged stair hall. Then the servant glided away into the house's interior. Maria was descending the right-hand staircase, carrying a pewter candleholder to light her way, for the beautiful chandelier was unlit.

"Ketch, is something wrong?"

It was not usual for him to enter the main floor except when he was invited to Sunday dinner. Not because he was unwelcomed there, but because he knew it was not his place.

"Yer husband summoned me."

58

"Oh…"

Her obvious surprise made Ketch wary. Her glance darted through the inner doorway, diagonal across the Great Hall to the rear library, as if expecting to see her spouse. Shadows lingered in her eyes from her child's death, and these days Ketch sensed a subtle tension between master and mistress. Since the time of Isabelle's arrival at Leighlin, things had been off kilter at the plantation. The peace that had settled upon them in the past year seemed to be slipping away.

"Well, I hope Jack doesn't keep you long. It's getting late. I'm sure you're tired." She bid him good evening and headed for the parlor.

Pushing his worries aside, Ketch entered the Great Hall, the clangorous fall of his worn shoes upon the wood floor heralding his arrival. The room served to welcome guests with its high ceiling and marble fireplaces, one on the north wall, one on the south. Light from a stand of candles at the rear of the Hall gleamed upon the broad pine floorboards, the quivering flames reflected in the windows that flanked the door to the west portico where Isabelle had been wed. Shadow and light played upon the fluted pilasters and the ornate moldings of carved magnolia and dogwood blossoms.

Thomas stood at the library door, which he opened upon Ketch's approach and closed after announcing and admitting him.

Jack Mallory sat at an oak desk strewn with papers, eyes as black as the night beyond the windows behind him. His face appeared darker than usual here in the dim lamplight, his loose hair draping forward to veil his features where he hunched over his work. The sight took Ketch aback, for he easily remembered James Logan in a similar posture, looking equally harried over Leighlin's paperwork and responsibilities. Both men had preferred a quarterdeck to a desk. Also like Logan, Mallory had an affinity for brandy, an attraction that seemed to have grown since the miscarriage. A decanter sat upon a serving tray on the corner of the desk, a single glass in front of the young man, nearly empty, with the glint of lamplight upon the wet rim.

"Sit," he invited him.

An upholstered chair in front of the desk had been moved from its usual location near the vacant hearth. Ketch sank into it, attention never leaving the boy. Mallory was unsettled, and Ketch searched through the past days for something he may have done to displease the pup and precipitate this meeting. No physical movement revealed the young man's unrest; instead, it lurked in his gaze, which did not remain long upon his guest, for Mallory was well-aware of Ketch's ability to read even the subtlest of moods. The boy had always tried to hide weakness

59

or indecisiveness around him, a defensiveness that harkened back to their early relationship.

"Elizabeth Archer," Mallory began, "has invited Maria and Helen to leave with her next week for Virginia to visit her family." He finished the last swallow of brandy. "I would like for you to accompany them." He eyed the decanter but refrained from pouring more; surely his restraint was not simply out of politeness.

"You won't be goin'?" Ketch's question was born of genuine surprise instead of the old desire to insult or wound the boy. However, Ketch could see that his inquiry did indeed pain the young man. Whose idea was it truly for him to remain behind?

"I can't go. There's too much to be done here."

And there was an overseer who lacked the master's full confidence.

At first Mallory's directive irritated Ketch, for going to Joseph Archer's tobacco plantation would offer nothing but boredom. Yet when he considered his foul mood since Zeke's marriage to Isabelle, he realized Virginia might offer a fortuitous change and erase the pointless distraction the girl had caused him.

"How long will we be gone?"

"You'll probably not return until September, after the worst of the heat passes."

Nigh unto two months. Ketch was astonished, though skilled enough to mask his reaction. Whose idea was this trip? Was the boy so terrified to lie with his wife and endanger her again that he thought this the only solution? Ketch knew such foolishness would pain Maria.

"Do you feel Gabriel capable of assuming the responsibility of your gang while you're gone?"

Ketch considered.

"I understand Zeke is a bit more…content since his marriage."

Ketch scowled. "Don't 'spect that to last."

"What, the marriage or his contentment?"

"That cur will never be content. He won't get no attention thataway."

"So, do you or don't you think Gabriel can handle him and your gang?"

Ketch grumbled, "For a time, I reckon."

"Very well. I'll let Willis know. I'll tell you more about your departure once the Archers inform me. Helen is very excited about the journey. I'm trusting you to keep her out of trouble, especially while at sea. She has it in her head she should be allowed to climb to the masthead whenever the whim strikes her."

An uncharacteristic nudge of pride in his entrusted role straightened Ketch's posture. "Do her good to get away, it will," he said. "She's been at Leighlin too long."

Mallory gave him a sharp look, as if he had been accused of something. Or was it envy that Ketch was going with his sister and wife? "Elizabeth Archer has younger siblings. I'm sure Helen will enjoy their company." He reached for the decanter and poured more brandy before he said, "That will be all."

CHAPTER 5

Isabelle knocked on door after door in the darkened settlement but received the same irritated response, "He's not here." Those whom she awakened were particularly gruff with their answers, some cursed her. With each rebuff, she grew more and more disturbed, but she kept anxiety from her voice lest someone laugh at her for losing her husband.

The last cabin she approached was where Hannah now lived with Jacob and Ester, who had been married last month. But when she stepped softly onto their porch, she halted. The sounds from within heated her face, and she wondered how Hannah could bear sharing such a small space when Jacob and Ester were grunting and moaning in their marriage bed. Some said Hannah joined them at times, and Isabelle certainly had no desire to interrupt or witness such a spectacle, so she quickly retreated.

Where was Ezekiel? There was no reason for him to be away from home. Perhaps she should go to Samuel and alert him. No, Samuel might cause a stir for nothing. Maybe Ezekiel had stolen one of Leighlin's small boats and slipped away to one of the other Ashley River plantations where he had friends and would be back before daylight. He had told her how he chanced that now and then. If she alerted Samuel to this possibility, it would only get Ezekiel in a peck of trouble. Surely he had not run off. As much as Ezekiel railed against his lot in life and those who enslaved him, Isabelle did not think him cunning enough or willing to take such a risk. After all, there was nowhere to run to here in the wilderness. Fleeing to Charles Town or another plantation would inevitably see him caught. The Indians who lived in the region would not harbor him, for they traded with Leighlin; they would not want to jeopardize their peaceful commerce. But what if he had gone into the swamps and taken a misstep? There were so many alligators and poisonous snakes. Perhaps she *should* tell Samuel.

But she ultimately decided against it. Best to wait a while longer. So she shuffled back to her lodgings—a new cabin built after their wedding—hoping that Ezekiel would be there when she arrived, but she found it dark. She stared at their home for a moment before climbing the porch.

They had been married nearly two months now. The first month had been nothing but happiness for Isabelle—having someone for whom to cook and someone with whom she could talk. And with Ketch gone to Virginia and Ezekiel assigned to Gabriel, she was even able to see her husband during the day and eat their midday meal together. In the evenings, they would join the others of the settlement around the central fire, and as usual Ezekiel was one of the most active talkers. At first, he tried to include Isabelle, and she did her best to join the conversation, but as time went by she was disappointed that most still cared little to befriend a mulatto, married to Ezekiel or not. And when some started to exclude Ezekiel, her husband became vexed, and in the past week he ignored her when they were at the circle.

She entered the cabin and stripped off her clothes; Ezekiel always insisted that she sleep naked. Her lips twisted at the memory of their first night together. She had done her best to avoid thoughts of Tom Clark, to be unafraid of her husband's touch, but Ezekiel had sensed her unease. He had chuckled in her ear and tried in his own somewhat heavy-handed way to comfort her, telling her how much she would enjoy him and how being with him would make her forget Clark. After those first few awkward nights, she grew used to his ways, and if not completely able to enjoy the experience, she at least lost some of her anxiety and became a more active participant.

Ezekiel had managed to acquire some old mosquito netting and had hung it about their bed. She pushed it aside now and crawled onto the rice-straw mattress, her heart still beating faster than normal, her thoughts running wild over her husband's fate. Again, she considered going to Samuel but remained in bed, her hands twisting the coarse sheet, staring up at the ceiling. What if Ezekiel had decided he had made a mistake marrying her? What if he had run away because of her? When she finally dozed off, her unsettling thoughts manifested themselves in dark dreams.

Dawn tinged the eastern sky a pale pink when a familiar, distant cough awoke Isabelle. She struggled beyond the netting, grabbed her shift and pulled it over her head. Her heart beat with anticipation as she rushed to the door. Ezekiel mounted the steps, clothing rumpled, eyes bloodshot. He failed to return her smile.

"Ezekiel, where have you been?" She reached for his arm, expecting a kiss, but he brushed past her into the cabin.

"Why isn't there food on the table?"

Dumbfounded by his abruptness, she followed him inside. "I'll get things started right away. I was fretting all night about you; I just now finally fell asleep. Where was you?"

"At Jacob's. Fell asleep there."

Remembering what she had heard last night, she frowned. Certainly, Ezekiel could not have slept through that. Was he lying to her? But why would he feel a need to lie? She should have knocked on Jacob's door. She thought of Hannah and her loose ways, but, considering Ezekiel's disparaging remarks about the woman since her arrival at Leighlin, he could not be interested in her. Besides, there was no need for him to stray; he had an attentive wife.

Ezekiel said little during their quick meal, and she could tell by his tired, irritable expression that to press him further on the issue would be pointless. Besides, he had given her an explanation. He was her husband; she should trust him.

When she and the others reached the south rice field that morning, her nose twitched at the lingering odor of mud and soaked vegetation from the harvest flow having been drained into the river. Now before them lay acres and acres of shoulder-high, slim green stalks bending to the river breeze, bearing untold numbers of grains of rice. It amazed Isabelle to remember the small pips just a few months ago and to now look upon the mature plants. She thought of her mother's tales of her home in West Africa and how every morning she used mortar and pestle to mill the rice she then cooked for her family, she and all the women of their village working together in an age-old tradition.

A wagon rumbled up, Jemmy at the reins, carrying dozens of short-handled implements. Jemmy halted the mules next to Gabriel, who wore two pistols today instead of one. Perhaps that had something to do with the blades in that wagon.

"Each of you grab one of them rice hooks," Gabriel directed, stepping back.

When her turn came, Isabelle took one of the crescent-shaped tools from the wagon and threaded her wrist through the leather strap on the wooden handle. Carefully exploring the sharp blade with her thumb, she retreated. Ezekiel also tested his blade, his gaze flicking to Gabriel, who sent Jemmy away with the empty wagon. In the morning sunlight, sweat already slicked Gabriel's face, and his right hand rested upon the butt of one pistol.

"Now," he began, "we have some newcomers among us, but I was told they already know about harvestin' rice. That right?"

64

Isabelle looked down, for the only thing she knew about rice harvesting came from her mother's stories, and she certainly remembered no practical details.

"We 'uns knows," Ester spoke up. "We 'uns was born and raised 'round rice afore we got brung 'cross the sea. But that mulatto there...she don't know nuthin' 'bout harvestin' rice. Reckon I show her."

"You show her, Ester." Ezekiel regarded the rice hook with contempt. "This be womenfolk's work, after all."

"Mebbe in Africa, boy," Gabriel said. "But in Carolina it's everybody's work."

Some of the women laughed at Ezekiel, which did nothing to lessen the young man's scowl.

Ester gave Isabelle a look of superiority before climbing the dyke, rice hook in hand, and descending into the field. The others perched atop the dyke, happy to have their work delayed. The saturated soil oozed between Ester's toes. She bent to the task and, with smooth accuracy, her hook severed the stalks near the bottom of the plant. She did this several times, each time binding the sheaves together with heavy twine from her apron and laying them upon the stubble. Then she straightened to see if Gabriel wanted further demonstration.

"You see how she cut down low?" He had directed his question at Isabelle. "After you bind it, you let it lay atop the stubble, so it can dry. Don't let it lie in the mud, hear? Take care, all of you, or you'll regret it, mark me. Each man has half an acre as their task today; each woman a quarter of an acre. That's how we marked off the field yesterday, recollect. See there? And with the harvest startin', that's the end of the afternoon break. Exceptin' dinner, you'll work straight through till your task is done. Understand?"

Well, Isabelle told herself as she stepped into the field, at least this was something different than weeding and hoeing or tending to Leighlin's other crops, and with the field drained she would not have to worry so much about water snakes. She had seen one of the ugly brown serpents swimming close a couple of weeks ago, and she had frozen in place, the handle of her hoe held in a death grip, ready to wield it if needed. But the snake merely flicked its evil eyes and tongue at her and continued on its way. When she called out to warn the other slaves, she nearly caused a stampede. Gabriel had been furious, for the scramble damaged some plants. He had warned her and everyone else that if such an outcry went up again, he would personally take the offenders to the swamps and throw them to the alligators. Isabelle figured his threat a mere bluff, for they were too valuable to kill, especially at harvest time, but she had no desire to test him.

The serpent had made her think of Ketch and the stories she had heard about his snake bite. Only the devil himself could survive a water snake bite, the people said. She considered his amputated arm and thought a devil would not have lost a limb to a mere snake. Ezekiel occasionally remarked how glad he was that Ketch was gone and how he hoped the villain would never return. Isabelle also thought of him whenever she looked at the trunk gate where she had been chained that night back in early June. That secret encounter still confused her, and she had to admit that the puzzle of his motivation continued to intrigue her. She liked the idea that perhaps she, though unwittingly, had been responsible for prompting goodness in someone believed to lack such a quality.

Although the brutal days of summer were just gone, the temperature still soared as Isabelle toiled with her rice hook, her back aching. Sweat soaked her clothes and headscarf, trickled down her face so she often had to wipe it away, eyes burning with the saltiness. The mud clung to her feet like lead. She was clumsy with the hook, more so than she had been with a hoe, and Gabriel often berated her, demanding she quicken her pace. Her lack of sleep from the night before slowed her best efforts.

When the midday meal break came, she cared more for the shade of the barn and bordering trees than food. She gathered her bowl of corn and black-eyed peas, her cup of water and hunk of cornbread, and found a comfortable spot, awaiting Ezekiel, who stood in line for his share. He appeared tired, too, but somehow had the energy to talk and laugh with Hannah in line ahead of him. Something unpleasant stirred in Isabelle's stomach as she watched the two. Ezekiel even reached out at one point and touched Hannah's shoulder.

Hannah accompanied Ezekiel toward the barn where most of the others sat. The young woman gazed up into his face with an expression far too familiar for Isabelle's comfort. As the two entered the edge of the shade, Hannah slowed so Ezekiel could move on alone, but the woman took the time to give Isabelle an irritating simper before turning away to find her own spot under a magnolia tree. There was something disturbingly triumphant in the way she carried herself and plopped down upon the ground, casting one last sly glance Isabelle's way before turning to talk to Jacob and Ester. Isabelle's blood began to race.

Ezekiel sat next to her, grinning to himself, and dipped his fingers into his bowl. Then he seemed to remember his wife and offered her a quick, half-interested smile.

"So, what you think of harvestin' rice, Izzy?"

Through tight lips, she managed, "It seems I'm not much good at it." She displayed several small cuts near her ankles.

"You'll catch on soon enough." He appeared oblivious to her clipped tone. "It'll take us days to cut this here whole field."

She kept her eyes on her food and barely veiled her spite when she conjectured, "Maybe Mr. Ketch will be back before we're done."

He studied her, the private smile now gone. "Mebbe. But it won't matter; I still be harvestin' and millin' rice like everyone else. Every hand will be from now till it all done months from now." A bit of reciprocated malice slipped through his words. "Nothin' like that housework you was used to at Mr. Tom's. You won't be able to move tomorrow when you get out the bed."

They said little else through the brief meal. Isabelle told herself that she should not act so jealous simply because Ezekiel had laughed with Hannah. He had a right to talk with anyone, just as she did. Well, tonight she would give him good reason not to venture from her bed again.

* * *

If ever images invaded Ketch's sleep, they came in the form of nightmares, but the image of Isabelle's naked form standing within reach certainly was no nightmare. He froze, terrified of her staying and equally fearful of her leaving. Her sepia eyes captivated him. When his gaze escaped downward to her small, round breasts, he became aware of the fact that he lay abed with nothing to conceal his arousal. Her attention remained on his face as she drifted down to straddle him, enveloping him in her moist heat, her warm fingers gliding up his belly, his scarred chest. Her mouth descended to capture his lips as she began to move. His hands caressed her shoulders, but instead of smooth, tight skin, he found the flesh dry and loose. Startled, he gasped at the sight of his mother now astride him, her head thrown back, red hair wild, mouth open to emit moans. He fought against the sensations, struggled and clawed his way out of the dream until he awoke in the night, winded, spent, soaked with sweat. Rolling over, he vomited over the side of the bed.

For some time, he lay there, calming his breathing so he could listen, hoping no one had heard any of the noises he may have made in the night. It took a moment to remember where he was—a small guest

67

bedchamber at the Virginia tobacco plantation of Elizabeth Archer's family. He strained his ears to detect any sign that he may have disturbed Helen and Maria in the next room, but he heard nothing. In fact, he heard nothing throughout the entire house except the distant toll of a clock near the head of the stairs as it struck three.

Too haunted to fall back asleep, he got out of bed, his nightshirt clinging to him. Determined no one should find any telltale sign of his ignominy, he wiped the floor clean.

His trembling persisted in the warm night. Near an open window, he stripped off his shirt and washed himself with a cloth from a basin. The faint night breeze cooled him as he looked down over the roof of the second-floor gallery then across the greensward, black in the moonless night, toward the nearby James River. Like Carolina, the Virginia peninsula had an abundance of rivers and swamps, and so the early September air held the heavy weight of humidity. The chorus of insects and frogs built a wall of peculiar noise, though not as deafening to him as that outside his chamber windows at Leighlin. How he missed his home; he had not expected to, nor had he ever thought of Leighlin as his definitive home before now. Nothing had been home to him since he had fled Southwark.

Here near James Town, he had languished for nearly two months with little to keep him occupied. No such boredom, however, touched Helen. She had been absorbed by the Archer family like a lost relative, and she ran and played amongst Elizabeth's young siblings as one of them. Maria, too, had been accepted by Elizabeth's kin, though at first her dark complexion had raised some eyebrows. But, in no time, her affable personality and grace pushed aside any prejudice and won the esteem of Elizabeth's parents as well as her crusty grandfather. The gnarled old man took great delight in showing and telling Maria all about the immense tobacco plantation as well as James Town.

From the first week, Helen had worked to make sure their host family received Ketch with respect, if not warmth. To do so, she had taken great pride in explaining how he had tried to rescue her from Leighlin's fire and had thus suffered his burns. Elizabeth Archer joined in the effort, for she knew only the so-called heroic side of Ketch. David Archer had thus far not exposed his naïve young wife to Ketch's past practices, which David himself had experienced firsthand. Their testimony impressed the austere grandfather enough for the patriarch to tolerate the unsavory-looking slave driver. The old man would be anything but gracious if he knew his guest had murdered his eldest son, Ezra Archer, with a pitchfork last year. Archer's brutal end had been well-deserved in Ketch's eyes, for the planter had been behind the fire at Leighlin, a plot to eliminate those who stood between him and his planned takeover of Leighlin Plantation.

A small sound drew Ketch's attention back to the Virginia night. He stilled his breath and listened closer. A night bird or some other creature perhaps. Again, it drifted to him, barely detectable but enough for him to recognize. His reaction was not instantaneous, though the duty with which he had been charged by his master dictated investigation no matter how much his nature struggled against it. Why would she be out of bed at this hour and obviously distressed?

Pulling on his breeches and shirt, Ketch cursed the nightmare that had awoken him and thus drawn him into this obligation. Silently, he slipped from the chamber.

The Archer home was much different than Leighlin House. Although three levels like Leighlin House, the floors of this wood frame structure had a sprawling quality with none of Leighlin's symmetry. On the first two levels, galleries wrapped around the entire house, accented with white railings and spotless white pillars. The upper floor, where the guests lodged, lacked access to a gallery, so Ketch knew she had to be on the next level down. He felt his way along to avoid a misstep on the stairs or bumping into anything in the hallways and awakening the Archers.

When he reached the gallery door, he cracked it an inch to listen again and to search the night. White wicker chairs crouched like ghosts. From the nearest one, he heard the muffled sound again and could make out a figure seated in pale clothing, long hair blending with the ebony night. Ketch frowned at the confirmation of his suspicion. Perhaps he should leave her to herself. Yet, to return to his chamber… Well, right now that held no comfort or appeal, especially when he was aware of Maria's presence here.

Stepping out upon the gallery, his weight creaked the boards. Maria started and peered around the wing of her chair before retreating into the chair's outline, sniffling a final time. A hand darted up to wipe her nose. Ketch sensed her unease as he moved to the railing. He did not stop directly in front of her but instead obliquely, then he leaned back, half sitting on the railing to portray insouciance. He waited for her to speak, but she remained silent, her gaze stabbing into the night toward the black river.

Just above a whisper, he asked, "Why aren't you abed?"

She turned her face away from him. "Can't sleep."

He was not one to meddle and was certainly no practiced shoulder upon which to cry, but he was here now and determined to keep her from further tears if by presence alone, for the girl had too much pride for a display.

"Why was you a-cryin'?"

"I wasn't…I'm not. It's the night air."

Although unable to see her features in the night, he kept his attention upon her face. She shifted in her chair, apparently determined to outwait him.

"Why are *you* out of bed?" she asked in almost an accusatory tone.

"I heard you."

"How could you? Your chamber is too far away."

But he knew she believed him just as her denial confirmed what he had heard; she, more than anyone, knew the acuity of his senses, especially when it came to her or Helen.

Attempting to sustain defiance, Maria started to sit forward and stiffen but then relaxed and sat back again. When she spoke, it was with cool control. "I miss Leighlin."

"Then why don't you go back home?"

"Helen is enjoying herself here. She would be disappointed if—"

"I can stay with her."

"Ketch…" She faltered, and he could feel her courage drain away into the night, replaced by frustration over his persistence as well as her own weakness. She made one last attempt at anger. "Go back to bed, Ketch."

He wished he could, but it was far better to forego sleep and avoid the nightmares. If they returned, the old agitation would return as well and build until it demanded a violent release. So now he focused on Maria, as much for his own sake as hers.

Knowing such propinquity would surprise her, he sat in the chair next to hers. The wicker protested his weight. Almost defensively, Maria turned toward him. Did his nearness disturb her?

"Are you afeared of goin' home?" The familiar old anger touched him. "Is it that boy?"

"Ketch." When his name emerged with force and volume, she checked herself. "You *must* stop referring to my husband that way. It's disrespectful."

He scowled.

"He's your master."

Ketch knew she never would have verbalized such an unsavory fact except to distract him. She would hope by rebuffing him that he would retreat, but he remained, and her desperation increased. Yet she remained, too, which told him much as well.

"*Are* you goin' back to Leighlin?"

"Of course. Eventually, when Helen's ready."

"And if she was ready on the morrow?"

"Ketch, this is really none of your affair—"

"It is."

"I think not—"

"Yer husband didn't send me here for me health. I was sent to watch out for you an' Miss Helen."

This at last cowed her, and she said nothing more for some time. Her hands rustled against the light shawl she wore over her shift. "The truth of the matter is," she said, barely loud enough to be heard, "I don't know if I'm wanted back at Leighlin."

Ketch forced down his initial bitter response, wondered if Mallory had said or done something cruel to her before she had left Leighlin. But he knew that suspicion was baseless, for Jack Mallory, though with many faults, dearly loved his wife.

"Why wouldn't you be wanted back?"

She sighed, and time slipped by. The night creatures seemed to soften their unearthly chorus.

"Have you ever been in love, Ketch?"

Her question nearly choked him, so unforeseen and ridiculous. "No."

Maria hesitated. Had she expected him to say otherwise? Surely not. "It's a wonderful and terrible thing all at once." She brushed away the hair that had drifted across her face. "I never realized exactly how much Jack wants a family until I lost the baby. And because it took so much out of me physically and emotionally, it frightened him; he's lost so much in his life. After that...well...things were...have been difficult. I guess I'm afraid to go back and find things the same. I hoped coming here would give him time to heal...without me there...to remind him."

"So comin' to Virginia was yer idea?"

"Partially. Elizabeth invited us, and Helen jumped at the chance. I knew Jack wouldn't leave Leighlin during the growing season, and I didn't want to disappoint Helen. And the more I thought of it, the more I thought it might be a good idea to leave Leighlin for a while."

"He's written to you."

"Yes. And he says he misses me, as I miss him. He tells me..." She faltered. "I shouldn't be saying these things."

But her confiding in him pleased Ketch; it reminded him of when

71

Ella Logan used to invite him to sit with her on the portico, rare occasions when she had been alone and he simply passing by.

"Do you miss Leighlin, Ketch?"

"Mebbe."

"Do you ever miss the sea?"

"Sometimes."

"I think Jack does, too. Being a planter hasn't come easy to him like seamanship did. Perhaps he would be happier aboard the *Adventuress*."

"He's not takin' Miss Helen to live at sea," Ketch grumbled. "Miss Ella wouldn't want that."

"No, he wouldn't. He knows." She studied him with unnerving penetration. "Are you two ever going to trust one another?"

Ketch gave a faint snort.

"You should go back to bed, Ketch, and forget everything I've said tonight. I'm just tired and far from home. I appreciate your concern, but you must not let Jack know the things I've told you. I shouldn't have."

Her regret unexpectedly wounded him. "I won't say nothin'."

"Thank you." She stood. "And thank you for indulging me." Her hand rested so lightly and so briefly upon his arm that he did not realize it until she removed it. "I can see that the only way you'll return to your bed is if I return to mine, so…good night."

Her soft, dark shape drifted into the house, but he stayed behind. And when the morning sun rose over the eastern trees, far out beyond Chesapeake Bay and the Atlantic, it found him still in his chair.

***

Isabelle hated to admit that she found her husband's tenderness in bed lacking, but what had started out as minimally romantic had grown perfunctory, an act as unthinking to him as the expectation that his meal would be prepared and set before him every night. Perhaps, she told herself, he was simply too tired from laboring all day to put forth added effort, or perhaps her expectations had been unrealistic, a young woman's fantasy. Maybe all men were this way. Yet, William had not been so indifferent in bed, according to her mother's subtle hints. Her mother had used her own experiences to assure her daughter that eventually she, too, would find happiness in a man's arms, that there was kindness to be had. Although Isabelle had been much younger at the time, she remembered William with great clarity, used those memories to help believe that she would find a good man. Even after so many years since William's death, her mother had still spoken of her lover's affection. But William, Isabelle knew, had never snuck off into the night and left his woman alone.

Several nights had passed since Ezekiel's first mysterious disappearance. And now he had left her again, this time after she had fallen asleep. When she awoke, she lay for some time, torn and twisted by doubt and anxiety. As exhausted as she was by the harvest, the heat, and the insects, Isabelle felt wide awake; sleep would elude her until she knew the truth. She would go to the one place where she had failed to knock that first night and would break the door down if necessary.

As she padded through the warm night in her shift, she feared what she might discover. Perhaps it was better to remain ignorant. After all, if Ezekiel was being unfaithful to her, what could she do about it? Yet, the mystery would eventually drive her mad, and she despised being made a fool. If everyone else knew, she had to know as well.

When she reached Hannah's cabin, she hesitated out of earshot, swallowed hard in a dry throat, her hands suddenly cold. She crept to the corner of the cabin, stopped. Over the hammering of her heart, she discerned the telltale sounds she dreaded—Hannah's quiet giggle, Ezekiel's low, crooning voice and deep chuckle then Hannah's moan. No mistaking them for Jacob and Ester; these carnal noises came from Hannah's side of the cabin. Fury welled in Isabelle, an anger greater than the pain of betrayal, and without another thought she rushed to the front of the cabin and threw open the door.

"Ezekiel!"

Jacob and Ester emerged from the sleep of the exhausted, their bed creaking. On the other side of the room, Ezekiel's shadow reared up against the paler background of the window.

"Ezekiel, I know you're here!"

Hannah's sharp voice shot through the darkness. "Get outta here, you half-cast little whore."

Blinded by humiliation and outrage, Isabelle rushed across the small space, but Ezekiel loomed before her. Without a word, he struck her a backhanded blow. She staggered with a gasp, a hand to her burning cheek. Ezekiel grabbed her arms, shoved her backwards.

"Get out of here, damn you."

She fought to regain her courage. "Let go of me."

Ezekiel dragged her toward the door. She tried to stop him, but she was no match for his hard strength. Jacob and Ester called out, Ester in amusement, Jacob trying to calm Ezekiel. But there was no calming him. Isabelle had expected some crumb of shame, some scanty denial or excuse, but instead her indignation seemed to fuel his wrath, his hold upon her painful.

"Let me go!" She tried to keep the tremor from her voice.

"I'll let you go," he snarled, and one hand came away from her arm long enough to deliver another blow across her face. She cried out, eyes stinging with tears.

As he yanked her onto the porch, she tried to reach him with her fingernails and teeth, but his tight grasp immobilized her. Behind him, from the safety of her bed, Hannah urged him on, throwing further insults Isabelle's way. Voices from the neighboring cabins called out for quiet, and a baby began to cry, but she kept yelling at her husband, determined to shame him in front of the others as he was shaming her.

Once outside, she expected Ezekiel to free her as she writhed against him, trying to kick him, but instead he cursed her a final time and with a growl flung her off the porch. Reaching out in vain for something to break her fall, Isabelle struck the second step and tumbled awkwardly to the ground, one ankle twisted beneath her. Sharp pain flashed up her limb, and she yelped.

"Go home, you stupid little fool! I can do as I please without your permission."

Isabelle wanted to claw his eyes out, or Hannah's, whomever she could reach. But when she tried to get to her feet, the agony in her ankle thwarted her, and she remained on hands and knees amidst pine needles and sand. Behind Ezekiel, Jacob appeared with a lantern.

"Looks like you done lamed her, Zeke. Mebbe you should take her back home."

"Like hell. She done this to herself. Let her crawl home. Little bitch. Thinkin' she can tell me what to do."

Jacob reached for his arm as if to settle him, but Ezekiel shrugged him off, gave Isabelle a last lethal look and returned inside the cabin.

The throbbing in Isabelle's ankle finally overpowered her inflamed senses. Her cheeks burned from Ezekiel's blows, and she tasted blood on her lips. Jacob hesitated upon the porch, as if considering helping her, then Ezekiel threatened something from inside, and Jacob retreated, shut the door behind him. The insults and grumblings from the other cabins slowly died away. Isabelle was left alone in the darkness, tears searing her eyes and tumbling down her cheeks as anger devolved into deep sorrow and helplessness. She could not walk, did not want to have to crawl all the way back to her cabin. But what choice did she have?

She struggled toward the porch, braced herself to stand on her one good foot. Pain stole her breath. From inside the cabin, she heard Ezekiel and Jacob talking, heard the women's voices. She hopped along the front of the cabin then the side, using the structure to support herself, wanting nothing more than to put distance between herself and Jacob's cabin, to drown out the cruel voices.

Desperately, she hopped toward the next cabin. Halfway, she fell. For a moment, she lay there in a heap, fighting back sobs. When she rose again, the agony worsened as blood circulated into the injured ankle. She gasped for air. Determined, she continued on her way. Two more cabins down then her own. Cold sweat soaked her by the time she collapsed, trembling, upon the porch steps. Away from the others now, she rested her forehead against a step and began to sob.

CHAPTER 6

Just past twilight, Wildwood Plantation's shallop nudged up against Leighlin's dock, and the slaves waiting there secured it with ropes. Torches glowed about the landing, lit the instant the shallop had rounded the river bend downstream. In the bow, Elizabeth and Maria stood close together.

On the dock, flickering torches bronzed Jack Mallory, his gaze fixed on his wife. Ketch thought the formality of the boy's attire odd— wine-colored velvet coat over a deep golden doublet, dark breeches, and silk stockings. James Logan had been one for finery while ashore, but never Jack Mallory except when an occasion called for such.

Helen's impatient voice pierced the air: "John!" She scurried forward from where she had been asleep. "Did you miss me?"

The young man laughed. "Have you been gone? I didn't notice."

"Did too!"

He laughed again. "True enough, the quiet has been deafening."

"Maria!" Helen protested with false anger. "Tell him I'm going to Wildwood with Miss Elizabeth if he's going to be cruel to me."

The tired women's laughter drifted to Ketch as the boatmen shipped the gangplank. Helen bounded past everyone and leapt into her brother's arms, nearly bowling him over.

At the top of the gangplank, Ketch offered his hand to Maria, but she hesitated. When at last she acquiesced, he understood her reluctance—she was shaking. He glowered down at Jack Mallory, willed him to have the proper reaction to her return. The young man looked only at his wife as he set Helen down. The child continued to chatter on about her trip. When Maria reached the dock, Mallory took her in a wordless embrace for longer than usual while in the presence of others.

When Ketch assisted Elizabeth onto the gangplank, the pretty girl's appreciative smile pleased him. He would miss her innocent civility after these many weeks together. He followed her down to the dock then stepped aside to allow the waiting slaves to retrieve the baggage. Ketch took Helen in tow, all the while the girl still narrating her adventure to her distracted brother. When Mallory remembered himself, he gave Maria a quick kiss and turned to greet and thank Elizabeth.

Maria asked, "Are you sure you won't stay the night with us?"

"Thank you, but I am eager to return home. It has been a long journey."

"Of course."

Maria embraced Elizabeth and thanked her for her invitation and hospitality.

Elizabeth's broad, easy smile returned. "You are more than welcome. I was so glad you could come."

The private look that passed between them, the quick squeeze of their hands, told Ketch that Elizabeth either knew or sensed the difficulties between Maria and her spouse.

Ketch tightened his grip on Helen's hand. "Come along, child. Let's get you up to the house." He bowed to Elizabeth.

Helen called her thanks and good night wishes to Elizabeth as Ketch urged her from the landing. She clutched her favorite toy close— a small stuffed bear that betrayed its longevity in the deepening dullness of its once-lustrous fur and in various patches sewn upon its hide. Helen's father had shot the black bear, her mother had created the toy from its coat, and her sister-in-law maintained it. Helen would never forsake it, her only possession left from her parents.

Before they reached the terraces beyond the ornamental ponds, fatigue claimed the girl, slowing her steps and drawing a yawn from her. Ketch crouched and pulled her close, so she could ride upon his hip. She offered no resistance, rubbed her eyes, and yawned again. By the time he reached the portico steps, she was asleep, limbs hanging limp, soft cheek pinning her bear against his neck, her hair tickling him. A far distant, painful memory of holding his newborn sister Sophia tainted the contented moment.

Mary, one of the house servants, met him at the door and took the child without a word. Ketch turned back to the portico steps where he paused to stretch. At the landing, the shallop was turning her head now upriver to carry Elizabeth Archer home on the remainder of the tide. Torches moved this way from the dock, and he could just make out the pale shape of Maria's dress, close to the dark form of her husband.

"Look who's back, gents," Willis said as Ketch entered the lower level.

All at the table turned from their supper. None offered a welcome, and Ketch was quite certain they had hoped he would stay in Virginia forever. He sat and snatched up a piece of roasted pork as well as the pitcher of ale.

"So, Doc," Gabriel asked Willis, "will Izzy be able to work on the morrow?"

"I should say give it another day. But I'll check her in the morn, if you'd like."

"Aye. Don't want her to get used to sittin' 'round. Learnin' lazy ways from Zeke."

Ketch kept his tone neutral. "What's amiss with the girl?"

"Nothin' that's your business," Gabriel said.

Ketch pinned a withering stare upon the young man who had apparently grown bold in his absence. As if suddenly remembering with whom he dealt, Gabriel erased the smugness from his face.

"Claims she fell off her porch," Willis answered. "Couple of days ago. Sprained her ankle so bad she couldn't walk."

"Or so she plays it," countered Gabriel. "Since she's been with that lazy bastard of Ketch's, she's even more useless in the field than before. No wonder Tom Clark got rid of her. He pulled the wool over the Captain's eyes with that one—she don't know nothin' about harvesting rice. Well, Ketch, you can have your boys back. Tired of having to ride 'em all the time. That Zeke, he's a champion at looking busy when he's doing nothin'.."

"If you stayed awake more," Ketch growled, "you might see more."

The others laughed, but Gabriel was undaunted.

"Like hell. I've been sweatin' me balls off workin'. More than I can say for the likes of you, playin' nursemaid up in Virginia."

The room fell deathly silent. No chewing, no drinking, not a twitch. Though Gabriel managed to meet Ketch's stare for a moment, he failed to sustain his courage. The agitation building in Ketch since Isabelle's wedding now flared like a fire stoked with fresh fuel. His fingers closed upon Willis's table knife.

Calmly, Willis said, "Ketch was just followin' orders, Gabe, like we all do. No need to insult the man for it."

Gabriel's attention took in the knife, and he swallowed. "Reckon you're right, Doc." He nodded to Ketch. "Beg pardon, mate."

They ate the rest of the meal in uncomfortable silence, and Ketch finished before the others. Without a care for his comrades' thirst, he took the pitcher of ale to his chamber. He lit the candle near his bed, stripped off his clothes except his breeches, and sat upon the bed with his back against the wall. He drank straight from the pitcher.

The chamber did not welcome him back as he had expected. In fact, it felt foreign and lonely, feeding his unrest and frustrations. Upon his return, he had had no desire to be immediately accosted by talk and reminders of Isabelle. His dreams over the past weeks had been reminder enough and a catalyst for the old black feelings within him, a violence that had nearly driven him to plunge the knife into Gabriel. If those dark emotions conquered him, as they always had, he feared what he would do to gain relief. And as he replayed in his head what Gabriel and Willis had revealed about Isabelle, he knew it was only a matter of time.

***

When Willis allowed Isabelle one more day of recuperation, Ketch knew the girl's injury was significant. So, while his gang busily gulped down their midday rations under a partial shroud of gray clouds, Ketch slipped away from the north rice field.

As he strode beneath the canopy of shade in the slave settlement, a carpet of fallen conifer needles muffled his footsteps. He had no idea which cabin Isabelle resided in, but he would find her easily enough since everyone was in the fields except two old women who minded the infants. During the harvest, even the half dozen children worked.

He found Isabelle sitting in a crude chair upon her porch, head bowed, fingers attempting to sew a sweetgrass basket; Ketch caught its hay-like fragrance as he drew near. Isabelle's concentration upon her challenging task deafened her to anything around her. Her slim fingers worked with a determination he admired as much as he admired her curvaceous form. It struck him again—after having not seen her for so many weeks—how slight she was to be working in the fields; surely her duties before coming to Leighlin had been inside a house. Perhaps a laundress or a seamstress. No, no seamstress, judging from the difficulty she was having with the intricate basket.

When he was nearly at the cabin's steps, she raised her head. With a small gasp, she dropped her work and scrambled to her feet, took a limping step farther into the shadows of the overhang. He considered picking up her scattered materials—yellowish sweetgrass, black rush, palmetto fronds and pine needles—but he let them lie. Although he did not relish her being afraid of him, he knew that fear would serve him well in discovering the truth, so he stepped close to her. Still she avoided looking at him. He stood speechless, for being close to her

79

again stirred him in a powerful, disarming way.

"Good day, sir." She curtseyed, unbalanced. "Mr. Willis gave me permission to stay home today."

Brusquely, he asked, "How did you hurt yer ankle?"

"I fell."

"Show me yer face, girl."

Slowly, she lifted her chin and revealed the bruises that the shade had hidden. A wave of rage swelled in him.

"And the bruises? How did you come by them?"

"When I fell, sir."

"I noticed the first day you came here you was a poor liar; you still are."

Alarm flashed in Isabelle's pale eyes, which she again diverted. He wanted to grip her chin and force her to look at him, but simply seeing her rekindled in him things that he should not encourage with the sense of touch.

"Has marriage made you clumsy, girl?"

"No, sir."

"Or did yer husband help you fall?"

"N-no, sir."

"Stop lyin' to me." He took another step toward her. She retreated against the cabin, wincing. Her breasts rose and fell with the rapidity of her breathing, and he remembered their symmetry from his dreams, the feel of them beneath his fingers, his mouth. He forced himself to demand, "How'd you get those bruises? And if you tell me one more time that you fell—"

"Please, sir—"

"Tell me the truth."

"What does it matter?" Anger and humiliation reflected in her moist eyes and in the tightness of her fine jaw. The spark of a repressed spirit.

"Don't question me! You may be his wife, but yer first and foremost Leighlin's property; yer husband don't have the right to damage that property so you can't earn yer keep, 'specially this time o' year."

"Please, sir," she said, the tears threatening to spill over, confirming what he suspected. Yet were the tears out of fear for her husband's safety or her own? "If he thinks I told you...if you punish him..."

"An' if I don't, you fancy he won't hurt you no more? Think again. You never should've tied yerself to that dog. I warned you about him."

Her gaze again fell to his feet.

"And it's made a mess I have to clean up." He turned to leave, but her voice caught him.

"Please, Mr. Ketch…please…"

He gave her one last look, forced disdain into his tone. "When I'm through with him, he'll durst not harm you again."

***

The world receded around Ketch as he marched back to the rice field. Sound became distant; vision narrowed; his skin did not register the touch of the elusive sun or the soothing flow of the breeze. It had always been this way before going into battle, whether amidst the roar of the great guns aboard *HMS Harwich* or while boarding an enemy from the deck of the *Medora*. Like a shield, the fog protected him during the bloody violence, a vacuous existence in which he struck men down in a blind rage, without fear, without emotion. The haze focused him, kept him single-minded.

He vowed to end all this now—Isabelle's suffering and his own torment. Like the burning desire for release found in battle, he needed another's pain to satisfy the old demons and thus purge the torment; otherwise, he would go mad, like his mother after Sophia's death, a madness that had driven her into his bed. He did not consider potential consequences; he knew only one course.

When he reached the rice field, he was distantly aware of the work that had resumed there, but it no longer had importance to him. Zeke and his gang were gathering the dried sheaves into Jemmy's wagon to be driven away for threshing. But he paid no further attention to the process. Instead, he crossed straight to Zeke and ordered, "Come with me," in a voice that belonged to someone else, deeper, colder.

Zeke replaced his glance of concern with a cocky grin to show his comrades how pleased he was to have an excuse to quit the field while they toiled onward.

Ketch said nothing as they climbed the bluff. He passed the gardens, avoiding Ella Logan's grave, and the house then headed toward the distant stables. Zeke began to lag, so Ketch ordered him to the front where the slave kept glancing warily back at him.

The stable-yard was quiet, for during the rice harvest even the carpenter, cooper, and blacksmith worked in the fields throughout the shortening days. All that met Ketch and Zeke were the meandering peacock and its mate as well as the chickens scratching in the yard.

81

Inside the barn, only birds gave the building life, for the horses were also hard at work. Swallows glided in and out in an acrobatic display of blue-green flashes, their high-pitched voices loud in the confines of the barn. Sparrows poked about among fallen grain from feed tubs or among the droppings in the stalls, searching for undigested morsels. They whirred up into the rafters when the men passed by.

At the tack room door, Ketch said, "In."

Although Zeke hesitated, he still possessed enough self-confidence to finally enter with a saunter.

The heady aroma of leather filled the small room, the single window closed, a number of flies tapping against the glass in a vain attempt to reach the outside. Saddles and bridles were arranged along the near wall, while across the room, shelves held all manner of items from brushes to hoof picks to cleaning rags. Jemmy's cot was against the far wall, neatly made. A table in the center lay bare, its surface discolored by oils but clean, just as the whole room always was under Jemmy's care. Zeke shuffled around it to the window, as if figuring the table would offer some barrier and the window an escape. When Ketch withdrew his knife from the sheath on his belt, he gained Zeke's full attention.

"I hear tell," Ketch rumbled, "you grew yerself a bigger set o' balls after I left."

Zeke watched the blade, said with false casualness, "Not sure what you mean, Mr. Ketch."

The slave's size, strength, and good fortune of owning two arms made Ketch very much aware of the situation's precariousness if Zeke decided to fight back, no matter how ill-advised that would be, but he continued. "Think I'll find out the truth for meself."

When Ketch advanced, Zeke stepped back, bumped into the shelving. Before he could shift direction, Ketch was upon him. He shoved the blade between Zeke's waistband and belly and, with a twist of the wrist, sliced the garment. The loose breeches slid toward the floor. The slave reached for them, but Ketch thrust the blade's tip under his chin and uttered, "Don't."

He lowered the knife to prod Zeke's cowering genitals. The slave held his breath.

"Looks like they was wrong; I only see two tiny things."

"Who 'they' you talkin' 'bout? That damn Spider? He jus' jealous 'cause I's gettin' me some and he not. Or was it Izzy what's been talkin'? You took a shine to her, I knows. Mebbe if you put that there knife away, we could talk about sharin' her—"

Ketch's elbow to the face staggered him against the shelving. Brushes tumbled to the hard-packed floor. Zeke's archness turned to anger, eyes narrowed, bloody lips tightening.

"She may be yer wife, but she's Leighlin's property, and you've no right to damage it."

"Who says I did?"

"I'm no fool, you whoreson black bastard." Ketch returned the knife to its sheath.

"She tol' you." Zeke wiped his lips, the blood smearing the back of his hand. He stared at it and mumbled, "She has a mouth on her, that one. Ungrateful mulatto bitch. She lucky I took her into my bed; no one else would've."

Another blow sent Zeke against the shelf again. In one fluid movement, Ketch gripped the younger man's shirt and slammed him face first upon the table. Blood poured from Zeke's broad nose. He started to push himself away, to roll out of Ketch's reach, but Ketch kicked his feet—entangled in the breeches—out from under him and sent him crashing to the floor. With well-aimed kicks, he kept the slave down, drove the air from his lungs. From a hook on the wall, Ketch snatched a riding crop and beat him until blood showed through the back of his shirt. Zeke could do nothing but try to protect himself by curling up and covering his head. When Ketch remembered the bruises on Isabelle's face, when he thought of her in Zeke's bed, the blows fell with killing ferocity.

"Mr. Ketch!"

At first, he paid no attention to the distant voice, figured his ears were playing him false.

"Mr. Ketch! Where are you?"

His arm halted mid-swing when he recognized Helen's voice echoing in the stall aisle. Dropping the crop, he wheeled into the aisle and pulled the door shut behind him. When she saw him only a few feet away, the girl stopped in her tracks, and the joy of her search died away. Ketch could only imagine what she saw on his face, what she sensed.

"Miss Helen," he managed, composing himself, almost breathless. "What're you doin' here?"

Her glance touched the tack room door. "Maria said she saw you walking to the stables, so I thought maybe you was coming to work on the crib."

"No," he stammered. "In fact, I'm on me way back to the field."

Her attention returned to the door.

"Why don't you fetch yer pony from the pasture and go out for a

83

ride? We'll work on the crib tomorrow. I promise."

She eyed his disheveled form.

"Off with ye, then. I'll fetch yer saddle."

"Not the sidesaddle. The hunting saddle."

"As you wish. Go on now."

Deflated, she finally left the barn.

Quickly, Ketch stepped back into the tack room where he found Zeke struggling to a sitting position, wincing, dazed. He froze, glared up at Ketch with hate-filled, bloodshot eyes. Ketch snatched him to his feet.

"You'll stay here and stay quiet till Miss Helen is gone, hear? Jemmy keeps bandages for the horses in that trunk yonder. Bind yerself up, damn you, and I'll be back."

Once he had helped Helen brush and saddle her pony, he sent her on her way with a forced smile then returned to the tack room. He removed his shirt and threw it at Zeke.

"Pull out them stitches from the right sleeve and put that on. Get back to the field." He gathered up the bloody, discarded shirt.

"What about my breeches?"

"Find somethin' in here to tie 'em up." Ketch stood toe to toe with the slave. "You say a word o' this to anyone, it'll be the last thing you do. Understand?"

Sullenly, Zeke nodded, his mouth loose and wet.

"You touch yer wife again, I'll cut off yer prick and feed it to you."

***

Ketch's departure had left Isabelle unsettled. She gave up working on the sweetgrass basket. It was a frustrating task anyway. Her mother had taught her, but she lacked her mother's skill. "What you lack, Isabelle," she had admonished, "is patience, not skill. When you get an idea in your head, you always want things direct-like instead of stopping to reckon if it's the right thing."

Isabelle longed for her mother's wisdom. She never would have gotten herself into this situation if her mother were here. Since the confrontation at Jacob's cabin the other night, things had gotten worse. When she had again voiced her displeasure and sense of betrayal, Ezekiel shouted her down and struck her, threatened her with worse. So she had submitted to avoid further pain. In bed, when he inflicted himself upon her, she closed her eyes, remembered someone warning her about his true character, sought to recall the voice, finally remembered it had been Ketch. Why had he bothered to counsel her?

She spent the afternoon in the small truck garden behind her cabin, thinking about Ketch's ominous visit. The malice in his eyes had been unmistakable, his final words to her unnerving. If her ankle were better, she would have followed him to see where he was bound. Had his words been merely a threat, something he expected her to pass on to Ezekiel to discourage further abuse? If he believed Ezekiel responsible for damaging Leighlin's property, why did he not simply tell Mr. Willis about it? Why had he come to her? How had he even found out about her injury, especially so soon after his return?

After harvesting what was ready in the garden, she retired inside to prepare Ezekiel's supper, all the while her stomach still in turmoil.

Voices eventually drifted through the open shutters as the people returned from the fields amidst the falling darkness. Isabelle had just set the food on the table when she heard her husband's heavy tread upon the porch. She turned to the open door and found him standing there with hunched body and crumpled brow.

"You told him, didn't you?" Nearing the table, he loomed over her and shouted, "Didn't you?"

"Told who what?"

"No one would do me thataway but you."

"Ezekiel—"

"Shut up." He pulled off his shirt—not the same one he had donned this morning—to reveal a swath of bandages. These, too, he ripped away and turned his red-striped back to her. "See what you brung down on me, you little bitch? Now get some water to wash me!"

Heart racing, she limped out to the pump to fill a bucket. By the time she returned, he had also removed his torn breeches. He threw them at her.

"Mend those."

Ezekiel gingerly lay on their bed, face down, wincing. Isabelle knelt beside the bed with her bucket and a rag.

"It was that devil Ketch what done this. But you already know that, don't you? Woulda kilt me sure if not for Miss Helen comin' in the barn. There was murder in his eyes, those lifeless black eyes of his. And you'd be to blame for it."

"I didn't tell Mr. Ketch nothing. I didn't even tell Mr. Willis when he tended me. I swear."

"Why should I believe you?"

"I'm your wife; I wouldn't lie to you."

He laughed harshly and complained further into his pillow as she wiped his wounds. She allowed her touch to be a bit rough. He flinched and cursed her. When she realized his pain pleased her, she concealed her satisfaction. The cuts were narrow and deep, perhaps caused by some sort of whip, something wielded with great force. She ignored Ezekiel's continued oaths directed at both her and his driver. Instead, she thought of what Ketch had said and hoped this would indeed be the end of her suffering, that perhaps the beating had knocked some sense into her husband. Yet her hope was too weak to overpower her growing dread. Beating or no, she knew Ezekiel would refuse to submit so easily to his driver's latest demand. He would find new ways to defy Ketch.

***

In the days that followed the beating, Ketch sensed a deepening of Zeke's hatred instead of a new growth of fear. The resentment would manifest itself somewhere, Ketch knew, so he made sure he had his pistol always at hand, especially when Zeke wielded a rice hook. The slave was, however, amazingly subdued. Stiff and sullen, he kept to his work. The others in the gang also said little, apparently afraid of Zeke's reticence and the reason behind it. Ketch suspected Zeke's pride kept him from revealing the truth or his torn back to his mates.

Ketch wondered of Isabelle's reaction to the bloody sight of her husband. Did she have feelings enough for Zeke to revile her husband's driver even more than she undoubtedly already did? Ketch forced away any further conjectures and neither returned to Isabelle's cabin nor sought her out in any way. By listening to Gabriel and Willis, he learned that she had resumed work and had not missed a day or shown up with any bruises since he had castigated Zeke.

The harvest proceeded day after endless day, and though it would be a long time until all was gathered and tallied, Ketch knew enough about the two previous harvests to calculate that this would be the most profitable of all.

Supervising the harvest kept Jack Mallory so busy that some evenings Ketch did not see him on the portico with Maria as usual. And this evening, as Ketch dragged up the rear lane to the house, hungry and worn, Mallory was absent again. Helen, however, kept Maria company, and when the child spotted him, she called out, her voice echoing beyond him down the sward.

"Hello, Mr. Ketch!"

"Hello, Miss Helen."

"Come sit with us." She jumped from Maria's lap and scurried

86

down the steps. "We're waiting for John."

She took his hand. The softness of her skin always amazed him, her grip as pleasant as a cool breeze on a stifling day, a privileged gift. Indeed, it had always been her touch that assured him that she, if no one else, cared about him. Maria had once used that bond as leverage against him—she had vowed she would help him recover from the snake bite so he could uphold his promise to safeguard Helen, but only if he forsook his violent ways. His promise troubled him now when he looked up at Maria on the portico; that promise, broken by what he had done to Zeke, had caused him to decline an invitation to Sunday dinner the other day and to now refuse Helen's invitation to sit with them. He felt no regret for what he had done to Zeke—the violence had given him both the relief he required and apparent safety for Isabelle—but, all the same, he felt uncomfortable around Maria now.

Helen tried to tow him up the steps.

"I'm intolerably filthy, child. You'll spoil yer dress just bein' hard by."

"I don't mind. My birthday is coming up soon; maybe I'll get a new dress." She grinned, and her hopeful blue gaze again put him in mind of Sophia. "When is *your* birthday, Mr. Ketch?"

"I don't rightly remember."

This astonished the child, and she set off detailing past birthdays and the gifts her father in particular had showered upon her. As he listened and grunted an occasional affirmation when the girl requested such, he chanced another glance at Maria, who smiled from her distant chair. Since returning from James Town, the young woman seemed happier and more active, though not completely so. Lingering problems with that damn boy, no doubt, though the couple obviously had no conflict the night Maria had arrived home from Virginia; Ketch had lain awake with thoughts of Isabelle and detected the faint, disturbingly private sounds drifting down the chimney from the master bedchamber. Apparently, the boy was capable of doing one thing right.

Ketch tried to shift Helen's focus. "Where's that brother of your'n, child?"

"I don't know, but he's late, and Maria said I can't stay up too much longer. Last night, he was so tired he fell asleep halfway through reading me a story." She giggled. "He started to snore. I've never heard John snore before, just like Daddy used to. Maria told me not to wake him, so he slept with me all night."

Finally, Ketch managed to excuse himself, beckoned by the smells of supper. He descended to the lower level and found most of the men

87

finished already and heading outside to smoke in the September breeze. Hiram Willis, however, lingered at the table. With a skeptical, dour eye, he watched Ketch devour his meal. Ketch could tell the man had something to say, something that would irritate him.

"I saw Zeke today with his shirt off. His back is a God-awful mess."

Ketch grunted over his turkey leg. "Mebbe he fell off his porch."

"Damn it, Ketch, this is no laughing matter."

"Bugger got what he deserved."

"And what was it he did to deserve it?"

"You know damn well what he did."

"You know the rules 'round here. If there's been an offense, it has to be brought to the Captain."

"The boy's soft."

"'Tis not your place to say. Zeke belongs to Leighlin, not to you. Same for the girl."

"Leave the girl out of it."

Willis leaned back. "Well, that's the rub, innit? The girl. 'Tis not what Zeke did but who he done it to."

Ketch dropped the turkey bone to his plate with a clangor and reached for his ale.

"There's talk, ye know," Willis continued, "'bout your interest in that girl."

"I have no interest in her."

"What happened to Zeke seems to prove otherwise."

Ketch guzzled the warm ale and brought the tankard down on the table with more force than he knew to be prudent. "He lamed her so bad she couldn't work. You know the truth; why didn't you go to Mallory if that be the way 'tis supposed to be?"

"She's Zeke's wife, you daft fool. A husband can do whatever he pleases with his wife. None of our affair, that."

"She couldn't work. That's our affair."

"Not your'n. I'm the overseer here, and doctor. 'Tis my discretion, hear? Mind your own affairs, damn it, or *that* I will report to the Captain."

Ketch scowled as he poured more ale. Willis eventually pulled from the lethal power of his glare and went the way of the others, leaving him alone in the common room.

CHAPTER 7

The sun rose beyond the Ashley, but its light could not reach Leighlin's west portico where Ketch stood, impatient and shifting his weight. The slaves belonging to his and Gabriel's gangs emerged from the distant trees. They came in groups and pairs, just fast enough to prevent a rebuke from him, many still looking worn from yesterday's tasks, yawning and rubbing their eyes. When he saw Isabelle, he experienced the now familiar stirring in his breast. For two weeks, he had been able to avoid her in all things but his dreams; there she visited him with disturbing regularity. Today there would be no escape.

She trailed her husband with lethargic steps, head down, face hidden until she reached the rear fringe of the gathered, murmuring slaves. From afar, he had thought she looked thinner than when last seen, and now he realized she had indeed lost weight. When Zeke muttered to her, Isabelle raised her head to see her substitute driver. Her cheeks lacked the characteristic smoothness from cheekbone to jaw, hollow now, and when Ketch met her dull eyes, she dropped her gaze as if to hide something.

Reluctant to draw attention to her, he pretended to be unconcerned by her appearance. Instead, he mentally checked off the last of the names on the roster.

"Yer driver is sick abed today," Ketch said with a scowl. "I'll be takin' over his duties in the south field."

Several of the slaves exchanged glances, though he knew their concern was not for Gabriel.

"You all took yer sweet time gettin' up here this morn. Anyone dawdlin' on the way to the field will regret it, hear?"

Today's work involved winnowing the threshed rice. Most knew their jobs well, but a few simple workers required Ketch's prodding. The air filled with flying chaff from the broad, shallow winnowing baskets. It coated Isabelle's blue headscarf and lighted upon her eyelashes and dusky skin where she stood in the shade of the storage barn. While the others sang to help pass the time, Isabelle said nothing.

With her circular basket, she tossed the rice, the pieces of broken stalk and loose husks carried away on the breeze, the grain left behind. She was slower than the others, but was her sluggishness due to a lack of skill or from weakness? Had she been ill since he last saw her? Was she ill even now?

When work halted for the midday meal, the slaves spread out in the shade of the oaks and magnolia trees on the western edge of the field. Many of the women who had been working in the darkened lee of the barn returned there to eat. Isabelle ate ravenously, careful not to let one morsel escape her trembling fingers. Once or twice, she glanced toward her husband a few feet away, who paid her no heed. When she saw Ketch watching her, she angled her body away from him. A faint outline of her backbone ridged her clothing. Realization crashed over him in a wave of outrage.

He went to the cauldron where the last of the parboiled rice clung to the bottom. "Give me the rest of it," he ordered Iris, the kitchen house woman in charge of doling out the rations.

He carried the half-filled bowl along with the remainder of his roasted chicken over to Isabelle and stood above her.

"Here." He set the food next to her on the rice mat where she had been working. "Eat it," he said. "Yer no good to anyone if you swoon from hunger."

"Thank you, sir," Isabelle replied, making an apparent effort not to snatch up the bowl but to instead reverentially take it in her hands. Again, she glanced at her husband, who was now watching. She hesitated.

"Eat it," Ketch ordered with a glare at Zeke, who looked away. For all to hear, he roared, "Five minutes! Then back to work with you God damned heathens."

He returned to his place under a nearby palmetto tree and tried to avoid looking at Isabelle but found it impossible as she wolfed the food. Rage boiled in him, but he forced it down, contained it for now, though he wanted to rip Zeke limb from limb. He thought of the past year, of the self-control he had gained, of Maria's trust, of Mallory's admission of surprise over his ability to become a valued part of Leighlin. But all those things faded from his mind as he watched Isabelle lick her bowl clean.

***

Isabelle had never wished harm upon anyone. Well, she admitted in the darkness of her cabin, perhaps upon Tom Clark and Hannah. Yet as her stomach cried out from hunger, she considered smothering her snoring husband with her pillow. To do any such crazy thing, however, required strength, and she had very little of that. In fact, she had spent all day in a crouch while winnowing, for she could not stand long. Gabriel, recovered from his illness, had chastised her and kicked her to her feet, but when she sank back down after a time, he seemed to realize any further effort on his part would be fruitless. If he noticed her weight loss, it failed to alarm him. He would only take an interest once she collapsed, unable to work, something she feared imminent. And then what would become of her?

Yesterday, when Ketch had given her extra victuals, his gesture nearly brought tears to her eyes, but she feared her husband's reaction. Ezekiel, though, had allowed her a small supper that evening. Perhaps Ketch's observation of her condition had concerned her husband. Ketch's unexpected presence that day could potentially be troublesome to Ezekiel's cruel game. Tonight, though, she had been allowed only a piece of bread after fixing her spouse's meal. In a vain attempt to avoid the torturous scents, she had fled to the porch, but her husband forbade fleeing farther afield.

Again, she considered the pillow. If she could somehow tie his hands to the bed… She closed her eyes and scolded herself for such a horrible thought. Her stomach, however, had no conscience and continued to encourage her mad ideas.

She wanted Ketch to intervene, if not directly then at least by notifying the overseer of her condition. Perhaps he had, but Willis cared no more than Gabriel. Or maybe Ketch had not suspected Ezekiel at all and attributed her weight loss to some illness about which he did not care. But he must, she told herself; otherwise, why would he have given her extra rations? He had not done so to anyone else. She frowned. Surely his displeasure was only because of the liability a sick slave would be to the harvest. Besides, she should dissuade his intervention, for his previous chastisement of her husband had caused her current suffering. Yet she continued to hope someone would help her.

The following autumn day carried the forceful heat of midsummer. The unending work and the draining weather finally claimed the last of Isabelle's strength, and midway through the afternoon, she fell face-first into her fanner basket. When she came to, Samuel and Gabriel were bent over her where she now lay in the shade of a palmetto tree. Someone had dashed water upon her face, and a cold rag lay draped across her forehead. Confused by Samuel's presence, she stared at him for a long moment before she remembered seeing him ride up on his mule just before she swooned. A line of concern furrowed Samuel's broad forehead.

"There," Gabriel said almost triumphantly. "She's comin' 'round already. I told you, Samuel, 'tis just the heat."

"I should take her to see Willis."

"Like hell. She has work to do."

Samuel loomed over the crouched driver, and for an instant his size seemed to intimidate the white man, whether Samuel intended such a result or not. Gabriel stood, avoided the man's eyes.

"You won't get any work from her," Samuel persisted. "Can't you see she's done in? How long has she been this thin?"

"She's always been thin."

"She should be seen by Willis."

Gabriel wavered, loath to show weakness to a black man or a slave girl. At last, Samuel's weighty stare won out, and Gabriel turned away with a wave of his hand.

"Bring her back here as soon as Willis is done with her."

Samuel turned to Isabelle. "Give me your hand."

Slowly, she sat up. Her stomach pained her and made her lightheaded again. She dreaded leaving the shade. When she took Samuel's hand and started to stand, dark spots danced in her sight again, and her knees began to give way. Samuel scooped her up and carried her over to his droopy mule, which did not even flick an ear when Samuel lifted her into the saddle. Although still unsteady, she managed to clutch the pommel and remain upright, hunched over, head down, as Samuel led the mule back up the lane.

Once in the shade of the trees alongside the river, Samuel asked, "Why have you lost so much weight? Have you been sick?"

"No, sir." Her eyes trailed thankfully up to the sheltering tree limbs. She was glad to leave the field behind but apprehensive about seeing Hiram Willis. "It's just the hard work; it caught up with me is all. And it's powerful hot today."

"I think it's more than that."

"No, sir."

"I'm not the only one who thinks this."

"Then you would both be mistaken."

"I've known Ketch for several years now, Isabelle; he is the keenest of observers and never wrong in his opinion of what he sees."

She tried to sound self-assured. "Mr. Ketch has been kind to me more than once. Perhaps he sees what he wants to see."

Abruptly, Samuel halted the mule and turned to her. "I understand if you are afeared of your husband, Isabelle, but we can't help you if you're not honest with us."

His sincerity and unexpected charity subdued her, made her feel almost foolish for the cowardly deception. She played with the mule's wispy mane near its withers.

"Ezekiel is my husband. It was my choice to marry him. The Captain married us hisself and gave us that big feast. If he was to hear I've caused trouble, he'd be displeased. He might send me back to Mr. Tom."

Samuel scowled and started forward again. "I have to at least talk to Zeke, if he's holding victuals from you. Husband or not, he has no right to starve you."

"Let me tell Ezekiel what you've said, and then if he don't stop…well, then you can say something to him. But please, Samuel, promise me you'll keep this between us. I don't want the Captain to know there's trouble. I'm sure he's already heard bad things about me."

Samuel fell silent until they reached the bridge and started over the creek, its surface carpeted by emerald duckweed. "Very well. Tell your husband what I've said. But if you swoon again, I won't be able to hold my tongue, and neither will Ketch. I'll be forced to tell Mr. Willis and see that Zeke is punished."

Isabelle's fingers ruffled the mule's sweaty coat. "I'm sure he'll listen once I tell him that. You'll see."

***

Willis reluctantly allowed Isabelle the afternoon off, and after she ate a small portion of food that Samuel provided from his own pantry, some of her spirit returned.

The temperature grudgingly declined with the dying of the sun and an increase of the westerly breeze. From her porch, Isabelle watched the people filter back through the purple twilight. Her stomach fluttered as she again reviewed what she would say to Ezekiel, how she would present Samuel's edict in a way that would not stir his blood. Then she admonished herself for being so afraid of him. When had she become such a coward? She despised her weakness and vowed to counter it by heeding Samuel's words—if her husband continued his ways, she would report his cruelty and hope for the best.

Lights blossomed in the settlement as night fell, so much earlier than during the summer. Still, Ezekiel did not appear. The meal Isabelle had prepared had long ago grown cold. She listened to the sounds of the community—quiet singing somewhere, a touch of tired laughter, the cry of a baby. All things she had hoped to feel a part of once married to Ezekiel.

Her dread of Ezekiel's return died away when she realized he was not coming home. Relief sent her back into the cabin. Salivating, she eyed the food left on the table, wanted desperately to eat it. But would he suddenly appear and find her with his food stuffed in her mouth? Why worry, considering what she had to tell him? But…she would not be telling him tonight. All the same, she would wait a little longer before risking a few mouthfuls of his meal.

The desperate emotions brought on by the desire for food and by her humiliation at the thought of Ezekiel now with Hannah drove Isabelle to bed. She sat in the dark, arms wrapped about herself, and rocked gently, listening to distant singing. It was soft, a lullaby perhaps. A great, unbearable loneliness welled up in her.

A board on the porch creaked. She held her breath to listen, heard another creak. She went to open the door.

"Ezekiel?"

A tenebrous form at the bottom of the steps, turning away before stopping at the sound of her voice.

The man's quiet response drifted to her, "There's victuals in that basket."

Confused, she wavered. "Mr. Ketch?" Searching the night, she asked, "Is my husband with you?"

"No. He won't be back tonight, so you go on and eat them victuals."

"But there's food in my cabin."

"Then eat that, too."

"Where is my husband?"

He stepped toward her and kept his voice low, frustration in his words. "If you don't take them victuals right now, girl, I'll fetch that basket back with me."

She rushed forward and crouched over the basket, pulled away the cloth and emitted a small gasp at the bounty within. Her fingers found a hunk of cold beef into which she sank her teeth, tearing at it.

"Why has he been starvin' you?"

Isabelle did not reply immediately, too busy gorging herself, afraid Ketch would change his mind and take the food back. "He says I need to learn my place, that I'm not obedient enough."

"He won't starve you no more."

"Then he will find something else to do." She tore into a hunk of cornbread.

"No."

The finality of his simple response chilled her, made her halt her feast. "Thank you for the food, sir. You've been kind to me more than once now."

"A man shouldn't use a woman so."

Some of her forgotten fortitude pushed her to bravery. "Even a slave?"

"Aye, even a slave." He turned to leave.

"Mr. Ketch," she called, this time with a new strength in her voice, almost a rebuke. "Has something happened to my husband?"

Ketch kept his back to her. "D'ye ask 'cause you care or 'cause yer afeared o' him comin' back?"

Slowly, she approached him, the basket in hand, the remaining contents left on the porch. "Do you *know* where he is?"

"You didn't answer me question, girl."

Isabelle returned the basket to him. "I am afeared of him, yes, but I'm also afeared of being alone."

"Is that why you married him?"

She hesitated then admitted, "Maybe," near a self-conscious whisper. It felt strange to be speaking so intimately with him. She should be afraid, but instead the familiarity pleased her. Perhaps the sightlessness of nighttime helped them forget their physical differences.

Ketch shifted his weight. He took a deep breath through his nose, as if smelling her. She could smell him, too; he had not just come from the fields, for the scent that drifted to her was of lye soap. Somehow, she could almost feel him as well, as if he stood closer to her than he truly did.

At last, he broke the spell. "You don't have to be afrighted no more." With that, he hurried back into the darkness.

***

Ketch slept sounder than he had in several months. Neither dreams nor nightmares disturbed him. He entertained no thought of what he had done to Zeke, no more than he thought about what clothes he had worn the previous day. His actions had been a necessity, a natural progression of events, a duty, an undeniable impulse, and so dwelling

95

upon the deed was as unnecessary as dwelling upon the last deer he had shot.

When wafting breakfast scents from the common room awakened him just before dawn, his stomach twisted in complaint. After leaving Isabelle last night, a profound desire for sleep had made him neglect his belly.

As always after the meal, he was the last of the white workers to leave the house. When he stepped through the back door, his gang awaited him. Mercifully, Gabriel and his crew had already left; Ketch wanted to avoid Isabelle after last night's encounter, for he figured from the girl's tone that she suspected him of killing Zeke. Well, she could loathe him if she so desired. At least she would no longer be starved or beaten.

Seeing his gang put him in mind of a conversation with Willis yesterday in which the overseer revealed that Jack Mallory planned to give him more responsibility, more slaves, more than even Gabriel had. Ketch could not deny the satisfaction he felt for the recognition. But that lingering pleasure quickly faded when he noticed that his gang was now missing more than Zeke. They shuffled their bare toes in the dirt of the lane, saying nothing. A twinge of alarm stirred Ketch.

"Where's Zeke and Spider?" he asked Asa.

Asa glanced sidelong at Jacob, wet his lips nervously. "Don' know where Zeke be, Mr. Ketch. Izzy say he didn't come home last night. An' Spider…well, Spider say he too sick to work today."

Anger blended with Ketch's sudden disquiet. "Did Willis examine him?"

"No, suh."

Agitation clenched his fist. "Go to the north field and get to work. I'll be there directly."

They scrambled to quit his presence, perhaps anticipating repercussions for their companions' imprudence. Ketch scowled. Spider had obviously spooked them. If that boy had revealed anything about yesterday, Ketch vowed he would have the bugger's hide. He had specifically chosen Spider for the task because of his weak mentality and because the slave feared his driver even more than the rest of the gang did, being youngest and slightest of build. Slightest, aye, but strong enough to restrain Zeke when needed, something Ketch could never have done lacking his right arm.

Hurrying back to the slave settlement, Ketch fully realized that if his master and mistress found out the truth, he could be banished from Leighlin. Yesterday he had not considered his master's rules and morals or his promise to Maria when he had taken Zeke into the swamps. Instead, he operated as he had for those two years with James Logan—an emotionless assassin on a mission to eradicate what needed to be eradicated, a man who had no consequence to fear. But that battle fog had lifted this morning when he saw Spider missing. Now thoughts of all he could lose bombarded him—his home, Helen, a benevolent mistress…and Isabelle.

Ketch burst into Spider's cabin and found him in bed, wrapped in a blanket. The slave quickly sat up, clutching the blanket to him as a shield, back pressed against the wall, eyes wild and wide.

"Please, Mr. Ketch. I didn't say nothin' to no one, jus' like I promised you. I didn't, I swear."

"Get up."

"I'm feelin' poorly, Mr. Ketch. I couldn't sleep, and my stomach hurt somethin' powerful." His trembling hands gripped the blanket tighter, and a haunted look darkened his eyes.

"Yer goin' to feel even poorer if you don't quit that bed." Ketch snatched the blanket away then dragged Spider's quivering form to his feet. "You yellow bastard, pull yerself together. You give me away with yer snivelin' and I'll flay you alive, hear?" He shoved him so hard toward the door that the young slave had to clutch the jamb to keep from sprawling. "What I did to Zeke, that won't be nothin' compared to what'll happen to you."

"Lord a-mercy, Mr. Ketch, I won' say nothin'."

"Damn yer eyes, get movin'."

When they reached the vicinity of Leighlin House, Ketch sent Spider on his way to the north rice field before turning for the river. Without haste, he crossed the front sward, for he needed time to think. The sun reflected its saffron glare off the river. Shading his eyes, he saw Willis upon his mule down at the landing, supervising the loading of the *Nymph*. He cursed to himself. Would Willis believe him? Damn it, he should have taken more time to plan all this instead of succumbing to his passions.

When Willis saw Ketch approaching through the line of birch trees near the landing, he reined the mule about and drew near with a scowl.

"What is it, Ketch?"

"That damn Zeke. He's run off."

"Run off or was runned off?"

Ketch returned the scowl. "You heard me."

Two of the closest slaves appeared to have also heard his

97

announcement, for they exchanged looks.

Willis gave an irritated sigh. "Put together a search party from Baruch's lot and search the swamps. If you don't find him by next tide, I'll send upriver for Archer's hounds." He glanced toward the house. "Christ. Not one runaway since I took over…"

Ketch knew Willis was thinking more of the embarrassment of reporting this to Mallory than of the production lost due to his slave's disappearance. The overseer's discomfort almost pleased Ketch as he turned back to the lane to carry out Willis's orders. But contemplating his own precarious position, he was wise enough to forego gloating over Willis's misfortune lest he bring bad luck down upon himself.

CHAPTER 8

They did not find Zeke, or any trace of him. When Wildwood's bloodhounds arrived, Willis went out with their handlers. The dogs' noses led them to the farthest swamp on Leighlin's western border, beyond the grazing land for the plantation's cattle, where the hounds milled about in snuffling confusion at water's edge.

"Fool must've gone into the swamp," Gabriel said when Willis returned at dusk. "But I don't reckon it'll do him no good, that. If a gator or snake don't get him, where's he gonna go?"

"Maybe he thinks he can go off and live with the Indians," Silas McBain offered, never looking up from his meal of fresh venison.

"Well, his black hide would stand out quite a bit," Latiffe said with a brief laugh. "He should know we would hear about it if he is with them. He knows we trade with those heathens."

Ketch saw Willis's attention upon him as the older man sank to the bench opposite him and reached for a tankard of ale. Naturally, the overseer was suspicious; Ketch would have been surprised otherwise. But with no proof, Ketch knew Willis would keep his mouth shut to avoid riling him as well as to circumvent any possible embarrassment if proven wrong later.

Ketch lingered at the table until the others had finished and departed for their usual smoke outside. Then he gathered the food that remained and stuffed it into a poke before stealing away into the early darkness.

As the night before, he found Isabelle's cabin dark. She sat in a rocking chair upon the porch. Without the weak flare from his lantern, he would have missed her entirely where she blended into the corner of the cabin. When he approached, she stood and curtseyed. He set the lantern upon the top step, so he could release the bag from around his arm.

"I brung you more victuals."

"I've eaten a bit. But thank you."

"Eat some more. Yer skinny as a stick, girl."

Her slender hands reached for the bag and pulled it to her midriff. She loosened the drawstring and peered inside, dipped an eager hand in and pulled out a corn biscuit.

Ketch tried to temper his natural gruffness when he said, "Sit down."

Slowly, as if wondering if his invitation was genuine, Isabelle returned to her rocking chair.

"No one has found my husband."

He said nothing. He knew he should leave but could not, did not want to return to the house, to see Mallory and his wife seated together upon the rear portico or to hear the exclusive conversation of his messmates. The nearby sounds from the other slave cabins—the tired talk and gentle laughter or songs, the scent of cook fires and food, the pervading feel of a community, however oppressed it may be— appealed to him tonight.

Isabelle breathed a gentle sigh. "No one *will* find my husband, will they, Mr. Ketch?"

"Do you want him found?"

She faltered. "Only if he came back a different man."

"Men don't change."

"Don't they?" The lantern light bronzed her skin and made her cheeks appear less hollow than the previous night. "If you mean to stop for a spell, sir, won't you sit?" Because she kept her eyes on the biscuit that she was thoughtfully tearing into bite-size chunks, he could not tell if her invitation was strictly dutiful or, in fact, sincere.

With only a moment's hesitation, he eased himself down upon the porch steps. He realized how much he enjoyed her voice. Soft and rounded, mysterious in its blend of white dialect and slave jargon. No harshness, though obviously her life had a sufficient amount of harshness in its past and present. No bitterness, even now. When he had first met her, he had detected hope in her, though tainted by anxiety over the unknown of her new home, but that hope had been disturbingly absent when he had talked to her after his return from Virginia. Now, though, he sensed the beginning of its return; something in her invitation for him to sit, to linger.

"May I ask you a question, Mr. Ketch?"

"Aye."

"How did you lose your arm?"

He laughed dryly. "I'm sure that story's well-known among yer kind."

"I've heard different stories, but there can only be *one* true story."

As she patiently watched him while finishing the biscuit, he felt a bit foolish for his evasion…and pleased by her interest to know only the truth. He cleared his throat and started anew, serious, "I got bit by a water snake."

"How?"

"Miss Helen got herself stuck in the swamp. When I went to get her out, that's when I got bit."

With mild wonder—or was it skepticism?—Isabelle said, "I don't know no one what lived after a water snake bite."

"Well, yer lookin' at one what did, and me missin' arm is proof." He said this with a certain proud ring, though he had never before felt proud about such a thing.

He detected a small, almost impish twist to her pretty lips when she said, "They say the snake curled up and died after it bit you. Some say it turned to ash right then and there and that you have poison flowing in your veins."

Ketch chuckled and decided to let the myth endure for now. A stifled sound, close to a low laugh stole through the night from Isabelle before she popped the last bite of the greasy biscuit into her mouth.

"Why is yer cabin dark?"

"Someone stole my candles." Isabelle reached into the poke again and pulled forth a sweet potato wrapped in a cloth. "The children, they sometimes play tricks on me."

Ketch could tell by her ruefulness that these tricks were not always harmless ones. With no husband now, such underhandedness would surely increase.

"Keep this lantern, then."

"I couldn't, sir."

"'Tis not a choice."

"Yes, sir." Isabelle prodded the sweet potato, perhaps afraid it might burn her, but all warmth was long gone by now, so she began to eat.

Blind obedience did not sit well with her nature, he could tell, but her intelligence and instinct for survival enabled her to repress any rebellion or sense of liberty.

Quietly, quite sober now, she asked, "Why have you been so kind to me, Mr. Ketch?" She hesitated. "Is there…something you want…from me?"

Ignoring the answer his body had already given this question when he had first arrived, he summoned the irascibility back into his tone. "If I wanted what yer referrin' to, don't you reckon I already would've took it?"

"Yes, sir," she murmured, no longer eating.

Reluctant to dampen her mood or encourage her to dwell on the uncomfortable subject, he said, "I do have a request, though."

As if eager to allay her blunder, she lifted her head. "Whatever I can help you with, sir."

"You was makin' a basket a while back."

"Yes. I'm learning. Selah's been helping me."

"Miss Helen's birthday is comin' in less than a week. I'd like you to make a basket for her so's I can give it to her as a gift. I'll pay you."

"Oh, Mr. Ketch. Wouldn't you like to have one of the other women make it? They have more skill than—"

"If I wanted one of them, I would've asked 'em." The moment the words left his mouth, he regretted the harshness.

"Yes, sir."

"It don't have to be fancy; she's but a chit. Anything colorful will please her."

"I will do my best, sir."

"I'm much obliged." He climbed to his feet, suddenly fatigued by the long day. If he did not force himself to leave, he would stay far too long. Perhaps he already had. Reminded again of his physical response to her nearness, he was thankful for the shrouding darkness. "I'll bring you some candles on the morrow."

"Even if Ezekiel is back?"

There was no coyness in her tone or upon her face. Did she believe there was still a chance for her husband's return or did she just not want to believe he had disposed of Zeke?

"Good night," Ketch said before he left her.

***

The next evening, Isabelle boldly went to her small garden and harvested everything she could. Then she cooked the vegetables in a magnificent pottage and ate it all, along with the cornbread she had baked two days ago for her husband. She ate by the light of the dying fire, for the lantern Ketch had left vanished during the day.

Afterward, she wandered out to her porch. The night promised to be chilly, and she considered retrieving a shawl from inside. She stared off toward the center of the settlement where the community fire freshly blazed, encircled by dark figures. No dancing or singing; the harvest left everyone too exhausted, even the children. During their work today, some of the people had continued to conjecture about Ezekiel's mysterious disappearance. Most believed he had indeed fled on his own; others were unconvinced, Hannah among them.

Isabelle returned inside and managed to scrounge up one last candle. Restless, as she had been these past two days, she retrieved her partially finished sweetgrass basket and decided to work a bit more on it before retiring. Sitting on her bed, she smiled at the thought of her work being presented to the Captain's sister. The task, however, held her attention only a short while, and her thoughts drifted to Ketch's last visit, to his continued solicitousness and his claim to want nothing from her. If he wanted nothing, why did he come? Perhaps he was lonely, like she was. She had heard that he had no friends among the whites except for the Captain's little sister—a strange alliance, but a telling one to Isabelle. Or maybe guilt brought him here, if he had indeed caused her husband's disappearance. Yet, surely, someone of Ketch's reputation experienced no guilt. He was a puzzle, to be sure, and puzzles easily allured her. She wondered if he would bring her more candles tonight, as he had mentioned.

As she worked, the realization struck her with stony finality that Ezekiel was truly dead. Not just missing. Dead. And her strange benefactor most likely responsible. Was it wrong, she wondered, not to mourn her husband? She had been foolish enough to fall for Ezekiel's early kindness, vulnerable enough and blinded by her own desires to believe his show, a mere trick to win himself a bride before his friends could marry. So perhaps she and Ezekiel deserved their fates.

A murmur of voices reached through the night to where she sat on her bed. Some of the people returning early to their cabins. But they drew ever closer to her cabin, which was at the farthest reaches of the settlement, and she detected a sharpness to those voices. Her heartbeat quickened, and she set aside the basket.

"Is'belle, you get out here!" Hannah called.

Isabelle hesitated, but then, with new strength provided by her dinner feast, she gathered her shawl and stepped onto the porch with her candle. She started at the sight of Hannah, Ester, and the men of Ezekiel's gang—except Spider, who lay sick abed—their angry countenances bronzed by the lantern Asa carried.

"You tell us," Hannah said.

"Tell you what?"

"Don't play all innocent. You might fool some, but you not foolin' me. Where be Ezekiel?"

"How should I know?"

"You know 'cause you done somethin' to him," Ester snapped, accompanied by nods from Jacob and Asa.

"How could I do anything to Ezekiel? I'm half his size. He's been starving me for—"

"You got what you deserved, makin' that devil Ketch beat on him." Hannah took a step closer. "He should've kilt you instead of makin' you go hungry."

Isabelle advanced to the edge of the porch, her indignation surprisingly strong, stronger than she had ever allowed it to be before Ezekiel's disappearance. "I don't know where Ezekiel is, and I haven't done nothing to him. Who's to say *you* didn't do him a mischief? You've been jealous since he first set eyes on me."

"Jealous? What's to be jealous of? He didn't love you; he loved me. Now he gone, 'cause of you!"

Hannah mounted the steps, but Isabelle refused to flinch when they came toe to toe. The others drifted closer. Isabelle could feel their tension. No doubt their suspicion had been brewing all day, and at the fire tonight, they had planned this move. What could she do against so many? She lacked the strength to fight even Hannah.

Hannah's teeth showed white in the lantern light as she growled, "You might not be big enough to hurt Ezekiel, but there be someone what is. Someone who done hurt Ezekiel times afore. That Ketch. He come see you last night, didn't he? Asa seen 'im. He brung you food. Now why'd he go and do that?"

Isabelle struggled to respond, afraid to say something that might bring trouble upon her protector. "So I'd be stronger to work. Mr. Ketch had nothing to do with Ezekiel running off."

Hannah gave her a slight push. "'Course he did."

"If you're so sure, then why not tell Mr. Willis instead of coming to me?"

Hannah laughed harshly, echoed by her companions. "What would Mr. Willis do to another white man, 'specially someone like Ketch? They's all afeared of him, too. And even if they wasn't, the Captain not gonna punish one of his own."

"But you can be punished," Ester said. "No one's gonna know."

"No one's gonna say nothin'," Hannah added. "You say one word to that one-armed devil or to Baruch or Amos about this and I'll take you into them swamps myself and you won't never come out."

"Get off my porch."

"I'll get off, but you comin' with me."

"I'm not going nowhere."

Hannah jerked her head at Asa. The large man came toward Isabelle, but she flung the candle and its spatter of hot wax in his face then leapt off the porch, avoided the reaching hands of the others. With her skirt gathered in her hands, she fled toward the lane, the outraged voices close behind.

When she raced around the corner of the next cabin, she slammed into what felt like a brick wall. The impact sent her heavily to the ground, her breath smashed from her. Scrambling to her feet, she bolted away, fearful of another ally of Hannah's. She thought only of getting away from the settlement.

A man's voice roared behind her, followed by Hannah's startled scream and the shouts of Asa and Jacob. Ester's fright-filled squeal pulled Isabelle to a curious, anxious halt. Near the distant fire circle, others stood in alarm.

Back near her cabin, lurid shadows broke from one another, lit by Asa's lantern. Its wavering light touched upon terrified faces before all fled into the safety of darkness. Before the stampede stole the light from the scene, Isabelle detected a singular shape between her and the fleeing group, a unique shape. Astounded, she stood frozen as the shadow came toward her. She took a step back from his approach yet felt no urge to flee as the others had.

"Are you hurt, Izzy?"

Ketch sounded different than ever before. Perhaps it was that intangible difference that left her dumb or the fact he had called her something less formal than Isabelle.

"Did they hurt you?"

"N-no," she stammered.

"What was they about?"

She hesitated. "They...they think I had something to do with Ezekiel going missing."

He cursed under his breath then paused before saying, "You can't stay here."

Afraid of exactly what he intended, she said nothing.

"I'll take you to Samuel's. You can sleep there tonight."

"But—"

"Do as I say."

Ketch led the way down the lane. Many had deserted the fire circle. Those who remained stood silently watching from their safe distance, poised to bolt. Voices whispered from inside some of the cabins, nervous, angry. A tangible foreboding lay over the settlement. A jumble of emotions engulfed Isabelle at once—anger, humiliation, fear, resentment. A part of her wanted to shout at all of them as she passed, curse them and spit.

She stayed close behind Ketch, who moved with long, purposeful strides.

"Why was you in the settlement, Mr. Ketch?"

"I was bringin' you some candles. Reckon I dropped 'em back there."

His thoughtfulness touched her deeply, his fortuitous timing amazing her.

"But, sir...what are you going to tell Samuel?"

"The truth, else he won't let you stay."

"But will he...will he tell the Captain?"

"I'll ask him not to."

"But will he?"

"I reckon that's his business. But you can't stay in the settlement, and besides Samuel's cabin, there's no place else for you."

"But I can't *stay* at Samuel's. I mean, more than just tonight."

"Let me worry about that."

Isabelle said nothing more, despairing. Ketch could have said perhaps Ezekiel would be found and then she could return to the settlement. Whatever had happened to her husband, Ketch knew the truth, and the truth could not be simple or anything less than repugnant since he refused to tell her.

A lantern illuminated the front room of Samuel's cabin, and as they climbed the steps, Isabelle saw him through one of the windows, seated at a table, bent over a book. At the sound of their approach, his head came up. When the door opened to Ketch's knock, light spilled forth from within, and Ketch glanced with concern over his shoulder at Leighlin House where one of the uppermost chambers brightly glowed.

Samuel's brow lowered when he saw Isabelle. "What's this?"

Again, Ketch glanced toward Leighlin House. "For Christ's sake, Samuel, let us in."

Ketch's emotional state seemed to alarm Samuel as much as Isabelle's presence. After a brief pause, he stepped back to admit them. As soon as Isabelle crossed the threshold, Ketch closed the door as if Samuel could not do it fast enough.

Isabelle took in the sparse room that stretched the width of the small structure. A low fire hissed in the fireplace where a cooking pot hung, but the scent of food was faint, the table cleared. There was a pantry to one side and a table with four chairs, and little else. She stared at the book left open on the table, marveled at Samuel's ability to read.

Samuel rumbled, "What's this about, Ketch?" He scowled as he watched Ketch move to the two front windows and close the shutters.

"The bloody animals came after her, they did. Was goin' to lynch her sure if I hadn't gotten there and scared the shit out of 'em. They think she had somethin' to do with Zeke disappearin'."

Samuel's lips pressed together as if to restrain a curse.

"'Tis unsafe there for her now," Ketch continued. "She needs a place to stay."

"She can't stay here. You know that."

"Just for tonight."

"Then what?"

"I'll think o' somethin'. Lemme sleep on it."

The distress on Ketch's face shocked Isabelle. How was this the same man who had beaten Ezekiel and perhaps killed him as well? Why was he so concerned for her welfare?

Samuel rubbed his chin as he considered Ketch. Perhaps his response was more for his comrade's sake than hers when he reluctantly said, "Isabelle, take the chamber back there to the right." He pointed, probably assuming she did not know left from right, which she did. "There's a bed there."

"Thank you." But she lingered, uncertain of what more to say. Ketch already looked as if a weight had been removed from his shoulders, and she regretted that he had become entangled in her troubles. Finally, she curtseyed and said, "Thank you, sir," before hurrying off to the rear chamber.

***

Come morning, Ketch made sure he was outside early, at the same time as Gabriel, for he wanted to see Isabelle before she started for the field. Just as important, he wanted to be seen by the others of her gang to convey through his presence a reinforcement of his actions last night, to discourage any further persecution and to make them think twice about sharing what had happened.

To his relief, Isabelle was among the first slaves to report for duty. Samuel had been wise enough to send her out of his cabin before anyone could see where she had spent the night, thereby appearing untouched by the controversy and neutral between factions. Her beauty drew a smile to Ketch's lips, an expression he was unconscious of until she smiled back, small and almost shy, quickly stifled behind a hand, a brief display that left him unable to breathe. He hoped she had slept well, unafraid and peaceful. God knows he had not, for he had spent the night cursing himself for not foreseeing the danger his disposal of Zeke would bring down upon Isabelle. He had also contemplated every possible solution to her predicament. Options, however, were virtually nonexistent. Only one idea had any chance of success, but it would require Samuel's assistance, something he was uncertain he could acquire.

As the rest of the slaves gathered, Ketch glared down at them from the steps of the portico. They glanced fearfully at him, probably still unnerved by his madman shouts last night. He had swung the small sack that carried the candles and victuals for Isabelle, striking a couple of the slaves in the head and shoulders, causing even further panic. In his rage, he had thrown the sack after the last of them.

Soon all of Gabriel's charges had appeared, and the young man led them off. The slaves kept a noticeable space between themselves and Isabelle near the rear of the group, some of them murmuring to one another, glancing from the girl to Ketch then away. Isabelle, too, chanced one last look his way before she rounded the far corner of Leighlin House. Did she suspect the truth about her husband's disappearance? She seemed clever enough to smoke it. Yet, if she did think Zeke had been murdered, why had she revealed no fear of his murderer? Was it a façade? Perhaps she had shared her suspicions with Samuel and encouraged him to report her concerns to their master.

The arrival of the last of Ketch's small gang pulled him from his speculation. Spider was absent. He scowled, but before he could question anyone, Asa spoke up, fingering his hat brim.

"Spider has a powerful fever, Mr. Ketch. Auntie June is tendin' him. She say to send Mr. Willis right quick."

CHAPTER 9

"Mr. Ketch, sir!" A harried voice reached him on the dock where he was supervising the unloading of rice from the mule wagon. Nahum—a young servant who worked in the main house—clutched his hat in his hands as he rushed to a stop several feet away.

"What is it?"

"The Cap'n sent me, sir. He bids you fetch Isabelle and come to the house straight away, sir."

The unsettling order gave Ketch pause before he acknowledged it and sent the slave back to the house. He directed Asa to continue with their work then started on his way to find Isabelle.

Mallory summoning them must mean he had learned of last night's disturbance. Surely Samuel would never have revealed such a thing without warning him. More likely one of the slaves had been bold enough to say something directly to Gabriel or perhaps the young man had overheard a remark and would be more than happy to see his fellow driver in trouble.

Near the south rice field, shelters had been constructed—open-sided, temporary sheds under which Gabriel's workers toiled, protected from the elements. The dull sounds of wooden pestles pounding into mortars filled the air with a monotonous rhythm, flavored by a Mende song that matched the slaves' almost mesmerizing movements as they worked the pestles up and down. The mortars—pine and cypress trunks cut and hollowed out by Ketch's gang—stood waist high and held the pecks of rough rice being milled, a grueling process that would go on for endless weeks. The tapping and rolling motion of the pestles removed the grain's hull, an art that required skill to achieve the best results. The women were always more adept than the men.

As Ketch moved along the line of shelters, he spotted Isabelle squatting next to her mortar, a flat sweetgrass basket in hand, moving in a circular motion. The husks and chaff from the pounded rice gathered toward the outside of the basket, and she paused in her work to remove these unwanted portions. Her movements entranced him as he admired her slender brown hands. Although the day was relatively mild, sweat from hours of difficult work slicked her face. She would be expected to pound and polish fifty pounds this day, an arduous task for any woman, let alone one so slight and not far removed from her forced starvation. Last night, Gabriel had complained that Isabelle's lack of skill resulted in far too many broken grains: "She produces midlings at best. But mainly small rice—fit for nothin' but slaves."

Ketch felt the eyes of other slaves upon him, caught a few whispers. The singers, momentarily distracted, struggled to recover the lost beat. He halted outside of Isabelle's shed, and the fall of his shadow garnered her attention and surprise.

Gabriel drew near. "What's this, Ketch? Don't you slow down this pea-wit no more than she already is. Worthless rag. She'll be lucky to finish by midnight."

"The Captain has need o' her. Sent me to fetch her to the house."

Alarm flashed across the young woman's face, and she quickly went back to her work, swirling the contents of the basket so forcefully that some of the rice spilled out.

"Mind your work, you useless cow," Gabriel snapped. He took a step toward her, but Ketch's hand clamped down on his wrist. Meeting Gabriel's pained glare, Ketch restrained him for only an instant then released his grip.

"Step lively, girl. The Captain will be vexed if we keep him a-waitin'."

Isabelle considered the pestle laid nearby. Ketch could not tell if she was relieved to be leaving her work or was worried about her ability to catch up later and complete her task before dark. But she set aside her basket and stiffly stood, wiped her hands upon her apron, and waited for Ketch to lead the way.

They remained silent as they headed up the lane, leaving the tedious noise of milling behind. Ketch felt Isabelle's anxiety as tangibly as if he had reached out to touch her.

At last, he said, "I don't know why the Captain's called for you; I'd tell you if I did. If 'tis about last night, let me do the talkin'."

Soon they passed through the tunnel of shade offered by the trees near Helen's favorite riverside spot, where she would search for fiddler crabs. Shortly thereafter, they crossed the bridge, Leighlin House looming upon the bluff beyond. Isabelle's steps slowed, and Ketch had to urge her forward.

At the front door, Thomas met them and ushered them through the Great Hall. Isabelle's wide eyes took in the spacious room, her mouth gaping.

After Thomas's announcement of their arrival to those within the library, Ketch gestured for Isabelle to enter ahead of him. Nervously, she looked at him, and he feared she might bolt. The best he could offer in the way of assurance was a shallow nod. She swallowed and stepped into the library.

The room was quite cool this time of day, for the sun's rays had yet to reach the windows. Ketch suspected even the sun would fail to ease the oppressiveness that hung in the room. Jack Mallory sat behind his desk with the stormy look of one who had suppressed something far too long and could no longer do so—dark hair flopping forward as it was wont to do whenever he worked at the desk, eyes even darker, almost black, beneath his lowered brow, small mouth even smaller with tension, hands clasped atop the desk.

Maria's presence surprised Ketch; she occupied a chair between the two south windows. Her expression concerned him more than Mallory's, for while Mallory's attention rested upon Isabelle, Maria's remained upon him. A pervading chill reached across the room from her and struck Ketch a blow. Her olive-toned skin seemed tight over her high cheekbones, and he was quite certain tears lurked somewhere very near. She finally turned from him as if to hide something.

"Shut the door," Mallory ordered then gestured for Isabelle to approach the desk. At first, Ketch thought he might have to shove the girl to get her to obey, but finally she moved forward and offered her curtsey. Ketch remained near the door, though he wanted to be close to Isabelle.

"Isabelle," the young man began with little volume as the girl clasped her dirty hands in front of her, head down. "Information has come to me regarding your husband."

Her gaze flashed from Mallory to Ketch before returning to the rug on which she stood.

"Your husband was murdered, and it is my understanding that you had a hand in it."

With an expression of horror, she said, "That's not true, sir. No, I—"

"Hold your tongue," Mallory barked, the foreign sharpness so much in contrast to his previous tone that even Maria started at the sound.

Ketch held himself in check, kept from jumping in without thinking, knowing the boy would only bridle even more if his ridiculous accusation was immediately challenged.

111

"I brought you to Leighlin to help bring harmony, not chaos, to marry someone like Ezekiel, not kill him. Have you any idea the value of a slave of Ezekiel's age and health?"

"No, sir."

"He was well-versed in many facets of working this plantation, and now I'll have to waste money and time replacing him, at the most crucial time of the year, no less."

"Please, sir—"

"I'll hear none of your excuses or lies." He stood. "I have no time to waste on troublemakers."

Maria beseeched, "Jack—"

He shot out a silencing hand, startling Ketch as much as Maria, for Ketch had never seen the young man behave in such an abrupt manner with his wife. Why was Maria even here? Judging from Mallory's demeanor, he did not desire her presence and would prefer to squelch her level-headedness and sense of fairness amidst his tirade. And why did the boy block Isabelle from speaking, from defending herself? Normally, he was no tyrant.

"I could see you hanged for this," Mallory continued, "but I can ill afford the cost of losing two slaves. So, instead, I'll commute your sentence to two dozen lashes."

All caution gone, Ketch started toward Mallory. As if expecting this reaction, the young man opened the desk's top drawer.

Maria jumped to her feet. "Ketch, no!" Her desperate tone, more than even the pistol that he knew rested in that drawer, halted Ketch in his blind rage, a rage akin to that which had gripped him when he had killed Zeke. Both Maria and Isabelle stared at him, Isabelle's quivering hands over her mouth as if to muffle her despair.

With a low, deep menace, Ketch snarled, "You have no proof she did this."

"Do I need any?" Mallory challenged before his tone slipped into something resembling slyness. "Perhaps you have proof she *didn't* do it. You seem quite interested, Ketch, interested in what happens to a slave, no less. Why would that be?"

The shine in the boy's coal-like eyes revealed the trap that had been set and which Ketch had just sprung. Mallory knew Isabelle to be innocent; Ketch suspected Willis had gotten the truth out of that weakling Spider. And now Mallory had the ammunition he lacked over a year ago when he had wanted to kill Ketch but for Maria's accord with him.

"That worthless piece of shit Zeke," Ketch growled. "He was

112

starvin' her."

"And why would he risk that? Punishing her perhaps? For what, I wonder?"

Ketch looked at Isabelle's tired, dirty, distraught face, remembered the bruises there, the fury and vengeance he had felt then and again later when he had sliced off Zeke's trembling prick.

"For what, Ketch?" Mallory demanded.

Ketch saw the deep disappointment on Maria's drawn face, and he realized for the first time that she had genuinely cared for him. Now she probably wondered why she had ever believed in him.

"Zeke was ill-usin' her when I was in Virginia," Ketch said.

Isabelle gave him a slight, dissuading shake of her head.

"So, I gave him a thrashin'."

"And then, when he retaliated by starving Isabelle, you murdered him."

"He got nothin' less than he deserved. But Isabelle had no part in it. She knew nothin'."

"You gave no thought to the fact that Ezekiel wasn't your property, wasn't yours to sit in judgment of?"

Mallory kept his hand in the drawer as Ketch stepped nearly to the corner of the desk.

"And what would you have done?" Ketch asked skeptically.

"I wouldn't have tortured and murdered him, you stupid animal!"

Maria appeared at the front of the desk without Ketch being aware of her approach. Only her physical presence kept the two men at bay. Isabelle remained frozen to the spot, eyes swimming.

Ketch could tell Mallory had considered his actions and words beforehand, which explained his exploitation of Isabelle. Obviously, the boy knew enough about his relationship with Isabelle to realize he would never let her take his place in the noose or otherwise.

"John! John, come quick!" Through the west windows came Helen's light, happy voice, accompanied by the drum of her feet on the portico then into the house. She reached the library door before Maria could and burst in with a smile on her cherubic face, as if she had brought the very sun with her.

"John, you must come see…" The sight of Maria's tears halted her.

"Helen, sweetie, your brother is busy right now—"

"Are you crying, Maria?" She resisted her sister-in-law's effort to turn her away.

To avoid revealing his flushed-face anger—if she had not already detected it—Ketch stared at the cluttered desk.

"Helen." Mallory closed the drawer. "Run along, and I'll come find you when I'm through here."

"But why is Maria crying, and Isabelle, too?"

Ketch was surprised Helen remembered Isabelle's name, what with the dozens of slaves at Leighlin. Yet the child always had been uncanny with details.

"Everything's fine," Mallory said. "Go on outside." When Maria started to escort her from the library, his voice halted her. "Maria, we're not through here."

She frowned over her shoulder at him, but he refused to yield. She bent to whisper into Helen's ear then guided the girl into the Great Hall. "Mary," she called. "Come take Helen to the garden, please." Once the servant appeared, Maria stepped back into the library and closed the door.

Silence stretched for a long moment as Helen's voice trailed away. Mallory turned back to Ketch, the stoniness returning to his stare.

"Tell me something, Ketch—why did Spider help you with Zeke?"

The coxcomb knew, of course, damn him, but he wanted to make this complete. "'Cause I told him if he didn't, he'd get the same as Zeke."

"You terrorized him into poor health and uselessness. You know this, of course. So, not only has this plantation lost Zeke's production, we've lost Spider's as well." He took in the women's guarded reactions. "When you first returned here after Logan's death, Maria saved your miserable life. And did you not make her a promise at that time?"

When Ketch answered in the affirmative, the weakness of his voice aggravated him.

"And what was that promise, Ketch? It seems you've forgotten."

He regained some of his rancor. "Damn you. If I hadn't killed Zeke, what do you reckon he—"

"You vowed not to harm anyone again. You promised to abandon your perverse path, did you not? Or was that not really a promise at all but instead a convenient lie?"

"Jack," Maria said at last, the silent tears conquered by her displeasure. "This has gone far enough." Her hot Spanish temper, so familiar to Ketch, showed itself when she stared at her husband, but she managed to stifle further admonishment in front of slave and worker.

"Please, Captain." Isabelle's trembling voice surprised all of them. "I know what Mr. Ketch done to Ezekiel was wrong, but…he was just protecting me."

"If Ezekiel was ill-using you," Mallory said, "you should have told Samuel or Mr. Willis, not left it in Ketch's hands."

"Mr. Willis knew, sir."

Maria took a step toward her. "What?"

"When Ezekiel threw me off the porch and hurt my ankle, Mr. Willis tended me."

"You told him about your husband?"

"No'm. I was ashamed, and it wouldn't have mattered; I am Ezekiel's wife."

"Willis knew the truth," Ketch growled. "He knew about Zeke starvin' her, too."

Mallory skeptically asked, "Did he tell you as much?"

Ketch gave a snort. "Any half-wit what saw her would've known."

"Then Isabelle should have gone to Samuel. He would have told me about it."

"Samuel knew," Isabelle said, "but I asked him not to tell. I was afeared if he did, things would be worse, or I would be sent away." She paused. "I don't want to be sent away. I believe the Captain is a fair and tolerant master."

Maria gave her husband an importunate look after Isabelle's artful supplication, and the boy sagged under this double onslaught. Ketch admired Isabelle's skill, yet her tone held sincerity, not manipulation. She would not want to take her chances with yet another master, one who might be more like Clark than Mallory.

With a frown, Mallory spoke in a gentler tone. "Go back to your work now."

"Yes, sir."

She curtseyed and wiped at the damp trails upon her cheeks, making her face even more of a smeared mess. She gave Ketch a fleeting glance, pale eyes filled with regret and apology, before she padded across the room and left. Perhaps he was mistaken, but he saw no revulsion for what he had done to her husband. Maybe she was too shocked to truly react. Later it would reach her, especially if she learned the rest of the details. At least Mallory had not been spiteful enough to divulge them, if Spider had indeed spilled all.

Mallory's fingertips rested on top of the desk as he considered Ketch with a different expression—still one of loathing, distrust, and intolerance—but Isabelle's pleas had diminished the anger and returned a lighter brown to his eyes. "What is your interest in Isabelle, Ketch?"

"Interest? I have no *interest*."

"Then why haven't I heard of you going to the rescue of any other slave at Leighlin?"

"It'd seem," Ketch said with tempered sarcasm, "no one else has needed rescuin'. Look at her. She's nothin' but a wisp. What could she do against someone like Zeke? You know what he was like. They shouldn't have been allowed to marry. She just wanted to fit in, and that bastard took advantage of her—"

Maria stepped around the desk, and her unexpected touch on his arm, so rarely hazarded, tripped him into glowering silence. "Go into the parlor while my husband and I talk."

"Maria," Mallory warned, but his wife ignored his irritation as she applied pressure to Ketch's shoulder to turn him toward the door.

Ketch knew he could add nothing more to the argument without making things worse, and he could tell that something he or Isabelle had said had dented Maria's resolve. If anyone could persuade Mallory to alter whatever ends he had planned for his rebellious driver, it was Maria. Yet, Ketch had little faith, figuring Mallory had awaited this opportunity for more than a year.

"I'll fetch you when we're done," she said quietly. While her gaze held a certain empathy, it also contained disappointment and anger. He felt ashamed, not because of what he had done but for the effect its discovery had upon her.

When he retreated to the parlor across the Great Hall from the library, he found Pip absently dusting. She displayed a guilty visage. The room certainly did not appear in need of dusting. Hastily, she curtseyed and fled through the short side passage that connected the parlor to the dining room. Before long, the whole plantation would know what truly had happened to Zeke.

Ketch paced in front of the west windows, wishing this were all over and he outside again. This room always made him uncomfortable. In the old house, Ella Logan had been laid out here after her death. He wondered now what she would do if she were here, if she were faced with what he had done to Zeke. Would he have gone to her beforehand about Isabelle? Perhaps he should have gone to Maria.

Mallory had been the second person to ask him about his interest in Isabelle. Ketch frowned at his own confusion, his continued denial at this inquiry. He was not one to think far ahead in life; there was no reason to do so. But now Mallory's question and the events in the settlement last night forced him to think of the future, at least the immediate future. Indeed, what was his interest in the girl? Why had he done something that could very well jeopardize his position, his very life here, his pledges to Ella Logan and Maria? Why had he been motivated into these dangerous actions for a woman—a mulatto slave, no less—when he knew he could never pursue her in any natural way? True enough, he could not tolerate a man's abuse of a woman, but he had never killed over it when such a murder would endanger himself.

The library door opened, and Maria beckoned him to return. Irritated by the whole process of being judged, Ketch crossed the Great Hall with the last vestige of indolence. He halted just inside the library door. Mallory stood staring out a south window, which had been opened to admit the breeze, hands clasped behind his back, fingers moving against his mother's leather bracelet. Maria stood near the hearth, positioned halfway between the two men, one hand toying with her locket. She looked dissatisfied with the conversation that had just occurred here and so did Mallory when he turned around, something that gave Ketch hope. Mallory crossed his arms against his chest, his smooth brow furrowed.

"If this decision were purely mine," Mallory began, "I'd see you removed from Leighlin this very tide and forbidden on pain of death from ever returning. But we both know my wife is of a kinder, more magnanimous nature."

With a harshness Ketch had not heard from her in some time, Maria added, "Don't think what you've done is anything but abhorrent to me, Ketch. You betrayed the trust I put in you. No one else at Leighlin trusted you, and now they never will. Maybe Jack's right and I *am* the biggest fool even now. But we're willing to allow that you're not the only one at fault in this, and that something besides evil made you kill Ezekiel."

"I'll let you choose your own punishment," Mallory said. "Either leave Leighlin or suffer the two dozen lashes I threatened Isabelle with, delivered under my own hand in front of all of Leighlin's people."

Ketch scowled. "You know I won't leave. You know I can't."

"The promise to my mother, of course. Aye. But I can't believe my mother would want you to remain after what you just did to one of her slaves."

The idea that Ella Logan would disfavor him flooded Ketch with true shame.

Mallory continued, "Before the people go to the fields tomorrow morn, then, you will report to the rear portico for punishment. And effective immediately you will relinquish your position as driver; you don't deserve such authority. You will work under Samuel on the new kilns. Furthermore, you will compensate Leighlin thirty pounds for the loss of Ezekiel, to be stopped from your pay. And if there is another such instance or anything whatsoever that displeases me, by God, even my wife's charity won't be able to save you. Understand?"

Ketch gave a small nod, more of a bow in deference, hiding his distaste.

"And if you have the foolish notion to seek retribution against Spider, save your effort; I'm removing him from Leighlin to another plantation, in exchange for another slave. He's worthless to me now, thanks to you." He moved to his desk. "Now, leave us before my wife's influence wears off and I change my mind."

Ketch knew he should mutter some sort of gratitude, if not to the boy, then to his wife, but when he again saw the deep disappointment in Maria's eyes, he remained silent.

CHAPTER 10

Ketch returned to the landing and instructed his gang to report to Baruch in the north rice field. Asa and the others exchanged curious looks but said nothing as Ketch turned his back on them and left.

He returned to his chamber where he lay upon the bed, staring up at the naked beams. Although he hoped to sleep, he remained awake, for his thoughts went to Isabelle. What was she thinking? He wagered that the gracious smile she had given him that morning would never be directed his way again. The monster she had heard about was no longer simply that of stories. Yet this was all for the best; she was free of Zeke.

The physical prospect of being flogged did not perturb him. He had been beaten enough between his stepfather, the Royal Navy, and the Spanish to view it with nothing but indifference. The scarring on his back would shield him from the worst of the pain for the first dozen, and then the agony would come, especially taking into account how that damned boy would take great delight in the delivery. No, the pain he could tolerate, but the humiliation of being made a spectacle in front of Leighlin's population, in front of Isabelle, would be more difficult to bear.

Considering Mallory's judgment, he knew he should not be too harsh on the boy. After all, Mallory had good reason to be shed of his driver. Ketch was confident Mallory would have exercised just such a verdict if not for his wife. What had made Maria send him out so she could speak privately with her husband? Was it simply Isabelle's revelation that both Willis and Samuel had done nothing with their knowledge of her circumstances? Or was it something more? Ketch doubted Maria had swayed the boy's decision strictly because of any misplaced loyalty she had acquired over the past year and a half. Maybe Helen had been behind her reasons. The child's appearance in the library may have been a bit of good fortune.

After a time, he left the house. At the top of the terraces, he settled upon a stone bench that faced the landing. The dogger had left long ago with the first of Leighlin's milled rice bound for a Charles Town warehouse. Waterfowl flew across the marsh opposite the landing, some descending to disappear among the tall reeds, others continuing to the far shore and vanishing among the thick trees. The vibrant greens of summer were beginning to fade.

"Mr. Ketch!" Helen's voice startled him. He turned to see the girl approaching from the house, holding Maria's hand. Nahum trailed behind with a valise in each hand. As Helen broke away from Maria to run toward him, Ketch got to his feet. Her broad smile told him that her brother and sister-in-law had once again shielded her from the truth about him. When he crouched down to greet her, she threw her arms around his neck for a quick embrace before taking a step back.

"Maria and I are going to visit Mr. David and Miss Elizabeth."

Relieved she would be absent when he was flogged, he forced a smile.

Helen lowered her voice. "Why was John so angry in the library? He won't tell me. Was he angry at Maria? Is that why she was crying? She won't tell me either."

Obviously, the child had been mulling this over in great frustration all day, troubled by the adults' reticence, and she had been bursting to cross-examine him before Maria or anyone else could deter her.

"Yer brother's not vexed with no one but me."

"What did you do?"

He gave her a tight smile and a wink in the hopes of not disappointing her too much with his evasions. "I reckon that's somethin' best kept betwixt yer brother and me."

Helen leaned close and whispered, "You can tell me, Mr. Ketch. I won't tell no one."

"I durst not. I'm in enough trouble as it is, child."

Ketch stood when Maria reached them, discomfort in her frown. He hoped his actions had not driven a new wedge between mistress and master.

"How long will you be gone?"

"We'll be back later tomorrow," Maria answered before sending Nahum on his way to the landing.

"We have to be back," cried Helen. "My birthday celebration is only three days away! Uncle Smitty's going to be here, too."

Maria absently straightened the blue ribbon on Helen's white hat. "Let's be on our way, sweetheart. The tide won't wait for us."

"Good-bye, Mr. Ketch." With that, Helen skipped after Nahum.

Maria started after her, but Ketch impetuously caught her arm. They stared at one another, surprised by the physical contact. He freed her, frowning with embarrassment.

"I'm sorry," he said, "for the trouble I've caused you."

His apology seemed to pain her more than if he had said something harsh or untrue. Without a word, she turned away and hurried down the terraces, the long braid of her hair tapping against her back.

***

Before sunrise, Pip knocked upon Ketch's door to awaken him for breakfast. He growled to be left alone. He wanted nothing to eat, not out of anxiety over the flogging but simply for want of an appetite, his belly sour from the rum he had drunk last night. While he lay there, contemplating birdsongs as the sun's faint eye weakened the darkness beyond his windows and within, he heard the quiet rumble of his comrades' voices as they ate in the common room. He made no attempt to decipher their words; blessedly, even his acute ears failed to discern them. This day would be great sport for them, to see the man whose very presence intimidated them humiliated and beaten to a bloody pulp.

If Helen were not a factor, he asked himself, would he remain here at Leighlin? Considering all that had happened since Isabelle's arrival, he would have to answer no. He should never have even looked at that girl. His attraction to her had nearly led them both to ruin, and any continued interest on his part would only lead to further frustration, the same frustration that had culminated in his recent crime.

A short while later, Willis opened his chamber door without knocking, his broad, whiskered face dutifully grave. "Get up with you. You'll need only your breeches, mind."

Ketch took satisfaction in Willis's dour expression, for he knew the man still chafed from Mallory's upbraiding yesterday for his own negligence in Isabelle's situation.

Once through the back door, Ketch's steps almost faltered when he saw Leighlin's slaves, including the children, massed on the opposite side of the lane that passed before the house. Their faces all turned his way, and their quiet murmurings hushed. Some regarded him with greater fear than before, others with greater hate. On the far left of the gathering, Samuel stood with Isabelle, and Ketch wondered if she had slept at Samuel's again last night.

Willis marched him to the whipping post newly fashioned by Leighlin's carpenter near the foot of the portico steps. Only one ring bolt, attached high on the left side. It would be a challenge to balance

121

against Mallory's blows with but one arm. He would have to plant his feet firmly and press himself against the post. He wanted to prevent the exhibition of losing his balance and struggling like a fish on a hook. The visibility of his amputation—the ugliness prominent without his shirt—would hopefully make Mallory squirm in his task.

Jack Mallory stood at the edge of the portico, the house staff in an orderly rank behind him. The stoic young man was dressed in a black and burgundy coat, not his finest attire yet fine enough to bespeak his wealth and authority, his station above them all. His dark breeches were spotless, his stockings equally so, the silver buckles of his shoes prominent even in the shadows of the portico. For a mere, disconcerting instant, his bearing reminded Ketch of James Logan.

While Willis tied Ketch's wrist to the ring bolt, Mallory began his address to all: "One of you recently called me tolerant. Perhaps that is true as masters go; I have little education or experience in the position. But my tolerance does not reach to those who put themselves above the rules of this plantation, who feel they know what judgment is best passed upon others. That is for me and no one else to decide."

His voice rang across the sward with such authority that Ketch was certain the boy had spent all night preparing this lecture. This trait of singular purpose Ketch had detected early in Ella's son—whatever he had to do, unpleasant or otherwise, he put his entire effort into it, driven to be as precise and correct as possible, to make sure there were no flaws on his part. As in the past whenever Mallory addressed the slave population, Ketch saw that having such attention focused upon him unsettled the young master. And this occasion provided even greater awkwardness because of the violence he would have to display. No surprise he had sent his wife away. Perhaps he had been concerned that such a spectacle might restore some of Maria's sympathy for their troublesome driver.

"Ketch is not the only one at fault here." Mallory's gaze lowered to Willis, who now stood near the steps, then to Samuel before returning to the group. "Perhaps I have not looked at things as closely as I should have. That will be remedied, I assure you." He toyed with the bracelet beneath the cuff of his coat. "You know my rules—if you feel aggrieved, you have ways to reach me. You have your drivers and if not your drivers, then you have Samuel. If what you see does not affect you but someone else, you are to report it just the same. In turn, I expect my men to come to me with your issues, not feel that they can solve them on their own. No one is to feel that I am beyond reach. That's not how this plantation will prosper. And if it prospers, we all prosper. If it fails, we are all cast adrift. I pray what you are about to witness will help all to remember this."

While Mallory's public acceptance of blame surprised Ketch, the fact that the boy took responsibility in the matter did not. Such behavior was in keeping with his penchant for self-flagellation and with the moral integrity his mother had instilled in him. And though Ketch could respect him for this, he stopped short of admiration.

With practiced deliberation, Mallory removed his coat and handed it to Thomas, rolled up his sleeves. The visible presence of his mother's bracelet made Ketch consider his and Mallory's relationships with her. What would she say about this moment?

James Logan had never practiced flogging even aboard his vessels—he had suffered its effects enough times himself while in the Royal Navy to abhor its use—thus Leighlin possessed no designated instrument of punishment. So the driving whip Mallory now picked up from the portico table would have to suffice. The fact that it was normally used upon animals was surely considered by all who watched.

As Mallory descended the stairs, no one made a sound—no coughs or whispers; even the birdcalls seemed to drop away, and the sheep and cows upon the sward grazed without a bleat or a moo. Perhaps some of the Africans had wagered that the master would never punish a white man, especially in such a degrading way, and now stood in shocked disbelief that this would occur. Tension tightened Mallory's freshly shaved face, as if he were the one to be flogged. He kept his gaze locked with Ketch's, showing no weakness to anyone, but Ketch surprisingly saw distaste there, a discomfort. Mallory was not shy—after all, he was his mother's son—but it appeared that delivering these blows would be difficult. He knew Mallory derived no enjoyment from playing the part of dictator, nor did he want to govern by the fear this whipping would put into the hearts and minds of those who watched. But perhaps their shared history of violence and distrust is what preserved the young man's resolve.

When Mallory took up his stance to one side, Ketch inhaled deeply, clutched the ring bolt, and braced his bare chest against the post, closing his eyes and bringing his teeth together. A slight chill to the autumn morning, accentuated here in the darkened lee of the house, tightened his skin, so when the first blow struck, it pulled a sharp grunt from him. He cursed himself and forced his mind away from the pain.

Willis counted off each stroke. Ketch focused on his gravelly voice, its dullness, the rhythm like an echo after each crack against his flesh. The blood soon flowed. Nothing prodigious, a trickle here or there in a lazy, meandering trail down to his waistband. He appreciated the coolness of the morning, for it kept sweat from the growing field of lacerations.

By the second dozen, he opened his eyes, face pressed against the post, and looked up to the portico, teeth clenched against any outcry, nostrils flared, forcing himself to breathe evenly. He imagined Ella Logan there now, seated in quiet privacy with a book. How she had loved to read. She could sit there for hours, speaking to no one, lost in the words of Shakespeare or some other author who offered her escape. A great mystery to him. She had even taught him. How well he remembered their lessons. He had refused to learn together with the other Medoras, making up excuses to cover his own feelings of inadequacy. So his mistress had one day tricked him into the *Medora*'s aft cabin with the pretense that she needed help lifting a chest, but once inside she had coerced him to the table where paper and quill awaited.

At last, the strokes of the whip ceased. Mallory sighed as if he had held his breath the entire time, then he tossed the whip aside and mounted the portico steps. From a distance behind him, Ketch thought he heard faint weeping. Willis stepped over and freed him. Quiet talk filtered through the slaves' ranks as they shuffled off to tend to the harvest.

"Go back to your chamber," Willis said. "I'll treat you there."

***

Isabelle had witnessed floggings before, had suffered a dozen lashes herself on a couple of occasions, but Ketch's punishment had upset her more than any of those other instances. He never would have suffered so if she had not been foolish enough to fall for Ezekiel's smooth flattery and lies. Each time the whip had struck Ketch, she had flinched until finally the tears came. The sight of him—half stripped, the pitiful stump of his limb exposed, the blood bright upon his raw flesh—had melted away all the stories she had heard about him, had reduced him from a shadowy, dangerous figure to simply a flawed man. She knew she should be repulsed by what he had done to Ezekiel, yet when she searched her heart for remorse and grief over her husband's death, she found only relief. He had been little better than Tom Clark.

"Samuel," she called with urgency as the man moved away. He halted, his own countenance heavy with guilt. She glanced Gabriel's way, knew she should hurry to join her gang but instead tentatively approached Samuel. The big man waited, said nothing. She wiped at her cheeks, gathered her courage. "May I tend to Mr. Ketch?"

He hesitated then requested Gabriel's permission. The young driver eyed her with disdain as he conceded. "But be quick about it," he grumbled.

She and Samuel entered the cool lower level of the manor house and stopped at the open doorway to the first chamber on the left. From just behind Samuel, Isabelle could see Ketch lying on his bed, Willis tending to the lacerations.

"Let her do it," Samuel said.

Isabelle was unsure who appeared more surprised by her appearance—Willis or Ketch.

Willis tossed his sponge into a nearby bucket of pink water. "Be my guest." He straightened. "Clean the wounds, then apply the sweet oil. Then smear this ointment on the cuts and cover them lightly with the lint; don't wrap 'em. Hear?"

"Yes, sir." Isabelle edged closer.

Willis stalked from the room. Samuel retreated as well. Ketch turned his face away from Isabelle, as if uncomfortable having the privacy of his bedchamber invaded. Isabelle half expected him to order her out, but instead he crooked his arm and pillowed his chin on the back of his hand.

"There's no reason to sniffle," he said gruffly. "'Tis nothin' worth cryin' over."

Collecting her resolve, she settled upon her knees near the bucket. After she had wrung the excess water from the sponge, she hesitated. Stray drops dripped onto the edge of the low pallet bed. "It will pain you," she murmured.

"No gettin' 'round that."

With a final sniff, she gingerly began to sponge the thin slices. The hard muscles of his back did not flinch. Why had he put himself into this situation? He would have known his murder of Ezekiel would have dire consequences.

"Why did Gabriel let you stay behind?"

"Samuel arranged for me to tend you. I'm responsible for this, so I wanted to...do something."

Ketch scoffed. "No one responsible for this but me. Get that outta yer head. And that boy can beat me till the cows come home 'cause I'm not sorry for what I did."

She soaked the sponge. "Neither am I."

Once the angry wounds were clean, she blotted his skin dry with a towel. In those few minutes under her ministrations, his body had relaxed, settled a bit deeper into the bed, and she almost wondered if he had fallen asleep, for his eyes were closed and his breathing had grown deep and measured. But when she began to apply the sweet oil with gentle fingers, a subtle tension returned to his muscles and he shifted as if in search of a more comfortable position.

"Am I hurting you?"

"No," he hoarsely said.

"It will hurt less if you're able to relax your muscles again."

"Just finish."

Her brow furrowed beneath her black and red headscarf. She could not blame him if he wished her gone as soon as possible. Perhaps coming here had been a foolish gesture. Then he looked at her with those dark, mysterious eyes, and she froze in her work.

In a softer voice, he chided, "You cry far too easy, girl."

His hint of a smile took her off guard. She blushed and exchanged the sweet oil for the aloe ointment. "My mama used to say that, too. She said I was soggier than a rainstorm."

"You miss yer mother."

Isabelle nodded. "I just wish I knew if she was well. I don't even know where she is."

She applied the aloe with the same care as the oil. Afterward, his eyes followed her hands as she set aside the jar and reached for the roll of lint bandages and a pair of shears. The color rose to her cheeks again as she busied herself with the bandages.

"'Tis kind o' you to nurse me."

"I'm obliged to you for all you've done for me, sir, though I don't know why you've troubled yourself."

"Did you sleep in yer cabin last night?"

"Yes."

"Was they cruel to you?"

"They left me alone mostly."

He hesitated. "I was thinkin' on askin' Samuel to see if Miss Maria would let you work in the house instead o' the fields. You wouldn't have to live in the settlement, then; you would live here in the house, in the chamber over yonder with the other maidservants."

Isabelle's gaze flew to his, wide and alarmed. "Oh no, sir. I'm no house slave." She turned away to place a strip of bandage.

"Yer no field hand neither. I seen that the first day."

Another couple of snips of the shears, another strip of bandage draped.

"Why don't you want to come in the house?" When she remained silent, Ketch's authoritative tone startled her. "Answer me."

Her heartbeat quickened and sweat prickled her skin. "They'll say horrible things about me if I work in the house."

"Who?"

"The others from Mr. Tom's plantation."

"Who cares what they say?"

"They'll lie. They'll make Miss Maria want to be rid of me."

"How would they do that? Miss Maria don't think ill of you. She keeps her own counsel 'bout folks. She won't listen to no flighty flock of mockin'birds."

Isabelle shook her head. He stirred, as if about to sit up, but then instead reached out to capture her wrist.

She gasped and blurted, "The Captain might take a fancy to me."

To her utter astonishment, he began to softly laugh, its unfamiliar sound fascinating her; had she perhaps thought him incapable of mirth?

"I assure you, the Captain don't have no designs on no woman 'cept his wife. You may be a...a comely wench, but I can promise you the Captain is a love-besotted dolt of a boy. I know it better than he does. And even if he did lose his head, his wife's not one what would tolerate bein' played false."

When he smiled, his appearance transformed into that of another man, a similar transformation to what she had seen during the flogging, when the myth had dissolved into a mere mortal. She could do nothing but stare, then felt embarrassed by her reaction and her outburst and reached for more of the bandages.

"Miss Maria does seem like a sensible lady."

"Aye, she is. And no mistake she's the reason why the Captain didn't hang me from a tree."

As Isabelle applied more of the lint to his back, he dropped the issue of her coming into the house, and she relaxed.

When finished, she asked, "May I get anything for you, sir?" She glanced at the half-empty rum bottle on his nightstand. "Water perhaps or more spirits?"

"No, you best get to yer task. I've put you behind enough today as it is."

She stood and curtseyed. "I hope you feel better soon, sir."

As she departed, his penetrating gaze left her with a feeling she could neither deny nor define.

***

127

Isabelle was the last of her gang to finish her task. Even Gabriel had left, cursing her as useless. Night had almost fallen by the time she stowed her basket and bagged the rough rice for tomorrow's milling. What others had accomplished in ten hours or less had taken her almost twelve. She stretched her sore, tired back and started up the lane with small, weary steps.

Her thoughts throughout the day had dwelled upon Ezekiel's death and Ketch's part in it. No matter how she puzzled it all, she fell short of understanding why Ketch had risked their master's wrath by committing the murder. And exactly how had he perpetrated the deed? With a macabre twist to her curiosity, she wanted to know how Ezekiel had died, if it had been quick like the flash of pain in her ankle the night he had shoved her off the porch or if it had been long and torturous like the days he had denied her food. Had Ketch killed him because of the ongoing animosity between the two, an animosity that had been formed long before her arrival at Leighlin? Or had he truly done it for the reasons he had talked about in the library, reasons related to the abuse she had suffered? She remembered Ezekiel's frequent insistence that Ketch fancied her, but she still doubted that, especially considering Ketch's outright denial of seeking any favors—sexual or otherwise—that night at her cabin.

Whatever Ketch's motivation, her own lack of fear around him puzzled her. If anything, she had felt the exact opposite when in his presence, whether that morning in his bedchamber or those nights he had come to her cabin. Perhaps that feeling of safety—so horribly absent since being separated from her mother—had overpowered common sense.

As she drew near the manor house, her drooping eyes took in the hulking square shape. The windows were dark save two. She remembered the interior grandness. What would it be like to work there, away from the sun and insects and snakes? Was Ketch right about the Captain's devotion to his wife? Would she feel safe there after all? Perhaps she should tell Ketch that she would like Samuel to approach the mistress and master to petition her change in status.

Isabelle turned onto the lane that ran past the rear of Leighlin House. Would Ketch be in his chamber and see her pass by? Perhaps he might be sitting outside on the portico steps as he sometimes did. If he spoke to her, she would inquire of his well-being, offer to tend him again if he so desired, because, whether good or ill, she was grateful for what he had done. But as she drew closer to the portico, she did not see him. Instead, she heard her master's voice, answered by his wife.

She should have known they would be seated on the portico, watching the last of the sunlight fade beyond the western tree line. Isabelle frowned and picked up her pace as she passed by.

"Isabelle."

Her master's hail halted her. A chill slid down her back, and she had to swallow her trepidation before she could turn toward him. She curtseyed, remembered his fury in the library, how his brown eyes had turned black.

"Come here, please."

His voice lacked anger, so she tried to take heart as she mounted the steps. She never thought him cruel for his judgment of yesterday. After all, he could have done much worse to her and to Ketch. When he had wielded the whip that morning, he appeared to take no pleasure in the task.

She curtseyed again in front of the couple. The young man hesitated, and Isabelle hazarded a glance at his wife, who appeared as intrigued by the summons as Isabelle. For a moment, Isabelle wondered if Ketch had pursued his idea of her working in the house.

"I have sent word to Mr. Clark's plantation. I've asked that he take you back and replace you with another slave."

Isabelle's mouth dropped open as did her mistress's, and she was certain her heart froze like water in winter, for it physically pained her.

"When you and the others from Clark's plantation came here, you were represented as having experience with cultivating and harvesting rice, an apparent lie I have since addressed with him. I might have overlooked that and kept you for the skills you have learned if I also thought you would provide Leighlin with children from your marriage. But 'tis obvious that the other people are set against you. For that, I am sorry. But I must first look to Leighlin's interests." He reached for his wife's hand, gave her a small, apologetic smile before turning back to Isabelle. "I'm sure you understand the value of children being born to Leighlin's people."

Somehow, Isabelle found her voice, though her answer of, "Yes, sir," could barely be heard over the common din of cicadas.

Maria leaned forward. "Jack—"

"I'm sorry if this news pains you, Isabelle," he continued with a sincerity that nonetheless had no power to soothe her. "I will wait for a reply from Mr. Clark to see if he has another suitable hand to replace you. Then I will let you know when you will leave."

Isabelle gathered her frayed courage and whatever scrap of self-confidence remained after these trying weeks. "If you please, sir, may

I speak?"

He hesitated then nodded.

Isabelle attempted to steady her voice. "I'm sorry for the trouble I've caused, sir. I don't want to leave. If you could just give me a second chance..."

"Isabelle, 'tis not just the trouble. I told you why you were brought here, but the others have made it plain that..."

That no man wanted her. Mercifully, the sentence went unfinished; he looked too ashamed to go further. But the reality still cut her deeply, and the tears welled up. Desperate, she considered telling him about Tom Clark's abuse, but she knew such a thing was of no concern to another planter, and she could not face the humiliation.

"Jack, please," her mistress implored. "There must be some other way."

"I could work in the house," Isabelle blurted. "That's what I done at Mr. Tom's. That's why I don't know about rice. I know I spoke false when I first got here, but I was afrighted."

"Isabelle," he gently said. "'Tis not just about the work. Now, enough of this. I'm sorry to have upset you, but this is what I must do. The matter is concluded."

Without thinking of her actions, Isabelle dropped to her knees and clasped her hands. "Please, Captain, don't send me away. Someone will marry me, after all this settles down. They'll see I'm not bad."

"Isabelle." Maria came out of her chair now and helped her to her feet.

The Captain stood as color rushed to his face, and Isabelle knew she had gone too far. "I said this matter is concluded, Isabelle. Go back to the settlement...now."

Seeing that his patience was at an end, that he would not change his mind, and fearing that he might do her harm, Isabelle fled the portico. She ran past Ketch's window, a hand pressed to her mouth to silence her sobs. Although she wished Ketch were there in his open window and perhaps had heard her fate, the chamber was dark. Maybe he was asleep; maybe he was away. It was just as well, for this time he could not save her.

***

The sun was already up when the scent of food from the common room awakened Ketch from dreams of Isabelle's nursing. Sunday breakfasts were served later than during the rest of the week when everyone had to be in the fields early. He lay there on his stomach for a bit longer, the burning pain of yesterday reduced to mild stinging. Listening to the servants preparing the table, he imagined Isabelle among them, no longer breaking her back with the rice harvest.

The other men were already eating by the time he joined them. The silence was not as strained as it had been over supper last night. None of the men had been bold enough to bandy remarks aloud about the flogging, but the wordless glances between Gabriel, McBain, and Latiffe had spoken volumes. The air of smug satisfaction still lingered this morning, but Ketch focused on his food. He made sure he avoided reaching too far across the table for anything, so he would not stretch the fresh scabs on his back. It pained him, however, to reveal his physical discomfort by asking the men to pass items to him.

Above them, he heard Helen's joyful voice as she raced down the stair hall to the dining room. Since she and Maria had returned late yesterday, he had avoided the perceptive child and cautioned himself to conceal his stiffness should she seek him out today as she did most every day.

"Josiah Smith's comin' in with the tide, lads," Willis announced, "so he can be here for Miss Helen's birthday on the morrow. So, I'm sure we'll have us a lively evening."

The others remarked favorably upon this news. Josiah Smith was captain of Leighlin's *Adventuress* and was also Jack Mallory's closest friend and surrogate father. He was not, however, a friend of Ketch's. Always protective of Jack and Maria, Smith had never warmed to the idea of Ketch living at Leighlin.

Gabriel's raised voice interrupted Ketch's thoughts. "Well, looky here, gents!" With a sly grin, he gestured toward the open back door. "Looks like your nurse has arrived, Ketch."

The men chuckled. Ketch nearly came out of his seat when he saw Isabelle waiting in patient silence to be acknowledged, a basket in her hands. With the early light outside silhouetting her, her face lacked definition, but what he did see concerned him.

"Ketch always seems to get all the attention of the womenfolk 'round here with his maladies," Gabriel continued. "Miss Maria nursed him last year through his trials, and now he has a mulatto wench to see to his needs."

Willis called, "What do you want, girl?"

"I...I brought Mr. Ketch the basket I made for Miss Helen."

"Very well. Set it down there and go on your way."

Isabelle started to speak again but then closed her mouth into a frown and set down the sweetgrass basket. She turned to leave.

Ketch sprang to his feet and called out, "Wait," though it drew everyone's attention to him. Strained silence prevailed. Isabelle looked back at him, and he stammered, "I need to pay you for yer work."

He hurried into his chamber and returned with a threepence coin. She lingered outside the doorway in the shadow of the house. Glad for an excuse to get away from his comrades' scrutiny, he stepped outside with the basket in hand and the coin inside. Now away from any tricks of light, he noted a bloated quality to Isabelle's face, a loss of color, as she stared at her bare feet.

"I hope the basket is to your liking. I don't expect no coin for my work."

Isabelle's haphazard technique had given the basket a slight lopsidedness, and the color pattern meshed only precariously, but Ketch admired the result just the same. "'Tis very much to me likin'. And you must take payment."

Hesitant, she obeyed with a flash of her eyes that revealed puffiness and redness.

"Here now. What's this? You've been a-cryin'."

She refused to respond.

"Why?"

Turning the threepence over and over in her hands, she stared at his chest, at the scar at the base of his neck. "The Captain is sending me away, back to Mr. Tom."

Ketch bristled. "What?"

"He told me last night. So, I come to bring you that there basket and say good-bye."

"Good-bye? By God..." He bit back harsh words for his master, saw that she was near tears again.

"Don't make no more trouble for yourself, Mr. Ketch. Maybe the Captain is right."

"Right?" he growled. "Is this what you want?"

"No, sir. I'd rather die than go back there."

"I'll talk to Miss Maria—"

"She already knows; she was there when the Captain told me." Isabelle forced a smile through her sorrow. "When I am gone, things will be better for you. I thank you for your many kindnesses, but I must say good-bye now. I hope you are feeling better soon."

With that, she wheeled about and started across the sward toward the settlement. When he called for her to come back, she picked up her skirts and broke into a headlong run into the distant trees.

CHAPTER 11

Ketch had never acquired the taste for tobacco that so many of his shipmates had, but this evening he stood outside Leighlin House's lower level and pulled on a clay pipe with the concentration of an enthusiast. His alternative was to drink, but this evening he needed a clear head. With a frown, he noticed his hand trembled when he removed the pipe and blew smoke upward between the flanking white-washed steps.

He listened to the contented drone of voices above him on the front portico, interrupted by occasional laughter—Maria and her husband along with Samuel and Josiah Smith. Helen was there, too, her sharp staccato bursts contrasting with the adults. It was her face that looked down at him over the ornate iron railing, her loose golden hair draping around her fleshy cheeks like Spanish moss, seeming to brighten her visage. When she saw who emitted the climbing, twisting smoke, she grinned.

"Hello, Mr. Ketch!"

"Hello, Miss Helen."

"You're coming to my birthday celebration tomorrow, aren't you?"

"Of course, child. I wouldn't miss it. I have a present to give you."

Her blue eyes widened. "What is it?"

"'Tis a surprise, o' course. You have to wait."

Her lips twisted in impatient disappointment, but then she continued in another vein. "Uncle Smitty is here."

"Aye, so he is."

"Why don't you come up and say hello to him?"

Ketch tapped the remaining tobacco out upon his heel. "Mebbe I should."

She beamed. If the child had her way, the whole plantation would be milling about the portico and she could avoid being sent to bed. Her face disappeared behind the railing like a turtle into its shell, and he heard her announce his impending appearance. A brief silence before conversation renewed. Ketch hesitated, considered his words, reconsidered them, thought of disappearing into his chamber to open a bottle of rum and forget this impetuous, desperate nonsense. But he screwed on his resolve and forced himself to move with measured purpose out of the shadows and up the portico steps.

"There he is!" Helen cried from Smith's lap, pointing. She grinned as if Ketch had been gone for ages and she had accomplished a great feat by convincing him to share their evening. Helen, however, appeared to be the only one pleased by his approach.

Josiah Smith—a hardened, blue-eyed former pirate somewhere in his late forties—watched Ketch with well-practiced caution, gently puffing on a pipe that protruded from a wiry dark growth of beard, a beard still devoid of gray. Smith, a cagey old bastard, studied Ketch with the acuity of an eagle protecting its nest.

"Good evening," Ketch addressed them as a group, incertitude in his own voice, a weakness that gave him pause, for he was a man who had learned long ago to hide any hint of doubt or fear. He was unprepared for his courage to fail him now.

They returned his salutation, Mallory and Smith quite coolly. Smith, here since this morning's tide, would already know every detail of what had transpired these past days. Only Maria, seated near the end of the portico, beyond the three men, showed a hint of curiosity over Ketch's uninvited appearance.

"Thomas!" she called over her shoulder into the house, and the servant instantly appeared. "Please fetch Mr. Ketch a chair."

"Yes'm." Thomas vanished back into the house.

"There's no need," Ketch said. "I just came to ask the Captain's permission in somethin'." He eyed Smith. "Private-like."

"What you have to ask me, you can ask me here."

Although Mallory's discourtesy did not surprise Ketch, it irritated him just the same. He forced himself to hide his emotions.

"Well?" Mallory prompted as if eager to be rid of him. "What is it?"

It took every ounce of Ketch's will and determination to hold Mallory's dark stare. "'Tis Isabelle…" He faltered.

"What of her?"

"I wish to marry her."

While very different in features and complexions, the four faces before him now looked amazingly similar in their shock.

Helen, however, sat up straight and with pure delight exclaimed,

"You're getting married, Mr. Ketch?"

"That's up to yer brother, child."

"Oh, John!" Helen sprang from Smith to her sibling, who sat in silent stupefaction. She placed her hands upon his knees and leaned toward his face. "Say yes, John. You must."

Mallory took Helen's hands in his. "You, young lady, *must* go to bed."

If this was a cue for Maria to remove the child, the young woman paid no heed. From the look on Maria's face, she could very well have been alone with Ketch, who thought he detected some fraction of justified relief in her eyes.

Helen rushed to Ketch's side and took hold of his hand to declare, "I'm not going to bed till you tell Mr. Ketch he can marry Isabelle."

Mallory sat forward and addressed Ketch. "Isabelle is returning to Tom Clark's the day after tomorrow."

"I know," Ketch said. "That's why I'm askin' now; normally, I wouldn't have asked...so soon after..."

Smith's laconic, cynical voice broke through, "Are you in love with this girl, Ketch?" Everyone looked at him in self-conscious silence, but Smith was impervious. "I mean, considerin' you, mate, this be...unexpected, to say the least." A small grin revealed his licentious nature. "I reckon I'd like to see this girl. Hear what she has to say about all this. What say you, Jack?"

"I haven't asked her to marry me yet," Ketch hurried to say. "I didn't see no point till I had permission."

Mallory countered, "And why would you think I would grant it, after all you've done?"

Ketch hid the storm that grew in his belly, fought against his natural tendency to strike back. Damn it, he was no great talker; negotiating was unfamiliar territory, as treacherous as trying to stand upon a log floating in the river.

"What I did," he began with a glance down at Helen's expectant face, "I'm sorry for; not for *why* I did it but for what it caused."

"That's hardly good enough," Mallory insisted.

Ketch glanced at Maria and saw the only person with a scrap of sympathy, someone who would want to hear an acceptable explanation for his actions, even as she knew there could be none. Perhaps she disagreed with her husband's plan to send Isabelle away. Whatever had driven her to talk Mallory down the day he had discovered Zeke's murder was there in her eyes now.

Ketch said, "Isabelle's suffered enough for things what aren't her fault. She shouldn't be sent away for what I caused."

Helen whispered up at him, "What did you do, Mr. Ketch?"

"Helen," Maria beckoned, "come here now."

Eager, as if thinking Maria would finally answer her question, Helen went to her. Providing no such satisfaction—much to Ketch's relief—Maria pulled the child onto her lap. Helen's head lolled against her shoulder, but her attention returned to Ketch.

"I acquired those slaves from Tom Clark for two reasons," Mallory addressed Ketch, "because they knew rice culture and because they were without husbands. For whatever reason, Clark deceived me. Isabelle has neither experience in rice harvesting nor the characteristics to make her suitable as a wife to any of the men."

"She works hard," Ketch insisted. "I'm sure if she's given a chance, she'll become as skilled as the rest."

Mallory studied him. "The other day you said you had no interest in Isabelle. What suddenly turned indifference into a marriage proposal?"

"I was never…indifferent. I didn't bring this up t'other day in the library 'cause you would've thought I did what I did just so's I could marry Isabelle, and that wasn't it at all."

In his casual way, Smith offered, "Jackie, why don't we fetch this Isabelle up here and find out what *she* wants. Seems like that would get to the heart o' the matter."

"Smitty," Maria scolded, "a marriage proposal is a private matter."

"I wouldn't reckon completely so since Jack be her master, eh? Me and Samuel don't hafta be here, but I think you and Jack should hear the girl's decision firsthand. Wouldn't want to think our man Ketch here would…intimidate or trick the girl for his own designs, now would we?"

Indignation brought hot color to Ketch's face, not simply because of Smith's brassy insinuations but because he had never considered the possibility of needing to acquire Isabelle's consent in front of others. Only when he had received permission had he planned to tell her of the ploy to keep her from being sent back to Clark, to let her know it was simply for her preservation. Now he deeply regretted that decision to delay.

Thomas arrived with a chair and set it next to Smith's. He had taken his time, perhaps to make Ketch stand longer.

"Thomas," Mallory said, "send Nahum to the settlement to fetch Isabelle here."

The tall black man's chary gaze flashed toward Ketch before he said, "Yes, suh."

"Jack." Maria leaned toward him. "Let's talk to Isabelle alone first, just you and I."

"I prefer to witness her reaction when she hears the proposal straight from Ketch's mouth. If there is no deception going on, then no one should have any reservations about speaking the truth in front of others."

Ketch knew Mallory saw through his plan, but it was too late to back down now. Maria's attempts, however, pleased Ketch, not just for Isabelle's sake but because it gave him hope that she had not completely forsaken him. Now he needed to conjure patience and forbearance, an air of convincing confidence.

He shambled over to the chair Thomas had provided and slumped into it. When he started to lean back, he thought of the lacerations and refrained, his awkward posture making him feel even more exposed and deficient among those upon the portico.

Smith knocked the remaining tobacco from his pipe and stood. "Maria, gimme that little one there an' I'll tuck her into bed. Samuel, I fancy the lads be expectin' us and our purses below." He grinned at the prospect of drinking and gambling.

"I don't wanna go to bed," Helen protested. "I wanna wait for Isabelle."

"You heard yer brother, missy; 'tis past yer bedtime, and you promised to read me a story, didn't ye?"

This reminder of reading to her illiterate surrogate uncle placated Helen, and she allowed Smith to take her by the hand. He grunted a comment on how her stubbornness reminded him too much of her brother. As Helen reluctantly said good night to all, Samuel stood and bade everyone good night as well.

"Tell the lads I'll be down directly," Smith said as he carried the languid child into the house.

Samuel threw Ketch an unreadable look before leaving the portico.

***

Isabelle felt a twinge of hope that her master had reconsidered sending her away. Why else would he summon her at such an hour? Maybe Miss Maria had somehow changed his mind; she had certainly seemed displeased with her husband's decision. That desperate wish

137

quickened Isabelle's blood as she followed Nahum out of the settlement.

All day she had searched for ways to escape her fate. The thought of seeing Tom Clark again, of feeling his stubby, fat fingers upon her flesh made Isabelle sick to her stomach. Probably, he had been pleased to hear that she would be returned to him. After all, it had been Mrs. Clark who had banished her, for she had long desired to be rid of her husband's concubine. She had come to Isabelle the night before the other slaves were to leave for Charles Town and told her that she and her mother were both to be sent away. Since Tom Clark was not at the landing when the women left the next morning, he would have had no idea that Isabelle and her mother were gone until he got up that morning. By then, his wife would have argued the justice of her decision. Isabelle wondered what the woman would do once faced with her return.

Isabelle had decided that she would do her utmost to avoid being taken back to Clark. She had been able to endure him only because of her mother's love and support. Without that, she would go mad. Her options, however, were limited; she could not swim, so jumping out of Leighlin's boat on the journey downriver could not be the answer. Her only chance would be when they reached Charles Town. Somehow, she would get away and hide until nightfall. She would steal aboard one of the ships at the wharf and hide herself. Not one of the larger vessels, for those might be sailing to far distant ports, spending weeks at sea. No, she would look for one of the smaller vessels and hope that it would take her north, perhaps far north, so far that she would never be returned to Tom Clark. A visitor at Clark's once spoke of New York, where he knew of free blacks and those who worked as paid servants. Perhaps she could find work as a laundress or a house servant.

She knew she ran the risk of discovery and rape aboard ship or wherever she ended up. But she struggled to hold fast to her resolve, for it was all that sustained her. If she failed, she hoped for a quick death. That would be far better than a return to Tom Clark's bed.

Total darkness had fallen by the time Isabelle and Nahum reached Leighlin House. Hanging lanterns illuminated the front portico and attracted a variety of insects that whirled in frenzied, suicidal flight around the glow. As they mounted the steps, Nahum's shoes tapped rhythmically while Isabelle's bare feet made no sound. She expected to see only her master, but when she saw Ketch rising from a chair, she halted with one step to climb. Her mistress was there as well, concern upon her face. But it was Ketch who captured Isabelle's attention. He appeared almost sickly, eyes troubled, two vertical lines between his eyebrows etched even deeper than usual. His lips were slightly parted, as if he were on the verge of saying something to her. His presence bolstered her hope for a reprieve, for why else would he be here with master and mistress? After telling him of her fate earlier today, she had hoped that he would somehow again come to her aid, for who else would?

"Thank you, Nahum," the Captain dismissed the boy.

Isabelle stepped onto the sandstone tiles and curtseyed. She found it difficult to look away from Ketch, though she knew she should focus on her master. Compulsion seemed to lift Ketch almost upon his toes, and through his intense gaze she realized he was attempting to convey something important.

The Captain leaned forward, hands upon his knees. "Isabelle, I will get straight to the point. Ketch has come to me with a request." He watched her in an odd way, and she sensed suspicion. "He has asked permission to marry you."

She gaped first at the Captain then at Ketch. Ketch shifted his weight, his lips silently moving, as if trying to form words. Something in his expression cautioned her to temper her reaction.

The Captain continued, "Do you wish to marry him, Isabelle?"

"But...but I'm to go back to Mr. Tom, sir."

"That's not the issue here," the young man continued patiently. "Do you wish to marry Ketch?"

Isabelle's mind whirled like a storm, trying to comprehend, to decipher. Her attention jumped from person to person, her mouth still open. What was it in Ketch's eyes? Desperation?

"Are you afraid of Ketch, Isabelle?" the Captain prodded. "You must be honest, for everyone's sake. No harm will come to you for it. We can speak privately if you'd prefer."

"Oh no, sir, I'm not afeared of Mr. Ketch. He's been kind to me, kinder than anyone." Her voice trailed off. She feared her words might be misconstrued as an accusation against her master.

"Then what is your answer to his proposal?"

Isabelle looked at Ketch with a hundred silent questions. He produced a weak smile. She could see that her continued hesitation made him uneasy. Surely he did not mean to make her his wife. Not his real wife anyway. This had to be his way of foiling his master's attempt to send her away. She could see the cleverness in it, for anything less than marriage would fall short. Yet, what if she were wrong and Ketch's proposal was not a ruse?

Considering her fate once she left this place, she decided that being wrong was still a better path than returning to Tom Clark.

Isabelle squared her shoulders and faced her master. "My answer is yes, Captain."

Isabelle caught Maria's smile from beyond the Captain's astonished face, a smile she quickly extinguished. With a soundless sigh, the tension left Ketch's shoulders. The Captain took significantly longer to recover. Isabelle was proud of her confident façade—chin lifted, back straight.

"Very well." Displeasure darkened the Captain's face as he sat back in his chair. Isabelle suspected that she had fallen short of convincing him of her conviction. He looked at Ketch. "I told Isabelle that I had decided to return her to Clark because of her inability to acquire a mate. It seems you have conveniently remedied that, Ketch. So, I must remind you both that by law the children she bears will belong to Leighlin."

Ketch swallowed hard, nodded. "Aye."

"And her ties to you will not exempt her from work in the fields."

"I understand."

The Captain eyed him with surprise and skepticism, as if he had expected Ketch to protest. "Then day after tomorrow the two of you will accompany Captain Smith to the *Adventuress*, and he will marry you right and proper since, after all, you would not be received in St. Philip's. My wife will be happy to accompany you, I'm sure."

"Of course." Maria stood with a smile. "Maybe Isabelle has someone among her people to accompany her."

"No'm," Isabelle said softly. "There's no one."

Maria frowned and drew closer. "Very well. I'll send word to Gabriel that you are to come to the house first thing tomorrow, so we can find a dress for you to wear. You and I aren't too far from the same size, I shouldn't think."

"Oh, no'm! Thank you kindly but I could never—"

"Consider it my...*our* wedding gift." Maria's tone offered no room for refusal, and Isabelle saw the wisdom in the gesture, for she could not wear the dress in which she had been married to Ezekiel.

The Captain appeared unhappy with Maria's enthusiasm, but before he could say anything, Ketch stepped forward. "I'll walk Isabelle back to her cabin." He bowed to their master. "With yer permission..."

The young man gave Ketch a curt nod and gesture.

Ketch extended his arm toward the steps, finally stirring Isabelle from her shock. She bid her master and mistress good night then waited for Ketch to proceed, but he remained in one place, arm still outstretched.

"Go on," he encouraged.

Suddenly comprehending, she descended the steps.

"Take one of the lanterns," Maria said.

Ketch thanked her and started down the steps to where Isabelle awaited. "Come along," he said quietly, and they left behind the raucousness that spilled forth from the lower level.

The cooling night soothed Isabelle's hot skin as they moved along the side of the house and farther into the darkness. The living sounds of the night soon overpowered the fading shouts and laughter from the lower level. Out of habit, Isabelle dropped a pace behind Ketch, unable to speak, though dozens of questions and concerns boiled in her.

The unexpected sound of Ketch's voice caused her to start. "I'm sorry I wasn't able to warn you. I didn't know if he'd give me permission, so I saw no point in gettin' yer hopes up for nothin'. And I never expected him to call for you tonight. I thought I'd have time to tell you meself."

Isabelle wished she could see his face. Uncertain which direction her words should take, she ventured, "You did this so I don't have to go back to Mr. Tom?"

"Aye. That's what you wanted, wasn't it? To stay here?"

"Yes, of course. But...you shouldn't have put yourself in this position on my account, sir. If you don't want—"

"There's no more need for 'sir' or else things won't ring true." The old gruffness had returned to his voice. "I'm Ketch to you now."

"Yes...Ketch."

The change of his mood left her even more unsure.

When they reached the lane that led back to the settlement, he continued, "You'll have to stay with me...share me quarters, I mean. You'll be me wife to everyone else but, in private, I don't expect you to play the part. I mean...there's no need for you to share me bed."

His bluntness left her discomfited. Although she appreciated his candor, she found her feminine vanity unexpectedly bruised. She should have felt relieved that he would put no demands upon her, yet she wondered if he found her so very repulsive. Perhaps the stories about his unnatural sexual tendencies were true. Since her wedding, she had spoken to Jemmy on more than one occasion, and each time her keen curiosity made her wonder what Ketch had done to him, if the stories of sodomy were true. But she knew even if the closest of friends,

141

she could never venture upon that subject with poor, reserved Jemmy, no more than she would invite inquiries from him about Tom Clark.

They arrived at the outskirts of the slave quarters where most were settling down for the night. A young dog barked at them from the shadows of the nearest cabin but then skulked away with a muttered growl. Ketch halted and turned to Isabelle, the lantern held between them like an illuminated barrier.

"Thank you...again...Ketch." She wondered if he found his name distasteful upon her lips because he frowned.

"You'll come to the house, then, like Miss Maria said?"

"Yes. It was very handsome of her to offer me a dress. She's most kind."

"Aye, she is. And I'm afeared I've taken advantage of that kindness for the last time."

"Maybe she will forgive you. Maybe she already has."

Ketch shrugged. "She has no reason to." He looked down the line of cabins where far away a couple of shadows wavered in the hint of a candle's light. Isabelle wondered if he already regretted his decision.

"Shall I tend to your wounds when I come to the house in the morn?"

"No." The answer came abruptly, but then he hesitated as if chagrined. "Tend to yer dress instead. Me back is doin' tolerable well." He faltered again, and his eyes could not find one particular place to land. Finally, he said, "Good night," turned on his heels and hurried back up the lane.

CHAPTER 12

Morning came too early for Isabelle. The developments of last night had kept her long awake. She had only just succumbed to sleep when a cock crowed outside her window. When did her mistress expect her at the house? What time did Maria arise in the morning? Would she rebuke her for an arrival too early or too late? Isabelle debated her choices and decided to report to the Big House with the rest of the slaves, as she would on any other day. How long would it take to be fitted for a dress? She would be so far behind in her task...

As she trailed through the early morning light up the lane toward the sward, the gray, murmuring figures of the other slaves moved along with her, some ahead, some behind, none of them close. Since Ketch's incursion the night Hannah had confronted her about Ezekiel, they all looked at her in a different light. Something akin to fear had replaced the old prejudices, a fear of Ketch meting out to them what Ezekiel had received if they but dared to look at her crossly. Even Hannah had been intimidated enough to hold her tongue. To Isabelle's amazement, she found that their unease empowered her. What would they say once they found out she was to be Ketch's wife? They would think her vile to marry anyone just days after her first husband's death, especially the white man who had murdered him; they would think her mad for accepting Ketch's proposal. Perhaps, though, they would speculate that the choice had been forced upon her. Her lips twisted with unrest; she should not care about their opinions.

Her steps slowed when she thought of Ketch. When she had contemplated the situation overnight, her brash decision terrified her, though she was also immeasurably relieved not to be returning to Tom Clark. Perhaps she was a complete fool for trusting Ketch, just as she had been proven a fool over Ezekiel. Yet, last night while walking back from the house, she had sensed more fear in Ketch than in herself. But what could possibly frighten such a man?

She wondered if Ketch had been married before. If so, what had become of his wife? Had he any children? Children... Perhaps that was why the Captain had agreed to this; he expected to get his future generations of workers. What would he say when she produced nothing? Well, she admitted with a frown, she had little faith that Ketch had meant what he said about separate beds. He was, after all, a man. By avoiding Clark, she could very well have fallen into a similar situation. However, she refused to believe the two men were at all alike.

What would her mother say to all of this?

Once Isabelle reached the house, she was pleased to see Maria on the lower portico. When her mistress spotted her, the woman smiled in welcome and gestured to her. Gabriel stood near the foot of the steps, and Isabelle hesitated before his scowling countenance.

"Go on with you." He jerked his chin toward Maria.

Isabelle felt all the slaves' eyes upon her as she picked up her skirts and climbed the steps. When she reached the portico, she curtseyed and bid Maria good morning. Her mistress returned the salutation with warmth and extended an arm toward the door.

"Come inside, Isabelle."

Isabelle allowed a backward glance at the slaves below and took great delight in the wide eyes and gaping mouths, the whispers back and forth. Then she turned her back on them and followed her mistress inside.

Unlike the last time she had been in the house, her trembling was born of excitement as her eyes roamed about the beautiful Great Hall. Her bare feet padded over the spotless pinewood floor as Maria led the way across the Hall and into the front stair hall with its towering ceiling. Early morning light poured through the sparkling clean windows and struck the magnificent chandelier there, making it appear lit. The matching staircases on either side bore mahogany handrails and balusters with decorative carvings of magnolias and roses. As she followed her mistress upward, she relished the polished feel of the wood beneath her fingers.

Maria was saying, "Don't fret about the time it takes for the fitting. I told Gabriel to adjust your task accordingly once you finish here."

"I'm much obliged, ma'am."

They reached the upper floor and entered a central room—the ballroom, Maria explained—which matched the size of the Great Hall except for a higher ceiling. Isabelle admired another chandelier, larger than the one in the stair hall. The carved trim and scrollwork upon the walls mirrored that of the Great Hall. The natural light that chased her through the doorway and spilled in through the windows opposite provided ample illumination. A rear door led to an upper portico, and

Isabelle wished she could rush out there and look down upon Gabriel's gang. Perhaps she would even wave and smile.

Four chambers flanked the ballroom, two on each side, the design in keeping with the house's overall symmetry inside and out, including the two fireplaces and their elaborate overmantels. Maria led the way to the rear chamber on the right, but before they reached it, the door diagonal to it opened.

"Isabelle!" Helen raced across the ballroom, still dressed in cap and shift, an excited smile on her pink face. "Today's my birthday!"

Isabelle crouched down as Helen stopped in front of her. "Why, happy birthday, Miss Helen."

"I'm eight years old!"

"Then you're already a young lady, aren't you?"

"John says I'm a little savage."

"Well, he is your brother; of course, he will tease you."

"Are you coming to my celebration?"

Isabelle laughed at her innocent enthusiasm, naiveté, and open friendliness. "No, I must work the harvest today."

"But you're getting a dress first, aren't you? I helped Maria pick them out for you. Now you get to choose."

"Helen," Maria gently scolded, "you must get dressed and eat. We have much to do before the guests arrive."

"Can I stay long enough to see which dress Isabelle picks?"

Pleased to find someone excited about her prospects, Isabelle looked hopefully at her mistress.

Maria smiled. "Very well. But then right back to your chamber. Mary will be up any minute to help you dress."

With an exclamation, Helen darted into the rear chamber ahead of them, urging Isabelle to hurry. The servant who awaited them curtseyed to her mistress. The black woman's eyes were dutifully unreadable, but Isabelle thought she caught a hint of distaste in the angle of her mouth.

"As you may know, this is Abigail, Leighlin's head seamstress, and she will make any alterations that you need. Here are the dresses."

The colorful sight of the garments laid upon the four-poster bed stilled Isabelle's breathing. To see them and know she would be wearing something so exquisite nearly brought tears to her eyes, and she forgot the folly behind all this. What would her mother say if she saw her in such clothing?

"I like the green one best." Helen hopped up on the bed to hold the bodice in front of her.

Maria added, "It would go well with your eyes. They are almost green, aren't they?"

"Yes'm, a touch." Isabelle hovered over the choices, hands clasped in front of her bosom.

"You may pick them up," Maria encouraged her. "There's a looking glass over here."

The three dresses were made of silk, satin, and velvet, all materials Isabelle had never before touched. She luxuriated in the feel of them. The first was a very pale pink, the bodice decorated with light gray embroidery and white lace; the second, a dark blue, like the deepest part of the ocean, with tiny black bows upon the bodice; the third, green; this was the one she picked up and carried to the looking glass upon its stand. She had not seen herself since leaving Tom Clark's house, and she almost started at her appearance. Her thin face still showed the results of her husband's starvation, and her eyes seemed much larger because of it.

"Perhaps it will be easier for you to decide if you try each one on," Maria suggested.

Thrilled at the prospect, she responded, "May I, Miss Maria? They are all so beautiful; I just don't know how I'll decide."

"Then trying them on is best. Come, I'll help you."

"But you have things to do, ma'am; the celebration. I shouldn't keep you."

"It won't take long. Don't fret."

Her mistress even provided a fresh shift for her, and soon she stood before the mirror in the pink dress, turning this way and that, enthralled by the incongruous sight of a slave in such finery. She laughed at herself. What a ridiculous plan this was. She almost felt criminal for her deception, yet she was enjoying the privilege too much to let it dampen her delight. And both Maria and Helen seemed as happy as she to be a part of this game.

After long debate, Isabelle decided upon the green dress. Maria was correct about its effect upon her eye color. As she stood before the mirror, she hoped the greenish flecks that the dress brought out would make her husband think more of her white origins than her black. The very wish made her remember her mother and feel ashamed of herself. How could she ever think such a self-serving thing when her mother had never begrudged her daughter's white origins, even when she suffered ridicule at the hands of others? And besides, what would Ketch care about her appearance?

Maria caught Isabelle's frown. "What is it? You don't like it?"

"No'm; I *do* like it, very much, but..." She turned away,

overwhelmed by everything—thoughts of her mother, Ketch's plan, standing in this chamber, the finery she wore, the unanticipated warmth and kindness around her.

Maria seemed to sense her quandary and guided her to a chair. Helen remained on the bed, curiously watching.

"Isabelle," Maria said, "if you don't want to do this, if you're afraid to marry Ketch—"

"No'm; it's not that. It's just…" She tried to laugh at her own absurdity. "This is so kind of you…you and the Captain. I don't know how I'll ever thank you enough. Letting me stay, taking me and Mr. Ketch out upon your boat to be married after everything that's happened. And the dress…"

Tears flooded in before she knew it, and she quickly tried to wipe them away, laughing sheepishly at her foolish display. Helen bounced off the bed and over to her side where she took Isabelle's hand.

Maria assured her, "You're just a bit overwhelmed by everything at once. I was the same way when I was about to be married. You've been through so much lately. Abigail, run into my chamber and fetch a handkerchief for Isabelle."

The goodness of her mistress shriveled Isabelle's heart in shame for the falseness she was perpetrating. Except her mother, no one had ever treated her with the graciousness Maria had shown her in just this short time. Perhaps she should tell her the truth and accept the consequences, go back to Tom Clark and endure whatever was to come.

"Don't cry, Isabelle," Helen said. "Aren't you happy? You're going to marry Mr. Ketch. He loves you. Maria said so."

Stunned, Isabelle stared at Maria, who blushed.

"Helen," Maria chided, "you are a little parrot, aren't you? Well, it's time for you to get dressed. Don't you hear Mary calling? Go on now." She ushered the protesting child toward the door and shooed her out. Then she turned back to Isabelle, who still sat in shock. Maria restlessly smoothed the front of her dress and gave Isabelle a wan smile. "Well then, it's the green dress, is it? Abigail will have it altered in no time. Not too much to do really, take the waist in a bit and the shoulders a touch; that's all. I really must be on my way with so many guests to prepare for."

Isabelle stood. "Miss Maria." When her mistress hesitated at the door, Isabelle continued, "Did Mr. Ketch tell you that? That he loves me?"

"No. He would never speak of such things to me."

Abigail had reappeared with the handkerchief and offered it with no sign of sympathy. Maria dismissed her then went to Isabelle.

"I don't want you to think Ketch was speaking out of place about you, Isabelle. What I said...what Helen heard was just me speculating to my husband. Intuition, perhaps misplaced. When it comes to Ketch, my husband—as you've seen—can be a bit...suspicious. I was just telling him that I feel Ketch is sincere, that he is marrying you not only to protect you but because he loves you."

Although Ezekiel had often teased her about Ketch's feelings for her, she had never believed it. To also hear Maria voice it caused a flutter in her stomach, one she could not quite interpret. She pressed the handkerchief to her eyes, forced the tears to stop so she could avoid making a complete scene in front of her mistress.

"Mr. Ketch...I mean, Ketch," Isabelle sniffed, "he thinks so kindly of you, Miss Maria. I know he feels bad about how angry he's made you lately. He's afeared you don't much care for him now."

Isabelle could tell her words took Maria by surprise and touched her as well, and she was pleased she could give something meaningful back to the generous woman. Although she understood Maria to be but slightly older than she, she seemed wise beyond her years. Isabelle admired her when she thought back upon Maria's troubles providing her husband with children, as well as the responsibilities of running this large house at such a young age. Maria could have dismissed her as nothing more than a necessary beast of burden, but instead she had stepped forward to influence her husband about a slave's plight and Ketch's as well.

"Here now," Maria said. "Dry your eyes and let Abigail take some measurements or your dress will never be ready by tomorrow. I must tend to other things." She offered a sustaining smile. "Don't fret about anything, Isabelle. I think your husband will take the best care of you and, even more so, I think you will take care of him. That's how a good marriage works. And don't concern yourself with your master." She winked. "He may bluster and stomp about when he's vexed, but I know how to cool him down."

Isabelle forced a smile and whispered, "Thank you, ma'am."

Maria patted her hand then called for Abigail. After giving final instructions to the seamstress, Maria left the chamber.

***

That morning, Ketch remained in bed until he was certain the other men were through with breakfast and gone from the house. Surely Smith had told them the latest news, and he wanted to neither see nor hear reactions. Willis had neglected to check his wounds, an oversight or deliberate negligence for which Ketch was grateful. He considered the wall between his room and the other men's bedchamber. It was not thick enough to keep his abstinence a secret once his bride arrived. The dogs would have their ears pressed to the wall nightly and high stakes wagered as to Ketch's true state.

Eventually, he trailed out into the common room and settled at the table before the servants could clear away what the men had left. He took his time eating since he had the day off for Helen's birthday dinner.

When a shadow fell across the open front door, he looked up to see Jack Mallory. Had the boy come to rescind his permission for marriage? Ketch forced himself to stand.

"Don't let me interrupt your breakfast." Mallory drew closer. "I'll be brief."

Ketch sat back down.

"I know Maria invited you to Helen's birthday celebration some time ago, but considering your hand in Ezekiel's death, you will only attend the meal and the opening of her presents. After that, you will not be a part of the festivities. Do you understand?"

Ketch felt no resentment, for he had agreed to attend the celebration only for Helen's benefit. At last year's affair, he had felt immensely uncomfortable; the other guests were far above his station. But he did rue the fact that his hasty retirement today might be misconstrued by Helen.

Mallory continued, "If it wouldn't grieve my sister and cause her to mercilessly browbeat me, you wouldn't be allowed to participate at all. But it is, after all, her day, and she remains ignorant of your many crimes."

Ketch forced down his distaste and managed to grind out, "I'm grateful for that."

Mallory scowled. "'Tis my wife, as usual, you should be grateful to, not me. She is convinced love is what motivated you to kill Ezekiel. I, however, am not convinced."

Stunned by Maria's belief, Ketch said nothing. Besides, what more could be said on the matter without jeopardizing his and Isabelle's precarious situation?

With one last look of disapproval, Mallory wheeled and left the house.

As Ketch finished his meal, Pip came to clear the table, moving with her usual tentativeness around him. She jumped when he asked, "Did Isabelle come to the house this morn?"

"Yes, sir. She upstairs right now with Abigail."

Satisfied, he went to the stable-yard to work on the crib. When it came time for Helen's birthday dinner, he returned to his bedchamber to don his meager finest, trim his beard, and make a vain attempt to tame his unruly brown mane.

Happy voices drifted through the open front door, laughter and the shouts of children at play. Such sounds gave him a feeling of insularity and made him think of Sophia.

When he stepped out into the afternoon sunshine, the sight of two dozen guests and their children greeted him and chased away the melancholy. The adults conversed in small groups near tables on the front sward. The skirts of the white linen tablecloths rippled in the breeze off the river. Vases full of flowers sat at measured intervals upon the tables. Bunting flapping on awnings used to shade the tables, along with streamers and ribbons fluttering upon poles, gave the scene a colorful, fluid feel. The gardens and waters of the Ashley provided a peaceful backdrop. In the gardens, children flittered in games of chase. Other giggling youngsters rolled out of sight down the terraces.

Among the guests, Ketch recognized such noteworthy folk as the Draytons—rich cattle farmers from downriver—and James Moore, a landowner prominent in the region's politics, who now stood in close conversation with Governor Thomas Smith.

Ketch knew none of the guests personally save the Archers from Wildwood Plantation, including the matriarch widow, Anna Archer, a once-frail woman who had regained strength and life after the death of her tyrannical husband, Ezra. Margaret, Anna's only daughter, was there next to her, helping her into a chair. The young woman wore a broad-brimmed white hat with a ribbon that matched the cheerful yellow of her gown, a favorite color and one that complimented her fair skin and blonde hair.

No man could look upon Margaret and be unmoved by her beauty. Ketch thought no woman more handsome than Ella Logan, but even he had to admit Margaret existed on the same plane. While Ella Logan had the quality of a statue or a finely painted portrait, Margaret's pulchritude was like that of a sleek animal—a well-bred mare or a yellow panther like the one he had come across devouring a deer last spring. Her blue eyes were as piercing as that panther's, and she had displayed a similar ferocity when protecting her trouble-prone brother,

David, who now assisted her with her chair.

Ketch was shocked to see Margaret's husband there, for Seth Wylder was no friend of Jack Mallory. No doubt his presence was solely due to his wife's insistence. Or perhaps he had simply come to appear gracious in front of men like Moore and Smith and to avoid any social whispers about his wife attending such functions alone. Seth, sitting in stolid displeasure on Anna Archer's left, was the son of a rich Charles Town merchant and one of the select few who knew Mallory's true identity and past profession. That profession had once nearly cost Seth his life.

Soon, all the guests were called to table, and conversation buzzed as they settled into their chairs. The ongoing promise of the harvest and the shipping season cultivated high spirits among the planters and men of business.

Ketch tried to approach the table unseen, but Helen spotted him and exclaimed, "Mr. Ketch! You must sit next to me. I saved this seat for you."

Her bold command surprised and mortified him, for it drew everyone's attention to him. But denying Helen's invitation was out of the question; after all, only his seat remained open now, and so he shambled to where she sat at the head of the rectangular table, a new hat upon her head, smiling at him with blissful ignorance.

Her brother sat on her right, her sister-in-law next to him, with Smith across from Maria. The empty chair was to Helen's left and thus directly across from Jack Mallory. Helen's arbitrating tactics were familiar to Ketch, and he knew she had as much to do with his placement as anyone. Whenever the child sensed a rift between people, she always worked like a skilled seamstress to thread the two parties back together. But perhaps now all was beyond repair.

Elizabeth Archer's large green eyes rested upon him, but then she turned away. Mallory had probably sent Spider to Wildwood in exchange for another slave, and so David Archer and thus his gentle wife would know of Ezekiel's murder. Ketch felt unexpected shame at the thought of having lost the favor of the one person besides Helen who had regarded him with innocent benevolence.

The servants carried out the various courses like drilled soldiers, their aprons sparkling white. Additional slaves from Wildwood had been recruited for today's meal because the regular staff were insufficient for this gathering, and thus things moved smoothly, dishes appearing and disappearing, wine for the adults and punch for the children seamlessly replenished. Ketch had never paid much attention

151

to the servants before, but now he thought of Isabelle among them instead of down near the south rice field under Gabriel's iniquitous hand. After the wedding—he choked on his sweet potato at the thought—he would see to Isabelle's inclusion in the house staff. After having spent time together today and later when they sailed, Maria would see the girl deserved such consideration.

Ketch partook in none of the conversation and kept to his food unless Helen spoke to him.

"Don't eat too much, Mr. Ketch, or you won't have room for dessert. Uncle Smitty! You have gravy in your beard!"

Indeed, even if he had eaten none of the food, Ketch's belly could never find space for the horde of desserts brought to the table. Tarts, pies, cakes, puddings, sugared fruits, and nuts. Helen was determined to have helpings of each. Before it was over, her party dress had a variety of samples upon its pale blue fabric, but no one fussed over her carelessness. Her brother was ever attentive to her. A joy reflected from him that only his sister's happiness provided. Ketch hoped Helen did not think about her parents' absence, but if she did, she said nothing to reveal it, too absorbed by anticipating her presents.

Soon, the servants paraded the gifts from the house's lower level where Maria had hidden them. Helen's bright azure eyes danced with delight, hands clapping in expectation, amusing the guests. The presents ranged from frocks to dolls to hats and shoes, storybooks and ribbons, and Ketch's basket in which lay two carved horses. She had an exclamation for each gift, but for Ketch's gift she left her seat to hug and kiss him, embarrassing and pleasing him. Afterward, she made a point to smile at her brother. She offered the same display to Mallory when she received his present—a new saddle, for she had outgrown her previous one—and then smiled at Ketch. Maria hid a laugh behind her hand, wise enough to douse her amusement when her husband turned to her.

After the presents, Helen and the other children rushed off to play again, taking the dolls and toy horses with them to the gardens. The adults broke off into groups, the women congregating in the shade of the portico while the men gathered at one end of a table to drink brandy and smoke. Ketch caught Mallory's stare and happily slipped away.

CHAPTER 13

The next day, the *Nymph* caught the tide just after it turned in the early afternoon. Lowering gray cloud banks threatened rain, but none fell. The marsh reeds along the Ashley River rattled with the westerly wind that sped the vessel along her careful course downriver.

The *Nymph* carried one more passenger than Ketch had anticipated.

"It was Smitty's idea," Maria had said when she saw Ketch's surprise and dismay at Mallory's arrival on board. "And I think it's a good one. Jack needs to get away from Leighlin for a couple of days; the harvest is wearing on him. And Helen has made him promise to take the *Adventuress* out of the harbor for a sail." Maria's smile revealed her own happiness at the prospect. "Besides," she tried to make light, "you were there for our wedding."

So he had been, though it had been an occasion of circumstance instead of will. He remembered the soft, attractive figure Maria had cut that day aboard the *Fortune*, adorned in a blue dress, kneeling on the quarterdeck over her prostrate groom to whom the sun, nerves, and heavy dark clothes had been unkind. The memory of Mallory's embarrassing swoon brought the shadow of an ironic grin to Ketch, for now he could fully understand the boy's debilitating tension. It had governed Ketch's every thought when he had arisen that morning and when he had trailed down to the landing. And now, standing aft upon the *Nymph*, the anxiety crawled into his stomach and made him queasy.

Mallory, Latiffe, and Smith stood near the tiller, carrying on a conversation Ketch ignored, while forward, Isabelle stood to starboard with Helen. They both appeared animated by today's adventure. They were peering toward shore where Helen pointed out a tall, gangly blue heron with one leg poised clear of the water, sharp beak aimed in its hunt for water-bound prey.

"You've not said a word to Isabelle since we got underway." Maria's voice snapped Ketch from his uneasy reverie. He wondered if she had meant her words as a rebuke. Her slight smile reassured him.

"I'm quite certain she's as nervous as you are."

"I'm not nervous."

"Then why aren't you with her instead of letting Helen prattle the poor girl's ears off?"

"She don't seem to mind."

"No. She and Helen got along wonderfully yesterday. In fact, Helen helped her pick out her wedding dress. I think you'll be pleased with it."

The idea of Isabelle's clothing being any of his business disturbed him. To look at her as his future wife seemed such wildly fantastic folly. For a crazy instant, he considered confiding the truth of the situation to Maria.

"Speaking of Helen," she continued, curbing his impulse, "did Isabelle make that basket you gave Helen for her birthday?"

"Aye."

"Helen used it this morning to take flowers to her mother's grave."

Isabelle lifted Helen atop a crate of melons, so the child could see better over the bulwarks. The slave girl's smile warmed Ketch.

"She just wants to belong somewhere," he murmured then realized he had spoken his thoughts aloud.

"She will in time. I know something about what she's going through. Being half French and half Spanish didn't exactly endear me to the English in Cayona, and it's gotten me a chilly reception from some of the people I've met since coming to Leighlin. You saw Joseph Archer's expression when Elizabeth introduced me. I suppose he expected a lily-skinned Englishwoman to be the spouse of a Carolina planter. If not for Elizabeth, he might well have been too scandalized to have me under his roof."

"That's why Isabelle married Zeke—to fit in. And 'cause she was young and foolish enough to believe that damned buck actually cared for her when he was a-courtin' her. I warned her…"

"We learn best from our own mistakes, unfortunately." Maria gave him a pointed stare.

Helen jumped off the crate and came bursting aft. Running into one of the black boatmen barely broke her charge. "John! Let me steer now. Mr. Latiffe promised me I could."

Ketch noticed the way the four slaves who worked the *Nymph* occasionally glanced at Isabelle, exchanging quiet words and grins that rankled Ketch. In response, she blushed and turned toward shore again. When Ketch finally moved to her side, her smile reflected her enjoyment of the day. A cruise down the river was ever so much more pleasant than winnowing and pounding rice for nigh ten hours. He did not flatter himself to think her happiness could possibly be derived from time spent with him.

"That big house yonder," she pointed, "through the trees...it looks like Leighlin House."

"Aye. 'Tis the Draytons' Magnolia Plantation, and 'twas Mr. Drayton's design what inspired Leighlin House. Ella Logan so admired it that her husband had their house built nigh the same. The first Leighlin House burnt down, you might know, but the second one looks much like the first, at least on the outside."

A vast garden stretched between the shore and Magnolia's manor house. Slaves moved about there, drawing Isabelle's attention. A couple of them paused in their work to wave to the boatmen. Impetuous and child-like, Isabelle waved back.

"Maybe that's where my mother is."

"Hard to say. There's a lot o' plantations she could've gone to. The fellow what took her off that day, I know who he works for, but he's no planter. Mebbe he knows where she ended up. I could ask, if you'd like."

Excitement sparked in her eyes. "You could?"

"Aye."

"Oh..." She smiled brighter than he had ever seen. "Thank you...Ketch." Self-consciousness tempered her smile when she said his name. She looked back toward Magnolia Plantation as it slowly slipped by and then astern, all the while her eyes upon any slave within sight.

"Was you and yer mother always together afore now?"

"Yes. We was lucky that way."

"And what would she say to hearin' yer married to a white man?"

Isabelle turned inboard. "Perhaps she would be...glad."

Skeptical, Ketch wondered how glad the woman would be if she actually saw what her son-in-law looked like with his pockmarked, battered face and missing arm. She would think her daughter had lost her mind or that he had forced her into the marriage.

"She once said to me that maybe I should marry a white man, since I look as much white as black. She hoped maybe then I'd have an easier life."

He hesitated, uncertain about his wandering curiosity, then pushed on. "Did you know yer father?"

"No. When the slavers brought Mama from Africa, a sailor forced hisself on her. He was my father."

"I'm sorry."

155

"In Barbados, there was a slave, William was his name. He was like a father to me." The memory generated a smile. "What of your father? And mother?"

"Me mother is dead. And I hope me father is, too."

"Why?"

Her bold inquisitiveness made him struggle to find an answer. "Truth is I have two fathers, one what sired me and one what married me mother. Neither was worth a damn."

Isabelle frowned as if ashamed she had asked. "Which is worse— to not know a father or to know a bad one?"

"Reckon one is as bad as t'other."

She nodded, and her gaze roamed the vessel as if she sought an easier subject to discuss. Her attention settled on Jack Mallory near the tiller. Helen stood on a box in front of him, her hands upon the tiller. Smith, actually the one manipulating the long, stout wooden device, stood on the other side. Mallory was instructing her how to watch the play of the wind upon the sails and to listen to the slave conning forward where he had a better vantage point to see the river's deviations.

"The Captain is very patient with her, like a good father, don't you think?"

Ketch grunted. The boy was good with Helen, true enough, always had been. Ketch did respect him for that.

"So few men take any care in children," Isabelle said. "They leave it all to women. Miss Helen loves her brother's attention, don't she? Wouldn't a daughter feel the same with her own father?"

"Reckon that depends on the father." He hoped she did not catch the regret in his eyes over the loss of Helen's father. Had she heard about his hand in the matter?

"Do you think the Captain came with us today because he don't believe you will marry me?"

"Miss Maria said he came to get away from the plantation for a while. That's all."

"Do you believe that?"

"Mebbe...partly."

She hesitated. "Does he have reason to believe you won't marry me?"

Her very real doubts deflated Ketch. Perhaps the nervousness Maria had spoken of in her was not because of the wedding but because she feared he would renege and leave her to Mallory's whim.

Injured by her lack of faith, he gave her a scowl and answered, "I promised you, didn't I?"

But who at Leighlin would have any faith in his integrity after what he had done to Zeke? Hopefully, she was not thinking this, and to avoid finding out, he returned aft.

***

The brig *Adventuress* had pleasing lines, Ketch admitted, and her mainmast—rising close to one-hundred-twenty feet—with its slight rake aft gave her an added air of dash among the other merchant vessels at the Charles Town wharf. Unbeknownst to the citizens of the town, the brig—formerly known as the *Prodigal*—had once preyed upon the shipping from this very port, captained by a pirate called Long Arm Jack. With the brig now back in honest employ, Jack Mallory had judiciously repainted her, reversing the colors so that her hull was now dark red and only her gunwales were black. Her original name again graced her stern, the name *Prodigal* forever banished. Although most merchant vessels forsook many guns for the sake of cargo space, Mallory and Josiah Smith had been loath to strip the brig's piratical armament and thus retained her original long six-pounders—four to a side—and four swivels. By the time she left for England, cargo would take up much of her 'tween decks and weather deck, but for now she still had a bit of breathing room for her new passengers.

With an exclamation, Helen raced past Ketch up the gangplank, urging Isabelle to hurry so she could show her all around the brig before they left the wharf. The Mallorys followed Ketch aboard, Mallory with his arm securely around his smiling wife's waist. The boy's love for Maria shone as obviously as his love for the brig. The couple looked renewed, all their stresses and heartaches momentarily behind them.

Ketch's emotions, however, went in the opposite direction. He never liked being aboard the *Adventuress*, for he could not help but look to the place on the starboard gangway where Ella Logan had lain dying in her son's arms.

After being dragged about the brig in Helen's whirlwind tour, Isabelle settled upon a forward locker to stay out of the crew's way. Helen, however, had no such compulsion; she raced about, generally hampering the tolerant crew as they prepared to warp the *Adventuress* from the wharf and ride the remainder of the tide out of Charles Town's vast harbor.

Not all the Adventuresses were present; since this was to be merely a pleasure cruise of a couple of days' duration, Smith had allowed half of the twelve-man crew to remain in town. His first mate, however, was aboard—Hugh Rogers, a small sailor aged before his time, who had served aboard the *Adventuress* since before the mutiny that had turned her from merchant to pirate. A fine seaman whose family lived in town. Having spent time at Leighlin on various occasions in the past year and a half, he was well-acquainted with Helen, and she treated him as she did so many others—as family. Now she trailed him everywhere in his duties, updating him on each bit of news that came to mind, including her birthday celebration.

As the *Adventuress* gingerly wound her way across the congested harbor, Ketch watched the sailors work around him and cursed the stump of his right arm. After sixteen years at sea, it was unnatural to stand idly by like some lubber while others hauled upon lines and climbed the rigging. So he took his black mood aft and stood glowering out over the larboard quarter at O'Sullivan's Island as the brig slipped past under reefed topsails then over the bar, and nosed her way toward the open ocean with the wind nearly dead aft. The breeze pushed his untidy hair diagonally across his face, carrying a hint of autumn in its breath. As the brig met the long, dying swell, he tried to focus on the pleasurable feel of the deck moving beneath him. The *Adventuress* was sluggish at first with her belly so full, but soon, with fore course set and the reefs shaken from the topsails, she gained a bold push into the offing, her bows rising in a slow climb, followed by an easy fall.

He lost track of time as he watched the sun die beyond the receding landscape of Carolina, the sky painted with streaks of salmon and violet. The scent of food reached him, and he turned to see smoke drifting from the galley's stack. Light glowed from the aft cabin's skylight, and Maria's laughter reached him, followed by the low rumble of men's voices. The Mallorys were sharing supper with Smith and Rogers. Ketch had been unaware that they had gone below. With a glance forward, he saw that half the crew were below for their meal as well. He had heard the orders for the brig to lie to for the night but had again avoided observing the crew work.

As Ketch watched their languid forms move about beneath lantern light, he realized Isabelle's contrasting small shape was nowhere to be seen.

He descended through the main hatch and paused to let his eyes adjust. The deeper gloom of the gun deck was brightened by the galley forward where the watch below huddled with their meal. When they saw him, all fell silent, the light glinting in their eyes. Then they went back to their conversation. This closer proximity to warm food awakened Ketch's appetite, but he ignored it as he scanned the deck for Isabelle. Surely she was not in the aft cabin or the wardroom—his quarters.

From somewhere nearby, he caught a low sound, barely heard above the men's voices and the creaks and sighs of the brig, the whisper of water along her hull. The incongruous sound emanated from down low. His vision softened and diverted so he could better determine shapes. The guns were black lumps, their ports open to allow the cooling breeze to ease the deck's stuffiness. Then, just abaft the number eight gun, he spied a small, balled protuberance that seemed alive. A quiet moan reached his ears, and he quickly stepped over and knelt, a waft of vomit rising to his nostrils.

"Izzy?"

The girl gave an acknowledging whimper. "I got sick," she managed, "on the cannon... Didn't mean to... Tried to get my head outside."

"Yer seasick; don't fret 'bout the gun. Let's get you up."

"No," she groaned. "Leave me here...by the...the breeze."

"You need a proper place to lie down."

Her one objection seemed to have drained her strength and will to argue except to say, "Can't get up."

"I'll help you." He cursed his lack of two arms to lift and carry the girl, and he would be damned if he was going to let one of the Adventuresses put a paw on her.

He slipped his arm between her and the gun carriage against which she leaned. She protested but with no more vigor than a sick goose. With his arm under her left arm, he bent his knees and stood, carefully hauling her with him. Now her moan came louder in his ear, and whatever power she had tried to summon into her legs immediately vanished. She nearly slipped from his precarious hold, but he tightened his grip, unwittingly squeezing her breast. Flustered by the accidental intimacy, he mumbled an apology that she seemed as oblivious to as his hand's intrusion.

"Put yer arm 'round me."

She did her best, but her upper extremities suffered the same faults as the lower. He frowned, could barely feel her arm around him. She would not be able to maintain her hold for long. He had intended to take her to the aft cabin where she was to berth with Helen and Maria while Mallory shared the modified wardroom with him, but he knew they would never make it those few extra steps between wardroom and cabin. So, instead, he pushed open the wardroom door and half carried, half dragged the limp girl inside.

The small space afforded privacy from the rest of the deck by bulkheads but bore very little resemblance to the brig's original wardroom. There were no interior cabins, just a space large enough for two hammocks, a tiny table, and a couple of lockers. The swaying canvas hammocks seemed to float and glow in the early night.

"Izzy, I can't get you into the hammock by meself; I need yer help, mind."

She offered a small sound that he took for an acknowledgement.

"Can you stand for a moment?"

With a gulp, Isabelle nodded.

"Put yer hands on the edge o' the hammock, so. Aye, that's it. Now I'm goin' to bend down and crook me arm so you can sit on it like a chair. Aye, just so." Her firm buttocks met his arm. "Now I'm goin' to lift you up into the hammock. On the count o' three…"

With a mournful groan, she managed to time the weak lurch of her body as he came up and spilled her into the hammock. He made an awkward attempt to straighten her dress over her slim legs, swallowing hard as he did so.

"I'll open the skylight to let in some air." Afterward, he retrieved a light blanket and spread it over her. "I'll fetch a bucket in case you get sick again." He did, and she did. When he returned from pitching the contents overboard, he set the bucket below her. "You just lean over and 'tis there if you need it. But don't move too fast else you'll spill yerself outta that hammock."

She gave a whimper that sounded close to appreciation. She lay still, and the swing of the hammock seemed to lessen a bit. From the aft cabin, happy conversation and laughter filtered through the bulkhead, a jarring contrast to her world. Ketch lit a lantern to hang where it would not shine upon Isabelle's pallid face. Her semblance to death troubled him, though he had yet to see a fatal case of seasickness. As a youth, he had suffered from it the first couple of days after he had joined the Royal Navy, but never again, and he rarely remembered the misery, followed too often and nearly obliterated by worse miseries. But he pitied her all the same and wished there was something he could do to offer solace. Distress seemed to take her away from him, making her aware only of the torture wracking her land-bound body.

He found a small cloth near the wash basin and soaked it, folded it, and gently pressed it against her clammy forehead. She stirred and studied him as if unaware of where she was or who he was.

"Thank you," she whispered before closing her eyes again and curling up into a loose ball.

"Izzy," he whispered. "You might feel cooler if you take off that headscarf."

She seemed to consider the effort versus the reward then finally crawled one hand up to painstakingly free herself. Ketch hung the damp cloth on a nail to dry. Her hair lay flattened against her head except the topmost part, which frizzled from the air's dampness.

"The sea don't trouble you?" she asked, barely audible, eyes closed again.

"No. I was a sailor most o' me life."

"Oh...yes. They said...you used to sail with Captain Logan."

Ketch lay the moist cloth against her forehead again. "Aye, *James Logan*."

"Why aren't you a sailor still?"

"No good as a sailor with but one arm."

"Oh...I'm sorry..."

"No need." He forced a smile. "Try to sleep. The sea should settle a bit more, then you'll feel better. When you wake up, you should try to eat a trifle; you wouldn't think so, but it'd make you feel better."

She groaned at the prospect. "Where will you sleep?" Her half-closed eyes dragged around the caliginous room, took in the other hammock nearby.

"I can sling me hammock anywhere." Ketch could not decipher the reaction in her tormented expression, so he ventured, "But I'm not tired yet. I can set with you a spell, if you'd like."

She produced a weary smile and nodded against the pillow.

"But don't tire yerself with talk or I won't stay."

She looked at him in alarm. He eased her with an unpracticed, teasing grin and shifted the cloth.

"Close yer eyes now. And imagine yerself someplace...nice." Ketch frowned, wondered if the girl could imagine any such place.

***

Isabelle floated as if disembodied. While vaguely aware of the shadowy wardroom, the roughness of the hammock, the meagerness of her pillow, and the rancorous odors of the *Adventuress*, she was acutely aware of the agony in her belly and the dizziness in her fuzzy head. She had lost track of how many times she had retched, doing so until she heaved dryly.

After each miserable bout, she sensed Ketch's presence, his scent, as he bent near, followed by the opening of the door with its inward sweep of new air and then the renewal of stuffiness when he returned with the bucket and closed the door once again. When he had first carried her here, a far distant fear had whispered a warning of vulnerability, but when Ketch spoke gently to her, all misgivings dispersed, and she knew he would take care of her. She was unsure why she felt so certain of this, but she did.

Isabelle had nearly drifted into deep sleep when a far-off knocking dragged her back to near wakefulness. But she kept her eyes shut against the unending sway of the deckhead. Desperately, she sought the peace offered by unconsciousness.

"Isabelle is to berth in the aft cabin with Maria." The Captain's voice, laced with displeasure. "Have you forgotten?"

Ketch remained at her side. "She got seasick and needed a quiet place to rest."

"Maria is putting Helen to bed now. We can carry her aft."

Aft... What did that word mean? Isabelle rummaged through her mind, hoped that "aft" was someplace close. Even one step seemed too far, indeed impossible. At the thought of it, she moaned and shifted onto her left side, desired to speak. She hoped her moan was enough to convince them to leave her be.

"The less movin' she does, the better."

"You're proposing she stays here?"

Yes, Isabelle wished to say. Please. But only a low mumble blurred through her dry lips.

"Just for tonight. I'll tend her so yer wife can sleep, and you can stay with yer family."

What felt like an endless delay tormented Isabelle as she floated into a darker, tumultuous place, perhaps within her own stomach, that heaving, unsteady hollow in her body.

"Very well," the Captain finally said. "On the morrow, we'll move her to the aft cabin. She can get more air there."

Air... Perhaps it would be good to move after all. A breath of air stole down from above, from the black sky. No, she was not outside. She was inside the *Adventuress*. A skylight. That was what Ketch had said; he had opened it. That was what allowed the trickle of breeze that occasionally caressed her warm cheeks.

The door closed. Isabelle retreated deeper within herself, tried to relax with the assurance of being undisturbed. But the knocking came again. How long had it been since the Captain had left? Or had he left? Had Ketch left? No, she could still smell him, feel him near. Softly, he cursed the knocking, and the air shifted again as the door opened.

Helen's voice, much too loud, "John said Isabelle is sick."

Ketch hushed her. "Aye, she is. She's sleepin' now, child. Come visit her in the morn. Mebbe she'll be more for guests then."

"But aren't you getting married tomorrow, Mr. Ketch? I brought one of my birthday dresses to wear special."

"We'll see how Isabelle feels. Now why aren't you abed? Yer brother said Maria was tuckin' you in."

"I promised I'd go right back to bed, but first I wanted to give Howard to Isabelle. He'll make her feel better."

"Well, yer a kindhearted one, just like yer mother."

Isabelle remembered Helen in the bedchamber at Leighlin House, there amidst those beautiful dresses. Dresses for her. She had picked one out. A green one... Her stomach clenched again.

"Are you sure you can part with Howard?"

Who was Howard?

"Just till Isabelle feels better," Helen said. "I'm sure she'll feel better in the morning. She wouldn't want to miss her wedding day."

Isabelle pushed away from the voices, from the smells and sounds of the brig. She burrowed down into the hammock, went to clutch the blanket tighter but instead felt something soft and furry. Her fingers closed around the small object, pulled it into her embrace, Helen's clean scent upon it. Its warmth and pliability eased some of her torment. Ketch murmured something. She wanted to respond, to tell him how grateful she was for his care, but she drifted away, thinking that the world no longer swung as wildly as it had just a short while ago.

CHAPTER 14

Ketch hovered nearby as Ned Goddard, the *Adventuress*'s boatswain, lifted Isabelle's slight form with no exertion whatsoever and carried her to the aft cabin. Overnight, Isabelle's color had improved enough to reveal the pink of self-consciousness at being physically transferred about the brig by a stranger—a particularly brawny, shaved-head stranger with a stoic expression. Her color drained, however, with the growing sea breeze that sent the brig capering, much to Helen's delight; Ketch could hear the child on deck, running about, shouting and laughing.

Once Isabelle was safely in a cot slung as close as possible to the open stern windows, Maria assumed the role of nurse and shooed Ketch out. Already humiliated by the sight of another man carrying Isabelle from the wardroom, Ketch was stung by being dismissed from her care, though it was not done maliciously.

He retreated to the wardroom after breakfast to try to regain some of his lost sleep. But he was unable to banish Isabelle from his mind, especially the memory of her clutching Helen's stuffed bear. The image disconcerted him, for it emphasized her youth and accentuated his age. There had to be fifteen years between them, though he was uncertain since he knew neither her true age nor could remember his own. Charade or not, the girl had been an impetuous fool to agree to this...and he to have conjured it.

Judging by Isabelle's lack of improvement and indeed her further decline with the wind's increase, Ketch knew she would make no significant recovery within the time allotted for Helen's brief pleasure cruise. Only the calmer waters of Charles Town harbor would see Isabelle out of her sickbed. And though Ketch was in no hurry to be married, he wanted nothing more than to see Isabelle freed from her misery. However, he knew her fate was out of his hands; only Helen had the power to return the *Adventuress* to harbor, for Jack Mallory would never willfully spoil the child's fun.

Late in the forenoon watch, Ketch went on deck. The stiff breeze out of the south struck the brig upon the starboard beam and pushed her, close-hauled, across the indigo Atlantic with exhilarating speed. The autumn sky was the sharpest blue Ketch had ever seen. Not a single cloud marred the cerulean dome from horizon to horizon. The song of the wind through the taut rigging pleased him, like an old, beloved melody. A perfect day that brought back the more pleasant memories from his days at sea.

Forward in the bows, a squeal went up from Helen when a dash of spray showered her. Unperturbed, the child continued chattering with her brother and was pointing at the bowsprit while she tugged at her sibling's sleeve. Well, she could tug until the sleeve fell off—that boy would never allow her out on the bowsprit with the brig's lively plunge and roll. Helen's mother had displayed the same caution, while her father had often indulged her more risky wishes. Many a time Ketch had positioned himself on deck so if Helen should slip from her father's grip aloft, he would be there to catch her.

From his place near the windward main topsail clew line, he watched Helen as she moved along the canted deck, holding her smiling brother's hand. The siblings seemed separated from the rest of the world, entirely happy and content with each other and their environment. Ketch had never seen Mallory so carefree. Strolling aft along the leeward pin rails, Helen touched belaying pins and flawlessly named off each corresponding line, her eyes sometimes following the line aloft. Ketch knew how much sailing meant to her, how it brought back such wonderful memories of life with her parents, especially before Leighlin when her father's vessel had been her true home. Ketch considered how much he had taken from her and detested what he was now about to do.

With false nonchalance, he crossed the waist so when Helen drifted aft she would notice him. When she did, she paused in her game.

"Are we going to have the wedding today, Mr. Ketch?"

He crouched in front of her, as much to get closer to her as to get farther away from Mallory's ears. "I'm afeared Isabelle's not farin' too well, Miss Helen. We'll have to postpone the wedding."

Helen's lower lip slid outward in a pout. "I thought Howard would make her feel better."

"I'm sure he's helped, but I reckon the only thing that's goin' to make Isabelle feel better is returnin' to calmer waters…to the harbor. She's not used to the open ocean like you and me."

"But we just left the harbor yesterday. John said we would sail for a couple days."

165

"Aye, so he did." He glanced up at the suspicious young man. "And so we will."

Tentatively, Helen offered, "Maybe Isabelle will feel better tonight."

"Mebbe so."

As if ashamed of her self-interest, she reached out to him and brushed a loose strand of hair from his right eye. "You must let me tie your hair back for the wedding. I brought a special ribbon for it. Maria said you should shave, too."

"Did she now?" He grinned, a reaction her touch often garnered. "And what else do the two o' you have planned?"

"You'll see." She grew wistful and looked up at the taut sails. "I hope Isabelle feels better soon."

"Me too, child."

He caught Mallory's knowing glance before the two continued along the pin rail.

***

"Just one more mouthful," Maria encouraged, holding a spoonful of broth without spilling a drop, though the *Adventuress* sought to defeat her balancing act.

The half dozen mouthfuls Isabelle had already struggled to swallow sloshed about in her stomach instead of absorbing. A precarious feeling, and she had no intention to contribute further to it, nor did she want to displease her mistress, who had so kindly nursed her all day.

"Maybe I'll try a little bit later, ma'am. Wouldn't want to make a mess of your clean boards."

"Don't fret about that. We have the bucket right here if you need it, but I think you'll find the broth helps; just give it a few minutes and try not to think about it."

The open stern windows brought the clean scent of the ocean as well as the bright sun to lift some of the oppression. Although the cabin was not large, the sparseness of Josiah Smith's furnishings allowed a spacious feel. It even boasted a tiny quarter-gallery that served as a privy to which Maria had helped Isabelle earlier. But even that short distance had been quite too much for her unforgiving stomach.

Back in the safety of her cot now, Isabelle absently fondled the soft bear, frowning. "Miss Maria, you should be on deck with your family. Sounds like they're having such a wonderful time, and you're

166

missing it all down here."

"I just had dinner on the quarterdeck with them. And, besides, it's good for Jack and Helen to have some time together. He feels guilty because his work often keeps him away from her. So today has been a blessing for them. That makes me happy enough."

Isabelle could tell that her mistress was indeed happy. She wondered if, like Maria, she would one day have a family of her own, perhaps a little girl to spoil like the Captain spoiled Helen. But who would be the father? Would she remain married always to Ketch or would a time come when he abandoned her for someone else, a white woman perhaps, once he grew tired of the prejudice his marriage to a mulatto would gain him? But maybe she was being unfair to him. After all, he had been nothing but considerate and honorable thus far in their arrangement. He was as much an outcast among his people as she was among hers, so perhaps he would have no other choice but to remain with her if he wanted a wife.

Last night, while she lay racked with nausea, she had sensed him always near. In her addled state, she had drifted in and out of bad dreams, some difficult to discern from reality. At other times, she lay somewhere between sleep and wakefulness, aware of the cool, moist cloth against her skin and the sound of Ketch's quiet voice. She could not decipher anything he said—nothing could penetrate the fog and her wishes to die—but to know he was close eased her. When she had first come aboard, the unfriendly stares of the crew had unsettled her, but she knew she had nothing to fear with Ketch in the wardroom with her.

Sometimes, she had dreamt of wearing her green dress, remembered how she had appeared in the looking glass. Would Ketch be pleased? Maria had said he loved her. Surely she was mistaken or misled, perhaps by Ketch himself in order to perpetrate their sham engagement. And what did love truly mean anyway? She thought back, found only her mother's love for her and for William to help define the word. Now, lying all day in this cabin, she had also heard it, heard it above in the voices of Helen and her brother. Never before had she considered that love had a sound, but now she knew. If Ketch did love her, would she hear it? And did she hope that she would? She had no answer; merely considering it confused her.

A knock upon the door, and Maria invited the visitor in. Ketch hesitated just inside, as if expecting Isabelle to be alone.

Maria welcomed him. "Isabelle ate a little broth."

"I think I'm feeling better," Isabelle lied. "I'm sure I'll be able to get up before nightfall, then we can be married."

Ketch frowned and drew near, and she knew he read through her dishonesty; he always seemed skilled at that. "The keenest of observers," Samuel had said.

Maria handed the bowl and spoon to Ketch. "Why don't you see if you can get her to take some more? I seem to have stalled." She smiled encouragingly at her patient. "I'll leave you two alone, so I can make sure Helen hasn't found her way to the masthead yet."

Ketch opened his mouth as if to say something to stop Maria, but the woman left before he could utter a sound. With a lost expression, Ketch stared down at the broth then at Isabelle, forced a smile. "You don't have to fret about the wedding. Whether 'tis today or two days from now, we'll still marry."

Isabelle knew her eyes betrayed her doubts. Weakly, she said, "I've been thinking... All of this is very selfish of me. I should release you from your promise."

"What you *should* do is rest," he said without irritation.

"Why don't I get used to the motion?"

"Some folks it takes a while; some folks never get used to it. You must've been at sea before, if you came from Barbados."

"Yes. Just that once. I had been sick then, too." The *Adventuress* suddenly dipped into a trough, and Isabelle muffled a belch. "It seems I didn't get my father's sailing blood."

"You should try to eat some more of this broth."

Her stomach clenched. "Maybe later."

The cabin door opened, and they both turned to see Helen. She paused there, a rare heaviness to her cherubic face. Isabelle feared that the child had come with some dire news. Helen looked disappointed to see her still prostrate. She frowned and shuffled near.

Above them on deck, Smith's harsh voice rang out, calling for all hands.

Helen stopped near the cot. Isabelle wondered why she avoided eye contact with Ketch. She appeared determined to say something and perhaps she feared Ketch would interfere. Her fingers—pink from too much sun—kneaded the edge of the canvas cot, and she stared at them instead of at Isabelle, whose concern grew into a question.

"What is it, Miss Helen?"

"I asked John to take us back to the harbor, so you won't feel sick no more, so you and Mr. Ketch can be married."

Isabelle struggled to sit up, but the attempt proved hasty and ill-advised. She sank back down, one hand upon the stuffed bear. "Oh, Miss Helen, you shouldn't have done that."

"Why? Don't you want to marry Mr. Ketch?"

"Of course, yes, but Mr. Ketch told me how much you love sailing, how much it means to—"

"I don't mind," the child said with adult-like maturity and perhaps a touch of her brother's stubbornness.

Isabelle could tell that this had been a difficult decision for her and suspected that her brother had left the choice entirely up to her, a prospect that astounded Isabelle.

"I don't want you to be sick." Helen shrugged. "My daddy used to say some folks are born lubbers; you can't help it."

Isabelle almost laughed, but the sobriety and sacrifice on the child's face stopped her and stirred tears of thankfulness, for now she knew she would soon feel human again.

Ketch set aside the bowl of broth and crouched next to Helen. Gently, he turned her toward him, but the girl kept her head bowed. The emotion on Ketch's face staggered Isabelle.

"Thankee, Miss Helen," he said. "This is very kind of you. Yer parents would be proud. I know there's nothin' what means more to you than bein' with yer brother at sea."

The child glanced at the bear in Isabelle's arms. Isabelle held it out to her. "You should take him back now. He misses you."

The fact that Helen accepted the toy into her embrace told Isabelle how much her decision troubled her. She wanted to insist that Helen tell the Captain to remain at sea, yet the terrible sickness roiling inside her head and stomach refused to allow her to produce any further words. Helen's melancholy saddened her. Ketch thanked her again before she said good-bye and trailed from the cabin with her bear hugged close.

Just then the *Adventuress* fell off the wind.

***

Ketch owned but one good coat, and that he had purchased a while ago to have something presentable to wear to Sunday dinners at Leighlin House and whenever he was sent to Charles Town on plantation business. Now he brushed off the dark gray broadcloth with its lackluster gold brocade on cuffs, collar, and buttonholes and stared at it in the late morning light streaming through the wardroom's skylight. The right cuff had been sewn against the side. He scowled at the useless sleeve, at the way it drew attention to his disability. He tossed the coat across his hammock and donned stockings and breeches—fawn-colored, worn but passable. At least the stockings were new, but somehow that newness detracted from his overall appearance instead of enhanced it. He slipped into his shoes—a bit shabby but clean enough, the buckles as polished as possible.

He held up a small looking glass to inspect his face. Regardless of Maria's suggestion, he had only trimmed his beard and mustache. On the left side where he had been burned, some of his beard would never grow, an unfortunate reality that gave him a slightly lopsided appearance.

Mercifully, the *Adventuress* rested easy at her moorings here deep in the harbor. As expected, the relative tranquility had restored Isabelle sufficiently for the ceremony to be carried out. When Helen had told him as much first thing this morning, the excitement of the impending wedding had tempered the child's disappointment of yesterday. Often last night, Ketch had reflected upon her sacrifice. He had known Helen to be mature beyond her years—how else could it be, considering her life thus far?—but, until yesterday, he had not realized exactly how mature and sensitive she was. For her to even consider another's feelings at such a time was remarkable, especially when they belonged to a slave whom she barely knew. Her pure goodness put him to shame.

Now the girl's insistent knocks drummed on the door. "Mr. Ketch, ahoy! Let me in. Hurry!" When he opened the door, the child rushed inward, a silk ribbon trailing from her hand. "They're ready for you. We must hurry. Quick, sit down."

He could have done nothing else, for Helen grabbed his hand and towed him over to a locker. She set to work gathering his unruly hair.

"Don't snatch me bald-headed, child."

She fussed over the tangle and general disorder of his wind-brutalized, humidity-curled locks, painfully tugging her fingers through like combs, incomprehensibly scolding him around the ribbon held in her teeth. She started and stopped several times in her attempt to corral as much of his uncooperative hair as possible.

"The ribbon matches the sun streaks in your hair," she observed cheerfully. "Now, hold still."

Her dexterity always amazed him for one so young, and soon she finished. When she retrieved his small looking glass, he gave himself a perfunctory glance. He preferred his hair loose; pulled back it did nothing to hide his imperfections and in fact seemed to call attention to them. But, he reminded himself, what did any of that matter in this farce? Smiling his thanks to Helen, he was relieved to see how happy all of this made her, for yesterday he had feared that she begrudged his part in her sailing disappointment.

"Your coat," she scolded. "Hurry."

He chuckled. "I don't reckon they'll start without me." He struggled into the unwieldy garment, Helen instantly there to button it, but he waved her off. "You want me to roast, child? Leave it unbuttoned."

"It's not hot today."

"Not to you in yer pretty cotton frock, no."

She grinned. "Are you afeared, Mr. Ketch? You won't swoon like John did, will you?"

"Why would I be afeared?"

"You're getting married!"

"I didn't reckon that was somethin' to be afeared of. Now, cast off."

It was all pretense because he was, in fact, very ill at ease, more so than he had anticipated. Masquerade or not, he had never expected such a day to come, and nothing had prepared him, not even the swigs of rum he had allowed.

"Here we come!" Helen trumpeted as they approached the aft cabin. She had a firm grip on his hand, tugging him along as if to make sure he would not escape.

She pushed the door open the rest of the way and allowed him to halt a moment to get his bearings. The incongruous scent of roses filled his nostrils, but he did not see the flowers; he saw only Isabelle, a sight that stilled his breath. Although nowhere near recovered, at least here in the relative calm of the inner harbor she could sit in a chair in front of her cot, which had been left slung perhaps in case of a sudden need. He recognized his own anxiety reflected in her pale eyes; somehow, this comforted him. She wore a stunning emerald-green dress, its tapered bodice accentuating her narrow waist and giving prominence to the rise and fall of her breasts. As usual, she wore a headscarf, this one matching the dress and shimmering in the reflective sparkle of sunlight playing upon the deckhead. She started to stand, but Maria's hand upon her shoulder discouraged her.

"You should stay seated," Maria murmured, "at least for now."

Smith and Mallory rose from a stern locker. Ketch had not even noticed them in his daze. Mallory, also dressed formally, his cravat tied precisely, gave him a stolid look. Undoubtedly it had been Maria and Helen who had insisted on proper attire for the occasion. He gestured for Ketch to join his bride then moved to stand as witness.

Ketch noticed the roses. Pinkish white, nearly the color of Helen's skin. They were spread in vases around the cabin, wherever they could be safely anchored against the gentle rise and fall of the brig upon the turning tide. He could tell by Helen's grin and the leading way she glanced at the flowers that she had had something to do with the flowers' appearance. For her sake alone, he regretted that today was nothing but a play act, another betrayal of her innocent belief in him.

When Ketch stood next to Isabelle, he could tell she still expected him to falter. He hesitated under Smith's shrewd perusal, then he took Isabelle's hand. Her cold fingers twitched and closed around his, taking his warmth. He was thankful for the morning land breeze that drifted in through the windows, cooled the sweat gathering under his collar and tickled the rose petals to increase their scent.

"Mr. Rogers made you a ring," Helen announced, stepping forward with a small object.

Amazed, Ketch tentatively took the unadorned ring—it had once been a guinea piece, he surmised. He knew it had not come from Hugh Rogers's purse, so that left but one source. Surely Mallory had plans to recoup the cost through his worker's wages, but Ketch found that he did not mind.

Smith held a Bible in his creased hands, but he had no more ability to read from it than the gulls that cackled and argued past the windows. Like Mallory, he appeared unconvinced by what he saw before him, yet he dutifully carried out his office, albeit in the fewest of words.

When Smith reached the critical pledges, he faltered after, "Do you…" and frowned in consternation at Ketch. His face mottled slightly. "I don't reckon I know yer full name, mate."

"Just…Ketch."

"No Christian name?"

"I said just Ketch."

Smith raised one eyebrow at Jack, shrugged and continued, "Do you, Ketch, take this woman to be yer wife?"

Somehow, the word came out with conviction. "Aye."

"And do you, Isabelle, take this man to be yer husband?"

Her fingers closed a bit tighter around his moist hand. "Yes."

Her response sent a small chill down Ketch's spine. The way she looked up at him, almost as if she had achieved something remarkable, made him wonder for an instant if perhaps this had been orchestrated. But he told himself he was being a cowardly fool.

When he presented the ring, Isabelle slowly rose to her feet. She appeared pleased with the object. She trembled—from seasickness or mere nerves, he did not know—as he slid the ring into place. They stared at it until Smith's laconic voice broke through.

"I reckon you could kiss her now, mate."

Ketch had not thought this far, so now he stood staring dumbly down into Isabelle's questioning eyes. As much as he was aware of her, he was equally, painfully aware of Mallory's close attention. To kiss her...here...in front of these others... The last woman he had kissed...so long ago and she dead by his own hand but a short while later. Awkwardly, he bent, hesitated, then briefly kissed Isabelle's lips. Just parted, he paused there, astonished by the softness of her mouth, the closeness of her eyes and how they appeared a different color than from afar. He almost kissed her again but straightened instead, unsure of what he felt or what he saw in her gaze. Her lips twitched at one corner—a half smile or a disappointed frown?

Helen's applause sent a shockwave into each of them, contrasting sharply with the graceless silence. The child's infectious happiness broke the spell, and the women smiled first, Isabelle laughing nervously. Then Smith and even Mallory could no longer deny a smile, at least for Helen's sake if not for the moment.

Isabelle, her color paling once again as the breeze stirred the brig, sank back to the chair.

Maria quickly offered, "Let me fetch you a glass of water."

Isabelle found Ketch's hand once again, and she smiled weakly at him. "Can we go ashore now?"

PART II:

Duo

CHAPTER 15

The cool, damp night conjured mist upon the Ashley River. The gray veil wavered just above the river's surface and gave a lighter, bluish hue to the darkness beyond the *Nymph*, the writhing mass ghostly and alive where the vessel's lantern light touched it. Beyond the river's bordering marshes, the calls of insects and forest creatures brought the night alive. Fish jumped nearby with disembodied splashes, reminding Ketch of days when he and Samuel used to fish the Ashley.

Wide awake, seated on a locker, he was careful to keep from leaning back forcefully against the bulwark for fear of disturbing his healing wounds. Isabelle stirred, nestled against his left side; he had not allowed her to sit on his right, for he feared the stump of his arm might revolt her. She wore his coat, nearly lost in its bulk, its warmth having lulled her to sleep. He pulled it close to her ear to keep away the night's clamminess.

Her willingness to be so near had taken him by surprise, indeed had alarmed him when she had drifted over earlier and sat next to him. He had had no choice but to put his arm around her as she fell asleep. At first, the unfamiliar posture agitated him—the sensation of another's touch so alien and so often avoided in the past. Her scent drove his senses to distraction, especially when he again revisited the wedding kiss, but eventually he gave in to his helpless position and concentrated on whatever else he could—the screech of an owl, the workings of the vessel, the gurgle of the water slipping along the hull.

He thought of the emerald dress that lay inside the locker upon which he sat, along with his and Isabelle's other meager items, of how lovely his...wife had looked in the dress. Maria had graciously allowed her to keep the garments, but when would Isabelle ever have need of such things? Married to him or not, she was still Leighlin's property and would certainly not be invited to Sunday dinners at Leighlin House.

In the rigging above him, a lantern swayed ever so gently and shed light upon the ring on Isabelle's finger where her brown hand peeked out from the edge of the coat. Since the wedding, Ketch had seen Isabelle admiring the pitiful thing, and he wondered why it gave her such pleasure. Certainly not because of what it symbolized, for that reality did not exist. Perhaps it was simple satisfaction for having been given something, for having a possession, something she could claim as her own. Or perhaps she viewed the ring as a symbol of security. While pleased to see her thus, he wished he could have given her something more than a battered guinea piece, especially since someone else had been the one to think of it in the first place. Did she know that?

The river shifted, the *Nymph* followed a bend to larboard, a familiar motion to Ketch; they were almost to Leighlin. The quiet voices of the crew rose slightly. Ketch and Isabelle were the only passengers because the Mallorys had decided to remain the night aboard the *Adventuress* and allow Helen some time in Charles Town to make up for her shortened sail.

A smile drifted to his lips when he remembered Helen fussing over him before the wedding. Her enthusiasm had continued afterward as well, unfortunately venturing onto a delicate subject in front of the Mallorys—talk of progeny. Isabelle's face had become as red as her dark skin allowed while Maria did her best to hide her ongoing disappointment over her own childlessness. Mallory had quickly scolded his sister and changed the subject.

Isabelle slept on even when the *Nymph* bumped against Leighlin's dock. Reluctant to wake her, Ketch knew how exhausted she still was from her long days of seasickness. And she looked so peaceful and content, safe from the world. At last, though, he gave her shoulder a gentle nudge, and she slowly returned to consciousness. As she took in her murky surroundings, she gave a small moan. Despite her bout with seasickness, perhaps these past few days had been a holiday to her, away from the monotonous demands of the harvest.

One of the crew set a lantern at Ketch's feet.

"We're home, Izzy." Ketch helped her stand. "No, keep the coat for now. 'Tis mortal damp."

All the way up the terraces and across the sward, he kept thinking how unprepared he was for this homecoming. He had not even arranged a place for her to sleep in his chamber before they had left for the *Adventuress*. Well, he was no stranger to sleeping on floors.

Perhaps it was the reality of what she had gotten herself into that brought Isabelle fully awake by the time they reached the house. She kept tugging the coat tighter as if to hide in it. When Ketch opened the door to the lower level and held it for her, she halted as if struck, took a step backward.

"There's nothin' to fear," he said. "This is yer home now."

She studied him, unsure. Then her eyes drifted up the dizzying height to the unseen roof.

"Izzy."

Swallowing hard, she finally stepped gingerly into the unfamiliar darkness beyond the door. She waited for him to take the lead and light the way through the common room. A slight, flickering glow came from beneath his closed bedchamber door, surprising him. Who could have known about their return in order to light a fire?

Not wanting to alert his white comrades snoring in the adjacent chamber, Ketch opened the door with care. He halted when the light from the lantern and the low fire in the hearth revealed an occupant.

Recovering, Ketch growled, "Samuel, wake up."

The large black man, obviously comfortable wrapped in a blanket in Ketch's bed, reared his head from the pillow to squint into the light. His bleary attention went from Ketch to Isabelle, and sudden life returned to him. He sat up, kept the blanket close.

Ketch demanded, "What're you doin' here?"

Samuel raised a finger to his lips and gestured for Ketch to draw near. Quietly, Samuel explained, "This is no place for a married couple. Better suited to someone like me. You and Isabelle will be more…comfortable in my cabin." He nodded to Isabelle, a small white smile greeting her. "Go. The cabin is yours." When Ketch started to argue, Samuel added, "Consider it a wedding present." Ketch caught a twinkle of delight in Samuel's patient expression.

Ketch could say nothing, do nothing. The concept of anyone, especially a man—black or white—giving him such an unexpected, generous gift left him dumbstruck. But, surely, Samuel knew him well enough to recognize this marriage for what it really was. Perhaps that was the reason he had offered the sanctuary of the cabin, keeping Ketch away from prying eyes and ears. This shadowy chamber where he had lived for well over a year seemed like a different room now, a foreign one, with Samuel here and Isabelle standing in the doorway.

"Thank you, Samuel." Isabelle's soft voice finally stirred him.

Again, the black man nodded, the fire sparking his eyes.

"Aye," Ketch mumbled. "We're…much obliged."

"Go," Samuel encouraged. "Your wife looks tired and cold."

***

178

Beyond the kitchen house and the smokehouse, Samuel's cabin sat dark and isolated in a clearing surrounded by conifers and hickories, towering trees that provided shade during the day. Samuel had told Isabelle how, after Leighlin House had burned, the three-room structure had been built to house the master, mistress, and Helen during the rebuilding process. Once they had moved into the new manor house, the Captain had given the cabin to Samuel as a gesture of gratitude for Samuel's agreement to assist him full time at the plantation. When Isabelle had taken refuge there last week, she thought the place lonely and felt sorry for Samuel's existence, a man stationed somewhere between slave settlement and Big House. Although she knew he had friends in both communities, no doubt maintaining his unique position was often difficult and required a certain distance from both parties, a self-imposed isolation. She admired him for his integrity and had been grateful for his aid, not only in taking her in that night but for granting her request to tend to Ketch after the flogging.

"Would you like me to see to your wounds tonight?" she asked her husband. His silence thus far during the walk concerned her, as did the reality of their impending coexistence, so stark and unavoidable now.

Blunt but not harsh, he replied, "There's no need."

Of course, there was a need—the wounds were not that old—but Isabelle refrained from persisting, assuming he was self-conscious of the marks and the humiliation they signified. Or perhaps he had been repulsed by the touch of a slave that day in his bedchamber.

They mounted the porch and entered. The lantern light fell across the front room—the modest table and chairs, pantry, and shelving which Samuel said Ketch had made, a skill that amazed her because of his disability. The hearth was cold and lifeless. Beyond, a short hallway provided access to the two bedchambers and a rear door.

Ketch paused near the well-stocked pantry and lifted the lantern. "Would you like somethin' to eat afore you go to bed?"

"No, thank you."

He led the way into the hall then paused outside the bedchambers that were directly across from one another. Isabelle's heart fluttered with anxiety. He gestured to the right with the lantern.

"That can be your'n. Take the lantern. 'Tis chilly tonight; keep me coat for an extra blanket should you need it."

"Thank you."

Abruptly, he said, "Good night," and turned to enter his chamber. He closed the door without even a backward glance.

Stunned by his actions—or rather his inaction—Isabelle shuffled into her own chamber and slowly closed the door. What had she expected of him? She set the lantern upon a nearby stand then crept back to the door and put her ear to it. She heard him move about just briefly then caught the protest of his bed and nothing more.

Frowning, she tiptoed to her bed and removed his coat from around her shoulders, held its heavy weight in her hands. She had breathed his scent upon it as she had fallen asleep on the *Nymph*, tired and still a bit overwhelmed by all that had happened in the past days.

When she had seen him seated on the locker during the journey from Charles Town, she had hesitated before approaching him. Perhaps he would reject her if she attempted to be so near him, yet he looked alone and pensive, the now-familiar pair of vertical lines creased between his eyebrows, his focus somewhere distant in the night. He appeared as confused as she felt, so she had gathered the courage to sit next to him, to offer him silent companionship, if he so desired. The space on the locker was small, so small that even if he had wanted to put more distance between them, he could not without getting up. But she was pleased when he remained and simply looked at her in bemusement. When he draped the coat around her, the comfort it provided made her smile and relax. Before she knew it, she fell asleep. Vaguely, she had been aware of his arm around her and responded with a natural tendency to move closer. She had never felt safer.

Now she put the coat upon the bed and undressed. The sleepiness returned as she lay down, not upon a tick stuffed with rice straw but one filled with goose down, for this had been Helen's bed. It had a luxurious feel. Instead of the bed's blanket, she used Ketch's coat as a cover, bringing it up close to her chin. She closed her eyes, but her ears still listened for any further sounds from across the hall. Would he truly not demand that she share his bed? Even if he cared nothing for her, why would he not take what was rightfully his? Did he find her so physically repugnant? Or did his carnal desires truly wander into the abnormal, as some said?

She played with the ring upon her finger, twisting it, its meaning undeniable. As she began to accept that Ketch would be true to his word at least this night, sleep crept closer. Perhaps Maria was entirely wrong about Ketch's feelings and she would spend the rest of her nights alone in this chamber, self-condemned to live with a man who looked at her as merely an obligation.

She remembered his kiss during the wedding and the look in his eyes afterwards. Had she only imagined his pleasure? Never had she kissed a man with facial hair; his bristly mustache had tickled her. His well-defined lips had tasted slightly of sea salt. He had been tentative yet tender, surprising her, and he had appeared to want to kiss her a second time. What had stopped him? Surely he was not a man governed by self-consciousness. Was it something in her eyes? The experience had been pleasant, and she had found herself wishing he had kissed her again.

Now Isabelle's hand drifted to her mouth, and a finger traced her lips. Perhaps, one day, her husband would kiss her again.

***

When Ketch awoke to the distant crowing of a cock, he thought he was back in his old bedchamber with the welcoming scent of breakfast teasing his nose. In anticipation of food, he smiled and stretched, but then the quality and size of the bed in which he lay alerted him to the change in his surroundings. He opened his eyes to the first hint of morning light and remembered. Instantly attentive, he reached for his shirt and breeches. Sweeping his disheveled hair back from his face, he left the chamber.

In the front room, Isabelle stood near the table as she spooned eggs onto two plates that already displayed bacon, potatoes, and onions. She wore her work dress, her small figure bringing back images from his dreams last night.

"Good morning," she said with a smile.

Ketch stood in stupefied silence, staring at her and the table.

"I found some tea. Do you like tea with your breakfast?"

"I…well, if that's what there is…aye; that'll do." It mesmerized him how at home she appeared, though he was unconvinced her comfort was genuine. He shuffled to the table and sat down.

"I must hurry." She poured tea for him; her cup held milk. "Mr. Gabriel will tan me if I'm late."

"He'll do no such thing, the bloody bugger, and yer to tell me if he tries."

Isabelle chanced a wary look at him and carried her plate to the hearth.

"Sit at table with me," he said with his common gruffness, ill at ease with the sight of her on the floor. "Yer me wife, not me dog."

Blushing, Isabelle sat at the end of the table. They began to eat in heavy silence, Isabelle with her fingers. Ketch's appetite withered, and he wished he had his usual small beer instead of the weak tea.

"Would you like me to tie your hair back before I go, like Miss Helen did?" she asked. "Then it won't bother you when you work today."

"No." Catching her frown, he scowled at himself and continued with his meal.

"Where will you be working today?"

"Out in the west woods. I'm to help with building kilns for makin' pitch and tar."

Another awkward silence. Ketch struggled for something more to say. He wanted to avoid talking about his new assignment, to keep her from knowing that he would be nothing more than a common hand, little better than the slaves who also would be working on the kilns under Samuel's direction. To steer Isabelle away from asking anything more, he said, "Thankee for the breakfast."

Her smile was small but triumphant enough to ease the distraction from her young face. She shoved one last fistful of eggs into her mouth and jumped to her feet, licking her fingers.

"I must go."

"You haven't finished."

"I'll be late." Then she was out the door.

Ketch stared at her empty chair and the leavings of her meal. Her portion had been smaller than his to begin with, yet much was left. Perhaps her appetite had been as shriveled as his by the uncomfortable morning. Well, there should be no waste, he thought as he shoveled her food onto his plate and ate it with little enjoyment. He would need it for the long day ahead.

He thought of her unexpected effort at married domesticity and scowled at his poor display of appreciation.

"Ketch," he muttered, "you are an awkward son of a bitch."

Well, he decided as he pushed his plate away, he would make it up to her tonight.

***

The weather was much more seasonal, the chill of the night already banished by the first rays of sunlight. Isabelle hurried across the grass to the rear portico. She enjoyed the feel of the dew wetting her bare feet.

As she joined the others of her gang gathered near Leighlin House, she absently played with the ring upon her finger. Her tardiness drew undesired attention. Gabriel appeared surlier than usual, and his attention, as well as that of others, went to the wedding ring. She started to put her hands behind her back but realized such concealment was unnecessary—she felt no shame. In fact, the weight of the ring on her finger gave her a new feeling of freedom and courage.

Gabriel growled, "You reckon bein' married to that murderer is goin' to get you special privileges from me, think again."

"No, sir, Mr. Gabriel."

He cast one last disapproving look her way before leading them down the lane. Isabelle fell in at the rear of the group, saw others cast looks over their shoulders at her. She stared back.

"She do think she special," Hannah's voice drifted to her. "But what kind of decent woman would go marryin' the man what murdered her husband? And right on the heels of his murder, too. But I told you all somethin' like this a-comin', didn't I? Ever since we come here. Just like at Mr. Tom's. She find her way into some white man's bed, then she don't have to fret none 'bout things like the rest of us."

Isabelle denied Hannah the satisfaction of a retort.

"What kinda husband he anyway?" the woman continued. "A fright to look at, that one. And a cripple to boot. Prolly scare his own mama if he got one."

Ester tittered; others grinned as they came around the manor house and caught the early sunlight upon their dark faces. Isabelle kept her steadfast gaze forward and away from Hannah.

"An' her set up in Samuel's house all fancy-like. Prolly that murderin' husband o' hers done kicked Samuel out. I still say somethin' smell."

"Tell 'em," Ester encouraged, "what you tol' me, 'bout the Cap'n."

"The Cap'n jes' playin' a game. He let that ol' devil Ketch take Isabelle into Samuel's house so she close-like and he can have his way with her. And Ketch can't make no fuss even if he wanted to 'cause the Cap'n'll throw him off the plantation."

Isabelle put as much confidence as she could muster into calmly saying, "You keep talking with that forked tongue of yours and I'll tell my husband. You just might end up like Ezekiel if you're not careful."

Perhaps the threat was hollow and foolish, but it got the desired results; Hannah left her alone. In fact, she seemed surprised by Isabelle's brashness, or perhaps the surprise was simply because she wondered if Ketch might actually care enough about his wife to defend her honor. Isabelle cautioned herself, though, for it might be unwise to threaten such things. Her comments might get back to the Captain, who could think the intimidation genuine. She feared causing more trouble for her husband.

Isabelle realized that marrying Ketch had permanently pushed her out of the slaves' realm. Although she may still work side by side with them in the field, in their eyes she was now on Ketch's social level. But for the first time since coming to Leighlin, she cared nothing for their opinions.

***

When Ketch went to work that morning with Samuel, driving the mule team into the forest, he contemplated seeking Samuel's advice regarding marriage. But he refrained once he considered the six male slaves riding in the wagon with them. Ketch had yet to decide if Samuel had guessed the truth of his married state.

They discussed pitch and tar production. Jack Mallory had given the latest naval stores project to Samuel. Naval stores in the form of oak and pine had always been one of Leighlin's major exports, and it had been James Logan's plan to also produce pitch and tar. When Samuel had resurrected the idea, Mallory had wisely embraced it. After all, Leighlin's eight hundred acres grew thousands of yellow pine and slash pine that could produce high quality products for England's vast array of ships.

"We've gathered enough wood so far for one burning," Samuel explained. "We'll start digging the kiln today."

Ketch looked forward to the work, for it would keep his hand and mind busy, more so than supervising his old gang. Perhaps this change would prove to be a boon.

The chosen site lay on Leighlin's western border, reached by a crude lane used by the cattle-herding slaves of the plantation. They passed some of the red cattle where they grazed to either side of the lane, occasionally standing stupidly in it, moving out of the way only when their herder appeared with a leafy branch to prod them off the path. Some of the land was open but most was tree-covered, the cattle leisurely roaming about, living here until they were to be slaughtered or sent to market. The herders, who protected them from predators like panthers, were Leighlin's most trustworthy hands, for their duties were so remote from the plantation house.

"After we finish the kiln," Samuel said, "it will take eight or nine days of burning to produce the tar, so we'll use that time to build another kiln, make barrels, gather more wood, and cut down trees. Four

184

or five years from now, we'll use the trees we fell now as lightwood for more tar."

"How much will we get from one burning?" Ketch considered the towering pines around them.

"Should be a hundred barrels, maybe more. But there's acres more of downed timber out there to be gathered and burnt. By January, we'll have some hands from the rice fields to help box trees. Thousands of those out there to give us sap."

The site of the first kiln was a clearing where the gathered wood covered the ground save for a small area in the center. The wood had already been prepared for burning—chopped down to billets two or three feet long and about three inches thick. Samuel dismounted from the wagon and proceeded to mark off the dimensions of the kiln while Ketch and the slaves unloaded the implements.

The slaves said next to nothing, and Ketch knew his presence had everything to do with their reticence. Perhaps they were unaware that he had no more authority over them than they had over each other. Once his position became clear, however, he doubted they would be so bold as to be smug about the equality.

They spent the rest of the day digging. The kiln would be constructed by building up a slight circular mound of earth about twenty feet across. Within that mound, an interior decline toward the center would be created, leading to a hole. From the hole, conduits would lead outward to a surrounding ditch where resin would eventually gather. Once the kiln was finished, the wood would be laid like rays, stacked until about ten feet high like a great wheel. Pine straw and other natural fuel would be strewn about it before all was covered with dirt. A cincture would be built to contain it. A fire built at the top would penetrate downward through the wood to allow gradual combustion.

To accommodate his disability, Ketch had long ago devised a short-handled spade-like shovel. He worked alongside the slaves and Samuel through the warm day, concentrating his attention on the outer trench, familiar with such work because of the hundreds of feet of trenches dug to irrigate the rice fields. Most of the time, he could concentrate on his task, but often Isabelle slipped back into his mind.

That evening, Ketch made sure he returned home well before his wife. Going to the kitchen house, he frustrated the women with demands for a meal to be cooked special, though they had just started to prepare supper for the main house. He barked and growled and prodded with threats until the last dish had been brought to his cabin and set upon the table.

Everything was still warm when Isabelle dragged herself through the door at sunset. She staggered to a surprised halt, completely different from the neat, clean young woman who had left that morning. Dust and chaff covered her loosened headscarf as well as the rest of her, all the way to her dusky feet. Amidst this veil of filth, her eyes looked even larger as they sought Ketch, who threw another log on the small fire. Although he wanted to smile at her, her expression troubled him.

"Good evening," he said.

At last, she found her voice, blinked, and said, "Good evening." She took in the two place settings across from one another on the food-laden table, swallowed, and started toward the back of the cabin.

"Izzy—"

"I must wash," she hastily said, disappearing in a blur behind her door.

Ketch stood, dumbfounded and deflated. He had expected her to be ecstatic to see the food all prepared, knowing that she was free from that wifely duty at least for one night. When she remained in her chamber, he shuffled to the table and slumped down, eyed the array of dishes spread there—duck, quail, sweet potatoes, collards, corn, peas, cornbread, and melon, even wine. Why had she looked so displeased? Or was she simply taken aback by someone doing a kindness for her? He listened to her moving about in her chamber. How tired she had appeared, perhaps too tired to want anything more than her bed.

When Isabelle emerged, Ketch stood. She had done her best to wipe off her dress and had donned a fresh apron. Her face and arms shone in the lantern light from her ablutions, and she had removed her headscarf and tried to restore some order to her short, frizzled hair. Padding over to her own chair, she stood behind it, staring down at her hands on the back of it, the wedding ring shining from the water.

"Sit," he said. "Please."

It seemed to occur to her that he would remain standing until she sat, so she obeyed.

Ketch tried to keep his tone light. "You must eat afore it all gets cold."

Her gaze snapped up as if she had been rebuked, but when she saw his encouraging smile, she murmured, "I've never seen so many victuals before, not even on Mr. Tom's table."

"Well, 'tis for eatin', not gawpin' at, so…dig in." To set an example, he filled his plate with robust enthusiasm until it overflowed.

"Where did it all come from?"

"Well," he said near a nervous laugh, "if you reckon I cooked it all, yer head must've been scorched by the sun today." The joke fell flat, so he stuttered to recover, "Why, it came from the kitchen house, o' course."

An unhappy line creased her forehead as she reached for the quail.

The rest of the meal passed in silence, save for the urgent sounds of their feast. Isabelle's first taste of the Madeira caused her to choke, but she recovered and tried to hide her surprise at the results of the alcohol. Ketch realized she might never have tasted any sort of spirits, the very idea foreign to him. Unlike this morning, Isabelle did not bolt early from her chair, busy until every speck of food had been sopped from her plate with the last of the bread. Eventually, the emptiness before her brought her up short, and she glanced warily at him, as if anticipating a reproach for her gluttony. A small belch managed to escape, which she quickly tried to disguise with a fist to her mouth. Ketch hid his smile.

The smile, however, vanished when Isabelle pushed her chair back and stood. Her fingers toyed with the wedding ring as her eyes swept over the carcasses and the empty plates.

"Would you like me to clear away the dishes now?"

"No. I'm not quite finished. And, besides, I'll have Rose take care o' things in the morn when she brings breakfast over."

As if horrified, Isabelle stared at him, and moisture raced into her eyes.

"What's the matter?" he asked, wondering what on earth he could have done to upset the girl. Or was it something that had upset her before ever returning home? Was it something from this morning? He cursed the futility of his new situation. Nothing had prepared him for this.

When she managed to gather herself and speak, he was stunned by the veiled anger in her words, the hurt. "Did…did you not like your breakfast this morning?"

The question threw him off for an instant. "'Course I did."

"Then why didn't you want me to cook supper for you?"

He struggled to find words.

"You went to the kitchen house, as if you didn't have a wife to cook for you, or at least one who *could* cook."

"Izzy—"

She sniffed back her tears. "Of course, you think I'm foolish. Well, maybe I am, but…but you've done so much for me. I just…wanted to do something for you."

"Christ, Izzy." He dragged his hand through his hair, felt foolish and blind. "This morn I thought I had done somethin' wrong, so I wanted to make it up to you with havin' food all ready when you got home."

"I'm your wife. It's my duty to cook for you."

"And if yer not seen doin' yer duty, then mebbe the truth will come out."

"That's not it; I know you will keep your word to me." Her voice dropped. "I want to repay you. You've done so much."

"I don't expect nothin' from you."

"But…everyone expects something."

The connotations seeping into this conversation compounded his frustration, and he got to his feet, bluntly said, "I reckon I'm done eatin' after all." He found his tobacco and pipe and fled to the front porch.

Once sitting upon the top step, he lifted his gaze beyond the kitchen house to the main house where light shone from the master bedchamber on the top floor. Surely the Mallorys had returned from Charles Town by now. Just then, Maria's slender form silhouetted in the window as she closed the sash and pulled the drapes partway. Her small shape reminded him of Isabelle, and he frowned, listening to his wife's movements from within, brisk and noisy with displeasure as she cleared the table.

Once he heard Isabelle's chamber door close, he tapped out his pipe and crept back inside. Is this how it was to be? Would they avoid each other whenever possible? Well, perhaps it was for the best.

He checked the fire one last time, poked absently at it to enliven the embers. Then he straightened his weary back and started for his chamber.

But when he reached his door, he listened to Isabelle preparing for bed in her room, her stray sniffle striking his heart low. Frowning, silently cursing himself, he lingered there. Finally, he sighed quietly, entered his chamber, and closed the door.

CHAPTER 16

"You know how to write?" Isabelle's wondering voice drew Ketch's attention from the piece of paper over which he labored.

"Well, I'm no hand at it but, aye, I know a bit about it." Her obvious admiration gave him as much pleasure as did her happy mood.

He had not seen her in the morning; she had already left after making his breakfast and awakening him. But that evening when he returned home from the forest, she was there ahead of him, supper just on the table. When she saw his pleased expression, she had given him a smile of relief, blushing. He could see that she was eager to leave yesterday's awkwardness behind, and so was he.

Now she left the basin where she had been washing their plates and bowls. Wiping her hands on her apron, she drifted over to stand at his left shoulder near the table.

"What are you writing?"

"A letter."

"To who?"

"To Malachi Waterston, the man whose apprentice took yer mother away."

"My mother?" Her hand clutched his shoulder.

"Aye. I'm askin' if they know what became of her."

"Oh...Ketch."

"You must tell me her name, so I can include it."

"Louisa." As if remembering herself, she released her almost painful grip on him. He tried to ignore his disappointment. "Will you read the letter to me?"

"Well, I reckon I can. That is, if I can read me own handwritin'. Chicken scratch is all, nothin' more." He squinted at the pitiful words. A dreadful presentation. He rarely had occasion to read or write, so his meager skills had never been polished, and to be forced to write with his left hand provided an even greater challenge.

"Who taught you?"

"Miss Ella, Leighlin's first mistress. She taught most o' Captain

Logan's—*James* Logan's—crew. Sure, she would cringe if she saw how poorly I kept what she taught me. Her handwritin' was a thing o' beauty, small and neat." He chuckled. "'Twas a trial for her to teach me how to move the quill across the paper to write them letters."

He curtailed his mirth when he remembered how Ella Logan had once reached to guide his hand but had stopped short and retreated. Her sheepish expression told him that she had hoped her diversion had gone unnoticed. Her reluctance to touch him then and at other times after she had nursed him back to health had wounded him deeply, an incongruous reaction, for with all others he shunned physical contact. Not for any base reason did he desire her touch but simply for the comfort it provided, the acceptance, things he longed for on occasion when around Ella or Helen. He had hidden his disappointment from her that day, and he certainly understood someone of her quality being reluctant to sully herself by holding the hand of a man who tortured and murdered. After all, she had an innocent child to shield.

Ketch cleared his throat and continued, "Lookin' out for us, Miss Ella was, in case our seafarin' days came to an end, like with me. I wish you could have met her, Izzy. She was a great lady."

"The people talk of her still."

"Aye, they would. She was kind to all, just like her daughter is. Ah, I wish she was here; she could have written this damned letter for the both of us."

"Read it to me," Isabelle urged. "Please, Ketch."

As he struggled back over the brief shamble of words, Isabelle listened without interruption, perhaps without breathing, frozen at his side. When he finished, she pointed. "Is that your name?"

"Aye."

"How do you say the letters?"

He dragged a finger beneath each letter, reciting: "K-e-t-c-h."

"What's this?" She pointed. "Before your name."

He hesitated. "That's an E."

"An E? What does it mean?"

"'Tis an initial. That's all."

"What's an initial?"

He struggled, shifted his weight in the chair, the low fire warm against his back. "An initial is...a letter what stands for a whole name."

"So, what does the E stand for?"

Ketch frowned as distant voices whispered in his head.

"It's your name," Isabelle said. "Your other name, I mean. Like other white folk; they usually have two names, like Mr. Tom. His

190

whole name was Tom Clark."

He hesitated. "Aye."

The puzzle seemed to excite her, as if it were something she had been waiting to solve. "So, what is your name with an E?"

He stared at that letter, written small on the page. He had thought long and hard about using it but signing simply his last name had seemed insufficient and crude for the cause. Including an initial made him seem more legitimate, more respectable, perhaps something that would help this undertaking.

"What is your name, Ketch?" Isabelle patiently repeated.

Hastily, he folded the small sheet of paper, mumbled, "Edward."

"Edward." A smile in her voice. "May I call you that?"

"No," he snapped.

Startled, she took a step back, blinking at him. The fire hissed for a protracted moment. Ketch pushed the chair backwards to stand, but Isabelle refused to retreat to her dishes. He did not want to speak on this matter, yet neither did he want to taint the goodwill that the evening had thus far provided them.

Softening his voice and trying to look at her, he said, "I prefer you just call me Ketch. 'Tis what I'm used to." He glanced at her curious face, surprised that she remained. She seemed to be waiting for something more. In the hopes of ending the discussion, he said, "Edward don't hold nothin' good, just reminds me of that bastard stepfather of mine I told you about."

Slowly, she nodded, almost apologetic. "Very well," she said near a whisper. "I'm sorry if I spoke out of place."

"You did nothin' of the sort." His fingers toyed with the letter. "I'll take this to Miss Maria on the morrow, so she can write it over for me proper-like and send it to town."

Isabelle's smile returned to her beautiful lips. "Thank you."

Fearful of further questions and the memories they would bring, he hastily retired to his chamber.

***

From where Ketch sat upon the top step of the rear portico, he watched Maria walk up the shaded lane from the stables. She had yet to spot him as she mopped sweat from her brow and neck with a lace handkerchief. Her riding attire was a self-designed curiosity, one she had also fashioned in a smaller version for Helen—a short jacket and a skirt that appeared to have been joined in the middle and sewn so that it formed something similar to a man's petticoat breeches. This invention was necessary since she went against convention and rode astride instead of sidesaddle, as did Helen. Much to Jack Mallory's relief, the two rebels relented in their unladylike behavior when visitors were at Leighlin, though Ketch knew their antics privately amused the boy. After all, he had the same rebellious qualities, and thus to judge them would be unfair. Mallory never could control those two and rarely tried. Helen had been the one responsible for teaching her brother and sister-in-law how to ride, and though Maria lacked Helen's natural ability, as did Mallory, she now rode about the plantation at least with confidence if not style.

When Maria drew closer to the house, she finally noticed Ketch. She would be surprised to see him this time of day when he should be at the kiln, having the midday meal with the other hands. She tucked away the handkerchief and made a hasty attempt to anchor some of her black hair that had fallen from their pins.

"Ketch, what are you doing here? Is something wrong?"

He stood, doffed his hat, and gave a slight bow as she ascended the steps. "I come to ask if you might do somethin' for Isabelle." He hoped that couching the favor thus would elicit more of a willingness to help.

"What is it?" Maria removed her hat, disturbed more of the precarious pins in the process, which led to more of her hair falling about her shoulders. Surrendering to inevitability, she freed the rest of it.

"I…I have a letter, one what I wrote, only…well, me own writin's not a thing o' beauty, you could say."

"So, you want me to rewrite it for you?"

"Aye. If not too much trouble."

She considered him with her dark eyes. He could tell her strong pride made giving up on him difficult after investing so much time in him over the past year. Also, she had enough of youth's foolish notions of love and romance that perhaps somewhere in her lived an appreciation for a man who would kill at great personal risk for someone he cared about.

"Come inside."

He followed her into the cooler house and into the deserted library.

"Do you have the letter with you or did you want to dictate it to me?"

He set his hat upon a chair, so he could dig out the crumpled missive. As she frowned her way through his composition, he stood in mortified silence.

"Has Isabelle never been separated from her mother?"

"No. They'd always been together. First in Barbados then at Clark's."

Maria shook her head and settled behind the desk. "How horrible to be taken away from your only family."

Ketch knew Maria understood the pain of being motherless, for her own mother had died after her birth. He was relying on that empathy.

"Jack would never do that to our people," Maria continued almost to herself as she began to transcribe.

Once finished, she offered him the quill, so he could sign his name; she and her husband were the only ones at Leighlin who knew his first name. Well, perhaps Samuel did, but if so, he had never admitted to it.

With a hint of suspicion, Maria asked, "If Mr. Waterston or his apprentice knows of Louisa's whereabouts, what will you do?"

"I'll write to her master to see if Isabelle could visit."

"And if they say no?" Before he could answer, she continued, "You've played me for a fool recently, so you must understand my concerns. If you don't get what you want from Louisa's master, I would expect you aren't going to take matters into your own hands, as you did with Ezekiel."

Anger clenched his jaw, but he knew he had no right to strike back at her lack of faith in him. "If they say no, they say no. That'll be the end of it. I promised Isabelle I would try, but beyond that I made her no guarantees."

Maria's glance reflected a lack of confidence, but she folded the piece of paper and melted wax upon it. Ketch was pleased to see her press Mallory's seal into the wax, for he hoped this, like his formal signature, would add credence to the request.

"We have other papers going downriver to Charles Town today for Mr. Waterston. I'll make sure this is delivered with them."

"Thankee." He bowed and reached for his hat. "I'll tell Isabelle of yer kindness. This means the world to her."

At the library door, he turned when she called his name. Behind the desk, she appeared ridiculously small and out of place.

"Don't make me regret this."

He fidgeted with his hat brim, frowned, and bowed again. "I won't." Then he hurried from the house and tried to forget her look of skepticism.

***

Three days passed with no reply from downriver. Isabelle talked of little else but her mother. The possibility of being reunited gave her a new buoyancy and energy. Even after working to exhaustion all day upon the harvest and further in preparing Ketch's supper, she was still full of life. Ketch lacked the heart to caution her that his inquiry to Malachi Waterston could very easily yield nothing. Waterston, a respected man of business, had never considered Ketch as anything more than Logan's dog. But Ketch would reveal none of this prejudice to Isabelle, for her excitement did him as much good as it did her.

After their meal each night, they sat on the front porch for a few minutes before retiring, Ketch upon the top step with a pipe and Isabelle in a chair. Ketch enjoyed those peaceful moments, surprised by how his unease ebbed away a bit more each day. He had feared that his years of social insularity, spent almost exclusively with men, would make living closely with her impossible, but he found himself hurrying home in the evenings, eager to see her and share their limited time together. He had also been afraid that Isabelle would miss living among her own kind, but at least for now, with the search for her mother providing a diversion, she seemed equally happy to see him each morning and evening and never mentioned her life in the settlement. Contentment eased him, and in it he found the ability to smile and even laugh at Isabelle's mannerisms and her stories about her mother. She seemed pleased by his reactions, at first almost shocked, as if she had never thought him capable of such, but she quickly hid that amazement.

Sometimes, when she was busy chattering away, her attention upon Leighlin House or the sheep grazing across the rear sward, he allowed himself to admire her slender shape and the way the last of the day's light shone in her large eyes and upon her easy smile. How did happiness come so readily to her after all she had endured in her brief life? Perhaps he could learn something from her in that respect—how to leave the past in the past. But as his gaze grew bolder, ignoble thoughts overpowered all others, and he hoped that when Isabelle's attention returned to him, she did not sense his base desires. Did she lay awake each night, fearing that he would break his word and invade her chamber? He wished he could somehow reassure her, for to think he frightened or troubled her in any way disturbed him. Yet, her brief touch when he had been writing the letter made him hope that perhaps he was not completely repulsive or intimidating to her.

"You must forgive me, Ketch," said Isabelle. "I know I've been carrying on for days about my mother and me like a selfish ninny."

She leaned slightly toward him, hands upon her knees. Her teeth caught the glimmer of faint lantern light through the nearby window.

"What about *your* mother, Ketch? Tell me about her."

Her question took him so off guard that he nearly choked on his pipe. He looked away into the night, coughed to delay. Instead of the blocky shapes of the kitchen house or manor house before him, he saw his mother, her red hair and green eyes, that wildness in them, that insanity he had brought down upon her by telling her of Sophia's death at the hands of his stepfather. Whenever his mother penetrated his thoughts over the years, he tried to remember her as she had been before Sophia's murder, the woman who nursed him through the smallpox, sang to him and did her best to keep him fed while her husband staggered from job to job. But he saw only the grief-induced madness in her eyes, heard her odd ramblings in his ears when she would lie with him and speak to him as if he were someone else.

"Ketch?" Isabelle's voice dragged him back to the porch. "Did you hear me?"

His answer came in a forced strangle, "Aye."

She faltered, and he feared that she somehow knew why he was reticent. Desperately, he searched for something to say, to satisfy her curiosity. "I was just a boy when I left home," he managed. "Don't remember much about her."

"You told me she died."

"Aye."

"How?"

"She was murdered. That's when I left."

"How terrible." Isabelle's chilled voice drifted to him from far, far off. "Did they catch the murderer?"

"Aye," Ketch murmured.

He had no idea how much time passed between his answer and Isabelle speaking again. For all he knew, she could have been talking for an hour before his senses cleared and returned to the present. The bending of time shook him, reminded him of similar lapses in the past, often during battle as well as other times, times like that night in the Plymouth brothel when he had killed that prostitute, ages ago but as fresh as yesterday.

"Someone's coming," he heard Isabelle say, bringing him fully back to his senses.

His breathing had quickened, and he felt sweat beginning to dry upon his skin. The pipe sat loose and cold in his hand, his mouth cottony. Alarmed, he glanced toward Isabelle, who was staring intently up the lane that passed between their cabin and the kitchen house. Fortunately, she seemed oblivious of his state. Perhaps the seemingly lengthy moment had indeed been a fleeting second.

Ketch followed her attention to a lantern bobbing through the night, two dark figures on either side. The smaller of the two moved with a noticeable bounce, an energy that only Helen possessed by this time of day.

"It's Miss Helen and Miss Maria," Isabelle said, getting to her feet. "Oh, I hope they have news."

"Is that you, Mr. Ketch?" Helen chirped as she hurried forward.

Relieved by the timing of their appearance, he stood, finding his legs unsteady. "What brings you out so close to yer bedtime, young lady?"

"We have a letter for you!"

Quickly, Isabelle stepped forward. "A letter?"

"Hello, Isabelle."

"Good evening, Miss Helen." She curtseyed to Maria. "A letter…?"

"Yes. Maria has it."

Maria held the lantern higher, so it shone upon all of them. "It came on the evening tide."

In an excited, impatient rush, Isabelle offered, "Won't you please come in?"

Inside, Helen buzzed about the front room with curious verve. "I've been wanting to come visit you in your new house, Mr. Ketch, but John wouldn't let me."

"Mr. Ketch is newly wed, Helen," Maria said. "Your brother wanted to allow him time alone with his bride before having a certain busy visitor underfoot."

The teasing remark had no effect on Helen, who returned her attention to their host. "Would you like me to bring you some flowers tomorrow, Mr. Ketch?"

"I'm sure Isabelle would like that."

Isabelle offered chairs. "Can I get you something to eat or drink? I have some sweet potato pie—"

"Oh, yes, please!"

"No, Helen," Maria admonished. "Thank you, Isabelle, but once we get back to the house, Helen will be off to bed." She gave her sister-in-law a chiding smile. "You don't need your belly full of pie or you'll never go to sleep."

With a frown, Helen slumped upon one of the chairs near the fireplace. But then her face brightened again. "May I read the letter out loud, Maria?"

"Well..." Maria glanced at Isabelle, who stood near the table, wringing her hands in her apron. "I suppose that's up to Mr. Ketch. It's his letter."

Ketch could not deny the child when she looked at him with her mother's blue eyes. So Maria placed a chair close to Helen and broke the Waterston seal on the letter before handing it to the girl. She leaned over the child to help her if needed.

Painfully deliberate, Helen enunciated each word, often looking up at Maria to make sure her interpretation was correct. Each pause caused Isabelle to emit tiny sighs of agonized impatience that Ketch hoped went undetected by their guests.

Dear Mr. Ketch:

We received your letter of the twelfth instant. The slave of whom you inquired, named Louisa, is a servant in my household. You may tell her daughter that she is well and sends her regards.

Helen looked to Isabelle, who stood with a bemused expression, obviously unsure how to react to this news.

"Is that all?" Isabelle asked.

Helen nodded.

Isabelle turned to Ketch. "She's in Charles Town?"

"Aye," Ketch said with a smile of reassurance. "This is good news, Izzy. Mr. Waterston is a wealthy man with the means to care for yer mother proper-like."

"I used to stay with the Waterstons sometimes," Helen said, "when Daddy and Mamma was sailing. They have a little boy named Robert. And soon he's gonna have a brother or sister, isn't he, Maria?"

"That's right," Maria said with a tight smile as she folded the letter and handed it to Ketch. "Perhaps that's why Isabelle's mother is there, to help with the children."

"She would like that," Isabelle said in a tempered tone.

Helen swung her feet to a private tempo. "We should go visit your mamma."

"Helen," Maria said near a laugh. "No wonder your brother calls you a savage. Where have your manners gone?"

197

Isabelle looked to her husband, and Ketch realized why she was not completely pleased with the news of her mother's proximity and welfare—she had hoped for much more. Ketch figured his reputation had discouraged Waterston from offering to allow a reunion.

When Maria saw Isabelle's crestfallen expression and the desperation in her eyes, she said, "If you'd like, I could ask Mr. Waterston if Isabelle might visit her mother."

Ketch assumed they would stand little chance of such an invitation, but he could not countenance Isabelle thinking he had not at least tried to acquire permission. And to have such a request come through Maria would offer better odds, for Malachi Waterston not only handled the Mallorys' business affairs but he held the couple in as high a regard as they held him. After all, Jack Mallory's mother had taken Sarah Waterston into her home and helped deliver Robert during a difficult birth, and without her aid Sarah could very well have died.

With a tremulous smile, Isabelle asked, "Could you, Miss Maria? Would you? How I would love to see Mama."

"Of course. I'll write the letter tonight."

"Thank you, ma'am. I'm much obliged."

Ketch thought Isabelle might impulsively clutch Maria's hands or embrace her, but she managed to refrain, smiling through a glaze of tears.

Helen poked about the pantry. "Maria, can I stay here with Isabelle and Mr. Ketch for the night? I could sleep in my old chamber."

"Helen," Maria scolded, "you must be invited; you don't invite yourself."

The child gave Ketch a sheepish, calculated look.

"Another night," Isabelle quickly assured Helen. "We would love to have you, if the Captain gives his permission, of course."

"Oh, John won't say no." Helen grinned.

"Before you go, you must let me give you a piece of that pie, Miss Helen. You can eat it tomorrow; can't she, ma'am?"

"Of course. Thank you. But we really must be leaving now, Helen. It's late, and I'm sure Mr. Ketch and Isabelle are as ready for bed as I am."

A certain hint of curiosity in Maria's glance made Ketch uncomfortable, so with relief he escorted them to the door, Helen with pie in hand.

***

With great anticipation over the next days, Isabelle awaited news from downriver. Every evening, she would rush home in hopes that Ketch had received word. When they heard nothing, she appreciated his efforts to buoy her spirits but sensed that the lack of response from Waterston failed to surprise him. She pressed him for details about her mother's new master and learned that Malachi Waterston was a stern but fair man, information that soothed her anxiety since coming to Leighlin.

"Helen came to see me today," Isabelle said one evening as she cleared the table after supper. "She asked me to teach her to sew a sweetgrass basket."

"The child loves makin' new friends. She has little contact with others outside Leighlin. 'Tis good that she's taken a likin' to you. That'll only help when it comes to our master."

"Helen's not at all what I expected. Any white child I've ever come across seemed mean-spirited. Well, at least to slaves."

"She's a sweet creature, true enough." His voice trailed off, and a powerful wave of melancholy swept over his face. His reverie was brief, and he appeared sheepish to find Isabelle studying him. A brief smile touched his lips. "I had a wee sister; Helen makes me think of her. Well, I mean, if she had lived to see Helen's age."

Isabelle drew closer, amazed to hear him reveal such a thing. "What happened to her?"

The smile vanished, and he stared at the table, suddenly hard and distant. "Her father drowned her. Tossed her into the River Thames like so much garbage right after she was birthed, the fucking bastard. We didn't have no money at the time to feed another mouth, he said. Claimed he knew a woman what could find Sophia a good home. But 'twas a lie. I followed him and saw what he did. It happened so fast, I couldn't stop him."

A chill invaded the room. Isabelle tried to think of something to say, but his revelation and obvious hatred for the man left her speechless. Ketch went to the hearth to absently stir the embers, prodding the coals to a glowing orange.

Isabelle could tell that he would volunteer no further revelations about his sister. She searched for a way to re-establish the feeling of goodwill that had thus far been pervasive. Gently, she suggested, "Helen is like a sister, isn't she? She loves you very much, like a brother. It's so plain to see."

Returning to his chair, he waved a dismissive hand.

Isabelle waited a moment before continuing with a confident, lighter air. "Mama told me that animals and children are good judges of a person's worth."

Ketch gave a dry laugh, though his tone lacked ridicule.

"It's true," she insisted. "You would think so too if you just thought about it for a minute."

"So, should I ask the chickens what they think of me new wife?"

Isabelle's face reddened. "Not a bird. She meant smarter animals like dogs and horses. Haven't you ever noticed? Not even with children?"

"Can't say I have. But then I'm a simple man. Only womenfolk care to spend time on such ideas."

"Well, I wager Helen is a good judge of character. Children are pure. They see the truth. And she sees you as good."

"Helen's mother sheltered her from the world's evil. She knows nothin' of cruelty beyond losin' her parents, so her judgment might not be as reliable as you think, Izzy."

Although usually careful to monitor any show of her true spirit around whites, she refused to hide her scowl at his cynicism. She put the last of the dishes into her wash basin and was about to turn away when he said her name again, this time with a harshness that pulled her attention to him.

"Don't make me into somethin' I'm not, Izzy. It won't serve neither one of us."

Footsteps on the front porch interrupted him, and Isabelle was glad to have a reason to turn away from his disturbing look. When she answered the door, her heart leapt with anticipation at the sight of Maria. But she remembered herself and took a step back to curtsey. "Good evening, ma'am."

"Good evening. Oh, I'm sorry; I didn't mean to interrupt your meal—"

Ketch came around the table. "We was finished. Come in." He sounded equally relieved to have been interrupted.

Maria entered. "I have news for you, good news."

"About my mother?" Isabelle asked in an eager rush.

"Yes. I received a response from Mr. Waterston. He said you're both welcome to visit a week from this Sunday."

"Oh..." Isabelle clasped her hands, eyes promptly brimming, lips tight together to refrain from an even more jubilant exclamation. Desperate to express her gratitude to Ketch and her mistress, she knew no words could suffice. So, without thought of anything but that need, she raised herself on tiptoe and kissed Ketch's cheek. It was but a fleeting thing. When she stepped back, he stood stiff as an old tree. Embarrassed, she wiped at her eyes and turned back to Maria, afraid her choice had been the wrong one.

"Thank you so very much, ma'am. Both you and the Captain. I can't tell you how much this means to me."

Maria did not seem as astonished by Isabelle's physical display as Ketch did. In fact, she tried to hide a grin with one hand until she managed to defeat it then said, "Before I go, I promised Helen that I would ask if she might spend the night with you tomorrow."

Isabelle welcomed the idea, for it would give her an opportunity to show Maria appreciation for her benevolence. But because she knew such an acceptance must come from her husband, she turned back to Ketch. He still looked out of sorts, but she could not discern whether he was angry because of her kiss or merely taken aback.

"I'll understand if you say no," Maria said.

Isabelle could not interpret with any confidence the hint of shyness in her mistress's tone. But it made her wonder if Maria suspected the true nature of their cohabitation. Ketch finally snapped out of his haze to assure Maria that Helen would be welcomed heartily.

After Maria left, Ketch said nothing while Isabelle washed their few dishes and utensils—she had her own set now, for Ketch had insisted that she no longer eat with her fingers.

She could barely contain her excitement over the news of being able to see her mother again, but she somehow held her tongue, sensing her husband's unrest. Was it her impetuous kiss that disturbed him or was he worried about Helen's visit, for what if the clever child figured out that they slept in separate beds? The girl might ask difficult questions and take her observations back to the Big House. Was it that reality that caused him to light his pipe and retire to the porch with a mug of rum? Or was it the memory of his lost sister? He did not invite Isabelle out with him, and his reticence tarnished her happiness. She decided it best to leave him alone, and so she spent the rest of the evening planning and preparing for the sweets she would bake for Helen.

CHAPTER 17

While Isabelle worked the next morning, she kept thinking about the coming evening when Helen would visit. She was so distracted during her milling that Gabriel often berated her slow pace. Thankfully, on Saturdays, the hands only worked half days, so in what seemed no time at all she was racing home to begin baking pecan pie and apple fritters for Helen.

She looked forward to the child's arrival and the ease Helen would provide to the household, especially considering the mild tension that remained this morning because of her impetuous kiss the previous evening. Helen stirred something deep within Ketch, something whose origins Isabelle could only guess were rooted in his brief and tragic relationship with his sister. If anyone truly held any power over Ketch, it was that golden-haired girl. Helen's love for him and, more importantly, his love in return gave credibility to Isabelle's belief that her husband was not the cold-blooded fiend the people claimed him to be. She also hoped Helen would so enjoy her visit that she would return to the Big House and give her brother and sister-in-law a glowing report. Isabelle wanted this not only for herself but for Ketch as well, for she sensed his desire to repair the damage he had caused with both master and mistress.

And what of the sleeping arrangements? Helen would be ensconced in her old bedchamber, leaving Isabelle no choice but to spend the night in her husband's chamber. Would he take advantage of this opportunity? Yet, even if tempted, he surely would abstain with Helen so close by.

That evening, just after an early, quiet supper, she and Ketch heard Helen's excited voice outside. Both hurried to the porch. To Isabelle's surprise, she found her master, not Maria, escorting Helen.

When the child saw them, she cried out and rushed up the steps with open arms. Isabelle bent down to receive the embrace and wondered what she had done to earn such affection. With pleasure over Helen's demonstration in front of her brother, Isabelle looked at Ketch, who smiled, obviously approving.

The Captain's expression was neither sour nor inviting as he handed a small valise to Ketch. With incongruous clarity, Isabelle remembered an Indian she had seen on one of the Cooper River plantations—a slave, for many Carolina planters chose to use natives to work their land rather than import Africans. The Captain, with his skin tone deepened by the brutal Carolina sun, his dark eyes, high cheekbones, straight nose, and defined lips, looked akin to that mysterious savage, a man she had thought graceful and attractive. Now those Indian-brown eyes reflected unrest. Obviously, tonight's arrangement fell short of her master's approval. Isabelle wondered if he also knew about Maria's letter to Mr. Waterston and their impending visit to his home. Would he be displeased?

The young man instructed Ketch, "Bring Helen by the house tomorrow morn. Don't feel obliged to let her monopolize your day off."

Isabelle hastened to assure him. "We don't mind, sir."

"Helen." The Captain bent down as his sister turned to him. "Mind your manners, young lady, and do as you're told." He kissed her cheek.

She indulged him with a sigh of capitulation and kissed him back. "I will."

"Right, then." He tweaked her fleshy cheek and straightened. "Good night."

As the Captain trailed off into the gray dusk of a cloudy evening, Helen swiped the valise from Ketch and hurried into the house. "I brought some toys, Isabelle," she called. "Would you like to play with me?"

Isabelle followed Helen inside, saying, "First, wouldn't you like some apple fritters and cider?"

Helen kept them up far beyond any prudent hour, first chattering over sweets and cider before showing Isabelle the toys she had brought with her, including the wooden horses Ketch had carved. Isabelle admired the detail, wondering how he had managed with his disability, though she repressed the question for fear of hurting his feelings and embarrassing him in front of Helen. What an artisan he must have been when blessed with two hands.

Helen also spent a great deal of time regaling Isabelle with tales of Ketch's heroic exploits, tales that made him squirm and caution her against exaggerating. She also wove stories about her brother, stories that revealed a special bond and humanized Leighlin's master, making it difficult for Isabelle to equate him with Ketch's flogger. From where Ketch sat in a chair near the fireplace, he did not appear to listen, perhaps lacked the desire, as he nursed a mug of rum and watched the two females at the table.

At last, Isabelle insisted the child retire. "What will your brother say when you can barely keep your eyes open at dinner tomorrow? He won't let you visit us no more."

"Will you read me a story? I brought some books."

"I can't read, Miss Helen."

"You can't?" The child seemed amazed. "Mamma knew how to read. So do Maria and Miss Margaret."

"My husband knows how to read," Isabelle proudly stated to distract. "Perhaps he'll read to you."

Ketch cleared his throat and sat up. "Miss Helen knows I'm no hand at readin'."

"We can read together," Helen pronounced. "I'll help you with the big words."

Isabelle stifled a giggle. She eased Helen from her lap, the girl's weight nearly having put her legs to sleep.

"Let's get you ready for bed, then my husband can come read to us."

Ketch tipped back his drink to drain it while Isabelle ushered Helen to her bedchamber. Once washed and dressed for bed, Helen shouted out to him, "Come read to me, Mr. Ketch!"

He shuffled into the chamber where the glow of oil lamp and candles fell across Helen in bed with her bear and a book. Ketch's smile seemed forced to Isabelle, who sat in a chair nearby, as expectant as Helen. She wished he were more engaged with Helen's visit, though she knew his mood was not in any way a reflection upon the child. Something else was troubling him, something that she realized went beyond her kiss. If only she understood him well enough to know for certain what that something was.

Ketch settled upon the bed, leaving ample space between him and Helen, but the child crawled over to sit as close as she could against his limbless right side. She showed no aversion to his stump, something Isabelle thought mature and kind for one her age. If anything, judging by her earlier narrative, Helen still felt responsible for her part in the loss of his arm.

Helen opened the storybook. "Can you see the words, Mr. Ketch?"

He squinted. "Aye."

"Isabelle." She patted the bed. "Come sit next to me."

Isabelle glanced at Ketch, who neither encouraged nor discouraged her. Warily, she joined them. The bed protested their combined weight but managed to support them. As if having accomplished something momentous, Helen smiled up at each of them before she instructed Ketch to commence.

To his apparent relief, Ketch's tenure as reader was short-lived. Helen grew impatient with his stops and starts and struggles with pronunciation and so took over reading aloud. Enthralled by the child's ability and by the dark squiggles and angles of the letters as well as the illustrations, Isabelle watched each page turn, wished she, too, could decipher what was written there.

Once, she caught Ketch's attention upon her, almost admiring. She smiled before returning her eyes to Helen lest she embarrass him. This small, odd, family-like moment filled her with contentment, reminded her of nights when her mother and William used to tell stories of their homeland and of trickster animal characters who outsmarted other animals and masters alike. Equally, she enjoyed the sight of her husband's obvious, albeit somewhat awkward, intimacy with Helen. Perhaps he was just as starved as she for tenderness, and Helen offered that to both of them freely and innocently. Maybe Helen's affection could help melt away some of Ketch's defenses.

Before Helen reached the end of her storybook, her eyelids drooped lower and lower, her words slowing, interrupted by yawns. She leaned even more into Ketch, and Isabelle could tell the child would soon fall asleep against him. Perhaps that was her goal. Gently, Ketch took the book from her.

"Time for bed, Miss Helen. Izzy looks as tired as you."

"Izzy…" Helen smiled sleepily at her hostess, who also yawned. "May I call you Izzy, too?"

Isabelle returned her smile. "Of course, you can, lamb."

Pure joy gave momentary life to Helen's blue eyes. "My daddy used to call me lamb."

"Miss Helen, would you like Izzy to sleep with you? You two could use t'other bed—'tis bigger—and I'll sleep here."

As Isabelle stood, Helen insisted, "I don't mind staying here by myself. I have Howard. This used to be my chamber before, remember."

"Of course. I just thought—"

She halted Ketch's words with a hug and a kiss on the cheek. "Good night, Mr. Ketch." She crawled up to her pillow, and Isabelle helped her settle beneath her blanket.

Ketch set the storybook on a dresser before shutting the two windows against the October night's deepening damp. Then he waited at the door for Isabelle, who picked up the lamp, said a final good night to their guest, and followed him into his chamber. Hesitant, she closed the door behind them.

Ketch moved to a chest under the side window. He opened it and removed a couple of blankets which he proceeded to spread upon the floor near the chest.

Without looking at Isabelle, he quietly said, "Take the bed."

"But it's your bed. I can sleep on the floor."

Gruffly, he said, "You'll sleep in the bed, damn it. Put out that light."

After such a pleasant evening, his curtness bruised her. She extinguished the lamp as a lump rose in her throat. He lay down upon the blankets without removing any of his clothes. She considered doing the same but decided in the blackness to strip to her shift before crawling under the blanket, knowing warm, restrictive clothes would keep her from sleep.

For a few minutes, there was only silence within and the sounds of crickets and tree frogs without. Isabelle lay on her side, curled up and facing the wall, Ketch's scent heavy upon the pillow and the bedding. She considered offering him the pillow but feared another rebuke. The harshness of his voice rang in her ears, pained her heart. Why was he so difficult? She had done nothing to earn such treatment. His unfairness stirred her pride, and she knew she could no longer be silent.

"Why do I displease you so?"

His blankets stirred but he made no reply, stoking her frustration even more.

"Is it because of my color?"

"No." He sounded almost rueful.

"Do you regret marrying me?"

"No."

"Is it—"

"Avast, Izzy."

She had no idea what that word meant—she had heard it aboard the *Adventuress*—but she could decipher its meaning in tone.

As if to make sure there was no movement in the other room, Ketch waited then quieted his voice before continuing, "The only thing that displeases me about you is yer always askin' questions. Now, quit yer frettin' and go to sleep, d'ye hear?"

She emitted a heavy sigh and said nothing more. Through the darkness, she felt his gaze upon her. Never had she known anyone so troublesome to figure out, especially a man. Just when she felt close to discovering who he really was, he turned a corner and doubled back on her, nearly frightening her with his obscurity and unpredictable nature. What made him lie in isolation across the chamber from her? What sort of man could deny such an opportunity? And would he remain there even if she invited him into her bed? What would he do if she went to him instead, if she removed her shift right in front of him and offered herself? But her fear of what she might discover outweighed her frustrated curiosity. So, she shut her mind to his peculiarities and closed her eyes.

***

Ketch spent most of the next day safely hidden away in the carpenter's shed, crafting a rocking chair for Isabelle. He hoped that by working on something destined for her enjoyment he would somehow feel less guilty about his uncivil conduct of the night before. But, as the day progressed, even the concentration required by this task fell short of providing the balm he desired.

Last night, he had slept little with her in his chamber, especially with the memory of her kiss still warm upon his cheek, a sensation that had taunted him ever since. Sharing the same house was temptation enough, but her sleeping in his bed had been an intolerable torment. When he anticipated detecting her scent left upon his pillow, he nearly flung his hammer across the stable-yard. Perhaps it was best that he had behaved in such a manner last night, for he needed to keep that distance, both emotionally and physically. While he held no delusions that she might now or later have feelings for him, he could not take the chance of letting down his guard lest his base desires send him along that dangerous path, a path that would only lead to pain for both of them.

By the time he returned home close to dark, Isabelle had already gone to bed, sheltered behind her closed door. He frowned at the sight.

The next night, he avoided her again by gambling with Willis, Samuel, and the others in Leighlin House's lower level until nearly midnight.

Come morning, Isabelle made his breakfast, and they exchanged a few perfunctory words before going their separate ways. Feeling defeated, Ketch vowed that this evening he would put on a cheerful face and bring her focus back to what had made her so happy—the upcoming visit to Charles Town.

For Isabelle's sake, he looked forward to the reunion with her mother, but, for his own part, he considered the coming visit with trepidation. While he was many things, an accomplished actor he was not. He regretted this deception in front of Malachi Waterston or anyone else, for that matter. It was not conscience speaking but instead his aversion to pretense. He had yet to speak with Isabelle about whether the truth of their union could be shared with her mother, though he suspected Isabelle would be reluctant to deceive her. Regardless of the reality being revealed or hidden, once Isabelle's mother caught sight of the abominable-looking one-armed white cur her daughter had tied herself to, she would either faint or burst into tears and demand that Isabelle end this. Yet, maybe after this visit they would see very little of Louisa. Surely Waterston would avoid allowing further intrusion. The fact that his response to Ketch's letter had lacked an invitation revealed his reluctance. No, Waterston's generosity stemmed from his relationship with the Mallorys, pure and simple. Maria might even have been so bold as to assert in her letter that her husband encouraged the reunion between slave girl and mother. Maria was, after all, tenacious in whatever cause she championed.

When he came home that evening, he had barely gotten through the door and washed his face before he heard Hiram Willis roaring his name through the open front windows. The overseer repeated the hail as he drew closer. Alarmed, Ketch hurried to the front room as uneven footfalls climbed the porch steps.

He opened the door to find Willis in front of him, face boiled red with anger, hand clamped around Isabelle's arm. The girl stood as far from the overseer as his grip allowed, and the anxiety on her dirty face deepened when her gaze swung to her husband, her right eye swollen and discolored. Her dress was torn and soiled, her apron gone. Before Ketch could utter a word, Willis jerked Isabelle forward against him. Ketch reached to steady her, but she pushed past him and fled to her chamber.

"What's the meaning o' this?" Ketch growled in the older man's face.

"That little…"

Ketch swelled above him, and Willis reconsidered his words.

"She caused a stir today with that sharp tongue of hers. She set upon one of t'other wenches like a she-bear. Nigh scalped the bitch and tried to put out her eyes, troublesome little…" His lips tightened into a straight line. "The Captain knows of it. I wasn't going to give him another chance to flay me, by God."

Ketch fought against his desire to throw the man off the porch. He said nothing, waited until Willis had given him a final glare and tramped down the steps.

He found Isabelle on the back porch, hunched upon the top step. The damaged neckline of her dress had slipped down to reveal her smooth, brown shoulder. With a start, she faced him, as if to ward off an anticipated blow. Her dread took Ketch aback. Obviously, someone had put the fear of God into her before she was returned to him, either the other slaves or Gabriel or Willis, tormenting her with ideas of being sent away for the trouble she had caused today or of the violence her husband would wreak upon her for it.

He calmed himself, never easily done once his blood had been stirred, and the sight of Willis manhandling Isabelle had certainly set it to boiling.

"Izzy, what happened?" in as even and non-threatening a voice as he could conjure.

Isabelle said nothing, seemed to blend into the falling night. To give her time to gather her thoughts, he returned to the house to retrieve a wet cloth.

"Here, put this against yer eye. 'Twill help with the swelling."

She studied the cloth and then him before taking it. Gingerly, she placed it against the red and purple eyelid and winced. To appear less intimidating, Ketch sat across the step from her, struggled again with the rage that demanded revenge. Perhaps that was what Willis and the others wanted—for him to lose control again and condemn himself as well as his wife.

"Izzy," he said, softer. "You don't hafta be afrighted o' me. I just want to know what happened. Willis told me you was in a scrap."

She took a deep breath, nodded.

"Why?"

Her left eye flashed at him with as much shame as apprehension, perhaps more so. "They're always saying such horrible things. I'm used to hearing it…when it comes to me, but…" She removed the cloth and frowned at it before holding it back in place. "Hannah…she hates me even more now because of Ezekiel. I finally had enough of her mouth. Shoved it in the dirt, I did, to shut her up."

Ketch smiled at her pluck. "And what was it she said that made her deservin' of a dirt feast?"

"It don't matter now. It's all just lies to hurt me."

"If 'tis all a lie, then why won't you tell me what she said?"

Isabelle frowned and looked off into the trees beyond the privy.

She muttered, "It was about you."

"Nothin' you haven't heard before, I'm sure." The idea of her protecting his honor amused and surprised him.

She fidgeted with her wedding band. Although the rest of her had been sullied from the fight, somehow the ring lacked any dirt. "I reckon things is different now. I mean, what kind of wife would I be if I stood there and let her tongue wag without giving her a piece of my mind?"

"Izzy, you don't have to try to convince them about our marriage. The only one we need to worry 'bout keepin' convinced is yer master. And he won't be too pleased to hear what Willis had to say about yer scrap. You need to keep out o' trouble lest he punish you. Remember, you may be me wife but yer Leighlin's property still, so I can't protect you from the Captain."

Fear returned to her eyes. "Do you think he won't let me visit Mama now?"

"Hard tellin'. We'll just have to wait and see. In the meantime, mind yerself. Let them wenches say whatever they like about me. They aim to rile you." With a tired sigh, he stood. "Now go change out o' that dress and soak that eye some more. I'll buy you some calico and you can make yerself a couple new frocks." He fabricated a smile to ease her. "That'll give Hannah somethin' to talk about, aye?"

Agape, she stared at him with the cloth limp in her hand and dripping onto the steps. She seemed to catch up with his words, and a small smile trembled on her pretty lips. He could see the nervous tension drain from her, leaving her exhausted and now fully aware of the aches and pains in her body.

"Thank you," she said near a whisper.

He paused in the doorway. "Tomorrow I'll talk to Samuel about gettin' you out o' that field and into the house."

Without waiting for her reaction or possible caution against such an endeavor, he stepped back into the cabin.

***

Ketch expected Jack Mallory to berate him for Isabelle's recent behavior, but two days passed with no summons to Leighlin House. In the meantime, Samuel took Ketch's petition for Isabelle to become a house servant before Maria. In like fashion, no reaction came from Leighlin House. But Ketch cautioned himself against discouragement, for if Maria were to champion Isabelle's cause, she would require some time to convince her husband of the proposal's merits.

Much to Isabelle's relief, permission to visit her mother was not rescinded, and when Sunday finally arrived, she emerged from her chamber wearing the green dress Maria had given her. When she had last worn the dress, she had been weak and pallid with seasickness yet had still looked beautiful. Now, even the yellowish gray bruising around her eye could not detract from her bright smile of anticipation. The sight nearly caused Ketch's knees to give way and drove his passion for her to new heights. For his own part, he had donned his finest as well, the same worn on his wedding day.

Self-conscious, Isabelle touched the hat that graced her head instead of the usual scarf. It had been dyed green, close to the same color as her dress.

"Do you like it?"

He smiled, more so because of her happiness than any opinion of the hat. "Aye. Miss Maria did a fine job."

Earlier in the week, Margaret Wylder had visited the Mallorys, wearing a stylish hat that earned Isabelle's admiration. She had mentioned this to Ketch, so he had decided to surprise her with a hat of her own to wear to Charles Town. He had approached Maria with the request to have one fashioned that would match Isabelle's dress. The result was this handsome creation with a dark blue ribbon around the crown and threaded down through the brim on either side to tie under her chin. Tucked in the crown were two peacock feathers, one longer than the other, nearly matching the blue of the ribbon. When he had presented it to her after breakfast, he feared another impetuous kiss, but Isabelle managed to refrain and instead danced about the room with her "going to town" hat in outstretched hands, admiring it and thanking him profusely.

"What a pair we are," he said now. "You with yer black eye and me with stripes upon me back."

"You must let me plait your hair like Miss Helen taught me."

She crossed the room, holding a dark ribbon, and Ketch could sense that resistance would be futile. His discomfiture was not simply from having his flawed face made conspicuous but from having Isabelle so close and almost intimate. His tie mates had always been shipmates or Helen while ashore and Maria on one or two occasions, which had been uncomfortable enough. But Isabelle looked so pleased when she finished her work and stepped back that he did not have the heart to show anything but gratitude.

"Now you look like a real gentleman," she declared, to which Ketch laughed heartily.

The *Nymph* lay tied up at the landing, empty and deserted as on most Sundays. Leighlin's smaller craft were gone, save for one, for Jack Mallory always provided passes to a select number of his slaves to travel the river and visit friends on Sundays. All that was left for Ketch was a small skiff, which lacked even a sail, so he had hired one of Latiffe's hands as oarsman. The young man awaited them on the dock. Having a third party for the four-hour journey would be awkward at best, but he had no choice. At least the tide and breeze would speed them along, and the temperature was moderate, made even more pleasant by a thin overcast.

When Isabelle stepped onto the dock, the oarsman's eyes nearly started out of his dark skull, and his mouth dropped open with shocked admiration. Seeing Ketch's glare, he quickly recovered and looked elsewhere.

During the uneventful journey downriver, Ketch often found himself dozing. Whenever he woke up, he found Isabelle either looking thoughtfully into the distance or staring down at her lap where her fingers moved nervously, often playing with her wedding ring.

He knew her concern over Louisa's reaction to her new son-in-law tainted her eagerness for the visit, though Isabelle denied any such anxiety. Isabelle had decided to tell Louisa the truth of their union, though the truth would exclude the fact that Isabelle's second husband had murdered her first. To Isabelle, concealing some of the facts was preferable to deceiving her mother completely. Ketch had his own reservations, for he feared Louisa might inadvertently expose the falseness of their marriage to someone like Waterston or his wife, who in turn might speak of it to Jack Mallory. Or, if she disapproved of her daughter's decision, such a revelation would be a way to free Isabelle from any rights he had to her.

During the final, sweeping bend of the Ashley River, Ketch gestured to his right. "That there's Albemerle Point, Izzy. Charles Town's first settlement was there one score and three years ago afore they moved across the river to the peninsula."

"Why didn't they stay there?"

"Lots o' reasons, I reckon, one bein' the place where the new town is settin' gives better access to the harbor and the Cooper River on t'other side of the peninsula."

That expansive harbor now opened before them as the skiff encountered choppier waters, causing the oarsman to apply greater strength to his duties. Isabelle paled and gripped the nearest gunwale but showed no worsening symptoms reminiscent of her wedding voyage. They stuck close to the shoreline, well clear of the traffic of sea-faring vessels and others of the river trade, all dimensions and rig, dozens of them, some leaving on the last of the ebb, others at anchor.

Once around the tip of the peninsula, the wharves came into view. By day, commerce occupied the waterfront while by night the predominant enterprises of the town were taverns and brothels, an astonishing number for a town of just over twelve hundred souls. Sailors made up a large transient population that contributed to the lucrative nature of the alehouses and what naturally came with them.

As they pulled toward shore just this side of the wharves, Ketch noticed the impatient flutter of Isabelle's hands in her lap. She nearly stood before the boat had been driven upon the shingle but wisely resumed her seat when she almost fell overboard. She flicked a sheepish glance at Ketch, and he remembered Helen's comical words about Isabelle being a hopeless landlubber. With the boat secure, she waited for him to disembark first, then he reached for her hand and assisted her over the gunwale. The shoes Maria had given her failed to help her navigate treacherous shingle, and so Ketch offered his arm to her.

"You don't have to," said Isabelle with a glance toward the flow of humanity around the wharves.

He tried to make light of her self-deprecation. "Aye, that I do, else you'll be draggin' behind me a whole cable length."

Although she probably did not know a cable length from a broom length, her demure smile vanquished the cloud of uncertainty. She rested her right hand on his arm. Her trusting touch pleased him as they continued to the opening of the wooden palisades that surrounded the small town. By then, they were among the bustle of the docks, though on a Sunday the activity was less frantic, and the sight of Isabelle drew the attention of every sailor within view. Some elbowed each other to draw eyes to the unusual sight. Isabelle kept her head lowered, the curled brim of the hat helping to hide her face. Ketch did not know if she was trying to conceal her bruises or if their stares made her uncomfortable regardless of her battered appearance. Either way, Ketch glared back with enough malice to discourage any comments.

Once inside the palisades, they moved along the busy street that ran parallel to the waterfront. Most of the citizens wore their Sunday finest, on their way home from church and other social gatherings. Ketch recognized several of them. When they eyed Isabelle, shock registered on many faces, distaste on others. Critical female gazes raked Isabelle, the white women apparently displeased by her audacity to dress like one of them. Often their attention touched upon the bruising around Isabelle's eye. At first, Isabelle kept her head bowed and almost removed her hand from his arm, but when he discouraged her retreat with a soft growl, she remained attached to him. He wondered if her attempt to separate was born of embarrassment for being seen in his company. But, when she finally brought her head up and gave him a tiny smile, he realized that she appreciated his refusal to show shame to the townspeople. While she did not emanate self-confidence, neither did she look ashamed of either of them as she eventually met the eyes of some of the whites.

This short, three-block journey would create a whirlwind of gossip in the small community. Ketch thought in particular of the reaction among the town's whores, women to whom he had once been a challenge and a curiosity, a curiosity that eventually gained their derision and barbs because he refused to patronize them when he came into town to drink and gamble. They never would have imagined that any woman—black or white—would associate with the likes of him. The thought of their prattle, or anyone else's, did not disturb him; in fact, it satisfied him to imagine the conversation that would arise. So much for eternal bachelorhood or the rumors that he was an irredeemable sodomite.

Charles Town's homes were varied structures ranging from simple clapboard houses to the brick of more wealthy citizens like Malachi Waterston. Waterston's home stood close to its neighbors, facing the harbor and affording a pleasant view from the second story. The sparkling windows with their colorful flower boxes and freshly painted shutters and trim were open to the mild sea breeze pouring in from the east, such a blessed relief from the swamp air.

As they neared the front door, Isabelle's hand tightened to a painful grip upon Ketch's arm, and he could barely be shed of her long enough to use the brass knocker.

One of Waterston's two indentured Englishwomen answered the door. Instantly, her glance went to Isabelle, particularly to her clothing and black eye, and the judgment there was quick and sharp but mute. The young servant invited them in, saying in her Yorkshire accent, "Mr. Waterston is expecting you, sir."

The scent of dinner still lingered about the house, stirring Ketch's stomach into an embarrassing growl. But he had little time to think about the turmoil of his innards, for Malachi Waterston appeared from his study at the rear of the house.

Waterston was a tall, reedy man, his thinness more from natural physical energy than from a lack of quality victuals. His hair was a blend of black and gray, as were his thick eyebrows above a hawkish nose. His eyes, close-set and dark, did not linger upon Isabelle as he greeted them. Never an expressive man, Waterston's lack of even a welcoming façade on his angular face did not surprise Ketch, and even beyond his usual lawyer's stoicism, Ketch sensed the man's reluctance to have them in his home. Perhaps reluctance was too strong; maybe lack of enthusiasm was a fairer term.

"Good afternoon, Mr. Ketch."

"Good afternoon, sir." Ketch offered a slight bow. "This is Louisa's daughter, Isabelle."

Isabelle curtseyed in reply to Waterston's lukewarm nod. "Pleased to meet you, sir."

"Isabelle and me…we'd like to thank you for allowin' us to visit. It means the world to me wife."

An artificial smile raised the corners of Waterston's thin lips, but he did not bask in their gratitude. He glanced toward the servant lingering nearby. "Molly, see to our guests' comfort, and I shall tell Louisa of their arrival." He begrudgingly gave a small bow. "Forgive me but I have work that I must attend to. Do enjoy your visit, and please give my regards to your master when you return to Leighlin." With that, he returned to the rear of the house.

Isabelle gave Ketch a nervous look before Molly led them through the dining room, the kitchen, and the pantry then out through a back door. There, in a small, shaded space between Waterston's home and the one behind his, sat a wrought iron table with four matching white chairs. Molly offered seats in a stiff, begrudging manner before returning to the house.

Isabelle looked upward in the shadows, studying the surrounding bricks and the blue sky far above, then she smiled at Ketch. "Thank you for bringing me here."

Before he could respond, the door opened, and the black woman whom Ketch had seen with Isabelle months ago appeared. Louisa halted in the doorway in disbelief before rushing to her daughter, who nearly knocked over her chair in her haste to embrace her. By the time they took a step back, tears trembled along their eyelids, hands still clasped, Isabelle's hat askew.

"Child…your eye…"

"It's nothing, Mama." Isabelle whispered further assurances into her ear and distracted her.

Louisa cradled her daughter's face in her hands and smiled

through her tears. "I never thought I'd see you again." She pulled her back into her arms.

Louisa was slightly taller than Isabelle and thicker of bone, and certainly darker, but it was easy to see that Isabelle was her daughter—expressive eyes, high cheekbones, and tapered chin. A brown headscarf concealed her hair, hanging almost club-like behind her head where it was knotted. Her clothing matched Molly's in neatness, but her dress was the same brown as her headscarf while Molly's dress was a pale blue with a white apron.

When they finally parted, Louisa seemed to notice Ketch for the first time. Her eyes widened with barely veiled alarm, and Ketch realized Waterston had not told Louisa of his coming, perhaps had neglected to even tell her about the marriage. He steeled himself for the inevitable distress.

"Mama," Isabelle said, one arm still around her mother's waist, the other outstretched. "This is my husband—Mr. Edward Ketch."

Louisa's astonished dark gaze returned to Isabelle's blackened eye then back to Ketch with accusation and conjecture. He could tell she was a woman difficult to intimidate. Just as plain to see was the origin of Isabelle's own spirit.

Heading off any possible show of indignation, Isabelle cheerfully said, "We have him to thank for today, for us being together again. He found you."

"Pleased to meet you, ma'am." Ketch fumbled over his words. "Won't you sit down?"

He pulled out the chair closest to her. Such a display from a white man so added to her shock that she remained in place, staring at him, trying to gauge him, to know whether to loathe him or thank him. Isabelle's hands drifted to her shoulders, their force revealed in the fabric's wrinkles beneath them. She whispered again in her mother's ear, and the woman slowly sat in the chair. Ketch hoped Isabelle would now dismiss him, but instead she sat down, eyes strongly urging him to do the same. Halfheartedly, he complied.

Louisa studied the tabletop. "So…Mr. Ketch…how did you come to marry my daughter?"

Removing her hat, Isabelle rescued him. "He works at Leighlin Plantation where I live now, up the Ashley River. You heard tell of it when we was at Mr. Tom's."

"Yes…yes, I remember."

Isabelle leaned toward her mother, glanced at the door, and lowered her voice. "I have a secret to tell you, Mama, but no one must know. If my master finds out, he'll send me back to Mr. Tom."

Louisa's gaze again slipped between Ketch and her daughter, the concern there deepening.

"My master was going to send me back to Mr. Tom, but you know I can't go back there, not for nothing." She took her mother's hand. "So, Mr. Ketch...Edward...married me so's I could stay at Leighlin."

Ketch wished Isabelle would stop using his Christian name.

"Edward's helped me in all sorts of ways, even before this, Mama." Isabelle proceeded to tell of the night in the rice field when he had brought her food and drink, and of how he had brought a lantern and candles to her house, given her extra rations, and paid for Helen's basket.

Regardless of Isabelle's glowing testimonial, Ketch could see Louisa's doubts, though any hostility had nearly faded. Her cynicism was understandable—he was a man, after all, and her daughter a comely, somewhat naïve creature.

"I know what yer thinkin', ma'am," he offered. "But I promise you I'd never harm yer daughter. She may be me wife in name only, but I try to honor her in the same way."

Ketch figured Isabelle's open, hopeful expression eased Louisa for now, yet fell short of completely comforting or convincing her.

Isabelle took hold of her other hand. "But what about you, Mama? Have they been kind to you here?"

"I reckon I can't ask for no better. They wanted another pair of hands to help take care of Robert and the baby when it arrives. Mizz Sarah, she not a strong lady. She nigh passed when she had Robert; she tol' me herself. The two wenches, though, they's a different matter, but I don't let 'em trick me into no trouble. I enjoy li'l Robert, and it'll be a happy day when the baby arrives. Mr. Waterston...he a stern man, he is, but I can tell he very excited about the baby. He do love Robert so." Her fingers touched Isabelle's wedding ring, and dread crept into her tone. "Is your master a fair man, Isabelle?"

"He seems so, Mama. After all, he let me stay."

"Why was he sending you back to Mr. Tom?"

"Well, seems I got myself into a peck of trouble, Mama. You see, there was this one fellow what I took up with, but it turned out to be a horrible mistake. He used me something terrible, hurt me more than once and starved me. I got shed of him, but the Captain didn't like the fuss I caused...that and I didn't know much about tending and milling rice like he was told I did."

"So, do you work in the house?"

"No. I'm a field hand."

Louisa made a small, forlorn sound as she turned her daughter's hands over and beheld the calluses. Isabelle withdrew them and offered a wan smile of reassurance.

Ketch said, "I aim to get her into the house."

Louisa's gaze held the same concerns that had blossomed in Isabelle's eyes that day long ago on Leighlin's dock when Maria had inquired of Isabelle's skills as a house servant.

"The Captain and his wife are good folk, ma'am. Isabelle wouldn't be poorly used. In fact, our mistress has taken quite a likin' to her. Same for the Captain's wee sister."

"The Captain's wife gave me this dress, Mama. She gave it to me for my wedding...and these shoes. Wasn't that handsome of her?"

All of this seemed too much for Louisa to fully take in, and she sat in silence.

Slowly, Ketch pushed his chair back and stood. "Mebbe this would be a good time for me to leave. Then you two can have some time o' yer own to talk. Izzy, I'll wait for you out front. Take as long as you like." He gave an awkward bow. "I'm glad I was able to meet you, ma'am."

Louisa recovered enough to manage, "I'm obliged to you for bringing my daughter here, Mr. Ketch."

"Happy to do it. Mebbe we'll be able to see you again."

"I hope so."

But her hope, he suspected, was more for her daughter to return than her son-in-law.

***

As Isabelle watched Ketch depart, she hoped her mother's doubts had not been too disconcerting to him. Her mother said nothing until his steps through the kitchen could no longer be heard, then she turned back to Isabelle, a pained expression aging her face.

"Isabelle, what have you gotten yourself into, child?"

"Mama, don't fret."

"Don't fret? You've only been gone from me a short time, and now here you are married to a white man and your face is all bruised. Why wouldn't I fret?"

Isabelle manufactured a small laugh in an attempt at disinterest. "Edward didn't give me this black eye. It was that vile Hannah. She's been nothing but a thorn in my foot since I got to Leighlin, saying false

218

things about me. She's one of the reasons why none of the men there would look at me. Well, she opened her mouth one too many times, so I shut it for her. But she did get one good swing in and used her claws on my dress."

"But this man… Has he hurt you in other ways?"

"No, Mama. He hasn't touched me."

"You mean for me to believe he hasn't taken you into his bed?"

Unexpected embarrassment warmed Isabelle's cheeks. "I told you—he hasn't touched me."

"But he will. I saw how he looks at you. What will you do then?"

"Mama, please—"

"I just want to make sure you've thought this through. I know you couldn't go back to Mr. Tom. I thank God you didn't, but—"

"I would've killed myself, Mama," she said with unanticipated passion. "I always had you to go to. What would I have done without you there this time? And Ketch…Edward…everything I told you is true about him, how kind he's been to me."

"But you are a child; he is a man, Isabelle. You've saved yourself from one man, but you've put yourself in the hands of another. And now that you are his wife—truthfully or not—you will have to answer to him, in all things."

"What else could I have done? I had to help myself. I couldn't go back to Mr. Tom. Edward was all I had to protect me; you wasn't there."

The accusation, conveying the pain Isabelle had never dared acknowledge, brought her mother up short. She tried to blink away tears. Isabelle instantly regretted her words. She apologized as she held her tightly, her own tears close.

"I just don't want to see you hurt again, child. I saw it too long, and it broke my heart, every time Mr. Tom touched you."

"But Edward isn't Mr. Tom." She sat back but still held her mother's hands. "I know you think I'm foolish, but I'm not afeared of him. I've never had someone be as kind to me as he is, not since William. We seem to understand each other. Maybe it's because his people treat him like ours treat me. He had no one, and I didn't neither. Now we have each other."

"I can see he cares for you, Isabelle. But if you care only for his protection, he may resent you. Then what will happen?"

Isabelle frowned, her hands falling away.

"Isabelle." Her mother's finger tipped her chin back up, and Isabelle recognized that penetrating stare that never failed to see through falsehoods. "Do you care for him, too?"

The question took Isabelle by surprise, flustered her. She stammered, "I feel safe when I'm with him. That's all I know. You think I'm foolish. You're ashamed—"

"I am not. Don't be a goose. You did what you felt you had to do, as we all do."

"At least he made it so we're together again. And I know he'll bring me back to see you. Don't that make it worth it?"

Her mother offered an unsteady smile in return, and a tear escaped her. "Yes. It do." Gently, she pulled her back into her embrace, and Isabelle wished she never had to leave.

CHAPTER 18

She had red hair like his mother. That should have served as a warning to him, but he—young and foolish—had allowed his half-brother, Dan, to sway him. With a seductive look and a lick of her lips, the prostitute straddled him. As the intensity of her movements grew, his body responded. When intrusive thoughts slithered in, he closed his eyes, did not want to see the wild red hair or hear the sounds she made. He wanted to retreat, to stop, but his body held him prisoner, as did she.

With a brief roar, darkness slammed down upon him. Silence followed, long and cold. He heard his own breathing—deep, labored, ragged. The girl's panting had stopped. Light returned, and he saw her, dead beneath his hands. But she was not the redheaded whore. The red hair...brown now, tiny curls glistening. Her eyes—pale brown, not blue—were wide in disbelief, lifeless. Beside her lay her green hat. He stared in horror, hands dropping away from her neck, leaving behind deep scarlet impressions. He mumbled her name, over and over, reached for her, shook her, called to her, louder. Her head lolled lifelessly, the eyes continued to stare with no recognition, no light. More vigorously, he shook her, screamed her name.

"Ketch...Ketch," her voice floated to him, yet the corpse's lips did not move, life did not return. "Ketch, wake up."

He sat bolt upright in bed, gasping, sweating. A flash of light, a startled gasp beside him, someone lost in the light. The lamp moved away as Isabelle set it on the floor. Relieved and horrified, he stared at her wide eyes, eyes that glowed with blessed life.

"You was having a bad dream," Isabelle said, her hand boldly upon his arm where she sat on the edge of the bed.

He pulled away, calmed his breathing, continued to stare at her very-much-alive face in the lamplight. Her beautiful, concerned face.

He croaked, "Go back to bed."

"You called to me. You was yelling my name."

"'Twas just a nightmare."

"You sounded afrighted. I thought someone had set upon you—"

"I'm fine, Izzy. Go back to bed now."

"No," she said with surprising forcefulness. "I've heard you having nightmares before. Is it the same one?" Softly, she added, "Tell me what it was about. Why did you call my name?"

He considered her hand on his leg, felt it so plainly even through the blanket, her warmth, her genuine caring. On the journey home from Charles Town, he had sensed a change in her. Seeing her mother had infused her with confidence as well as contentment, and she looked upon him in a different way, as if some great revelation had come to her. In the skiff, when she had grown sleepy, she had asked if she could sit next to him. Not wanting to deny her in front of the boatman's ever observant eye, he had granted the request. She sat on his left side, which forced him to put his arm around her. Removing her hat, she rested her head against his shoulder.

Her lack of hesitation had taken him aback, and he knew she was becoming far too comfortable with him, a comfort encouraged by his generosity in taking her to Charles Town. Did she feel the need to reward him? Whatever her motivation, he had not known what to do about the predicament…until now, sitting here with the memory of the prostitute's death so fresh and with Isabelle awaiting his explanation. Perhaps if she knew more about the truth of him, she would not feel so at ease or so willing to touch him.

"There was this girl," he began deliberately, "she wasn't much older than you. We was in bed together. I don't know what happened, but things went black on me, and when I came to, she was dead. I had strangled her."

Isabelle's eyes widened.

"That's what I was dreamin' about, but this time in the dream it wasn't her that was dead but you."

To his consternation, Ketch detected neither revulsion nor alarm. Instead, Isabelle looked confused, as if mulling over a frustrating puzzle. "Had you quarreled with her?"

"No. She done naught to me but what I paid for."

"But there must be a reason why you don't remember, why you did it."

"Aye, there's a reason. 'Tis in me blood. The terrible things I've done, the things you've heard about…'tis all true. I didn't want to kill that girl, but I did. That's why yer not safe here. Now, please, go back to yer chamber."

"Is that why you was cross with me that night Miss Helen was here? You was afeared of me being in your chamber."

"Izzy…just go back to yer bed."

"I'm not afeared of you. I don't believe you'd hurt me."

He could see that his tactics were failing. She would remain here debating unless he did something more drastic.

"Izzy…these things, these…hopes you have in yer head about me…they're false." Brusquely, he pushed her hand away. "Now do as I say and go back to bed."

"If you was the same man what done all those things, you wouldn't have done so many good things for me."

"Don't be a fool. I did what I did for no one's sake but me own."

"I don't believe you. What purpose did it serve *you* to let me see my mother?"

He could imagine no favorable end to this ridiculous argument. He needed to remove her scantily-clad person from his sight, from his reach before her close presence, her scent drove him to regrettable action which in turn would force him to remember things he wanted only to forget.

Abruptly, he stood and pulled her to her feet. She gasped at his painful grasp. He thrust his face close to hers, spoke through bared teeth, "Get out."

She stood her ground, unnerved yet almost challenging. He towed her to the open door.

"Don't never come in here again. D'ye hear?"

Before she could recover, he pushed her out and slammed the door.

***

Demoralized, Isabelle retreated to her bed and drew her blanket close. Her heart hammered in her ears as she rubbed her sore wrist. She heard Ketch pacing in his chamber like a caged animal and wondered if he would punish her further for her intrusion. When his door abruptly opened, she held her breath, fear tightening her muscles. But he did not come after her. Instead, he fled through the back door. Perhaps he was merely going to the privy, but as time passed, she realized he had no plans to be back that night. What if he never returned? The prospect terrified her because of what it would mean for her, but more so she worried about him, about what had truly driven him from his own home.

She had been foolish to press him, especially when he was in such a vulnerable state following the nightmare, his intimate space invaded

223

without warning. She had grown to trust him, but when he had taken hold of her, the darkness in his eyes making him almost unrecognizable, she had been frightened and reminded of Ezekiel, a comparison she never wanted to make, for that would be admitting she had made the same mistake twice. She regretted her impulsive decision to touch him, but she had been desperate to reach him, to show that she wanted to help him. Considering her mother's words as well as Maria's about his feelings for her, she had thought her actions sound.

She wondered about his nightmare, of the story he had told her. Why had he killed that girl? There had to be a reason he had done it, as well as a reason why he could not remember the act. The distress that the memory still caused him told her much. Deep fear dwelled in him, a fear of himself, a self-loathing. Perhaps the nightmare explained why a man in his position of power over her had refused to act upon his base desires. And those desires were there, she knew, because his body often betrayed him in her presence.

The next morning, she awoke to a silent cabin. Outside, the kitchen house chickens had wandered under her east window, and she listened to them scratch and cluck quietly, a contented group. Far, far distant, the peacock wailed from the stable-yard. With a soft moan, Isabelle crawled out of bed and dressed for another day of work.

She found Ketch's door wide open and his bed disheveled. Where had he gone and why had he not come back? Anxious over the possible answers, she made his bed, all the while hoping he would return for his breakfast. But he did not, nor was he there a short while later when she could tarry over the meal no longer and left for the fields.

Her concern deepened when, partway through the day, Samuel rode to the south field and drew her aside to ask of her husband's whereabouts.

"He didn't come to the kiln today." Samuel accompanied his statement with a look far too probing for Isabelle's comfort.

Afraid to reveal details lest they humiliate her husband, she murmured, "I'm not sure where he is."

Thankfully, Samuel did not press her, yet she could tell he knew something was amiss. After all, he could have sent one of his hands to inquire but had come himself, showing great discretion as well as respect for his friend's privacy.

When she returned home at twilight, the cabin was quiet there in the fading light and shadows of the tall trees. Inside, the space was cool; no fire lit. Her heart sank into despair. She started for her chamber but halted when she saw Ketch's door closed. She remembered leaving it open that morning. She pressed her ear to the door and detected faint snores. Reluctantly, she retreated to her own chamber to tidy herself. Perhaps when she started dinner, he would awaken.

But Ketch never emerged. Feeling utterly defeated and responsible, Isabelle retired to her own bed after dinner and lay there listening to his snores. No dreams or nightmares awoke him. Outside, a gentle rain began to fall.

Somewhere deep in the night, before she drifted off into her own troubled dreams, Isabelle succumbed to a fateful decision.

***

When Ketch awoke the next morning, far later than normal, his head still pounded from the rum and ale he had consumed in no small quantity yesterday in Charles Town. He remembered only a few things about the spree. After drinking himself unconscious, he had awakened in the street, only to drag himself into another establishment and drink some more. The whores had baited him, said cruel things about Isabelle until he threw his tankard at them. Somehow, he had ended up aboard Wildwood's shallop, waking only after one of the crew gave him a solid nudge with a toe upon reaching Leighlin's landing. How he had found his way to his bed from there was a complete mystery.

He groaned and put his hand to his forehead, knew from the light trailing through the windows that he was already tardy for work. The scent of any breakfast that may have been prepared for him had long since been extinguished. How he wished he could remain in bed and sleep, the blanket pulled over his throbbing eyes. But he knew it would be imprudent to miss a second day of work, especially since his flight downriver had been neither sanctioned nor explained. Although certain he would pay for that impulsive indiscretion, his escape, however temporary, had been necessary after the disturbing nightmare and his discreditable treatment of Isabelle.

He fumbled his way out of bed. Having slept in his clothes, he now took the time to don a clean shirt before he left his room. The cabin was silent, Isabelle long gone to the fields. She had made breakfast. As he stared at the plate with crapulous regard, he wondered if his disappearance yesterday had relieved or worried Isabelle. Had his most recent actions convinced her that her belief in him was unfounded and ill-advised? The new stubbornness in her voice that night concerned him, that spark of spirit since seeing her mother. What had the two women talked about when he had walked away from them? Obviously, any words of caution or warning from Louisa had been ignored.

His stomach refused breakfast, so he wrapped a biscuit and some bacon in a cloth and put the food in one of Isabelle's small, lopsided sweetgrass baskets. Then he began a painful journey to the stables where he was to work with the cooper on more casks for the kiln. He was glad he could avoid traveling back into the forest today, not only because he felt so wretched but because he could postpone Samuel's displeasure. He would have time to sober up a bit and think of some excuse for shirking his duties yesterday. Revealing the truth was out of the question. He wondered if Samuel had reported his absence to Jack Mallory. Hopefully, he had held his tongue until he could speak with his wayward worker.

The day was long, the noise of hammer and adze paining him far into the afternoon. Slowly, his ears lost their sensitivity, and he began to feel human again. The cooper—a slave about Ketch's age—spoke to him only when necessary. Late in the afternoon, one of the slaves from the kiln drove up with the wagon to load the thirty-gallon pine casks that had been completed. When he saw Ketch, he looked a bit surprised but relayed no messages from Samuel.

Ketch worked until the very edge of darkness. When he dismissed the cooper and his growling stomach, Ketch stood there in the shed row for a time, allowing the sweat to cool upon his skin. The pounding in his head had receded to a dull ache, and his belly protested its emptiness. Running his sore hand through his hair, he sighed and began the trek home.

From the chimney of his cabin, a thin line of smoke ascended in a serpentine in the windless night, and the flicker of the fire within animated the front windows. The prospect of seeing Isabelle stirred him in two diverse ways. He had missed her this day, yet what would he say to her after his long absence? Would she ask her endless questions? Would she dare pick up where they had left off in their conversation about his nightmare? If so, he would have to be prepared to treat her as he had the first time, no matter how wretched it made him feel, for he could not hazard explaining the catalyst behind the prostitute's death.

When he neared the porch, he noticed a dark form sitting there, pressed up against the house, next to the chair in which Isabelle usually sat after dinner. A shapeless lump beyond the reach of the outward shine from the fireplace. Ketch's steps slowed. He heard a faint sniff, and the form moved slightly. Isabelle was sitting with her knees drawn up, dress wrapped about her legs, her arms encircling them. She remained unmoved when he said her name and stepped toward her, but her voice reached him, hollow and seemingly from another person.

"Someone is coming."

A lantern bobbed from around the kitchen house, growing brighter, larger, until Ketch made out Nahum's form. The young slave halted at the foot of the steps, lifted the lantern high so the light would reach Ketch.

"Good evening, suh," he said with a nervous bow. "Beg pardon."

"What is it, boy?" he growled.

"The Cap'n wants to see you."

Ketch glanced at Isabelle, felt a chill crawl over him. "Now?"

"Yes, suh. Directly, he say. Not a minute later."

"Very well. Tell him I'm on me way."

"No, suh. I's sorry, but he say for me not to come back without you."

Ketch realized from Isabelle's lack of reaction to Nahum's presence that she had been expecting this summons. With black misgivings, he descended the steps and started toward the looming house, Nahum trotting ahead.

***

Shifting his weight from foot to foot, Ketch waited in the Great Hall while Nahum entered the library to announce his arrival. Ketch's mind raced with wild ideas as to the reason behind the summons. One thing was certain—the revelation would be unpleasant, for there could be no positive reason for Mallory calling for him so late and with such apparent urgency.

Beyond the open door, Jack Mallory stood in the middle of the library, upon the Persian rug with its rich colors of dark red, black, and gray, colors that matched his mood. He stared sidelong at Ketch as Nahum scurried out. Then he waggled a beckoning finger, turned his back, and moved to the front of his desk. Ketch dutifully stood before him, cautioned himself against reactionary responses, come what may. A low fire had recently been started, and it crackled with fresh energy, warmed Ketch's back and threw golden light against Mallory's tanned face. The young man leaned back against the edge of the desk, hands lightly gripping the wood, the unbuttoned cuffs of his shirt draping over them, hiding his mother's bracelet. His ebony hair, parted to one side, fell forward over his left eye.

"Have you seen your wife tonight, Ketch?"

"I was just gettin' home when you sent for me."

Mallory moved behind the desk and picked up something from the floor. He carried it back to resume his same stance, this time with the item held in front of him, something once green but now crumpled and muddy. When Ketch recognized the object, his heart sank.

Mallory's monotone continued, "Why would Isabelle wear such a thing to the fields?"

"I...I don't know."

"Did you know she had worn it?"

"No. If I'd knowed she was goin' to wear it, I wouldn't have let her. It weren't meant for that."

"Why didn't you see her with it this morning? Surely you are up before she leaves."

Ketch stared at Mallory's shoes. Normally, by this time of night, Mallory dressed more casually, often wearing deerskin slippers when he sat on the rear portico with Maria. But here, when he needed to play the master and not the relaxed husband, he remained dressed almost formally except for his unbuttoned cuffs and lack of a coat.

Ketch answered, "I slept late."

"Because you got drunk in Charles Town."

"Aye," he muttered. There was no sense in lying; he had plenty of witnesses, from the crew of Wildwood's shallop to whoever may have carried him to his bed.

Mallory set the battered hat aside and crossed his arms. "You shirked your duties. You go missing and your wife's showing away incites a brawl between her and another field hand."

The realization struck Ketch now—Isabelle had worn the hat for the very purpose of instigating jealousy, perhaps spoiling for a fight over the frustration her husband had caused her.

"'Twas not Izzy's fault. I mean...'twas mine. Whatever she did, I take responsibility for it. She's upset with me, and rightly so."

"What of the time before? Was that your responsibility as well?"

"I reckon when it comes to marriage, I'm a bit akin to a landsman first put to sea—I need to find me sea legs. It has caused some trouble 'twixt me and Izzy. But she's not to blame."

Some of the hardness left Mallory's gaze. Perhaps he reflected upon his own marital difficulties in the past. It was then that Ketch was reminded of the things he and the boy had in common—their love for Helen and her mother, and now marriage, both to challenging women. If nothing else swayed Mallory toward clemency, perhaps their shared trials as husbands would.

The young man moved around the desk at a slow pace perhaps

calculated to make his worker sweat. With a tired sigh, Mallory sank into his chair, and Ketch again considered how much the boy had aged since taking over Leighlin.

"A few days ago, Maria came to me and said she wanted to bring Isabelle into the house as a servant. You can imagine I wasn't overly receptive to the idea. With the trouble surrounding Isabelle since she got here, it might look to the others to be a reward for bad behavior. And now there's this."

Ketch fought down the immediate urge to offer his own petition on Isabelle's behalf, for he knew this had to be anyone's idea but his own. Was Mallory's apparent ignorance of the idea's origin due to Maria's discretion or Samuel's? Perhaps both.

"I told Maria I would consider it, after the harvest. But now..." He looked past Ketch, toward the fire. "Gabriel feels his hands are tied when it comes to disciplining Isabelle, because of you being her husband, of course. The other drivers will feel the same if I put her with another gang, so... It appears my hand has been forced."

Ketch held his breath.

"With Maria and Helen united in this crusade, I stand little chance. Seems I've been in this position before, haven't I?"

The chastisement was not lost upon Ketch. Anxiously, Ketch stroked his beard, awaiting the final decision, forcing himself to remain passive.

"'Tis against my better judgment, and my resources, to give Isabelle this chance, but...I will grant her a fortnight here to show her true colors. If there is one whiff of trouble, by God, that will be the end of it, and I'll be left with little choice but to replace her with a more productive servant and suffer the wrath of my family. Do you understand?"

"Aye."

"I'll leave you and Maria to impress this upon Isabelle."

"I will, straight away." He saw the boy's familiar unease with the whole reality of governing the lives of so many others. Perhaps that discomfort had helped stay his hand with Isabelle, now as well as before.

"I expect improvement from you as well. Neglecting your duties won't be tolerated. If a squabble with your wife sends you diving into a bottle, you will find your liver pickled in a month's time and yourself off this plantation. Am I clear?"

"Aye." The ease of his humility amazed Ketch, but Mallory's decision so relieved him that he would have kissed the boy if it would have helped. "I'm sure I'll...learn the ropes eventually, and things'll smooth out."

Something close to good-natured skepticism twisted Mallory's lips. "When it comes to marriage, don't bet on fair-weather sailing."

***

As Ketch returned to the cabin, he caught distant singing from the slave settlement. A small, sad sound, almost haunting. He shivered. He could not discern whether they sang in their native tongue or not. Could Isabelle hear the song? Did she miss being among her people? Is that what had driven her into today's confrontation, the frustration of forever being caught between two worlds?

He was surprised to find her where he had left her on the porch. She remained unmoved by his approach. The firelight from within the cabin burnished the top of her head while throwing her face into shadow.

Before he could speak, she softly asked, "Is the Captain going to send me away?"

"No, but he was vexed 'bout what happened today...and before." He paused. "Are you hurt?"

She wiped at her eyes, mumbled, "Just some scratches."

Tentative, he stepped past her to sit in the chair. He leaned forward, stared into the night then down at her, tried to see her face. "Izzy. Why did you wear yer goin'-to-town hat to the field this morn?"

Her feet shuffled beneath her skirt, and she swiped a hand under her nose. "They said you runned away and got drunk, and that I must be no kind of wife for a man to do that."

"Izzy—"

"Why did you run away?"

Without thinking, he left the chair and knelt before her on one knee. He stopped short of taking her hand. "Izzy. What I did wasn't 'cause o' you, hear? 'Tis just...well, I'm no hand at bein' a proper husband. If what you did today was on purpose, because o' me, to get sent away...well, I reckon I wouldn't blame you if you wanted to leave."

"I don't want to. But it seems whatever I do upsets you." Her voice fell. "I'm sorry the hat got ruined."

To keep from touching her, he rubbed his beard in agitation, wished he could pull her to him, but after what he had done two nights ago, he had no right to consider anything of the sort.

"Do you know why Hannah hates me so much?" she quietly asked. "I'm sure you've heard."

"I don't listen to no gossip."

"Ever since we was young 'uns in Barbados, she's hated me. She was an orphan, and she was jealous of me having a mama, and William was like a father to me. Then, when we was at Mr. Tom's…" She hesitated, bowing her head, her voice growing faint. "She reckoned I let him have his way with me just to gain his favor, but…I had no choice. If I hadn't done what he said, he'd have killed Mama. But Hannah made everyone think it was all my idea. Mr. Tom's wife, she spent most of her time in town at her sister's in the summer 'cause she couldn't abide the heat and swamp air and bugs. So there was no one to stop him."

Although Ketch had heard the rumors about Clark, to hear the truth and its direct impact on Isabelle set his blood racing and clenched his fist, but he held his tongue, sensing she had more to say.

"I thought I'd been ruined forever, that I'd never be no good to another man and that I wouldn't…that I couldn't be with another man. But Mama always told me it didn't have to be that way, that it hadn't been that way with her, even after what my father done to her, 'cause she wouldn't let it be that way. And that's how she fell in love with William when we was in Barbados."

"What happened to him?"

"He died right before we left. Got burned so bad by the water used to boil the sugar cane. He lived a couple days. It was horrible."

"I'm sorry."

"We all have secrets, Ketch. Now you know mine."

He suspected her statement to be purposeful and leading, as was her revelation. Her undying curiosity about him was no casual desire to learn his secrets but was born of true concern, a realization that puzzled Ketch. Clearly, she was clever enough to know his troubles stemmed from more than the inexplicable murder of the prostitute.

He got to his feet, sore from the day's work, and put a safe amount of distance between them. "Tomorrow yer to report to the house. The Captain's decided to give you a chance to work there. A fortnight, he said. If you stay out o' trouble and tend to yer duties, then he'll keep you at Leighlin."

Stiffly, Isabelle stood and smoothed her apron.

"Are you still afeared to work there?"

"No," she murmured in a tone from which he could detect neither displeasure nor relief. "Not no more."

"Good." He started toward the door but hesitated. He knew he should say nothing more and enter the cabin, but he felt compelled to offer some kernel of concession for having put her in this precarious situation. "Izzy, I don't mean to be cruel to you, but there's some things I can't tell you. It'd serve neither one of us. I hope you can understand that."

With no desire to tarry for her response, he retreated into the cabin where his cold supper awaited.

CHAPTER 19

Ketch's offer to escort Isabelle to the Big House pleased her, for she found herself exceedingly nervous come morning. The surprising announcement of her new occupation had prompted a mixture of emotions. Although thankful that she would no longer need to endure the harvest and the hostility of field hands like Hannah, she was apprehensive about the unknown—not the work itself but those who inhabited the house, both black and white. And being under special scrutiny for a fortnight added further anxiety.

"Don't fret about the Captain," Ketch had reassured her over breakfast. "He'll have little to do with your daily duties. Miss Maria will be in charge o' you. But whenever the Captain does need something, make sure you jump right to it, hear? Don't give him no reason to be vexed with you." He toyed with his food. "Izzy, you seem to have it in yer head that I want to be quit of you. That's not true. What I want is for you to do yer best for Miss Maria and her husband. I want you to be happy."

His candor filled her with hope and confidence, helped ease some of her tension. But now, as they neared Leighlin House, some of that poise slipped, and she almost reached for his hand in search of strength but managed to refrain.

When Ketch knocked upon the rear door, Thomas answered then led them into the Great Hall where the scent of breakfast drifted to them from the dining room. The tap of Isabelle's shoes on the floor startled her. Because she had not worn shoes since the wedding, they felt uncomfortably foreign.

As Thomas glided to the dining room to announce their arrival, Isabelle's wide eyes roamed the hall. Tom Clark's house was half the size of Leighlin House and was neither awe-inspiring nor decorated. She and one Cusabo Indian woman had been the only slaves to serve the Clarks. Here, there were Mary, Pip, and Abigail, as well as Thomas and Nahum. Where would she fit in? She felt the urge to flee, to return to the familiarity of the rice harvest, but Helen burst into the Great Hall from the dining room

"Izzy! You're here!"

The child rushed to them, Maria trailing behind. Helen took Isabelle's hands and danced about, causing Isabelle to laugh at her energy and exuberance.

"John just told me you was coming." As if just noticing him, Helen added, "Good morning, Mr. Ketch."

Isabelle curtseyed to Maria, who spoke with a smile. "Well, good morning to both of you." A spark of mischief brightened her dark eyes. "Were you planning on helping Isabelle with her duties, Ketch?"

He stuttered and stammered and finally said, "I just thought I'd come with her to make sure things was set with you, that you knew she was a-comin'."

"Yes, my husband informed me last night, and I was very pleased to hear the news. I'm sure this will be a blessing for everyone."

"Well, then," Ketch mumbled, "I'll be on me way." He gave Maria a small bow. Then, with a quick, hopeful glance at Isabelle, he turned and left the house.

Helen tugged Isabelle's hand. "Come along, Izzy, I'll show you the house and where everything is."

"Helen," Maria said. "We must finish our breakfast first. Isabelle can wait for us in the parlor."

Maria gestured to the room to Isabelle's left before returning to the dining room. Isabelle entered the parlor. No fire glowed there, but she could smell a fire on the opposite side in the dining room. The night had been chilly, so now a blaze would offer comfort to those at table. As her gaze roamed about the parlor, taking in the coral-colored draperies, she could hear the voices of master and mistress on the other side of the wall, punctuated by Helen's bright tones and the muted clash of utensils and dishes. She considered the childless Captain and hoped Ketch's assurances were correct.

Soon Helen appeared in a rush through a passageway door to Isabelle's left, along the north wall, surprising her; she had been unaware the dining room and parlor were connected in such a way.

"I'm done eating, Izzy! Are you ready to see the house now?"

"Helen," the Captain's smooth voice drifted through the passage, "wait for Maria, young lady. Let her finish her breakfast."

Helen made a playful face for Isabelle, who could not help but giggle. Then the child bounced onto the settee, sitting close to her.

"John's going to get a virginal and put it here in the parlor."

Helen's language astonished and alarmed Isabelle.

"Don't you know what a virginal is?" Helen asked. "It plays music. Miss Margaret has one, and she's going to teach me how to play once I get my own. Maybe she can teach you, too."

Relieved, Isabelle laughed. "I don't reckon your brother will want me spending my time learning music, Miss Helen. I'll have so many things to learn here in the house now that I'm going to serve you and your family."

When Maria arrived to take Isabelle through the house, they started on the lower level. It was strange to think of Ketch living here not long ago and of the time she had come to nurse him after the flogging. How things had changed in such a short time!

From there, they returned to the main floor where they toured the withdrawing room and the library, with a quick trip through the parlor and the side passage into the dining room. Pip and two of the women from the kitchen were clearing away the table. The women cast unsettled glances at Isabelle but nothing more. Maria frowned at them but revealed no other displeasure as she told Isabelle the times of the various meals.

When Maria saw Isabelle's attention upon the servants' dark green livery with sparkling white aprons, she said, "We shall fit you with a dress today. One of Pip's should do for now."

The young slave girl's eyes darted to Isabelle, but Isabelle could not tell if Pip was insulted or angry or both.

Like the other floors, Leighlin's topmost floor had two rooms on either side of the central ballroom. These were all bedchambers. She remembered this well from the day she had come to have her wedding dress fitted.

"We're going to have a harvest ball, aren't we, Maria?" Helen said as she danced and twirled like a butterfly across the large floor. "Mr. David and Miss Elizabeth are going to come, and Miss Margaret, and the Waterstons, too. Maybe they'll bring your mamma with them."

"Now, Helen, don't get Isabelle's hopes up. I doubt Mr. Waterston will bring Isabelle's mother. She'll be in town watching over Robert."

"They won't bring Robert?"

"Of course not, silly. The ball will be for adults only."

Helen's expression fell. "You mean I can't come?"

"You can, of course. You're going to be hostess with me, remember?"

Helen's joy returned, and she twirled until she was dizzy, morning sunlight through the upper stair hall glistening upon her golden hair. Taking Isabelle's hand, she wobbled toward the southeast bedchamber, on the river side of the house, which belonged to her. She showed Isabelle all around, introducing her toys. The horses Ketch had carved stood proudly upon one of the window seats, emblazoned with sunlight.

After Maria had shown Isabelle all the chambers as well as the tight spiral staircase that led from the master bedchamber down to each floor, the young mistress shooed Helen into the ballroom. To Isabelle's surprise, Maria closed the two of them in the master bedchamber and invited her to sit in a chair near the hearth. The night's fire had nearly faded to ashes but still emitted a subtle warmth. Maria stood near the foot of the four-poster bed. She rested her weight against the edge of the lofty mattress, and Isabelle imagined how soft the bed must be, considering its fluffed appearance. When she thought of her master and mistress together in that bed as a husband and wife should be, she felt a twinge of loneliness and almost hopelessness when she reflected upon Ketch.

"Isabelle, I'm going to have you spend the day with Mary. She's been here the longest and will give you a good overview of the duties you'll be expected to perform."

"Yes'm."

"If there are any questions you have that she can't answer, come to me before you go home tonight." She studied Isabelle before continuing, "You said before that you worked in the Clarks' household. Is that true?"

"Yes'm."

"Why didn't you tell us this when you first came to Leighlin?"

Ashamed and afraid her deception had angered her mistress, Isabelle lowered her eyes. "I was afrighted."

"Of what?"

Isabelle faltered. If she told the truth about Tom Clark, perhaps Maria would think her a threat to her husband's fidelity and send her back to Clark.

"I...I didn't know you and the Captain, ma'am, if you was kind folk or cruel. So, I thought I'd take my chances in the fields."

Nodding shallowly, Maria appear unconvinced. "I see." She toyed with the beautiful gold locket around her neck. "How much experience do you have?"

"At Mr. Tom's, it was just me and one other servant, so we did most everything 'cept cook."

"Very well." Maria paused again, and Isabelle could tell she wanted to say more but for some reason used restraint. "You don't need

236

to be afraid here, Isabelle. You will find my husband is a good man, if a bit stubborn and sometimes judgmental. As you know, he's had a couple of opportunities to turn you out but hasn't."

"Yes'm. I'm much obliged. And to you, too. I know you spoke for me. My husband told me."

"I'm sure Ketch wouldn't want to see you go any more than I would."

"Yes'm, that's what he told me."

"You can believe him, Isabelle. You're good for him, and he knows it, as do I and even my husband, though he might not admit it. Our husbands share a...difficult history. But they want the same thing—for Leighlin to flourish, especially for Helen. Sometimes, though, because of those difficulties, it's hard for them to remember that they actually have the most important thing in common."

"You care for my husband, don't you, Miss Maria?"

"Granted, your husband has caused many problems, but he's also done considerable good. Knowing him, he's not said anything to you about it but, truth be told, if not for him, Leighlin might not exist as we know it today and my husband could very well be dead. Because of Ketch, I'm standing here as Jack's wife and Helen has a bright, secure future. Even my husband understands that."

Isabelle's pride, and curiosity, swelled. "Thank you, ma'am, for your kindness, to both me and my husband. I promise I won't disappoint you again."

Maria returned Isabelle's smile. "I know you won't."

***

The weather was unusually warm and humid for November, even beneath the towering trees of the western forest. Ketch's sweaty hand took a tighter purchase on the leather lines before he pulled the mule team to a halt near the kiln. The mules willingly obeyed, tired from a long morning of hauling loads of downed timber from deep in the forest. The paths they had traveled were crude at best, barely cleared enough for the wagon to pass. Now and then, they were delayed when a wheel caught against a tree or got wedged against some other obstacle. This load would be added to what had already been gathered during the previous days when Ketch had worked with the cooper. Perhaps by the end of today there would be enough to completely fill this latest kiln. The previous burnings had yielded nigh two hundred and forty casks of tar, a number that had put a smile on Samuel's face.

237

Samuel climbed down from the wagon as the slaves trudging behind caught up with them in the clearing. "We'll break for dinner before we unload," he announced, swiping a muscled forearm across his brow.

Ketch saw to the mules' thirst with buckets of water dipped from a cask that was kept replenished at the site for both man and beast. Then he joined Samuel beneath a tall yellow pine, relieved to rest his weary back against something solid. He reached into the basket between them to retrieve his allotment of beef, peas, and cornbread packed that morning by the kitchen staff. The work gang hunkered down near the wagon, their voices low.

For the first few minutes, Ketch and Samuel were too engrossed in their food to converse. Although they had been working together for close to a month, most of their conversations had been limited to their work. The few times they spoke of private matters the subject was usually limited to the Mallorys or others of Leighlin or gossip from Charles Town and the other Ashley River plantations. Any discussion of Ketch's married state covered only innocuous topics, an appreciated discretion on Samuel's part. Samuel had never revealed whether he believed Ketch's union to be the genuine article or a concocted plot for Isabelle's safety. Whatever he believed, he reflected no judgment. If anything, Ketch sensed Samuel's relief that Isabelle was out of the settlement and the fields, not simply because it caused fewer problems but because he had a genuine affinity for Isabelle.

The sound of hooves lifted Ketch's focus from his food—a light sound, more of a patter than a drumming on the loamy ground. Helen rode toward them on her dark bay pony, bobbing with the mare's short-strided trot along the crude lane. When she saw Ketch's attention upon her, she grinned and called to him but never slowed the sweaty pony until she reined in next to the tree.

"Miss Helen," Ketch chided. "You been runnin' that pony?"

"No, sir!" She slid from the pony's bare back, wearing the unique pantaloons Maria had fashioned for her. "Cinnamon's just fat is all, and it's hot."

Indulgently, Samuel grinned, "So it is," with the air of one wanting to keep Helen from chastisement.

"I can barely get my legs around her."

"All the more reason to ride sidesaddle like a lady," Ketch responded. "What would yer mother say?"

"Daddy wouldn't have minded." She plopped down next to him, the pony's reins entwined in her fingers.

"Would you like an apple, Miss Helen?" Samuel offered the fruit.

"Oh, yes, please." She reached across Ketch, inadvertently almost knocking the bowl of peas from his hand. "Thank you." Her eyes had a teasing glint for Ketch when she withdrew, showing favor to Samuel for not admonishing her about her riding. Ketch gave her a patient but knowing glance, and though she looked away, her delight in the game was obvious. The bright-eyed mare robbed her attention by trying to steal the apple.

"What brings you way out here, by yer lonesome?" Ketch maintained his slightly judgmental tone, for the child was forbidden from riding far from home alone.

"Izzy said I have to ask you."

"Ask me what?"

She bit into the juicy apple and answered around her mouthful, "If I can visit after supper tonight and learn to make baskets."

"Hmm. I don't know if I should associate with a girl child what rides like a boy. Me and Izzy is civilized folk."

Helen pursed her lips and narrowed her eyes in a look of false ferocity. Samuel chuckled.

"Right, then," Ketch relented. "Reckon it wouldn't pay for me to say no to the likes o' you. You'd just go tell that brother o' your'n, and then I'd be in the soup."

All pretense left the child, and she smiled that beautiful smile so painfully reminiscent of her mother. She went back to crunching into her apple, juice dribbling down her chin. The pony's velvety lips sought the apple again. Helen tried to brush her away and squealed as the mare licked the juice from her face. Finally, she surrendered the rest of the apple to the greedy pony.

"So, you was talkin' to Izzy today?"

"Oh, yes. She helped serve breakfast this morning."

"And how did she fare?"

"She was very nervous around John and almost dropped eggs into his lap. He pretended he didn't notice."

Ketch appreciated the boy's patience. He had feared Mallory's distaste for him and resentment over the current situation would color his behavior toward Isabelle.

"T'others in the house treatin' her respectable-like?"

"They'd better. Maria told 'em."

"Told 'em what?"

"That they'd best not be cruel to Izzy or they'd find themselves out in the fields."

"You heard her say that?"

"Yes." She looked at her dirty bare toes. "Maria didn't know I heard, though. You won't tell her, will you, Mr. Ketch?"

"'Course I won't tell, child."

Helen's voice grew quiet, as if to keep Samuel from hearing but loud enough to ensure that he did. "I have another secret, too. But you must promise not to tell a soul 'cause I'm not s'posed to know."

"Sounds like you know most everything yer not supposed to know." Ketch's falsely rebuking tone resurfaced. "And why am I not surprised?"

Helen grinned. "I reckon I just have good ears."

"And a chattery mouth like that squirrel up yonder. Mebbe you should keep this secret a secret."

She feigned insult with crossed arms. "Very well. I won't tell you I'm going to be an aunt."

"Maria's going to have a baby?" Samuel asked.

"Yes. I heard her talking to John. They didn't know I was outside their door." When she saw Ketch's eyebrow raise in disapproval, she added, "It was partway open. John saw me and said I shouldn't say a word, but I'm so excited, Samuel."

"Of course, you are. Don't you fret; your secret is safe with me and Ketch."

"Why don't yer brother want no one to know?"

"He said it might bring bad luck, after what happened before. But I don't believe in bad luck. Do you, Mr. Ketch?"

He hid his cynical reaction, swallowed a laugh. "I'm sure yer brother has nothin' to fret about, child."

She launched into a litany of things she was going to do when the baby arrived. Ketch half listened, his thoughts instead going back to his last meeting with Mallory. It made even more sense now. Once the baby was born, Maria would require additional help inside the house, so adding Isabelle to the staff had been foresight on his part.

Helen tugged on his sleeve. "We have to finish the crib now!"

Ketch chuckled. "Miss Helen, that babe won't be here tomorrow."

"But we're almost done. We just need to paint it. Maybe it'll bring good luck if we finish it. Maybe not finishing it last time brought bad luck."

"I thought you didn't believe in bad luck?"

"Can we finish it this Sunday? Izzy can help us."

"I reckon we can find the time."

She got to her feet. "I'll go find us some paint right now." She swung the reins over the pony's head. "Can you give me a leg up?"

A leg up was all he could do since he had but one arm and thus had no other way to lift her. Helen sprang onto the pony's back with lightness and grace. She said farewell, dug her heels into the chubby pony and reined her about to gallop back down the lane.

***

The unseasonable warmth of the day lingered into the evening. Not a leaf stirred, and Ketch sensed a storm to come later. He sat on his front porch, his back braced against a support, the pain from the flogging long gone and the scabs shedding. Their itchiness caused him to slowly edge back and forth against the post. Contented—an uncommon state at which he marveled—he smoked his pipe and listened to Helen and Isabelle. They huddled close together in the light of two lamps set on the porch as Isabelle explained the craft of sewing a sweetgrass basket.

Ketch studied his wife's pretty face. She was tired from her long workday, yet he could see she did not want to disappoint Helen. She was still no skilled hand at basket-making, but Helen admired her work all the same and eagerly asked questions, fingers impatient to put into practice what she saw.

"What will this one be, Izzy?"

"This will be a tray. I thought we'd start with something simple."

"Can I take it home tonight and show John?"

Isabelle softly laughed. "No, Miss Helen. We won't finish this tonight. Something like this will take many hours. I'm not skilled like my mama. And you're just learning, too. So, you must be patient." She reached for the nailbone in her lap—a piercing tool made from a cow's rib.

"I love the basket Mr. Ketch gave me for my birthday. It's so very pretty." She picked up a handful of the sweetgrass spread on the porch and pressed it to her nose. "It smells so good, like fresh hay." She put the grass back down and in turn fingered the long-leaf pine needles. "What are these for?"

"We'll use that and the black bulrushes to add color to the pattern. You'll see."

"And these?" Helen lifted the strips of palmetto fronds.

"We'll use those to sew the coils together."

Helen turned to Ketch. "Izzy helped scrub the floor in the ballroom today. We're getting the house clean from stem to stern,

241

aren't we, Izzy?"

"That's what Miss Maria wants."

"'Cause soon we're gonna have the harvest ball. Won't that be exciting? We haven't had a ball since before John came." She giggled. "John can't dance, though, so Mr. David and Miss Elizabeth are going to come over to teach him next week."

Isabelle smiled. "Do you know how to dance, Miss Helen?"

"Oh, yes! Daddy and Mamma taught me. They was very good dancers, wasn't they, Mr. Ketch? You should've seen 'em, Izzy. Would you like me to teach you? Then you and Mr. Ketch could come to the ball, too."

Isabelle and Ketch laughed, but Helen's perturbed expression made it obvious that she found no humor in the moment, so Isabelle explained, "That's very kind of you, Miss Helen, but...I'm a slave and my husband is a...a hired hand. Folks like us don't get invited to the parties of folks like your brother and the Archers."

"Why not?"

"Well..." Isabelle looked to Ketch for help, but he was just as confounded as she, so she struggled on. "There's different types of folks in this world. You'll see that more once you're growed and away from Leighlin more. And those different types of folks don't...share things."

"What different types? You mean black folks and Indians?"

"Yes, but not just. There's different white folks, and there's free black folks. Different types of each kind."

"But you're a slave and you're married to Mr. Ketch. You're different but that don't matter."

Isabelle smiled sadly and touched Helen's arm. "You'll understand better when you're a bit older. Now, I think it's about time my husband takes you home. It's past your bedtime."

Helen frowned and considered the beginnings of their tray. "May I come back tomorrow?"

"How about Sunday? I'll have some free time then."

"Sunday we're painting the baby's crib. Mr. Ketch said you could help us."

"Baby?" Isabelle turned to Ketch.

He headed Helen off from possibly spilling her secret to an even wider audience. "Recollect the crib I told you I been workin' on for the Captain and his wife when they was expectin' their baby? 'Tis done save for the paintin'. I promised Miss Helen we'd finish it on Sunday."

"And you can help us," Helen repeated as they stood. "Then we can come back here and work on the basket. It'll be so much easier to see during the day."

After Helen hugged Isabelle good night and thanked her for the visit, Ketch allowed the child to clamber onto his shoulders. In this way, he carried her through the darkness, her warm hands alternating between his hair and his ears to stay balanced upon her lofty perch.

As they neared the rear portico, she whispered into his ear, "I hope you and Izzy have a baby soon, Mr. Ketch. Then your baby could play with Maria's baby, and they could be best of friends. I could be an aunt for your baby, too."

Ketch chuckled. "You do have a busy imagination, don't you, child?"

Near the steps, he crouched down, so she could dismount. She thanked him and kissed his cheek before scrambling up to where her brother and sister-in-law sat in their usual chairs. Ketch gave the couple a brief bow and wished them a good evening before Helen could launch into the news of her basket-making prowess.

Maria said, "I'm sorry she kept you so late, Ketch."

"'Twas our pleasure." He was about to depart but remained longer, resolute. "I want to thank you both for lettin' Izzy work in the house. Done her a world of good already, it has."

Mallory considered him, quietly shushing Helen, who was determined to tell him about her visit. When he addressed Ketch, his tone was genuine. "She's a hard worker. We're glad to have her."

As Ketch turned away, he had a feeling Maria's satisfied smile was not simply because her husband found value in Isabelle. She would be just as pleased by the fact that the two men's relationship appeared to be progressing in a positive direction.

Strolling back toward the cabin in the heavy night, he reflected upon the expressions he had seen on the Mallorys' faces there in the lantern light. Relief. Happiness. Peace. As it had been months ago. The anticipation of a son or daughter would buoy them and help ease the young man's harsh attitude about his troublesome slave and his former driver. Then Ketch remembered what Helen had said about bad luck, so when he reached his porch, he knocked upon wood.

***

Isabelle was unsure if it was the lightning or the thunder that had awakened her, but she knew the minute she opened her eyes deep in the night that a storm was bearing down upon the cabin. She tensed,

243

and her heart raced. The wind in the trees had yet to reach a roar, but the moaning giants lamented what was about to stretch them to their limits. A bright white flash, followed by a deep, still-distant rumble, the anger in the sound warning that the impending storm would be a violent one. Rain already tapped upon the roof—thick, heavy drops, promising a deluge to come. Isabelle whimpered and rolled onto her side, facing the interior wall, close, her breath bouncing back against her. Regardless of the room's warmth, she pulled the blanket up to her chin, drew in her knees.

Minutes later, the storm arrived in its full fury. It charged through the trees to the west of the cabin, sending branches and debris upon the roof, then slammed into the house, shook it. The rain increased to a downpour, a deafening drumming. The thunder spoke in sharp cracks immediately upon the heels of the blinding stabs of lightning. Her bed trembled. She cried out and pressed her hands to her ears, clenching her teeth. The reports exploded one after another. The atmosphere changed in an instant from humid to flowing chill, and she realized she had left her windows open. One was somewhat protected by the roof over the rear porch, but the east window, even though on the opposite side from the rush of the storm, allowed the swirling winds to push rain inward. But terror kept her from closing them.

She thought of Ketch in the next room. How could he sleep through such a cacophony? But, of course, he was unafraid of storms. He had braved the fury that night long ago when she had been chained in the south rice field. When another blast of thunder pained her ears, she called his name without thinking, as if the power of the thunder had shaken it from her lips. When the next flash bathed the wall before her in white, she tossed her blanket aside and dropped to the floor. She struggled beneath the low bed and lay on her back. But the closeness offered little solace, instead making her feel claustrophobic and suffocated. The dampness from the rain pooling below the window made her shiver in her thin shift.

"Izzy?"

Ketch's voice came amidst the deep after-growl of this latest thunderclap, or had she imagined it? With the slats of the bed a mere inch from her nose, she remained rigid, held her breath, strained to hear as the floorboards beneath her vibrated, not just from the thunder but from Ketch's steps. Yet she remained under the bed, too afraid to leave its protection. With the next flare of lightning, she saw his bare feet in the doorway. She spoke his name, but it came out in a strangled whisper. He mumbled something, crossed the room and sharply closed the windows. Then he drew near again. A blur of his long nightshirt as he knelt.

"Izzy, what're you doin' under there? 'Tis only a storm. Come out."

"The trees will fall," she managed to squeak out.

"Hidin' under this flimsy bed won't make no difference to a tree. Now come out afore you catch a chill."

She saw his hand near the edge of the bed frame, open and inviting.

"Come on out. There's nothin' to be so afeared of. 'Twill pass soon."

His offer gave her the strength to inch away from the wall but no farther, and she realized she had tears streaming along her cheekbones, down into her hair and ears. She told herself he was right, that she was being foolish, but still she could not force herself to leave the protective burrow. With a sigh, Ketch climbed to his feet. Impulsively, she reached out a hand.

"Don't go," she cried. Although she knew the desire was silly, she nearly clutched his nearest ankle to tether him. "I'll come out."

Extricating herself was indeed a struggle, and he knelt back down to take her hand and assist her.

"I was beginnin' to think I'd married a gopher."

His unexpected humor drew a nervous laugh from her as she sat up, straightening her hair and shift, sniffing back tears.

"There now. Hop back into bed and I'll cover you up safe."

But she remained balled up on the floor, pressed against the bed frame. He tried in vain to free his hand from hers.

"Stay here," Isabelle pleaded. "At least until the storm is gone."

He said nothing, halted his resistance. When the next illumination brightened the room, she saw the two vertical furrows between his eyes. His hand warmed hers, squeezed a bit more firmly.

"Please," she said, knowing her weakness would convince him against his better judgment.

"Let go me hand, Izzy."

She refused.

After a roll of thunder, he said, "Very well." The rain seemed to ease a bit. "But I'll only stay if you get back in yer bed and cover up against the damp, hear?"

She hesitated, tried to judge the storm's progress. Perhaps he was correct, and soon it would pass. The last thunderclap had not seemed so deafening. Still holding his hand, she crawled into bed.

"I'll fetch me pillow and blanket and sleep here on the floor, but you have to give me back me hand, Izzy. Yer clawin' into me."

Sheepish, she obeyed and instead clutched her pillow, the tears shoring up at the thought of him remaining near. As he left, she tried to regain some scrap of nerve, knowing he must think her a ninny, but she cautioned herself against appearing too brave lest he return to his bed. The cabin shuddered again, and she pressed her eyes shut. When she opened them, Ketch had returned to spread his blanket on the floor near her bed. The grunt he emitted as he settled against his pillow told her that the situation displeased him.

"Thank you," she said, hoping her gratitude would ease him. She wanted to say more, explain why storms frightened her so, but the pounding rain and intermittent thunder made sustained conversation impossible. With the next flow of light, she saw that he lay on his side, facing her, his attention close. Before she could read what lay in his eyes, the blackness swallowed him again. She curled up tight, facing him, her blanket up to her ear. The urge to take his hand again was so strong that she wondered if he felt the same desire.

"Close yer eyes, Izzy. Afore you know it, 'twill be morn."

"You won't go nowhere?"

"No."

"Promise?"

"I promise."

A smile crept to her lips, and she nestled deeper into the pillow, closing her eyes against the next flash and the sight of him watching her, unblinking and enigmatic. Like that night aboard the *Adventuress*, she felt a warm, secure wave wash over her and conquer the storm.

***

When Ketch awoke with the cock's crow, the first ephemeral grayness of early dawn brought the room into focus. He lay on his right side, facing the rear window, and watched the rhythmic drip of water from the porch roof, more seen than heard. A cardinal chirped in the stillness left behind by the storm's passing violence, a sharp contrast to the unearthly din. Ketch sensed something out of place in the chamber. He frowned and waited for the significance to penetrate. His attention shifted from the dripping water to the equally metrical cadence of Isabelle's breathing...close...so close he swore he could feel its warmth against his neck, could feel *her*. He should have left long ago but had foolishly fallen asleep. Wary, he slowly rolled onto his back and tugged his nightshirt down once aware that the blanket no longer covered him. Instead, it lay beneath Isabelle, who was curled up in sleep next to him.

Raising himself on his elbow, he raced backward in thought to try to remember how she had gotten there, if he had been aware, if he had somehow invited her. She had brought her pillow with her, and her profile was soft against its cushion, her bruised right eye hidden, curled eyelashes beautiful and dark, her cocoa hair disheveled and revealing one small, delicious ear. She breathed through her slightly parted lips. Her cheek was no longer taut with fear but smooth and inviting. How he longed to touch her. He should get up, leave her chamber instantly. If he had a choice, he would stay here all day just looking at her safely sleeping, peaceful and unaware, alluring, close.

The cock crowed again, this time nearer, having strutted over from the kitchen house, for he took his morning duties very seriously and would grow petulant if movement went undetected within the dwellings for which he felt responsible. As if in response, Isabelle stirred against the pillow and gave a small sigh. Her nostrils twitched before she opened her eyes. Her attention rested on his arm directly before her on the blanket, and he froze in uncertainty, expecting her to gasp in surprise or push away. But her gaze lifted to his face, and a smile raised the corners of her mouth.

In a low, hoarse voice that fired his blood even more, she said, "Thank you…for staying."

Stupefied by the situation, he offered a tight smile then remained there, equally helpless as she languidly rose upon her elbow. Her left hand drifted to his cheek to further impale his senses. Her lips brushed his other cheek in a light kiss. She hesitated there, just parted from his flesh, and he both feared and willed her withdrawal. But her warm mouth found his, captured him with incomparable tenderness. He closed his eyes, gave in to the kiss with appalling weakness, and when he opened his eyes, he found himself precariously above her, supported by his arm alongside her pillow. She smiled again and brushed the curtain of wild hair away from his face. Her fingers against his ear sent shivers across his scalp.

He struggled to find his voice. "Izzy…"

Her finger silenced his lips, then she kissed him again. When her arms encircled him, he could no longer maintain resistance and balance upon his cursed single arm. The firm softness of her breasts through his nightshirt drew a quiet, unwitting moan from him. He struggled to shift his weight back over his arm, but Isabelle took his face in her hands.

247

She whispered, "You won't hurt me."

"Izzy—"

"Just...look at me." Her leg drew him back over her, brought the weight of him against her. Her thumbs touched the outside corners of his eyes. "Keep looking at me, just me." She slid his nightshirt over his head. Her persistence, her onslaught finally destroyed the last of his defenses as she drew up her shift and arched against him.

If he faltered, if he started to speak during their union, Isabelle kissed him back into silence, caressed his sweaty face, and whispered, "Look at me," with a smile of the sweetest self-assurance. And afterward, when he lay beside her in exhaustion, she rested her head next to his on the pillow and draped her leg over his helpless body.

"Now," she whispered, "I am your wife."

CHAPTER 20

Isabelle lay against Ketch's side, her head pillowed upon his shoulder, his arm around her, warm and strong, his eyes closed. Beneath her hand, his chest rose much shallower now, his breathing returning to normal, her own breath disturbing the dark hairs on his chest. Her index finger gently traced the inner edge of the burn scar where hair no longer grew. A pleased expression altered the corners of his mouth. Drawing a long draught through his nostrils, he finally looked at her with brown eyes that had lost their darkness. Although Isabelle had much she wanted to say, she held her tongue and allowed him to absorb what had happened.

Quietly, he said, "What have you done?"

The question, which came more as a statement, caused Isabelle to blush and smile.

"We must get up." Briefly, she kissed him.

His hand caught her as she sat up, drew her back, kissed her long and deep, stealing her very breath. If only they could remain here the rest of the day…

Isabelle was nearly late getting to Leighlin House. She raced up the rear portico steps at the same time the kitchen staff were bringing breakfast over for her master. As she flew into the Great Hall, Maria entered from the stair hall opposite. Isabelle slid to an abrupt halt, nearly tripping herself, and curtseyed and said good morning. Maria returned the salutation with a bemused look then continued on into the dining room.

After Isabelle and Pip served breakfast and cleaned up afterward, Mary set them to the task of scrubbing the floor of the Great Hall. Isabelle was thankful for such a mindless task, for thoughts of her husband and their brief though gratifying encounter distracted her.

She had not planned to seduce him. Before the thunderstorm had ended, he had drifted back to sleep, turning away from her and quietly snoring. Purely on impulse, she had left her bed, too frightened to remain alone while the storm still raged. She told herself that she would lie near him just until the lightning and thunder had died, then she would return to bed. But once she had carefully lain beside him, she had relaxed, his broad bulk between her and the windows blocking some of the flashes, especially when she edged as near as she dared to his back and closed her eyes. The scent of him and his warmth reached out to her, and she concentrated on his breathing instead of the storm, counted each exhale until her own breathing calmed. The next thing she heard was the cock crowing. Before opening her eyes, she realized she had not made it back to her bed, and she expected to find him gone, but there he was, staring at her with amazement and that desire he so often tried to hide from her. For the first time in her life, she had felt needed, knew she had made a difference where no one else could.

As pleased as she was to have gained Ketch's intimate trust, she was equally satisfied with her own reaction, for she had thought of neither Ezekiel nor Tom Clark during their lovemaking. Now, she truly understood what her mother had assured her would happen if she kept her heart open.

As Isabelle worked the scrub brush in a circular motion on the pine boards, she smiled. Was Ketch even now thinking of her as she was thinking of him? How she wished the day would fly.

When she no longer detected Pip's scrubbing, she noticed the girl staring at her, but when their eyes met, Pip went back to work with renewed fervor. Isabelle's private smile broadened. She knew the gossip—her husband was nothing but a depraved sodomite who would never share her bed. Well, maybe now when one of those cruel troublemakers from the fields snuck to her cabin window, as Hannah had taunted they had, they would see how wrong they were, the spiteful villains.

Isabelle's new-found happiness made the drudgery of mopping and scrubbing bearable through the morning as the autumn sun lifted over the house and chased the chill from the Hall. Before she knew it, it was time for the servants' midday meal in the lower level. Leighlin House's servants always ate dinner before master and mistress because, as Mary had explained, "The Captain don't want his staff hungry while serving his family."

As usual, the meal was eaten quickly and with few words, a strain that Isabelle suspected had everything to do with her presence. Although she had experienced no open hostility from the other servants since she had started, neither did she receive any outward fellowship. They would have heard the rumors about her and her previous master and were no doubt waiting to see if she would work her way into their master's favor by the same methods. Isabelle was glad the Captain paid her no special heed, particularly in front of the others. Perhaps in time they would realize she had no intention of currying favor with master or mistress. Maybe then she would make an extra effort to seek their friendship and thus eliminate any friction that might displease her master.

Once the Captain and his family had been served, the meal eaten and cleared away, the household resumed its routine. Helen galloped upstairs to her room while Maria called Thomas into the withdrawing room to rearrange furniture. Before returning to her duties in the Great Hall, Isabelle made sure the Captain's brandy decanter was well supplied and near at hand on his desk in the library.

"Thank you, Isabelle." His voice turned her, his entrance unheralded because of the soft moccasins he wore.

She had been about to disappear through the side passage into the withdrawing room but now hastily curtseyed.

"I see you are learning my habits quickly."

It was not the first compliment he had paid her and, like before, she now blushed. "Is there anything else you need, sir?"

"No, thank you. You best return to your scrubbing lest Pip think herself ill-used."

His covert grin took her by surprise, warming her cheeks even more and pulling a small smile from her as she left the library. His facial expression gave her a glimpse of his youth, an expression that lacked the slyness of Tom Clark, a fact in which she took comfort. Indeed, the Captain had thus far been nothing but kind and patient with her, and the hint that he was aware of her struggle for acceptance among the staff also encouraged her.

The Captain's kindheartedness made her puzzle even more over the hidden history of rancor between her master and her husband. While she knew nothing more than rumors, she vowed to be an instrument in mending their relationship. If she could see the good in both of them, they must be able to as well. She could learn a thing or two from Helen's efforts to unite the two men. It seemed the child was always singing Ketch's praises to her brother at the dinner table or making a fuss over him when he stopped by the house in the evenings to escort his wife home. And during Helen's visits to their cabin, the girl often found a way to bring the topic around to her brother and some benevolent thing he had done. Isabelle had already fallen in love with Helen, but the child's attempts at reconciliation had endeared her even more.

Isabelle was not long back to work in the Great Hall when a knock sounded upon the front door, pulling Thomas from the withdrawing room. The arrival of a guest puzzled Isabelle, for no one was expected today. Mary had taught her that whenever guests were anticipated, Maria would notify the staff to be vigilant.

In the Hall, Isabelle was too far removed to hear what the stranger said to Thomas, but when Thomas came back into the Great Hall, agitation furrowed his high forehead. Maria came out of the withdrawing room, wiping her hands on her apron.

"Who is it, Thomas?"

"It the sheriff, ma'am. He askin' for the Captain."

Confounded, Maria managed to say, "Fetch him from the library." She entered the stair hall to greet her visitor.

With deep interest, Isabelle met Pip's gaze, but when their master emerged, they went back to their work until he had passed. Then Pip stopped scrubbing and strained to hear what was happening in the stair hall. Isabelle inched her way closer to the doorway, taking her bucket with her.

The Captain asked, "What can I do for you, Sheriff?"

"My apologies, sir, but…I have a warrant for your arrest. I must ask that you come with us to town."

"Arrest?" the Captain echoed. "There must be a mistake."

"I'm afeared not, sir."

"On what charges?"

The sheriff hesitated, and Isabelle detected unease in his answer, "Piracy and murder, sir."

Isabelle's breath caught, and she glanced at Pip's wide eyes.

The Captain scoffed. "Preposterous."

Maria interjected, "Surely you have the wrong name, Sheriff."

"I'm sorry, ma'am, but I do not."

"Who would make such an outrageous allegation?" Maria demanded.

"I'm not at liberty to say, ma'am. Now, Captain Logan, if you please… I do regret this, but I must discharge my duty."

Fear in Maria's voice now. "This is a mistake, Sheriff."

"That's not for me to say, ma'am. As I said, I'm sorry. Captain, I will wait for you on the portico with my men while you say good-bye to your family, but I cannot allow you to tarry."

"I understand, Sheriff."

The man left the house.

"Jack," Maria said, "I'm coming with you."

"There's no need. I want you to stay with Helen."

"I'll go to Mr. Waterston. He'll get to the bottom of this."

When Maria beckoned, Isabelle found her mistress with a pained look upon her face, one hand on her husband's arm to stay him. The shadow in her master's gaze worried Isabelle and made her wonder if the charges against him were somehow true.

He produced a wan smile and kissed Maria, whispered, "Stay here," before he left.

Isabelle saw two men who had come with the sheriff follow her master down the portico steps. Both shouldered muskets. Isabelle's attention shifted to Maria, who stared after her husband, one hand upon her belly. Maria turned to Isabelle with sudden resolve.

"Isabelle, I want you to find Mr. Willis and tell him Jack's been arrested."

"Yes'm, I will."

"I need to go with my husband. Don't tell Helen anything except that we had to go to town. I'll be back tonight."

"She can stay with me and my husband till you return, if you'd like."

"I would. Thank you, Isabelle."

***

From his chair at the table, Ketch pulled contemplatively upon his pipe and watched Isabelle and Helen where they sat near the fireplace. They worked upon the sweetgrass tray, heads bowed to the task, saying little except for Isabelle's quiet instructions. The fire bronzed them both, softened their features even more. The scent of the fire mingled with the lingering aroma of apple pie. Although usually rapacious when it came to sweets, Helen had eaten only a few bites of the pie.

He watched his wife's fingers move over the sweetgrass tray. Her handiwork seemed more confident tonight. His musings went from the extremes of Jack Mallory's situation to the morning's seduction, a memory that had dominated his thoughts all day. Equally consuming was his relief that he had not harmed Isabelle in any way, yet these concerns remained. Having lain with her now, he knew he could no longer deny his need for her. Would she remain safe? Had she somehow broken the curse? Perhaps the riddle had been solved by her insistence that he not close his eyes and invite the darkness in. And the daylight…it had been like a barricade against that darkness. Tonight, though, there was no soothing sunlight.

Footsteps on the porch sent Helen scrambling to open the door before Ketch could even rise from the table.

"Maria!" Helen threw herself into her sister-in-law's embrace.

When Maria could pry the child away, she took her by the hand as Isabelle offered, "Please come in, ma'am. Set for a spell and have some pie. You look tired."

"Thank you, but it's late; I need to get Helen to bed. Ketch, could I have a word with you on the porch?" Once outside, Maria quietly asked, "Isabelle told you Jack was arrested?"

"Aye." He gestured toward the chair where Isabelle often sat at night, and Maria accepted. Her pallor concerned him. "What'd you find out in town?"

"It's as Jack and I suspected—Seth Wylder. It's no coincidence that the charges were filed while his father is in England. Unfortunately, Seth lacks his father's honor."

"I've never trusted that bastard. Figured 'twas just a matter o' time afore he showed his real stripes."

"I'm sure his wife doesn't know. Margaret is at Medway Plantation, visiting the Smiths. She isn't due back until late tonight. I sent word to her; I would have waited but I wanted to come home for Helen. Jack wants me to stay here until he or Mr. Waterston sends word. He doesn't want Helen hearing any of the rumors flying along the river." She had paled a bit more, perhaps considering how Helen could very well end up without her brother for much more than a couple of nights. "I asked Margaret to come to Leighlin as soon as she gets my message. I'm sure she will do everything she can to help us."

Ketch lacked confidence in Margaret's ability to sway her husband, not after more than a year of Seth Wylder waiting for this opportunity to destroy Jack Mallory.

"How was Helen tonight?"

"She knows somethin's afoot, but me and Izzy kept mum."

"Thank you for taking care of her. I may have to impose upon you again."

"'Tis no trouble. We'll help however we can."

Ketch saw desperation in her eyes, as well as an unspoken plea. Last year, when she had learned of Ezra Archer's murder, Ketch knew without question that she had celebrated the freedom his suspected actions had afforded her husband. And her appreciation had been at the root of her benevolence toward him ever since. She would never openly ask him to commit any crime, let alone murder, yet if killing was necessary to safeguard her spouse and the father of her unborn child,

254

he knew she would do everything in her power to shield him, as she had after Ezra Archer's death.

"Wylder won't get away with this." Ketch's cold voice conveyed his understanding.

Maria smiled tightly and nodded before she climbed to her feet. "I need to get Helen to bed. I only wish I knew what to say to reassure her."

"She's a smart one. Mebbe she should be told the truth about her brother's past now that she's a bit older."

"That's a decision for Jack to make," she said wearily. "He would want to be the one to tell her."

"Aye, just so."

Once Helen and Maria had departed, Isabelle sat at the table, a thoughtful expression upon her bruised face. "Those charges against the Captain...are they true? Do you know?"

Ketch sighed and moved to sit across from her, his pipe now cold. He considered relighting it but felt too tired to do even that. Isabelle watched and waited, that unquenchable curiosity shining in her eyes.

"What I'm goin' to tell you, Izzy, can't be repeated to no one. Understand? 'Specially not to Miss Helen."

"You know you can trust me."

It was almost a question, and Ketch hastened to convince her of that trust with a nod. The sincerity of his belief in her surprised him. When had that trust manifested? He could think of no one in his life besides Ella Logan whom he had ever completely trusted.

"Afore James Logan owned Leighlin, he was a pirate. 'Twas over eight years ago when he attacked a merchantman sailin' from England, long before I sailed with him. Our young master and his parents was aboard that ship. Just a boy, he was. John Mallory was his name then. He never was no Logan like what you know him by. His father was killed, and he and his mother—Miss Ella—was taken by Logan. Not long after, when the Royal Navy captured Logan's vessel, Mallory was accused of piracy. He wasn't no pirate, o' course, not then. Logan got away, took Miss Ella with him and later married her."

Isabelle's lips parted with unspoken shock. "But what happened to the Captain?"

"He was in jail for seven years. Seven years spent plannin' how he'd kill Logan and rescue his mother."

"You mean, Miss Ella didn't want to be with Mr. Logan?"

"'Twas not me place to know what she wanted. I didn't meet her till five years after Logan took her. By then, to me, she seemed a willing

255

wife. Later I suspected otherwise, but I never asked her. Like I said, 'twas no place o' mine to be buttin' me nose."

"So how did our master find her?"

"Well, that's where these charges against him come from. He got hisself a brig—the *Adventuress* we got married aboard—turned her into a pirate and came trollin' in these waters, lookin' for Logan. Made a noise about it, too, provoking Logan by takin' ships what Logan wanted for hisself. By then, Logan was leadin' a double life, one at sea and one here at Leighlin. Leighlin was Miss Ella's idea. She wanted Helen to have a life here, an honest life. She had convinced Logan to give up piratin', but he owed a debt to a right bastard named Ezra Archer, David Archer's father. Until that debt was paid, he had to keep on piratin' and givin' Archer his share o' the purchase we hauled. About that time was when Jack Mallory showed up off Charles Town harbor. Stole Miss Ella right out from under Logan's nose after he parlayed with Logan."

Ketch remembered James Logan's fury that night when he awoke to find his beloved wife gone. No man aboard the *Medora* soon forgot Logan's curses and blows and the way he drove them and the brigantine until they caught the *Prodigal*. Ketch had not begrudged Logan's judgment, for he recalled his own desperate rage over Mallory's audacious stroke.

"We finally overhauled the *Prodigal*. Logan knew those waters off the Outer Banks better than any man, and he drove that boy upon a shoal. That's when we boarded him. Logan would've killed Mallory sure if not for Miss Ella puttin' herself betwixt the two. That's when she was shot by one o' Mallory's men, me own half-brother, he was. He didn't live long enough to regret shootin' Miss Ella—he was wounded in the fight and Logan hacked him to bits."

"Oh, my... Was he dear to you?"

"Once, but not then. Like I said, Dan sailed with Mallory."

"So, what happened then? Why didn't Logan kill the Captain?"

"'Cause o' Miss Ella. She begged Logan to spare his life. And Logan couldn't deny his dyin' wife. He loved her like I've never seen no man love a woman. And the boy...well, findin' out he had a wee sister just then, he couldn't go on tryin' to knock Logan on the head. Miss Ella made the both of 'em promise to take care o' Miss Helen. So, Mallory gave up piratin' and assumed a new identity. The only folk 'round these parts what know about his past are the Archers and the Wylders, and they'd never betray his secret. Well, except for this cove named Seth Wylder—David Archer's brother-in-law—what holds a grudge against Mallory. The only thing that's stayed his tongue all this time was his father. But it just so happens his father has gone to England."

"Why would he want to harm the Captain?"

"Mallory nigh killed Wylder...and his parents. 'Twas not Mallory's idea; he was ordered to it by Ezra Archer. With Logan dead, Archer had lost his partner, so he found a way to entrap Mallory into takin' over Logan's role. Archer hated the Wylders and wanted 'em dead; they was competition to him in both politics and business, so he ordered Mallory to kill 'em. Mallory came damn nigh to doin' it, too, though he didn't want to. But Archer up and died, and that was that. Seth Wylder's not forgotten, though."

Ketch halted there. Perhaps Isabelle had already heard rumors of her husband's alleged role in Archer's demise, but he had no plans to confirm that tonight, not after gaining so much this morning.

Isabelle, while still puzzled, seemed to accept this as the end of his exposition. She looked down at her wedding ring, and he could see something else simmered inside her.

"Miss Maria said you and the Captain have always had...difficulties with each other. Why?"

"Truth is, I didn't know that boy existed till the day Logan nigh killed him right in front o' me. Miss Ella mentioned a son once—not by name, mind—and she said some other things over the years, things that made me wonder if he was still alive. But even she didn't seem to know, till he came for her."

"Why didn't she know?"

"I reckon Logan wouldn't let her search for him. He was a possessive man. I think he feared that boy ever showin' up, 'cause o' course Mallory would have murder in his head and, worse, a plan to reclaim his mother. And that's exactly what happened. When all was said and done, 'twas his mother what paid the price." He picked up his cold pipe and stood to place it upon the mantel, remained with his back to Isabelle. "Like I told you before, I loved Miss Ella. No one in life was kinder to me. Losin' her...'twas a mortal blow. I had to blame someone. 'Course at the time blamin' me own kin was somethin' I couldn't do. So, I blamed Mallory. Truth be told, I reckon I still do."

Isabelle came to stand near him. "What will happen to our master?"

Ketch stared down into the fire. The day had been a chilly one after the storm had stolen away the previous day's warmth and left behind thorough dampness. The fire did its best to banish the clamminess.

"If they can find enough witnesses to speak against him, the boy could hang."

Isabelle's breath caught. "Oh...poor Miss Helen...and Miss Maria."

"Aye. But yer mama's master, Mr. Waterston, he's a powerful friend o' the Mallorys and a lawyer as well. He'll represent the boy if it comes to a trial, I'm sure. And there are others who'll help Mallory, too, men what was friends o' James Logan, like Governor Smith and James Moore. After all, they think Mallory is Logan's son, and the boy's done nothin' to discredit hisself in the community since takin' over his false name."

Isabelle stepped closer still and rested a hand against his back, so light that he barely felt her touch. "If the worst should happen, what will become of Leighlin, and us?"

"Hard tellin'. Leighlin might be used to pay back some o' what Mallory took from the merchant ships he plundered." He offered a small smile. "Don't fret, Izzy. Miss Maria would see after folks like us."

His words drew Isabelle from her sadness. She smiled tightly and nodded. A silence stretched between them. The desire that had ruled Ketch's thoughts all day rushed back. Her expression, her fingers still upon his back revealed a similar yearning, which pleased him. He had been concerned that her actions of that morning might have been a mere duty she felt she had to perform to reward him for the benevolence he had shown her these months, including staying with her during the storm.

She murmured, "Would you like me to share your bed tonight?"

"Izzy..." But no true resistance dwelled in him. Even if he were able to bar the two bedchamber doors, he knew he could never stay away from her. The fear of memories, his fear of hurting her was still there, nearly as strong as before—it caused a sick feeling in his stomach even now—but his lust overpowered even that. She patiently watched him, her hand sliding down his back.

"We could light all the lamps," she suggested softly, "so it's not dark, so we can see each other."

She had no need to see him; the need for revealing light was all his own. How she had arrived upon illumination as his saving grace, at least so far, he could not fathom. But he appreciated her efforts to understand him. To turn her away now would be to insult her, and he wanted that no more than he wanted to retire alone to his bed.

Seemingly of its own volition, his hand touched her cheek. She covered his hand with her own. Then he leaned down to kiss her.

CHAPTER 21

Perhaps it was the fact that now they lay in *his* bed or that their union was willful, not merely impulsive as the first encounter had been. Whatever the root cause, Ketch's fears won out, and he found himself lacking after their initial lovemaking.

Unperturbed, Isabelle kissed his ear and whispered, "It'll just take time," then curled up against him like a contented cat.

He marveled at her optimism and wondered how she could push aside her own inhibitions after Tom Clark's violations. How much stronger she must be than he. Although she claimed to have simply refused to let Clark's abuses determine her future, Ketch knew overcoming such things took far more than a mere decisive thought. For this, he admired her even more than before and lay awake, watching her sleep in the lamplight, afraid to drift off lest her warm nearness awaken the demons of his past and the ignominy of his Southwark bed.

Isabelle awoke when the sun brought the first hint of daybreak into the room. She stretched and smiled at him, a most beautiful, arousing sight. With the banishment of the darkness, his confidence rallied, and he took her into his arms.

Afterward, with no time for a hot breakfast, Ketch tossed an apple and a pear along with a piece of pie into a basket to take with him to the kiln. Isabelle darted from her room, dressed in green and white livery, face hastily scrubbed, and hair contained by a green headscarf, her expression open and bright.

As they left the house, Ketch said, "Reach inside me basket here and give this note to Miss Maria first thing."

"What is it?"

"I've asked her to send for me when Margaret Wylder arrives. If she forgets, you must remind her, aye?"

"I will, but," she bit into her apple as they hurried along, "why is Mrs. Wylder coming here? You said her husband had the Captain arrested."

"Miss Maria sent word for her. The Mallorys are good friends with Mrs. Wylder. She had no hand in what her husband did to yer master, and I'm sure she'll do what she can to help him."

"Does she have any power over her husband? You said he's a wealthy man…"

"When you see Margaret Wylder, you'll understand the power she has over any man." He faltered. "But the fact that her husband was bold enough to do this makes me wonder if she's lost some o' her charm over him."

Isabelle rushed to keep up with his long strides. "Is there something you can do to help the Captain?"

He heard hope in her tone; she was more certain of his assistance than he was. It unsettled him to think that perhaps she knew him better than he knew himself. Overnight, lying awake for so many hours, he had indeed devised a plan, but he needed to keep the details from her, for the sake of her own safety.

"I'm not sure what I can do," he replied. "But I'll do whatever Miss Maria might ask me."

Once they reached the steps of the rear portico, Isabelle turned to him with a child-like smile, and he could see that his willingness to help pleased her greatly. She stood on her toes and kissed him, the touch of her lips sending heat rushing through him.

Her open display amazed him. "Why are you so good to me, Izzy?"

The smile reappeared, quick and knowing, and she said, "Because I love you," then blushed and ran up the steps into the house.

He remained there, slack-jawed and staring after her for a long, numb stretch of time. Almost dropping the forgotten basket, he stumbled toward the stables, Isabelle's words humming in his ears.

Love? How could she love him? Love. Was that the heady feeling he got whenever he was around her or thought of her? How would he know? What previous knowledge did he have of its existence in his life? His mother had loved him, at least before he had unwittingly destroyed her life and ultimately his own, and he had loved her. He had also loved Ella Logan. And then there was Helen. But that type of love was different from the love of which Isabelle spoke; it was not what had shined in her pale eyes along with hope, a hope that he would reciprocate those feelings. But was he capable of such? And could he sustain it? He feared disappointing her as Zeke had, nor did he want to blurt some foolish sentiment without knowing if true meaning lay behind it, for she would detect any falseness and be grievously injured.

When he reached the stables and found Samuel and the hands next to the wagon, eying him warily, he wondered what he must look like.

Samuel asked, "Is there something wrong?"

Ketch tried to recover but when he replied, "No," the word came out strangled and deficient. So he avoided Samuel's gaze and climbed onto the wagon seat. With a sideways glance, Samuel settled next to him and took up the lines.

"Looks like you've seen a ghost," Samuel said then slapped the lines against the mules.

***

Ketch watched the sun climb ever higher in the morning sky, aware of when the tide would reach its flood, the latest time for Margaret Wylder's arrival. His concern that Maria might fail to send for him was dispelled when Jemmy rode to the kiln on a mule, leading along the placid bay gelding, Curly, saddled for Ketch's use. Ketch would have preferred the stability of the wagon, but it was needed at the kiln, so, with Jemmy's assistance, he hauled himself astride the gelding and started back along the lane at the fastest pace he could manage without toppling off. Fortunately, Curly knew the way back to Leighlin perfectly well, so Ketch needed to do little more than clutch mane.

At Leighlin House, Nahum led him to the withdrawing room. A low fire burned in the hearth to ward off the last of the morning chill, sunlight flowing through the river windows to splay across the Persian rug. Ketch paused in the doorway and bowed to Margaret Wylder and Maria, who sat on the far side of the room, a tea table between their golden green upholstered chairs. The women's contrasting beauty struck him—Maria small and dark, Margaret tall, blonde, and fair. So different physically but not so disparate in strength of character.

He read distaste upon Margaret's exquisite face, her blue eyes darkening upon him like a turbulent sea. Unlike most others, she refused to allow her fear of him to show and had courage enough to instead reveal her scorn. Like her brother, Margaret suspected Ketch to have been her father's assassin.

"Ketch," Maria welcomed him, looking very drawn, whether from worry or her pregnancy he could not guess. She gestured to a chair across the large rug from them. "Come in. I told Margaret I was expecting you."

Obviously, the two women had been talking at length before his arrival, but the urgency in Maria's tone told Ketch that Margaret had not brought the words of certainty that she sought regarding her husband's freedom. Surely his cryptic note had piqued Maria's interest. With ease, he remembered the expression on her face last year when she had received word of Ezra Archer's murder—a jumbled mass of emotions ranging from horror to amazement to pure joy, and eternal gratefulness. Now the dire anxiety that her countenance betrayed assured Ketch that she would be open to any suggestion he may have, lawful or otherwise.

Isabelle appeared so silently that Ketch nearly started. She carried a sweetgrass tray with a teapot and matching cups and saucers, which she carefully set on the spindly-legged table next to Maria.

"Thank you, Isabelle," Maria said as the girl poured tea. "Perhaps your husband would like a cup as well."

When Isabelle turned to him, Ketch could tell she was trying to maintain the decorum of her station, but all the same a small smile captured her lips, and the blush that had colored her cheeks after her declaration of love that morning returned.

Although Margaret tried to hide her shock at Maria's revelation of marriage, the way she stared into her tea exposed her.

"No, thankee," he said with upheld hand. His own self-consciousness left over from the morning display made him perspire. Isabelle appeared a bit crestfallen, so he forced a tight smile.

Isabelle curtseyed to her mistress and left the room.

Maria took a prolonged sip of tea, as if waiting for Isabelle to move far beyond earshot before she spoke. "Margaret is sending word to her father-in-law about what's happened with Jack."

"That'll take weeks," Ketch grumbled, "and by then it may be too late."

Margaret scowled at his opinion. "I will do everything in my power to see the charges dropped."

A certain hint of culpability colored her words, and the private glance she shared with Maria confirmed Ketch's suspicion—Seth Wylder's charges against Jack Mallory were as much to affront his rebellious wife as they were to punish Jack. Over these many months since Mallory's arrival in Carolina, Wylder's grasping nature had nurtured jealousy over his wife's friendship with the former pirate whose youth and looks far outshined his own. Yet, regardless of Margaret's frustrating loyalty to the Mallorys, Seth would never consider forsaking his wife. Margaret Wylder was an important jewel to Seth for more than just her beauty, for if anything unpleasant were to happen to David Archer, the family fortune—no small consideration—would devolve to Anna Archer's only other child. Ketch was counting on this greed.

A small but conspicuous silence followed Margaret's declaration. A silence heavy with enmity between Margaret and Ketch. Maria hastened to bridge the tension.

"You mentioned in your note, Ketch, that you had an idea you wanted to share with us."

He held Margaret's cool stare, which shockingly told him that no matter how she felt about him, she was open to any path that would free Leighlin's master, even if that avenue were to come from her father's murderer.

"Aye," Ketch said, "but 'tis a drastic measure that would require secrecy and risk."

Maria set aside her cup. She crossed to the door and shut it as well as the door to the side passage leading to the library. Then she perched on the edge of her chair, one hand grasping the locket around her neck.

"Go on," she said.

Ketch lowered his voice. "I propose a staged kidnapping, of you, Mrs. Wylder. Yer safe return in exchange for Jack Mallory's freedom."

Maria stared. "Ketch...you can't be serious."

To Margaret, he said, "Did yer husband know you was a-comin' here?"

"No. We argued and I left. I did not tell him where I was bound."

The truth, Ketch knew, and common. The couple's quarrels were legendary in Charles Town. Equally unsurprising was the spark of interest in Margaret's eyes, for well he knew her ability to carry out clandestine schemes.

"Then I suggest you don't return to town," Ketch continued. "When the tide rises this evenin', you'll go to Wildwood. We'll send one oarsman with you, someone trustworthy, who can honestly say when he last saw you, you wasn't with neither of us."

"You mean for her to hide at Wildwood?" Maria said. "That would mean involving David and Elizabeth."

"Aye."

"But even if they agree, Seth knows David's loyalties to me and Jack. He might suspect."

Margaret interceded with muted enthusiasm. "I have ways to conceal myself at Wildwood, should the authorities come there. And you know David will do anything to help."

"I can write the ransom note," Ketch continued. "Yer husband won't know me handwritin', and 'tis wretched enough to convince him yer captor is a low, desperate type."

"What will it say?" Margaret returned her cup to the tray, the tea quite forgotten.

"That yer husband must drop all charges and not pursue the matter again, that you won't be released until Jack is returned to Leighlin. He'll have three days to comply or else he'll never see you again."

Maria let go of her locket and clasped her restless hands in her lap. "But how can the demands be delivered without exposing anyone?"

"I'll have one of Latiffe's boatmen take it downriver, sealed, and offer coin to any sailor at the wharf to have it delivered anonymously."

Margaret eased back in her chair and regarded him with something close to surprised respect. "It seems you have this all figured out, Mr. Ketch."

"'Tis a simple plan."

Maria asked, "What if he doesn't comply?"

"He will," Margaret said. "I am of greater value to him alive than Jack is dead."

"Then 'tis settled." Ketch stood. "I'll see to the letter afore I go back to the kiln."

"Use the library." Maria hurried to open the passageway door. "You'll find what you need on Jack's desk."

Ketch bowed to Margaret before entering the short passage. Maria followed, stopped him with a hand upon his shoulder just before he reached the library. Light from the passage's single window fully revealed the deep concern on her face.

"I'm ashamed to admit I've felt...helpless over this." Her confession brought color to her face, for they both knew she was normally anything but helpless. Ketch suspected her pregnancy had much to do with her current state. "I just want to say...thank you." Her hand had again drifted unconsciously to her belly.

Concealing his satisfaction, he bowed again before retreating to the library.

***

Margaret Wylder stayed at Leighlin through the remainder of the day. After supper with Maria and Helen, she left for Wildwood, ferried through the moonless night by Leighlin's most trusted boatman. This same slave rode the turning tide downriver to Charles Town where he would ensure the anonymous delivery of Ketch's note to Seth Wylder.

265

That night when Ketch returned home from the kiln, dragging from lack of sleep, he did not share with Isabelle the plan he had concocted. Tomorrow the search parties would inevitably come, and he wanted her to be able to truthfully say she had no knowledge of any wrongdoing by anyone at Leighlin.

To Ketch's relief, Isabelle carried on through supper as if she had never uttered her declaration of love. He sensed that she was not indifferent to his reaction; if anything, she probably feared it, and that contributed to her avoidance of the subject. Instead, she talked about Helen's sadness regarding her brother's absence.

When they retired to Ketch's bed, neither had the energy for anything more than an intimate embrace. In the orange glow of two lamps, Isabelle murmured on for a short time about Helen and Maria, but eventually her words grew slurred and spaced until she relaxed completely against him and fell asleep. Ketch knew he could never remain awake two straight nights, and to think he could go on that way forever was ridiculous. He contemplated slipping out of her soft hold and taking up a nearby chair, but before he could begin to extricate himself, exhaustion and the soft warmth of his wife dragged him into sleep.

The next morning, Ketch walked her to the house and kissed her good-bye. She smiled before she hurried up the portico steps. Although she had not mentioned it, he knew she felt vindicated after two complete nights together without any manifestation of the violence he feared. Ketch shook his head at her unwavering belief in him.

It was late in the afternoon when Helen rode out to the kiln, surprising Ketch with her galloping appearance but not with the reason behind her arrival.

"The sheriff's here, Mr. Ketch." Confusion filled her blue eyes. "He wants to talk to you, so Maria sent me to fetch you and Samuel. Mr. Wylder's here, too. He seemed very angry, but Maria wouldn't let me stay to hear what he was saying."

Although Ketch knew the main reason why Searle had returned, he was taken aback by Wylder's presence. The fact that Wylder had come with someone else was less shocking. Ketch's blood stirred at the thought of Wylder harassing his mistress, but he did his best to conceal his displeasure.

"You ride back to the house, Miss Helen, and tell 'em we're a-comin'."

At first the child seemed reluctant to leave, her fingers fidgeting with the reins. She chewed her bottom lip in thought, and Ketch feared that she would ask unanswerable questions, so he again urged her on her way.

Once Samuel had the mule team trotting down the lane, he studied Ketch sidelong before speaking. "Why do you think Wylder's here? I'd think he'd want to stay clear of Maria after what he's done."

Ketch grunted.

"Odd that Sheriff Searle would come back. Do you reckon Wylder's after us now, too? Maybe whoever he thinks will speak against Jack will speak against us as pirates."

"I reckon we'll find out soon enough what they want," Ketch said.

Samuel's speculation was certainly a possibility. They had never skulked in the background when the *Medora* had raided Charles Town vessels during James Logan's reign. There had always been the risk that some sailor might recognize them on land, but Samuel had always avoided Charles Town as much as possible, and if anyone had entertained thoughts of taking Ketch to the authorities, they had yet to be so bold, and with so much time having passed, Ketch had lost any concern for it.

Samuel urged the mules into a canter. The breeze created by the motion soothed Ketch, and he observed the dappling fall of sunlight through the forest's canopy.

"I told Maria last night," Samuel said, "that if there's anything I can do, all she has to do is ask." He paused. "And I say the same to you."

Ketch hazarded a look at his companion and found Samuel's gaze intent. But there was no solid knowledge there, just fervent willingness. Maria would never have dared intimate their plan to anyone, not even Samuel, a man Maria had known for as long ago as when she had lived in the Caribbee with her father.

When they reached Leighlin House, Thomas directed them around to the front of the manor. Finding Searle and two of his men along with Seth Wylder on the portico instead of in the comfort of the house please Ketch. He admired Maria's refusal to offer the intruders any hospitality, not even a cup of water.

The other men got to their feet. Ketch's attention remained on Maria only long enough to see that her temper camouflaged fear.

Casually, Ketch spoke before anyone else could. "Afternoon, Sheriff. Didn't expect to see you back so soon."

Although a man almost of Ketch's height, Searle was of average build, and the softness around his middle made it plain that Charles Town required little of its sheriff. He looked uncomfortable here on the frontier, and the warm swamp air produced beads of sweat from beneath his hat. Searle's unremarkable brown eyes lingered upon the muscles of Ketch's arm as Ketch wiped away his own perspiration, perspiration that had nothing to do with nerves.

"I'm investigating a crime, Mr. Ketch." The confident authority in his voice rang false. "I need to ask you some questions."

"You mean the charges against me master?" He flicked a dismissive glance at Wylder, who remained slightly behind Searle.

"No. A different matter."

"Seems you have a right parcel o' things to keep you busy these days."

Searle scowled, and his men shifted their weight, coats open to reveal pistols. Searle was a bit subtler, keeping his coat closed. Ketch suspected Wylder had more than one pistol on his person, though he doubted the fool would know how to load one, let alone fire it.

Wylder spoke up, his voice almost cracking. "Where were you yesterday, Mr. Ketch?" The question came with a certain amount of contrived force, as if he had been practicing it the entire journey upriver.

Ketch's brow lowered, and he turned his full stare upon the merchant, all sarcasm gone. Wylder took a half step backward. To have the man so close now, all of Ketch's impulses screamed for him to thrash him or worse.

He rumbled, "How durst you come here and trouble this woman? What you've done to her husband is enough, but to show yer pasty face—"

Samuel's restraining hand fell to his arm, though Ketch had not moved an inch, and Maria's calm voice halted him. "That will do, Ketch. You'll please answer these gentlemen's questions, so they can be on their way. I'm sure they will apologize for interrupting your work."

"Of course, Mrs. Logan," Searle said with a slight, uncomfortable bow. "Forgive our intrusion, Mr. Ketch, but I must insist that you answer Mr. Wylder's question."

"I would think you askin' would be sufficient," Ketch growled. "After all, yer the lawman, aye? That is, unless he's the one pullin' yer strings."

"Ketch." Maria's sharp voice broke through his unrestraint.

He realized that prolonging this was becoming an agony for her, so he reined in his passions just as he caught sight of Isabelle in the doorway. It was a moment so brief that he almost questioned his vision, but it was enough to settle him and make it possible to regain control. How much of this had she heard? Did she linger somewhere just out of sight but still within hearing?

"You asked where I was yesterday. I was out in the woods, workin'."

Searle spoke before Wylder could interfere. "Can anyone corroborate that?"

Not completely sure what Searle's word meant, Ketch hesitated. Maria came to the rescue. "Samuel can. Can't you, Samuel?"

Searle turned to Samuel, who had freed Ketch and eased closer. He viewed the black man with suspicion. "I'm to believe the word of a Negro?"

Maria, who until then had stood slightly apart from the men, now stepped toward Searle with a scathing look, and Ketch could tell Searle, for the moment, was more afraid of her than of anyone else on that portico.

"I would trust Samuel's word before your own, sir. Now, if you are only here to insult my men—"

"Mrs. Logan." Seth Wylder cleared his throat, his use of her false name like that of a weapon. "Surely you can understand our skepticism. After all, these men work for your husband. They will feel obligated to say whatever they feel duty-bound to say."

"Mr. Wylder. It's only because of my faith in my husband's innocence that I've even allowed you to set foot on his property. You will ask your questions and accept these men's answers as the truth. If you question their integrity, you question mine, and I should caution you against anything so foolish. Do you understand?"

All the men looked uncomfortable now, and Searle's glance at Wylder begged for a quick conclusion to the visit.

"Ketch was with me yesterday," Samuel said. "At the kiln. He came back to the house once."

"For what reason?" Searle asked Ketch.

"Miss Maria had sent for me. She couldn't find some o' her husband's paperwork about the tar we've produced so far, so she wanted me to give her the information meself."

"Did you see Margaret Wylder yesterday, Mr. Ketch?"

"Aye. She came to visit Miss Maria nigh the end o' the forenoon tide, about the time I come to the house."

"Did you see her leave?"

"No. I didn't tarry after me errand. I went back to the kiln. But I reckon Miss Maria already told you all this."

Searle sniffed. "'Tis my duty to question anyone who might have seen Mrs. Wylder."

"Is she lost?" Ketch quipped.

Wylder scowled. "She's been kidnapped, damn you."

"What concern is that o' mine?"

"It just so happens," Wylder continued, "the kidnappers are demanding Captain Logan's release in return for Margaret's safety."

"Like I asked, what does that have to do with me?"

"I think it obvious, Mr. Ketch. You work for the man, and your reputation lends itself to just such an outrage."

"I work for the man, aye. But that be the extent of it, mate. If you really knew the truth of things, as you seem to think you do, you'd know me and the Captain don't see eye to eye much. Whether yer charges see him swing or not, I'll still be here."

Wylder stepped next to Searle, his hand brushing back his coat and resting on the butt of a pistol. "You may not be loyal to your master, Mr. Ketch, but I know you to be loyal to his sister. And when your master is convicted, Leighlin will no longer be her home, or yours. Mark me well, sir."

The astute mention of Helen nearly pushed Ketch to undeniable action, but the gleam of satisfaction in the merchant's small eyes stayed Ketch as much as Maria's incensed voice.

"That's enough, Mr. Wylder."

"I have just one more question for your trained dog, Mrs. Logan," Wylder ground out, his indignation causing his temple to subtly pulse.

"Ask it," Maria tersely said. "Then leave."

Wylder's nostrils flared and his chin trembled just slightly. His voice raised a pitch. "What have you done with my wife, you crippled fiend?"

Ketch leaned toward the man's face. "You asked yer question. Now do what the lady says and leave."

Wylder looked at Searle, but the sheriff offered only strained silence, a strong swallow, and a wistful glance toward the landing.

"If you have anything more to say to me or my workers," Maria said, "you will do so only through Mr. Waterston. For you to accuse anyone at Leighlin of doing harm to your wife is an outrage. Margaret is a dear friend, as you should know, regardless of her husband's suspect honor. Now, good day to you, sirs."

His face a brilliant red, Wylder appeared close to another outburst, but the intimidating bulk of both Ketch and Samuel dissuaded him. Searle touched his hat to Maria, apologized for the intrusion, and hastily circled around Ketch to descend the steps, followed closely by his men. With his protection now fleeing, Wylder made his own swift retreat, as if afraid the sheriff would leave him behind.

Maria held her ground until the men trailed from sight down the terraces, then she leaned against the portico railing, her knuckles paling with the strength of her grip. Samuel stepped closer as if to physically assist her.

"I'm fine." Maria waved him off. "Thank you both." She straightened and offered them a wan smile. "Would you care for a drink before you go back to work? Some of Jack's brandy?"

Although Ketch's mouth watered, he and Samuel declined. He had a feeling Maria desired nothing more than to lie down, judging by the relief and fatigue dulling her eyes, the fire now gone. She thanked them again and retired to the house.

When they left the portico and mounted the wagon, Samuel eyed Ketch curiously. The strain had left the black man's muscles, and he almost smiled when he said, "Whatever you've done, Ketch, I hope to hell it works, you damned fool."

CHAPTER 22

When Ketch returned home that evening, Helen was there, helping Isabelle with supper. Isabelle informed him that Maria had returned to Charles Town to see her husband and to try to champion his cause. Although Ketch wondered how much Isabelle had heard of Seth Wylder's inquisition, he was thankful that Helen's presence discouraged her from questioning him.

Ketch manufactured happiness in his greeting to Helen and told her how pleased he was to have her as their guest again.

The child smiled back, but in her eyes yesterday's worries had been compounded. During supper, she asked, "Why did the sheriff visit today? Maria wouldn't tell me."

"'Twas nothin' for a child's concern."

"It was because of John, wasn't it? He's in trouble."

"That's not it at all. Now, eat up or you won't have much time to work on yer basket afore bedtime."

"Why won't Maria let me go to town with her?"

"'Tis a long sail down the river, as you know, and even a longer one back in the dead of night."

He hid his concern for the young woman's travels. Normally, he would think little of Maria braving anything alone. During Mallory's days as a pirate, Ketch knew she had toiled above the tops like any able seaman, and he had witnessed the flash of her blade in a ship-to-ship action. Before that, he had been well-acquainted with her father's tavern in the West Indies where Maria served drinks to pirates and other wayward men. But she had changed much since then. The rough edges were all but smoothed away by her maternal role with Helen as well as her duties as wife and mistress of Leighlin. Even the way she spoke had been refined over time, though he knew the change had been an unconscious one. Now her pregnancy made travel to and from Leighlin anything but mundane, and Samuel—far wiser in the line of expectant mothers—had mentioned to Ketch how stress from Mallory's incarceration could further add to the danger. Both men knew, however, that discouraging Maria from going to Charles Town would only result in stubborn words and dismissive gestures.

As if reading his thoughts, Isabelle remarked, "Miss Maria is sick most every morning lately. She must be in a family way, but she hasn't said anything, and it's not my place to ask."

Helen gasped and looked with anxious suspicion at Ketch.

Ketch shook his head and paid attention to his venison. "If she was, Izzy, I'm sure she would've told everyone. Somethin' that excitin' for her...well, she wouldn't be able to keep the news bottled up, 'specially now."

When Helen searched Isabelle's face for her reaction, Ketch gave his wife a discouraging look and a shake of his head.

Isabelle murmured, "You're probably right."

Later, on the porch in the mild evening, Helen and Isabelle worked on their sweetgrass tray while Ketch relaxed in a chair. How different the two were but how pleasant to see them close together, Helen distracted from her troubles if only for a brief time.

The child shocked them when she announced, "I asked John if you and Izzy could come to the ball."

Isabelle laughed. "Miss Helen, you did not."

"Did too. But he said no, so I called him a tyrant. That's what Mamma used to call Daddy sometimes when she didn't get her way." Her fingers trailed over the palmetto fronds before her. "John said you're serving in the house that night with all the guests coming."

With a wink at Isabelle, Ketch asked, "And did he say why I wasn't invited?"

Helen frowned as if sorry she had brought up the subject. She kept her attention on Isabelle's hands as they worked. "He said you've vexed him too many times."

"Aye, I reckon I have."

"Why?" she asked with startling frustration. "Why don't you and John like each other?"

"Well," he stammered, "yer brother and me...we're just very different, child."

"Maybe...a little. But *I* love you both, so why can't you love each other?"

Touched by her fervor, he quashed his impulse to laugh at her absurd idea. "Love's not that simple, child. You'll learn in time."

Once she grew tired from her lesson, Helen climbed onto Ketch's lap and snugged her toy bear between them. A short while later, she fell asleep, one of her hands clenched in his shirt. She had not clung to him so the previous night. Her distress gnawed at him, made him dread her reaction should she indeed lose her brother. Surely she would not look to him for anything more than comfort. If so, she would find him woefully lacking.

When he rose to carry her inside, she accepted Isabelle's offer to sleep with her. Ketch relinquished his larger bed and retired to Isabelle's chamber. There he lay, his wife's scent all around him, tossing and turning for some time before finally drifting off.

Come Sunday morning, Helen awoke first, and she roused Ketch with running feet and shouts, wanting to rush to the house because Maria should have returned in the night. But Isabelle convinced her to help with breakfast and eat with them so Maria would have more time to sleep.

When they started for Leighlin House, Helen bolted ahead, calling back, "Maybe John came home!"

But only Maria greeted them on the rear portico, as if she had been waiting all night for them. She wore one of her husband's dressing gowns, looking weary, though she did her best to smile with conviction when Helen threw her arms around her. Once Helen learned that her brother was still in Charles Town, her shoulders slumped. Maria kissed her cheek.

"Have you eaten?"

"Yes," the child muttered.

"I saw your mother, Isabelle," Maria said. "She's doing well and sends her love."

A bright smile banished Isabelle's troubled expression.

"Would you take Helen to the garden and cut some roses for her mother's grave?"

"Yes'm." Isabelle ushered the child into the house to gather the usual basket and shears.

Once they were out of earshot, Maria quietly asked Ketch, "Have you told Isabelle of your plan?"

"No. I reckon the fewer people know, the better."

"Yes." She gestured an invitation toward the nearby wicker chairs. Gazing out over the sward where the grass had lost the deep green of summer, she said, "I shouldn't have put you in this position."

"'Twas me own decision. Wasn't much else for a choice, was there?"

"From what I've gathered in town, Margaret's right about Seth— this is more about his marriage than it is about Jack." She made a small, wry sound close to a strangled laugh. "Margaret's been quite the challenge for him."

"Aye, she's a stubborn one, like someone else I know."

She blushed. He nearly scolded her for traveling up and down the river. Surely her husband admonished her daily, but there would be no stopping her efforts to have him freed. Hopefully, between Margaret's sham kidnapping and Maria's undaunted efforts, Seth Wylder would cave in. He was not, after all, a man of nerve and ruthlessness, though he liked to fancy himself so.

"I was thinking," Maria said, "if you could write another letter, something even stronger…"

"I'll do it directly."

She smiled, and for the first time since the discovery of Ezekiel's murder, Ketch saw true forgiveness there.

"I told Jack the truth—about Margaret, that is, so he wouldn't fret about her. Of course, the news is all over town. Everyone is in an uproar." Maria faltered then continued with deep emotion. "Jack has more friends than I realized, powerful men. James Moore came to see him when I was there and pledged whatever help he could provide to see him freed."

"Aye, Moore and Logan knew each other well. I don't know for sure, but I always reckoned Moore knew the truth about Logan's piracy and secretly supported him. Moore knew pirates brought more good than harm to Charles Town 'cause of the money they spent and the goods they brought, back when Sothel was governor."

Maria laid her hand upon his arm, unable to speak for a moment. Ketch patiently waited, felt her desire to show strength where she had little left. "Jack said to thank you, for trying to help him…us."

In the past, such sentiment would have caused him to point out that he had not done this favor for Mallory but for his sister and his wife and Miss Ella's unborn grandchild. But when he considered Isabelle, he realized that he had indeed done it for Jack Mallory, that he owed the man a debt even this effort could never come close to repaying.

***

Isabelle awoke deep in the night. The lamp had been dimmed, but she could not remember if she had adjusted it or if Ketch had. Naked, he lay asleep on his back, gently snoring. Close against his side, she enjoyed the tranquil sight of him. He looked truly at peace only when asleep, the lines gone from his face, the shadows in his eyes hidden, his

275

jaw relaxed. Even his scars seemed faded or lost completely in the night. The vertical creases often present between his eyes, lines she wished to wipe away forever, were far too deep for someone his age, though she could only guess how old he truly was.

Before meeting Ketch, she had naïvely thought that being a free person meant a better life, a life devoid of fear and concern. But now she knew even freedom could never guarantee such things. Perhaps, she told herself, if she knew all of Ketch's secrets, she would not be so drawn to him. Maybe she loved the mystery more than the man. Yet now, silently watching him, she knew her declaration to him yesterday morning had been for the man. Although he had not voiced his love in return, the trust he had shown her signified that his feelings ran equally deep, if not deeper.

She thought of his words to Helen: "Love's not that simple." Indeed, it was not, she reflected as she watched the golden lantern light play across Ketch's wild hair. Careful not to wake him, she brushed it away from his eyes.

Her finger drifted down past his ear, along his neck, across his shoulder to his muscular arm resting between them. She imagined him whole, with two arms to hold her as he had once lamented. His head rolled slightly on the pillow. His lips formed quiet, incomprehensible words, but he remained asleep. The animal strength of men, their muscle mass, had intimidated her in the past, but now she admired Ketch's strong arm and thick chest, thought of the burly sailors aboard the *Adventuress*, imagined him there among them, whole and active in his duties. She wondered if he missed that life. He spoke infrequently of it, usually only when Helen brought up the subject, hoping aloud that they would one day again sail together, and Isabelle would not get seasick.

When Isabelle remembered Helen's words and Ketch's subsequent chuckle, she smiled. How good he was with the child. She had mentioned it to him again the other day.

"I think she looks to you as a second father."

"No," he had quickly insisted.

"Why not? Don't you think you would be a good father?"

"I don't know the first thing 'bout bein' a father."

"Who does till they are one?" Although he failed to answer, she refused to abandon the discussion. "If we have a child, someday, what would you want—a boy or a girl?"

"You and yer questions, Izzy—"

"Don't you want children?"

276

"I haven't given it much thought, truth be told."

"But which would you like? Most men want a son."

"I can see you won't let me rest till I give you an answer."

Although afraid she had angered him, she offered no apology for her inquiry. He would not be foolish enough to think they could share a bed without ultimately producing children.

Finally, he replied, "I don't want to bring more cruelty into this world, so...'twould have to be a girl. And she must look like her mother." With a sly glance, he offered a grin of concession.

From someone with an expression usually guarded, his grins often caught her unprepared. True, he was not a man of uncommon beauty, but when he smiled, the scars and imperfections were less pronounced. Happiness had visited his countenance infrequently—no creases lay in the corners of his eyes like those of happier souls Isabelle had known, those accustomed to regular mirth, like William.

She looked now at the smooth corners of his closed eyes, wondered about the laughter he had been deprived of in life, hoped that she could provide such lost joy.

Her hand glided downward across his flat belly, her finger tracing the narrow trail of hair below his navel. Again, he garbled distant, sleep-induced words as his body reacted to her exploratory touch. Down low he bore a scar that she had noted before—an ugly, pale, diagonal line where hair would no longer grow. She had yet to ask him about it, nor had he offered any explanation. Ever so gently, her finger traced the two-inch mark...

The blow struck from nowhere. White light exploded in her head, blinding. She tumbled from the bed with an outcry unheard amidst Ketch's roar—an animal sound, a mixture of rage and fear that caused her to push away from the bed. He had reared upward, poised now to spring from the mattress, fist clenched, teeth bared, eyes wild. But the rapid motion had brought him back to awareness, left him teetering there as consciousness eroded the fury and cleared his eyes. His elbow had caught her full on the mouth and split her lips. Her teeth had cut a gash on the inside of her lower lip, and blood flowed hot and salty down her throat.

Ketch's shoulders rounded in despair as the air rattled out of him. He crouched before her, his trembling hand poised between them, as if afraid she would recoil. The part of her where memories of Ezekiel lived urged her away from him, but sensibility allowed her to hold her ground. She saw that his unconscious actions had horrified him and brought home all his previously revealed dread about harming her.

"Izzy…I'm sorry…I didn't mean to…I was dreamin'…"

She took his hand in hers while discreetly staunching the flow of blood. Her lip was already swollen.

"I'm sorry," he whispered again.

The way he leaned toward her bespoke his desire to hold her, to offer physical consolation, but indecisiveness restrained him. Isabelle reached for him, and he pressed her so tightly against him that her ribs protested, the pounding of his heart almost painful against her.

"You should go back to yer own bed tonight."

She pulled just far enough away for him to see her resolve. "I'm not going anywhere. We must give it time. That's all."

Ketch's thumb gently wiped away the blood.

She recaptured his hand, whispered, "Come back to bed." She hid any uneasiness she felt, cautioned herself to never again let her fingers wander upon him while he slept.

Ketch's obedience to her request, though slow with reluctance and uncertainty, assured Isabelle that she had indeed made progress these past days. Once in bed, he remained near the outside edge of the mattress. Undeterred, Isabelle moved close to his tense body and laid her hand upon his chest, which still rose and fell strongly. He studied her, shame deepening those familiar lines.

"T'other day, when you said what you said to me… Well, you know I'm no great hand at sayin' things right or sayin' 'em when they need to be said, but… Truth is, I love you, too, Izzy."

The pain slipped away. She kissed him then rested her head upon his shoulder, quietly asked, "What was you dreaming?"

"Nothin'. 'Twas but a jumble."

"Won't you tell me about it?"

"No."

"Why not?"

"I'd rather forget those things."

"But you can't."

"No. How do you do it, Izzy—how do you forget the things they done to you?"

"When I'm with you, they don't matter no more." She considered his pensive expression. "What is it you want to forget?"

He stared up at the ceiling, said, "Everything."

***

The next morning Maria was still in bed when Isabelle arrived for

278

work. She was not surprised to hear her mistress retching behind the closed bedchamber door, for Ketch had told her about Maria's pregnancy after Helen had left last night. Now and then, Mary emerged from the room, carrying a chamber pot to empty and return. From the kitchen house, Rose brought a tray of her concoctions used to help ease their mistress's troubles. When Helen came to check on her, Rose shooed her out, but the child was concerned their trip to Charles Town would be postponed. By afternoon, however, Maria's sickness had passed, and Helen's excitement over their trip downriver returned full force. The girl rushed back and forth between her chamber and Maria's while Isabelle and Mary helped them pack.

"We're going to stay with the Waterstons tonight," Helen announced. "I'll get to meet your mamma."

Envious, Isabelle smiled. "You must tell her I said hello and give her my love."

"I will."

When Maria and Helen left, sadness weighed upon Isabelle the rest of the day. Not only did she already miss them, but she worried over the fate of Helen's brother. For the child to have lost her parents then to possibly lose her brother... Isabelle had often wondered what it would have been like to have siblings or even half-siblings if William had lived. Thinking of William made her think of her mother and wish that she could have accompanied Maria to the Waterstons, but she knew Maria could not show such obvious favor to her, especially so soon after her inclusion in the household. Any display of partiality would only increase the other servants' prejudice.

The next day, the house was even more melancholy. No meals for the servants to serve, no happy chatter from Helen echoing off the walls. The void was felt by all, including Ketch, who mentioned it when he came to escort her home. Isabelle knew the situation with their master was wearing on him, especially since the sheriff's last visit. She had heard part of the conversation on the portico, enough to know that her husband was suspected of meddling. But she had refrained from questioning him about the accusations, not only because she sensed he did not want her to but because a part of her was afraid to know the truth. Thinking back upon what he had done to rid her of Ezekiel, she shuddered.

Restless, Ketch left their bedchamber partway through the night and spoke little during breakfast. On the way to Leighlin House, he was distracted, staring far from her, brow low. Isabelle shivered and pulled her shawl tighter about her. Desperate to shake him from his dark thoughts, she took his hand and squeezed it tightly.

"Ketch," she said, "I know you want to help the Captain and his family, but... I'm sure Mr. Waterston and Miss Maria will find a way...and...and I'm sure the Captain wouldn't want you to get yourself in a fix trying."

"You might be surprised what the Captain wants; whatever it takes, I'm sure, to keep him with his family."

"But..." The words died upon her lips when he tossed a discouraging look her way. She was being selfish, but a rush of dread pushed her onward. "I don't want to lose you."

"Nothin's goin' to happen to me."

When they reached the portico steps, she was reluctant to free him, and she hoped what she failed to convey with words could at least be seen in her eyes.

"If you come home tonight and I'm not there, I don't want you to fret, Izzy."

She restrained her protest only with great difficulty and took his hand again, tried to speak, to assure him of her support, but nothing came except silent tears.

He gently protested, "Now, Izzy...damn it..."

"Mr. Ketch! Izzy!"

Helen's shout from the doorway above turned them. The child burst forth from the house and ran down the steps.

"We're home, Izzy. Did you miss me?"

The child bounded into Isabelle's embrace before she or Ketch could respond. Isabelle hurriedly blinked away her tears before Helen could notice.

"I met your mamma, Izzy. She told me to give you this." Helen bestowed a noisy, wet kiss upon Isabelle's cheek, making her laugh.

Someone appeared on the portico, moving at a much more restrained pace, and halted at the top of the steps. Isabelle gasped, for there, looking down upon them with satisfaction and something close to pleasure, stood her master as if he had never left.

"Captain!" She curtseyed. "Good morning, sir. We're so pleased you're home."

Ketch stood dumbfounded as the young man descended the steps, a smile raising the corners of his thin mustache, eyes tired but bright with the light of freedom. He stopped before them, one hand resting on Helen's shoulder.

"Thank you, Isabelle. I'm pleased to be home as well. And I have many people to thank for it, one of whom is your husband."

He held out his hand to Ketch, who hesitated in surprise. Almost mechanically, Ketch took the young man's hand and shook it. Helen's eyes lifted from the men's clasp to Isabelle, her expression alight with pure triumph and satisfaction.

CHAPTER 23

The scandal over Jack Mallory's arrest and release failed to deter Maria from having Leighlin's ball as planned. The young woman was determined to show the community that she and her husband viewed the arrest as merely a misunderstanding and that her spouse was still a respectable, honest, civilized man among them.

During the week leading up to the Saturday night ball, she drove Isabelle and Leighlin's staff in a feverish effort to have the house spotless and decorated from top to bottom, inside and out. Isabelle welcomed the work because it made the days fly, and the preparations provided something cheerful to occupy master and mistress after the recent drama.

By the time the anticipated day arrived, the house had been transformed. The clean smell of fresh paint lay just hidden beneath the scent of fresh-cut green boughs above some of the doorways. The perfume of flowers in vases and baskets throughout the house helped mask the paint odor as well. Every window sparkled in the autumn sun, and the floorboards gleamed "like the deck of a man-of-war," her master had proclaimed, though Isabelle had no idea exactly what the phrase meant.

Isabelle and the other women served the Mallorys their breakfast earlier than usual, and after they were done Maria rushed off with Rose to the kitchen house, Helen shadowing them.

The Captain stood from the table, said, "After you're finished here, Isabelle, please lay out my riding breeches and boots; Thomas is busy with other duties. I'll be taking Helen riding for a bit this morning to get her out of Maria's way."

A short while later, as Isabelle climbed the stairs to the master bedchamber, she had a feeling Helen would have little desire to go riding with her brother. The child had been as determined as her sister-in-law to make sure everything was perfect for their guests' arrivals this afternoon.

In the master bedchamber, morning sunlight through the river windows had already chased away most of the night's chill. Mary had made the bed, everything perfectly smoothed and tucked, and had opened one of the windows just enough to allow a small flow of fresh air. Isabelle went about her business, humming a tune her husband had been whistling that morning.

Upon the bed, she laid out a gray pair of riding breeches, the deerskin seat reinforced more than once. Isabelle wondered if Ketch had hunted the deer that had given its hide for their master's comfort.

The Captain's riding boots were made of calfskin, as soft as butter from the master's hours in the saddle and Nahum's close care with oil and cloth. Although they were clean, Isabelle took a moment to buff them with a soft rag. So intent was she on bringing out the highest shine in the boots that she failed to hear her master's approach. His chuckle startled her, and she almost dropped the boot.

"Don't worry about appearance, Isabelle. My boots have no one to impress this morning."

The old fear struggled to overcome her here in the Captain's bedchamber. Up until now, she had managed to avoid being alone in this chamber with him. She told herself that her misgivings were foolish, reminding herself of the devotion between master and mistress as expressed by Ketch as well as seen by her own eyes. But that familiar dread kept her immobile, knowing that if she moved right now, it would be in an embarrassing rush to flee.

The young man moved past her to one of the river windows and opened it. "Thank you, Isabelle. That'll be all."

Her body relaxed, and breath entered her lungs once again. She gave the boot one last swipe before setting it down. In the doorway, she glanced at the Captain, who still stood staring toward the river, hands clasped behind his back. She wondered what he was thinking but was happily confident that it was not about her.

"Captain?" The word slipped from her mouth before she realized it, turning him. Although she knew she should just excuse herself and leave, she gathered her courage. "May…may I ask you something?"

"Of course."

Isabelle felt perspiration gather under her collar. "Well, since you came back…" She faltered. "When you came back to Leighlin, you thanked my husband for helping you."

"Aye."

"He hasn't told me what it was he done to help you, but I reckon that's business between you and him, sir, but…well, I could see how grateful you was, and I know my husband would have done even more than he did to get you back to Miss Helen and Miss Maria." She hesitated.

"Go on."

"Well, sir, I know this isn't my place to talk about such things, but it's been laying heavy on my mind since, and I…I just wanted to say, I know you and my husband had troubles in the past and that he's done many things to vex you, but I truly believe he aims to make things better between you…'cause of all you've done for us."

The Captain considered her with a hint of satisfaction on his dark face. "I believe you, Isabelle. And 'tis true we've had our troubles and no doubt will have more of them, but don't think I haven't appreciated the better side of your husband. He's served Leighlin well in other ways. And, thanks to you, I believe he will continue to serve my family for a long time to come. That's my hope."

Relief washed over her. "Oh, sir, that's my hope, too."

"Rest assured, I know I have sometimes been a bit unfair in my bias toward your husband because of our history but…well, from now on I'll try to leave the past in the past."

"Thank you, Captain." She curtseyed. "I do hope you have a pleasant ride with Miss Helen."

***

During Ketch's work at the kiln that morning, he swore he could smell the harried work of the kitchen staff even at that distance. The guests would be served a supper hearty enough to fuel the evening's dancing. There would be finger foods to maintain stamina. Afterward, the visitors would spend the night, so Leighlin had to provide space and sleeping arrangements—a difficult proposition with two dozen visitors. Helen's bedchamber would be used by some of the guests while she would share her brother and sister-in-law's bed, though Ketch was quite certain Helen would let neither of them sleep after such an exciting evening. He smiled at the thought of her circulating among the guests like a tiny goodwill ambassador, blissfully ignorant of the danger her brother had so recently faced.

When Ketch returned home in the early afternoon, his house was dead and lonesome, so he sought out Maria to help with the preparations. Once the guests began to arrive in the late afternoon, starting with David and Elizabeth Archer, he returned home to wash and shift his clothes. He let his hair fall loose. Isabelle would be displeased with him looking so unkempt when in Leighlin House, but he would be seen only by Samuel, Willis, and the other white men of the lower level, so he felt little guilt for being remiss.

As he crossed over to the main house, passing behind the busy kitchen house, darkness closed in. A perfect evening for that time of year—dry and warm, little humidity. The towering house sparkled with an illumination from within that he had not seen since Ella Logan had been alive. The sight made him smile and forget that they had come close to possibly losing all of it. Instead, he remembered his former mistress's great joy at hosting social events. Her husband, purposefully a cautious, reserved man in this region, had looked with disfavor upon large gatherings but had tolerated them for the sake of his wife and for his daughter's future in this expanding community.

Leighlin's dining room was particularly refulgent and lively, the north windows open to alleviate the heat generated by so many bodies and the piping hot food, which he could smell as strongly as if he were in that room. His mouth watered. A considerable feast awaited him in the lower level, for though he and the others would not be a part of the festivities upstairs, the Mallorys would see that their workers enjoyed themselves tonight as well, that all could celebrate the harvest. Even the slave settlement would be enlivened this evening, the workers having been allowed to slaughter a steer for their own jubilee.

Willis and the others were already at table when Ketch arrived. Except for Samuel's nod, he received no greeting or acknowledgement, the others far too deep in their meal and in their drink—wine tonight instead of the usual beer or ale. They knew nothing of his part in Jack Mallory's release and thus in their own preservation. He wondered if they would have offered any thanks.

Once the meal was through and the table cleared, Latiffe produced a deck of worn cards, and all settled in for a long, enjoyable night of dice and cards.

Shortly after they started, music from far above could be heard as musicians recruited from Charles Town kicked the evening off with a lively reel. Often, subconsciously or otherwise, one or more of the men at the table would tap fingers, cards, or feet in time with the tunes that sifted down through floorboards and chimney. Willis hummed whenever a tune came that he recognized. The happy sounds from two floors up reminded Ketch of his days at sea when the men would gather on the forecastle in the evenings to sing and dance. Although Ketch had offered neither a step nor a note—he had never risked knowing if he could sing or dance—he enjoyed the sights and sounds, sometimes even clapping or stomping his feet. Now, that same joyful ring inside

Leighlin House dispelled all memory of the gloom of a week ago.

Occasionally, he heard Helen's voice. She would be in her glory, wearing her new pink gown that she had insisted upon donning to show him last week, one Isabelle had helped Abigail sew.

Thus, distracted by these musings as well as by thoughts of his wife, Ketch realized his winnings were rather meager. If he was ever to square his debt with Jack Mallory for Zeke's loss, he needed to be attentive to his cards. So, while he forced himself to focus, he also began to pay more attention to the conversation around the table, conversation increasingly colorful and opinionated with the wine consumption.

Having drank the most, Gabriel headed much of the talk, rattling off slurred gossip about the various guests. Ketch offered no opinion, but when he heard Tom Clark's name, he looked up from his cards. Never had he considered that Clark could be one of the invited. To avoid giving Gabriel the gratification of having known about Clark's presence before he did, Ketch hid his alarm.

"Maybe he came to reclaim his former property." Gabriel chuckled. "I hear tell he's done well in the last quarter. Maybe he can afford more slaves again." He downed the last of the wine from his cup. "Maybe he regrets sellin' Isabelle. You know what they say about her and him, lads. But then that was hearsay, wasn't it? I wager Ketch could tell us the real story, eh, Ketch? I'm sure by now your wife would've told you."

The others cleared their throats, or shuffled their feet, or coughed.

Ketch stared at his cards as he discarded one, spoke in a flat, dismissive voice. "That's me own business and none o' your'n."

"My, my, my, Ketch," Gabriel tsked. "What's become of you? That little mulatto wife of yours cut off your balls?"

"Seems marriage agrees with Ketch," Samuel rumbled. "Maybe it's something you should consider, Gabe. It'll give you something to do other than gossip like an old hen."

The others laughed and turned their remarks to the young man's lack of prospects in the female line, teasingly encouraging him to consider a slave wife as well. Ketch hid his tiny smile of appreciation for Samuel's distraction.

He allowed any talk of Clark or Isabelle to drift far away as he waited impatiently. When the men had gathered in a crouched circle on the floor with dice rolling about and hoots and hollers filling the room, he could no longer bear to remain there. He slipped outside on the pretense of going to relieve himself.

Outside, the music came louder and clearer, voices above him on the upper portico, laughter. He paused near the steps, forced calm into his racing mind, cautioned himself against succumbing to his desire to crush Clark. But he could not deny his concern for Isabelle being confronted by the villain. He must see her, just a quick view to gauge her state of mind. Surely Maria would relieve her of her duties if she knew the truth.

In the illuminated Great Hall, two couples stood in close conversation. All other activity was above him, but as he crossed over to the dining room, the music and rumble of dancing feet halted, followed by applause. Entering the empty, dark dining room where the faintest scent of supper still lingered, he stealthily squeezed his way into the cleverly hidden winding staircase near the hearth. With some difficulty, loathing the smothering darkness and musty odor of the space, he wound his way up to the next floor. Before opening the narrow door to the master bedchamber, he paused to listen, and when he detected no sounds from within, he peeked out. No one there, the door to the ballroom closed.

No music. Perhaps the musicians were being allowed a breather before the next set. Jumbled conversations buzzed beyond the door. Isabelle would be busy offering refreshments to the guests. As softly as he could, Ketch moved to the adjoining ballroom door where he paused again. He inched the door open and peered with one eye into the vibrant crowd beyond.

Bunting, wreaths, ribbons, and flowers lavishly decorated the room, along with bowers over hearths and doorways, all flooded by dazzling light from the beautiful crystal chandelier used only when master and mistress entertained company. The guests stood in small knots, talking gaily, faces open with cheer and flushed from dancing. Among them was Margaret Wylder in a stunning red and black gown, her blonde hair pulled up, revealing diamond earrings. Her husband was nowhere to be seen. The door to the rear portico had been propped open to ventilate the warm space. The musicians stood near the door, instruments set aside, mopping their brows and guzzling punch, except for one fiddler who was showing Helen his polished instrument, allowing the curious child to touch the strings. Maria flowed from group to group in an indigo gown, her smooth shoulders shining like mahogany. She looked a bit off her color but otherwise happy and only slightly tired. Mary and Pip offered trays of sweets to the guests, their forest-green livery with immaculate white aprons a sharp contrast to the guests' varied silks and satins.

Ketch looked for more of that deep green and found Isabelle on the far side of the room, holding a tray of champagne glasses. She wore a troubled expression as Jack Mallory took a glass and spoke to her, then her eyes went to the man with whom Mallory was conversing, a man whose wide posterior faced Ketch. The distantly familiar shape and the concern on Isabelle's face told Ketch who this guest was.

Tom Clark was an unattractive man—his head too round and big, his facial features too small, the wig that covered his sparse hair ill-fitting, his neck barely discernible upon his shoulders. And he was shorter than Jack Mallory, who himself towered over few men. Isabelle seemed to be listening to Clark, who had squared his shoulders to her. Suddenly, her eyes widened, and her mouth gaped. The silver tray fell from her hands with a prodigious crash, glass and champagne flying in all directions. Conversations ceased as everyone turned. With a gasp, Isabelle dove to the floor and started plucking at the wreckage.

"Captain," she cried, "your stockings! Oh, I've ruined your stockings."

Tom Clark laughed. "I see she has lost some of her grace since she left my house, Captain. Perhaps you treat her too gently. If you let her return to me, I will straighten her out in no time."

Ketch shoved the door open and crossed the room with long strides, pushing past guests. Seeing his bull-like approach, Isabelle scrambled up just in time to put herself between him and Tom Clark, who stared at Ketch with feral gray eyes and astonished recognition. Ketch halted, unsure what he had intended to do, though acutely aware of what he desired to do. Realizing the foolish impetuosity of his advance and the attention he had drawn, he held himself rigidly in check.

Amazingly, Jack Mallory stood unmoved by Ketch's unheralded advance and his guests' shocked silence. He spoke with incongruous calm, something Ketch certainly did not expect, as if they were the only ones in the room. "Mr. Clark, I believe you know Mr. Ketch."

Clark regained some of his smugness when he realized Ketch would not pounce upon him. "Aye, I'm familiar with Mr. Ketch…and his ways."

"Well, if you're indeed serious about reacquiring Isabelle, you'll need his permission as well as mine."

Ketch stared at Mallory, an oath upon his tongue, but the mischief in the young man's dark eyes and the wry lift of one corner of his mustache quelled any outburst. Although Ketch now realized Mallory was simply making game of Clark, the terror in Isabelle's eyes told him that she was ignorant of the ploy.

"Why would Mr. Ketch's permission be required?" Clark asked with barely veiled disdain. "You are master of Leighlin, Captain."

"Just so, but Mr. Ketch is Isabelle's husband."

No one gasped in the room, but Ketch felt the wave of scandal just as keenly. He could hardly conceal his own surprise that Mallory would so publicly volunteer such knowledge, for it would reflect unfavorably upon anyone at Leighlin, especially the master.

"Her husband?" Clark said. "What sort of trumpery is this? Really, Captain, you astound me. James Logan would never have countenanced such a disreputable union."

"Are you questioning my judgment, sir?" The private amusement had fled Mallory's face, and Ketch wondered if he meant to call the scoundrel out. In that moment, Ketch saw a man instead of a boy.

Clark bowed slightly with a careful glance toward Ketch, as if to make sure he had not moved closer. "Of course not, Captain. My apologies if I misspoke." Sheepishly, he looked around at the guests, and Ketch realized Clark's wife was not among them. "I had no idea Mr. Ketch had such a bride. I would never have entertained the thought of reclaiming her if I had known."

Some of the tension left Isabelle's features. Ketch calmed at the welcomed sight of Clark's discomfiture.

Maria had drawn near to her husband, and with forced cheerfulness she said, "Come now, Isabelle, there's a mess to be cleaned up. We wouldn't want our guests slipping. Pip, bear a hand." She turned a smile upon her friends. "We'll have more champagne directly. Please, sample the punch in the meantime."

Taking Maria's cue, the guests turned politely away from Ketch and Clark and resumed their conversations, though far more subdued and with occasional glances over their shoulders. Clark retreated swiftly to the portico, and Mallory moved toward Malachi Waterston and his wife, a fabricated smile upon his face as he joined their conversation.

Helen wound her way across the room, oblivious to the tension. "Have you come to dance with me, Mr. Ketch?"

Flustered, he managed, "No, child. I can't stay. I shouldn't have come to begin with."

"Why isn't your hair tied back? And your shirt is untucked—"

"Ketch." Maria stepped next to him with that same thin smile, saying in a voice loud enough for those near to hear. "Will you help me and Thomas break out more champagne?"

Isabelle raised her head from the disaster upon the floor long enough to urge, "I'm fine. Go."

Ketch nodded to Maria and made his excuse to Helen, who eyed him with disappointment and a good bit of disapproval.

He followed Maria down the left-hand staircase in the stair hall where another chandelier, also rarely lit, filled the tall space with a burst of light, chasing away the familiar shadows and making it seem almost daytime. Maria's stiff shoulders reflected her tension, and when he thought of the child she carried, he again regretted his brashness.

"I'm sorry. I didn't mean to cause a fuss. I just came to check on Izzy."

Near the front door, she halted and turned back to him. "Check on her? Whatever for?"

"'Tis Clark. When she was servin' in his house…" He hesitated, knowing Isabelle would prefer he keep her secret.

"What about Clark?"

Considering that perhaps if Maria knew the truth, she would release Isabelle for the night, Ketch said, "Clark raped her. When I heard tell he was here, I just had to see her, to make sure she was well. We didn't know he was goin' to be here."

Maria's face crimsoned with familiar anger, and she seemed to struggle with her emotions before speaking. "That's why she begged Jack not to send her back to Clark."

"Aye. He's a first-rate whoreson of a swab…" Ketch caught himself. "I didn't come here to knock the bastard on his head, though I'd like to. I didn't aim to come bargin' in like that. I just saw how frighted Izzy was and—"

"Go back downstairs. I'll ask Isabelle if she'd like to be excused. Don't worry about Clark. Jack would never let her go back to him, not after what's happened the past week or so."

A wave of relief swept over him. He thanked her and reluctantly left the house.

290

CHAPTER 24

1694 arrived and with it colder weather, the chill reminding Ketch of Southwark and the dampness that would emanate from the Thames. After the harvest ball, Leighlin Plantation settled into winter routine. Once the last of the rice had been milled and stored or sent downriver to be shipped, the slaves were rewarded with a week off. Afterward, work resumed in full force. Field hands were reassigned to help with the production of naval stores as well as to prepare the rice fields for spring planting. The stubble was burned off, and canals were cleared of excess mud, their sides fortified, and new ditches dug where fields were expanded.

Once a month, with Malachi Waterston's permission, Isabelle visited her mother. At Isabelle's request, Ketch accompanied her, and the time spent with Louisa seemed to erode the woman's initial misgivings about him, though he could tell she remained unconvinced of his devotion to her daughter. No such question, however, remained in Ketch's mind.

As each day passed, his love for Isabelle grew. Each night spent in her arms brought healing to his soul, and the violence of that one instance never resurfaced, though he refused to hazard dousing the lamps yet. Perhaps he never would. After supper, they would sit together in front of the fire, Ketch gazing into the flames or at his wife as she worked away at her sewing or basket-making, a struggle that she was winning with emerging artistry. Isabelle chatted happily about her mother or about happenings in the Big House where she had established herself as a valued member of the household. While not intimate friends with the likes of Mary or Pip or the other servants, they seemed to have accepted her. Ketch hoped that one day she would find a particular friend among them.

On one of those dark winter evenings, when Ketch had just carried in firewood and knelt to prepare the fire before Isabelle arrived home, he heard the drum of small feet upon the front porch steps. Only one creature at Leighlin had the energy that late in the day to move at such a furious gallop. The door burst open before he could fully turn. Helen raced through the house without a word. The door to Isabelle's former chamber slammed shut behind her. Ketch found her on the bed, face down, sobbing into a pillow.

"Miss Helen." He sat on the edge of the mattress. "What's amiss, child?"

"It's all my fault," she sobbed into the pillow.

"What's yer fault? Come now, tell me what's happened."

"I shouldn't have told you. I shouldn't have told anyone. It was bad luck just like John said."

The wintry feel of the cabin reached even deeper into him as he grasped the issue. "You mean Miss Maria…?"

Helen faced the wall. "She got sudden sick, and there was nothing Mr. Willis could do to save the baby. He died, and it's my fault."

"Miss Helen…now don't be thickheaded. Come here." His invitation was all she needed—her arms went around him, and she wept even harder. "Hush now, child. Yer goin' to drown the both of us, sure. And you runnin' here without even yer cloak. 'Twixt the damp outside and the damp yer causin' you'll catch cold, you will."

"John'll hate me for telling."

"Oh, what stuff," he gently admonished. "I've said nothin' to no one, Samuel neither, 'bout the secret you told us, so there's no reason for yer brother to think ill o' you, as if he ever would."

"But I have to tell him, so he knows why the baby died. If I don't, he'll blame himself."

"You don't need to tell yer brother nothin' o' the sort. That baby dyin' had nothin' to do with him or you. These things just happen."

"But why?"

"I don't know. They just do."

They were still sitting together on the bed when Isabelle arrived. Helen's tears had finally halted, but she still held Ketch close and trembled.

Ketch asked, "How's Maria?"

Isabelle shook her head. "She's resting, poor thing. Mr. Willis said she lost a bucket of blood, but she'll be fine."

"Miss Helen." He tried to extricate himself from the girl. "You must let me go start a fire afore we all freeze. Why don't you set a moment with Izzy whilst I do that, then she can get supper started? I'll send Iris to tell yer brother yer eatin' with us."

"I'm not hungry."

"Just the same, you'll eat. Now cast off, child."

At last, she surrendered herself to Isabelle, who folded her into her arms.

Supper was a gloomy affair, though Ketch and Isabelle did their best to hearten Helen, but the girl listlessly picked at her pork and sweet potatoes. And when a knock sounded upon the front door, Helen bolted for the bedchamber. Isabelle frowned at Ketch and followed the girl.

Ketch found Jack Mallory standing on the porch, swallowed by a dark coat, lantern in hand. Shadows lent him a particular gauntness, skin drawn tight over pronounced cheekbones, eyes haunted, hair disheveled.

"I've come for Helen."

Moved by his young master's appearance, Ketch said, "Izzy and me...we're sorry 'bout what happened. If you'd like, Helen can stay here the night, so you can tend to yer wife."

The mere mention of his loss renewed the film of moisture in Mallory's eyes, and he quickly looked away as if he could hide the grief. "I should speak with her."

But Ketch could see his master had no more strength to talk to Helen about their loss than the child did.

"She said she don't want to upset you with her cryin'."

He considered telling the whole truth, so Mallory could dispel Helen's fear, but he did not want Helen to find out that he had exposed her secret, nor did he want to take the chance that Mallory might feel vexed by his sister having gone against his wishes.

The young man lingered there, his expression revealing his pain and worry over his sister's behavior. Since the charges Seth Wylder had brought against him had been dropped, he had shown Ketch a willingness to forgive past offenses, and their relationship—though certainly not warm—had returned to the way it had been before Zeke's death. Perhaps, Ketch reflected, it had even been strengthened by mutual respect and the shared bond of marriage. He saw that esteem now in his master's dulled eyes, a gratitude for Ketch's continued assistance with his family.

"Helen will be fine," Ketch said with more of a softening to his tone than usual around Mallory. "I'll bring her by in the morn."

The young man nodded, shoulders rounded, appearing completely at a loss and uncomfortable with his helplessness. He turned back into the darkness, his footfalls hollow upon the wooden steps.

Later, when they tucked Helen into bed, Isabelle lingered until the child fell asleep, then she crept across the hallway. She and Ketch lay awake for some time as she told him how she had found Maria unconscious on the portico that afternoon, how she had stayed in the bedchamber to tend her mistress after Willis had examined and treated her.

"There was so much blood. And Miss Maria was in so much pain for a time, till the baby… Poor thing, only the size of a strawberry, it was, but Mr. Willis said it passed." Her voice diminished to a distant whisper, and she sought Ketch's hand. "Miss Maria cried, but when she heard the Captain coming, she made herself stop. She told me to fetch her a cloth, and she had me wipe her face as fast as I could. When the Captain came in, he sent me out for a time. He was so sad, the whole house was, the women all crying, even Thomas." Her grip upon his hand tightened, and some of the warmth left her fingers. "It isn't that way with all women, is it? I mean, the way it's been with Miss Maria. I don't recollect it happening that way so often with others, but then I reckon I've never paid much attention to such things. Do you have to lose babies before you can finally hold just one?"

"'Tis not the way with all, just some. Think on me own mother— she had several little 'uns after me." As he thought of how criminally short their lives had been, he drew Isabelle's hand beneath the blankets where their bodies had created a wonderful pocket of warmth. He kissed her and whispered, "Won't be that way if yer time comes, Izzy."

She drew in a long, quivering breath and slowly exhaled. "I reckon we'll find out soon."

"Soon?"

"Yes."

Speechless, he raised himself upon his elbow.

"I haven't been able to tell you. I've known for a while, but… Silly, I know, since it's nothing I could hide forever. But maybe it's a blessing now, something I can tell Miss Helen that will cheer her."

His words remained trapped somewhere deep in his whirling mind or buried in his tightening stomach. Seeing how his silence concerned her, he finally uttered, "A baby?"

"You've hardly spoken about us having a babe of our own. So, I've been afeared, ever since I realized I'm with child, that you would be angry or displeased. That's why I didn't saying nothing till now."

"How long have you known?"

"A couple months now. So, Miss Maria and me…our babies would've been born not far apart. Maybe they could've even played together." She turned onto her side. "Are you displeased?"

"O' course not."

"But you're not happy neither. I can see that. I can hear it in your voice."

"Izzy." His fingers played with her small, tight curls upon the pillow. "'Tis just…you've caught me betwixt the wind and a lee shore. Call me daft but I had no idea, no suspicion. But I'm not unhappy with you. Don't think that." He could tell, however, that he could neither convince her nor hide his feelings from her as he could with others, so he drew her close and kissed her. "Yer right about Helen. You must tell her in the morn. That will cheer her a bit. But we should warn her against tellin' her brother and Miss Maria for now. It might pain them."

"Yes, but I think Miss Maria already knows." She yawned. "I've been unwell sometimes, and I know she's noticed. Pip was complaining about it, the little fool, worried I had some sickness that I was going to pass onto her."

"Well, all the same, considerin' today, we won't say nothin' for a bit, aye?"

"I won't," she murmured, suddenly relaxing and an instant later asleep.

She had been this way for several weeks—it came to him now—and he felt like a buffoon for his lack of observation about his own wife. But what did he know of such things? He had avoided all contemplation about the possibility of children—his children—so perhaps he had seen and sensed the signs but had immediately denied them. He again thought of his forsaken siblings, of his brutish stepfather and father, and more than anything in life, he feared what sort of parent he would prove to be and what sort of offspring his blood would produce.

***

The news of Isabelle's pregnancy buoyed Helen somewhat, and she vowed not to breathe a word of it to anyone lest she curse Isabelle as she had cursed Maria. The fact that she kept such a thing secret—a child who delighted in being the first to tell everyone any bit of news, great or small—revealed to Ketch the depth of her guilt over her sister-in-law's loss. A month later, Ketch freed her to spread the word to whomever she wished, which she promptly did with tempered zeal and hope. When Maria and her husband congratulated Ketch and Isabelle, they concealed any pangs of envy. Ketch thought it a cruel twist that he, who dreaded nothing greater, should have a child before the Mallorys, who had been trying with such high expectations for so long. But life's brutal unfairness never surprised him.

Maria often found ways to surreptitiously lighten Isabelle's daily burdens in the house, though Isabelle pleaded with her not to show her any favor over the others. She told Ketch every night of one kindness or another from the Mallorys.

"Perhaps if I'd listened to my husband," Maria had confided to her, "and not worked so hard over the ball, I wouldn't have lost our child. So, you must listen to me."

Ketch enjoyed his daily work in the quiet of the forest, listening to the lofty pines whisper when the wind blew, for it soothed his growing worries over his impending fatherhood. Much of his anxiety he hid from Isabelle. She was so easily set to tears nowadays, an unsettling phenomenon that Samuel insisted was typical for a woman in her condition. These bewildering changes only unnerved Ketch more, made him feel inadequate in his ignorance.

He dreamed often of his stepfather, of his callousness and the murders of his own issue, especially Sophia. Then Ketch would awaken to memories of his own crimes. He had always believed that much of his own tendency to violence was something bred into him, that he lacked complete control over his actions. He had but to think of his own half-brother's lifetime of violence, murder, and rapine, behavior that their father had bred into Dan. The thought of passing such disreputable qualities on to his offspring aggrieved Ketch. How could he love such a thing, knowing what it would eventually become, knowing he had brought it into this world? Perhaps Isabelle's goodness would somehow prevail, just as his mother's greater qualities had provided some small portion of humanity in him.

"Why, Ketch," Isabelle said one evening when she walked in upon him donning his best clothes, "you can't go to town now—the tide is rising."

"I'm not goin' to town." He finished buttoning his coat. "I'm off to see the Captain." He turned. "Would you fetch that ribbon yonder and tie me queue?"

She obliged. "What do you need to see him about?"

"Just a bit o' business 'twixt us." He felt his evasion necessary. If he revealed his purpose and Mallory denied his request, Isabelle would be disappointed, so he held his tongue and quickly departed.

Because Ketch's request for an audience had been written and delivered the previous day, Thomas now awaited him at Leighlin House's back door at the appointed time. The servant led him to the library where the Mallorys awaited, both with puzzled expressions, especially when they saw his washed, trimmed, and brushed appearance. Mallory offered him a chair within the warm glow of the fire, which held the creeping evening at bay. Then the young man joined his wife on the settee opposite. Ketch cleared his throat, stared beyond them to the west windows, shuttered and draped, and wished he had stayed home, wished he did not feel impelled to do this, wished that there was no child in his wife's womb. Perspiration beaded on his forehead.

"I've come to ask somethin' o' you. A favor, ye might say. But not just for me—for Isabelle more'n me really, for her baby."

Baby. How he feared that little being.

Maria's concerned voice pulled him back. "What is it, Ketch?" and he realized he had been staring for too long at his hand in his lap, fingernails nasty from tar and pitch.

"I..." He cleared his throat. "I want to ask for...for Isabelle's freedom...so it...the babe can be free-born." He berated himself for his deplorable practice of referring to the child as "it." Perhaps if he called it "she," he would be blessed with a girl.

Mallory showed no surprise at the request, nor did he reflect displeasure. In a matter-of-fact tone, he said, "As freehold property, Isabelle belongs to Leighlin more than to me. And if she was to be manumitted, Leighlin would lose yet another hand."

"You wouldn't lose her," Ketch quickly insisted, sitting on the edge of the chair. "She'd still work in the house. We wouldn't expect no wages. This is just 'cause of her babe, so it...she...whatever 'twill be...won't be a slave. If you want work from the creature, you'll get it, boy or girl. You have me word."

"Then why bother with manumission?"

Agitated, Ketch rubbed his beard. "If somethin' was to happen to you and Maria, what would become of Leighlin and its people? I'd have no legal right over Isabelle or her child."

Mallory exchanged a look with his wife, a familiar look of discomfort often displayed over matters relating to his slaves. Perhaps having recently lost his own freedom for a time had made his position over others' lives even more difficult. Or maybe any empathy he had stemmed from his awareness of Isabelle's pregnancy and her unfaltering service to his family. She was no longer some faceless field hand but, instead, a kind-hearted member of his household who tried her best to please him. Helen, no doubt, had a big hand in championing Isabelle's cause.

Mallory said, "You understand, of course, 'tis not as simple as me stating or even writing that Isabelle is free?"

"Aye, there be…legalities."

"I'd have to petition Governor Smith, maybe even the Assembly."

Smith, Ketch hoped, would surely honor any request from James Logan's stepson, especially something as benign as manumitting one slave. Smith's wife, Sabina, had died the same year that James and Ella Logan had come to Carolina, and when Ella had learned of it, she had invited Smith to Leighlin one Sunday afternoon. The Logans had been friends with Smith from that day forward.

Mallory asked, "Have you mentioned this to Isabelle?"

"No. I don't want to get her hopes up. And if it happens, I want to surprise her."

Maria's expression reflected clear hope and assurance, yet she prolonged her unusual silence, as if afraid a word from her might dissuade her husband.

"Well," Mallory said at last, standing, "I'll consider the matter and have an answer for you when you come to the house tomorrow morn."

Ketch impulsively stepped over to offer his hand, saying, "Thankee."

Mallory hesitated only an instant, long enough to remember to bring his left hand forward instead of his right. Then Ketch gave Maria a small, tight smile and bowed before leaving the library.

CHAPTER 25

The breeze had died away, leaving the *Nymph*'s sails limp and only the tide to ghost the vessel up the Ashley River. Ketch stared at the distant stars as the approaching clouds overtook them, extinguishing their crystal pinpricks like a drawn curtain. Frequent heat lightning lit up the western sky beyond the wilderness, but no thunder could be heard in the peaceful, humid July night. Thinking of Isabelle's terror of storms, he hoped they would not encounter any while here on the river, out in the open with little shelter.

He shifted his weight with care where he reclined against covered bolts of calico, afraid he might awaken his wife, who rested against him. Latiffe and two of the crew were sleeping aft—he could hear their snores through the odd music of insects and night creatures as well as the whisper of water slipping along the hull. A third boatman tended the tiller while his mate forward watched the turn of the river's course, though these slaves needed little conning on a waterway known so intimately.

Isabelle slept serenely, one hand resting on her distended belly. Frequently, in the past few weeks, Ketch saw the baby within kick against his wife, a disturbing sign that the creature was quite formed, quite viable, and indisputable. Sometimes, its blows would stop Isabelle mid-sentence, and she would pause with a veiled look of alarm before smiling and often laughing, saying, "He's going to be strong like his father."

He had tried to dissuade her from going to Charles Town for their monthly visit, but she had wanted to see her mother one last time before the birth.

"'Tis a four-hour journey first down the river then back again in the dark of night," he had reminded her. "What if you have some sort o' trouble? I wouldn't be no help to you. And who's to say anyone where we might put ashore could help neither?"

Isabelle had assured him that all would be fine, but he would not rest until they were safely back at Leighlin. Her confidence and calm, her burgeoning maturity over these past months put him to shame.

Louisa had been overjoyed to see her daughter. Ketch spent his obligatory few minutes with them at the table behind the house before leaving them, so they could speak freely of the mysterious workings of the female body and of the baby's life to come. Ketch tried his best to appear enthusiastic around Louisa, but he feared she could see through his act. She was a tough, wise woman, he knew, one who was still unconvinced of his worthiness when it came to her daughter, no matter his declaration of love. After their initial introduction, Ketch suspected Louisa had found out all she could about him from whatever gossip she could glean around town, and nothing she could have heard would have set her at ease. Quite the contrary. Perhaps Isabelle's happiness with him and her life over the past months would ultimately win over her mother. And if he could have Isabelle manumitted, Louisa's last bit of skepticism might fade away.

Jack Mallory had petitioned the governor for Isabelle's release from bondage. But, as the calendar drew deeper into summer and ever closer to his child's birth, Ketch despaired of ever hearing from Governor Smith.

Isabelle jerked and gave a small gasp, suddenly awake, her hands on her belly.

Ketch stiffened with alarm. "What is it?"

She hesitated, sighed and relaxed against him. "Nothing. He's just kicking again."

"Izzy, must you keep callin' it a 'he'? If he pops out a she, you'll be sorely disappointed after all this time."

"No. You know I'd love a girl just as much. But I think the first should be a boy, then you'd have a son to learn things to."

"And what pray tell could *I* learn him?"

"Why, all sorts of things. How to hunt and fish. How to read and write. Maybe he could be a—what was that word?—a scholar."

Ketch laughed at the idea of fathering a scholar. An absurdity.

"Or a carpenter," she forged onward, unperturbed. "That's a fine trade. I'm sure it would please the Captain to have another skilled worker. And when our son isn't working at Leighlin, he could hire hisself out to other plantations and make enough for hisself to live a comfortable life."

"Aye, or he could always work as carpenter aboard the *Adventuress* if she still swims by then."

"He can't go to sea."

"And why not? I was a sailor."

"It's too dangerous, and he would be so far away all the time."

Ketch chuckled, pulling her even tighter against him. "Yer gettin' the cart afore the horse, Izzy. Like I said, it may be a wee girl you'll be havin' instead of a sailor."

They fell silent for a time, and Ketch thought she had drifted off until she spoke again, this time softer, more contemplative. "Mama said she's worried 'cause she reckons you don't really want this child."

Ketch hid his reaction. "Why would she say such a thing?"

"She said it was just her...feeling."

"Izzy, must we get into this again? I told you—"

"Yes, you've told me, but what you've told me isn't the truth. I see it in your eyes, too, but I don't understand it. Why won't you tell me what afrights you so?"

He rested his cheek against her head, thus keeping her from turning to look at him again in the weak lantern light. For months, he had avoided this conversation, aggravating her whenever she tried to broach the subject, but now he heard more than frustration and hurt in her voice—he sensed deep concern as well as fear. Perhaps she and her mother were apprehensive that he would abandon her once the child was born.

"Izzy," he said. "The blood that runs through me veins... Well, you know what I'm capable of. Me birth father was a right cruel bastard, almost as bad as me stepfather. He passed on his evilness to his sons—me and Dan. When I was a lad, I looked up to Dan. He had a powerful hate o' women, though. His mother deserted him, and he never knew why she did till later, when we both learnt about our father and me mother. Well, his mother couldn't abide her husband bein' an adulterer. That's why she left 'em. That was years afore we knew the truth. But Dan..." Ketch shook his head, saw his half-brother as a young man, angry and resentful. "I came home one night, found me mother dead. Raped and murdered, she was. I was terrified, o' course, didn't know what to do. I went to find Dan. He said everyone would think I'd killed her, so he convinced me to run away. That's when we joined the Navy." He swallowed in a suddenly dry throat. "For years, I wondered...mebbe I *had* killed her, especially after I killed that whore in Plymouth. Mebbe I did it and couldn't remember doin' it."

"Oh, Ketch. You can't blame yourself for that. Of course, you didn't kill her."

"Well, that's what I thought at the time. I didn't know the truth, not till after Dan died. One o' his old shipmates said Dan had told him, after he had deserted the Navy and we was separated for several years."

301

Ketch looked upward at the sagging sails. "'Twas Dan who raped and murdered me mother."

Isabelle made a small, distressed sound, brought his hand to her lips and gently kissed it.

"But I don't much blame him for it no more," Ketch murmured. "'Twas in his blood, like I said. The same blood what flows through me own veins."

Isabelle turned his face toward her. "You're not the man you used to be. You've said so yourself. Miss Maria says the same thing, and I think the Captain believes it now, too. You always talk about the bad things you did, but we think of the good things. I don't think what you once was will have any bearing on our son."

"You can't know that, Izzy. Men are capable of all sorts of evil. You should know that. If you had told me as a lad the things I'd do as a man, I wouldn't have believed you."

"Our son won't hurt no one. You're talking foolishness." When he tried to debate her point, she hushed him. "If we have a son, he will grow to be a good man because we will love him. You're *not* your father. You're my husband, and you will be a good father to our son. I have no doubts." She kissed him. "I want you to be as happy as I am when the baby comes."

He caught a burst of heat lightning upon his face. Over her shoulder, Isabelle noticed the bright illuminations for the first time. She uttered a worried sound and pressed tighter against him.

"Are we far from home?"

"No," he said distantly as he watched the brilliant explosions of light. "You'll be there soon."

***

Sweat coursed down Isabelle's face in the August stifle as she sewed. She glanced at the chamber's open windows, caught a waft of the southerly breeze, but its furnace-like qualities offered no relief to Leighlin House's upper floor and, worse yet, it brought the unpleasant odor of the harvest flow. How glad she was to no longer be a field hand, especially this time of year when the stagnant water lay over the crop and another harvest loomed near. Even her most arduous day of housework held no comparison to the field work she had endured. Sometimes, she looked back upon those times and wondered how she had suffered through it, especially when Ezekiel had starved her. How amazing to think that only a year had passed since those troubled times.

She smiled at the thought of her husband's role in her deliverance. Realizing Abigail had fallen silent, Isabelle glanced up and found the seamstress's attention upon her, one eyebrow cocked.

"I'm sorry," Isabelle hastened to say. "What was you saying?"

Abigail breathed a sigh of mild frustration, used to Isabelle's penchant lately for drifting off into reveries. Isabelle could not help it, for her time of confinement drew nearer and nearer and she had much on her mind. Abigail showed no anger, however, and simply went back to her chatter, the conversation meant to pass time more than to engage Isabelle as they sewed. Maria had curtailed much of Isabelle's work, confining her to mainly sedentary tasks such as sewing. These garments they worked upon were clothes for the children of the slave settlement. November was the month when the Captain doled out clothing allowances for the year, so they had only a little more than two months to have everything ready for distribution.

The baby within Isabelle's womb gave a swift kick that nearly made her prick herself with her needle. She smiled again and waited to see if he would move some more, but he appeared content enough with his current position, one that did not make his mother too uncomfortable, so Isabelle resumed her work. Abigail had taken no notice of her pause; the older woman did like to talk and not always about things that interested Isabelle, but Isabelle was happy to listen, to be included.

During these last couple of months, Isabelle had been pleased to notice changes in Abigail and the other house servants. It could not be said that they were warm to her, but at least they conversed with her more willingly and openly. Pip even went so far as to share some of her coveted gossip when they worked alone together, gossip about those in the Big House as well as those in the slave settlement. It was Pip who told her that Hannah had finally found a husband—a man whose wife had died of yellow fever in the spring—and would be married within a fortnight.

Thoughts of her own husband distracted Isabelle. Soon their child would be born, a fact both exciting and terrifying to her. She hid most of her fears from Ketch, particularly because she knew of his own concerns. How she wished he genuinely shared in her enthusiasm instead of just pretending he did. She told herself that he would come around once the baby was born. In fact, she fully expected fatherhood to give Ketch a whole new, positive purpose in life. She had told her mother as much during their last visit. Once the baby was born, Isabelle could not wait to return to Charles Town and present her mother with her first grandchild.

Isabelle's ears were always attuned to her mistress's approach, which she now heard, but with her body so unwieldy she could not get to her feet before Maria appeared in the doorway. The bright, open expression on the woman's face stirred Isabelle's curiosity. Maria seemed to be suppressing something exciting, her fingers turning the locket at her neck, her breathing noticeably increased as if she had run up the stairs.

"Isabelle, your husband's here to see you. He's on the rear portico." A smile flashed upon her face before she stifled it, as if afraid its very existence would give away whatever had so moved her.

Curiosity propelled Isabelle across the chamber. She wondered why her husband would leave his work in the forest this time of day to come to her.

"What is it, Miss Maria?"

"You'll see. Now, go on. He's waiting."

Isabelle thought Maria would accompany her but then realized she was to go on alone. What could this mean? Well, whatever it was, Isabelle's perpetual curiosity was thoroughly aroused, and she hurried down the stairs.

On the portico, she found her husband, a piece of paper in hand. She saw him rarely during the week except before and after their work hours, and for him to visit so unexpectedly now brightened her day.

"Ketch. What are you doing here?"

Appearing incapable of speech, he held up the piece of paper then gestured toward a wicker settee. Surely the paper's contents were significant since it had interrupted her husband's work and had stirred her mistress so. Ketch sat next to her, a warm, tight fit, but one that pleased her nonetheless.

"What is it?"

"This is somethin' the Captain wrote afore he went to Wildwood today. You must listen carefully."

"Very well." Eagerly, she waited, her hand resting upon his thigh, and regarded the document with a desire to be able to read it herself. Her son would learn how to read and write.

Taking a deep breath, Ketch slowly, carefully read:

Know all men by these presents that I, John Logan, of the town of Charles Town in the province of Carolina have manumitted, emancipated, and set free a certain Negro woman named Isabelle Ketch, so that the said Isabelle Ketch shall be and remain free from

304

this time henceforth forever. In testimony whereof, I have hereto set my hand and affixed my seal this 10ᵗʰ day of August, one thousand, six hundred and ninety-four.

John Logan

Isabelle's attention remained upon the words, lips silently repeating some of them, trying to understand what they meant. But one word—free—she certainly understood. Did the words that she failed to understand contradict or in any way diminish that single, most important word? She stared at her master's signature, at his seal, gingerly took the document from Ketch, studied it further.

"Yer free, Izzy," Ketch quietly stated. He took her hand, her ring finger now too swollen to accommodate her wedding band. "'Tis very handsome of the Captain, I hafta say. He had to get permission from the Governor hisself. We've been waitin' all summer to hear from him. Truth be told, I'd about given up hope. I didn't want to tell you 'bout it ahead o' time in case it didn't happen."

She whispered, "I'm free?"

"Aye, you *and* yer babe."

Uttering a long, low gasp, she pressed the paper to her bosom, a bosom larger than it had once been. She breathed deeply as if overcome with fresh, cool air. All the love she had ever felt for him magnified until her eyes filled and spilled over.

***

In his bedchamber, Ketch awoke with a start. It had not been a dream that had awakened him. A pressure in his hand. Quiet panting. The pressure grew, and he realized Isabelle was clutching his hand.

"Izzy? Are you unwell? Is it the baby?"

"Birthing pains," she said tightly.

"I'll fetch the midwife."

"No." Relaxing, she sounded amused by his concern. "It'll be some time yet. Mama told me about babies coming. No need to wake no one up yet."

Knowing he would never get back to sleep, he replenished the lamp's oil and brought water and a wet cloth to cool her skin, passing it over her to keep himself occupied. With deep agitation, he watched helplessly and held her hand whenever a contraction gripped her. He fanned her, though she insisted he not fuss and instead return to bed; she would awaken him when the contractions came closer together.

Regularly, he asked if he should fetch someone. He did so as much for himself as for Isabelle, knowing he would be worthless if something terrible were to happen, and having someone like Maria near would ease some of his anxiety.

By daybreak, the contractions were coming about five minutes apart. Isabelle already looked exhausted by the effort, the heat, and lack of rest. Ketch prayed the process would progress swiftly now and free her from such suffering.

"I should make your breakfast." She struggled for the edge of the bed.

"The hell you will. I'm goin' to fetch Miss Maria and the midwife."

When Ketch burst into Leighlin House, he found no one yet stirring, so he raced up the stairs to the master bedchamber. Maria answered his urgent knock, having just gotten up, her husband half-dressed behind her. Initially, the young man gave him a displeased glance, but when he heard Ketch's purpose, he said, "Fetch Mary. She'll already be up."

"I'll be right behind you," Maria said.

Mary had enough birthing knowledge to have earned the title of plantation midwife, but Ketch ignored any dignity she may have felt such a position merited; he clutched her arm and hurried her significant bulk along. Eyes rolling uneasily at him, she rushed as best she could, insisting that all would be well with his wife.

Ketch lingered in the front room of his home until Maria arrived and sent him on his way with instructions to notify Willis to be available in case an emergency arose outside the scope of the women's skills. When Ketch found Willis in Leighlin House's lower level, the overseer was about to leave on his morning medical rounds to the slave settlement.

Predictably peevish over the idea of having to attend a birth, Willis grumbled, "Simple enough thing. No different than—"

With sudden fury, Ketch snatched a fistful of the man's shirt. "If you even think to compare me wife to some barnyard beast, I'll have yer balls off afore you can finish yer sentence, damn you."

Threatening the man felt cathartic...and unnervingly familiar. How dangerously tight his nerves had become over these long months, when he had thought of little else but Isabelle and that child in her womb...his child. An incredible tension that he fully recognized only now.

"Easy there, mate," Willis said with forced calm.

Ketch desperately wanted to strike the man, or worse, but he freed him with a shove. "If the time comes when they need you, if they do, and somethin' happens to Izzy under yer hand, by God, there won't be a scrap o' you left to find."

Willis scowled and straightened his shirt. Ketch served him a final warning glare and stalked out of the house.

The morning dragged endlessly. Ketch had no ability to focus upon his work in the forest as each minute he anticipated a messenger. Even now, it was difficult to comprehend that soon he would actually see and hold the mysterious result of his love for Isabelle. To Samuel, he berated himself for neglecting to learn more about what to expect when Isabelle's time came. Was it normal for it to take so damnably long? Glancing at the sun's climb through the swaying green tops of the pines, he guessed her labor had been going on for nigh ten hours at least. His concern deepened, but he could neither express it nor alleviate it through his work.

Close to noon, he heard a distant call and turned as Helen, riding bareback, galloped up on her lathered pony. While he had expected to see happiness on her face, he saw anything but.

"Mr. Ketch! You must come quick!"

His sweat turned to ice. "What's amiss?"

"The baby won't come."

"What?"

"That's all Maria said, and just to bring you quick."

Ketch bolted for the wagon and mule team dozing in the shade. He clambered up and snatched the whip before the reins, cracked it sharply upon the team's dusky, fly-dotted rumps, continued to strike them and curse until they lurched into a trot after Helen's pony. Only then did he bother to gather the reins in his well-practiced grip, the whip held there as well. He applied the lash again and flapped the lines with merciless insistence, all the while shouting at the top of his voice, frightening Helen's pony to greater speed. Finally, the team broke into a clumsy canter.

All the way, he tried to imagine what Helen's odd explanation signified. How could a baby not come? Had it perished in its mother's womb? His mind raced on with further conjectures as the forest and swamps flashed by on either side in a green blur.

Once at the house, he leapt from the wagon, Helen in his wake. When he reached his bedchamber, he halted as if struck. Isabelle lay transformed from the woman whom he was accustomed to seeing in that bed. She looked drained of life. Pain-filled eyes beseeched the women around her. Sweat drenched her hair, her legs drawn up but discreetly covered with a stained sheet. Iris from the kitchen house tried to cool Isabelle with a palmetto fan, but she, like the other women in the room, was a mere shadow, unimportant and half seen.

When Ketch spoke his wife's name, it came out in a hoarse whisper. She looked to him with the same confused disbelief. Her lips formed his name, yet no sound came forth. Mary vacated the chair next to the bed, but Ketch ignored the offer and sat on the edge of the bed, reached for his wife's seeking hand. Before either could speak, she cried out, her fingernails nearly drawing blood from his flesh.

Frantically, Ketch looked to Maria, who had drawn closer, and demanded, "Why hasn't the baby been birthed yet?"

Maria, her own face drawn and slick with sweat, touched his shoulder with authority. "Come outside with me."

"What the hell have you done to her?" he snarled at Mary, who fell back. "Why haven't you gotten Willis? Where is that God damn lobcock when—"

"Ketch," Isabelle gasped through the pain. "Please, go with Miss Maria. Hurry. Please."

Torn, Ketch hesitated until she started to whisper another plea, then he submitted to Maria's request. She led him to the back porch where he was surprised by the harried sight of Hiram Willis at the far end, forearm braced against one of the supports. Willis turned in a defensive posture when he saw Ketch.

Maria asked, "Is it true you threatened Willis this morning?"

"What in damnation is this? There's no time for…" Ketch fought to keep himself from the man. "God damn you, get inside and help me wife, you cowardly son of a—"

"Ketch!" Maria's sharp anger stifled him. "Willis *has* been helping, but so far we haven't been able to deliver the baby."

"Why in hell not? By Christ, this should be over by now. She's so exhausted she can't even lift her head."

Willis seemed prepared to vault off the porch if need be, but his voice at least came with some confidence, "'Tis a breech birth. The midwife tried to turn it in the womb, and so have I, but 'tis a stubborn, resistant thing. There's but one choice left, and that's to open her belly."

"By God, you'll do no such thing."

"Ketch," Maria desperately said. "There's nothing else to be done. Isabelle is exhausted and in danger, and the baby will die if something isn't done right now."

"Why hasn't it been done already if yer so sure?"

"Willis said you threatened him earlier, so he wants your witnessed word that there will be no repercussions if he operates."

"Repercussions?"

"I've only done this once before," Willis said. "And 'tis difficult to say what complications there may be, during or after; she very well could die."

"Just what you'd like, you God damn butcher."

Willis's broad, whiskered face flooded red. "How dare you? I'm no murderer like you."

"Stop it!" Maria ordered. "We're wasting time. For God's sake, Ketch, give him your word."

Ketch's fist clenched. From the house, he heard Isabelle's cry, the agony and fear in the sound twisting his guts into a hopeless knot. *She very well could die.* He forced the possibility from his head.

"Is this what Isabelle wants—for Willis to do it?"

"Yes. Please, we must hurry."

Ketch ground his teeth together. "Fine. You have me word."

Maria clutched Willis's arm, dragged his skeptical form past Ketch. She even gave him a significant shove across the threshold before turning back to Ketch to say, "Leave here. If you stay, Willis might still balk. Take Helen and go to the stables. Keep her with you. I'll send for you as soon as Willis is through."

CHAPTER 26

Ketch heard the baby's cry the minute he set foot upon the porch. The animal-like sound slammed him to a halt. Helen, however, gave an excited exclamation and darted through the cabin.

He focused upon the cries that gradually ceased by the time he reached the open bedchamber door. A lingering odor of blood. No one saw him at first. Mary was wiping Isabelle's pallid face with a wet cloth while Iris waved the palmetto fan with the unseeing, mechanical stiffness of someone who had witnessed far more than she had been prepared for. Maria sat in a chair near the crib, holding a bundle, Helen now hovering over it. A tiny hand appeared from the swaddling, the minute size alarming him, amazing him. Isabelle lay as motionless as death save for the shallow rise and fall of the sheet covering her. Relief flooded him, and he must have made some sort of sound because everyone turned.

Maria smiled and quietly said, "Come see your son, Ketch."

Helen came to take his hand and tug him across the room. Maria stood and pulled the edges of the blanket farther away from the baby's face, murmured, "Isn't he beautiful?"

Ketch was astounded by how pleased she was to hold a baby that was not her own, especially after all she had endured with her own pregnancies.

Helen protested, "He's not beautiful, Maria—he's *handsome*; he's a boy. Girls are beautiful, boys are handsome."

The little creature's limbs twitched, his pink face—neither broad nor narrow—twisted in a perturbed, almost comical expression. An outrageous amount of dark hair lay flat and damp against his head. The smooth flawlessness of his skin astonished Ketch, as well as its color, certainly not pale but really no darker than his father's. Would that change? Would Izzy be displeased? He glanced at his wife.

"She'll be fine," Maria said near a whisper, though unconvincing. Her own pallor reflected the shock of witnessing the delivery. "She fainted, of course, poor thing. She was just now able to feed him then drifted off. It's best for now. The caudle Willis gave her should help her rest."

She shifted the baby in her arms as if to distract him, and the child's eyes opened, small and misty, wandered without true focus, pausing but an instant upon his father's face. Ketch's breath caught.

"Here, you must want to hold him."

Ketch took a step back and shook his head. "I can't hold 'im with just one arm."

"Of course, you can. He's so small. Just crook your arm like this. Go on."

Her tone and stare gave him little choice but to obey. He protested a bit more, broken and low, as she tenderly transferred the swaddled bundle to him. The baby made an unhappy squeak.

The boy proved surprisingly easy to hold, so small and light, certainly no more than six pounds, all warmth and softness. The child made another quiet noise, scrunched his face in a humorous frown then relaxed and appeared to fall asleep.

"What's his name, Mr. Ketch?" Helen asked, straining to curb her naturally boisterous voice as she stood on her toes to see the baby.

Ketch looked to Isabelle. The amount of blood she had lost, the pain she had suffered and would suffer still troubled him. How he longed to be alone with her. Their bedchamber—such a private place— seemed so mortally crowded.

"William," he said. "That's the name Izzy wants for him."

"William Ketch," Helen proclaimed. "I like that."

Ketch swallowed hard in a dry throat. Half desperate, he looked to the crib he had crafted with the aid of Isabelle and Helen.

"Miss Helen. Open the crib. You recollect how, don't you?"

"'Course I do."

Proudly, she demonstrated to everyone how Ketch had designed one side of the crib to hinge downward so he with his single arm could easily move the baby in or out. Not his desire but Isabelle's, thus the idea had been hers.

"Are you going to put him to bed already, Mr. Ketch? Can't I hold him?"

Maria directed her to the chair near the crib. "If you sit down here and stay still. Then Mr. Ketch can give him to you if he doesn't mind."

Relieved, Ketch transferred the baby to Helen. As she began talking to the infant, Maria turned Ketch to Isabelle.

"Willis said to leave the dressing on today and tomorrow and for her to stay in bed, to move as little as possible. She'll be in considerable pain for a time."

"Can't we give her somethin'? Laudanum or—"

"Willis doesn't think it wise. He's afraid it might harm the baby through nursing. For now, the caudle will have to do. I'll show you how to make it."

Ketch hid his surprise that Willis cared enough about the child's health to offer such advice, or was he merely afraid? Glancing between Isabelle and his son, Ketch considered the suffering of one against that of the other. Isabelle would want it this way. For his own sake, he wished she would wake up. He wanted to hear her voice, he wanted to know she was going to be fine.

"Why don't we give you a little time alone? I'll come back in a bit." Maria touched Mary's shoulder, and the woman stood, obviously eager to leave. "Helen, let's put William in his crib. You can come by before supper with your brother, after Isabelle gets some rest."

At the prospect of their departure, Ketch swayed between relief and apprehension, but he said nothing to dissuade them. He had Iris leave the palmetto fan behind. Once they were gone, he took up Mary's seat with the basin near at hand and continued cooling Isabelle's face with a wet cloth. A dread of his wife never waking crept over him, made him feel alone and lost. William stirred and began to fuss then cry, arms waving in the air above his contorted, toothless, purpling face. Regrettably, Ketch considered, William seemed to have inherited his father's temper.

Isabelle moaned and slowly opened her eyes, studied Ketch from a puzzled distance until the baby's cries penetrated her haze. Ketch took her hand in his, but she lacked the strength to grip back. Her tortured gaze cleared and went to the crib.

"I thought it was a dream," she murmured, hoarse and weak, followed by a winced groan. "Please…bring him to me." When Ketch laid the boy upon her full bosom, his cries softened to strange, foreign chortles. A pale smile brought some life back to Isabelle's eyes. "Isn't he beautiful, Ketch? Our son…"

He kissed her. "Not as beautiful as his mother."

"He's hot with this blanket. That's why he's fussing."

Her intrinsic ability to know the infant's voiceless needs unnerved him. Gingerly, he unwrapped the boy, felt somehow self-conscious about his male nakedness, though he knew the aversion was foolish.

"Maria said you fed him."

"Yes, before I dropped off again. Mary showed me how. It…it wasn't as easy as I thought it'd be, and I'm so weak, but…he seemed to know what to do. Isn't he the sweetest thing?" Her finger caressed a fleshy cheek. "And thanks to you, he's free."

Ketch dropped his gaze, his frown returning. "Maria said we can't give you no laudanum 'cause Willis thinks it could pass from you to the baby."

"I'll be fine." Faintly, she smiled again, this time with a touch of her usual good humor to hide the misery in which she swam. "But I'm afeared I won't be able to make your supper tonight."

Although he felt close to tears, he managed to laugh at her joke, saw how pain kept her from joining in.

"Are you hungry now? Can you eat somethin'?"

"No." Her voice trailed away, eyes half closing upon William as if the mere sight of him could keep the agony at bay. "Just some water, please."

When Ketch brought a cup to her dry lips, he saw the suffering even this small movement caused her, tears filming her eyes.

"I wish there was somethin' I could do to make you feel better."

Looking at the sleeping infant in her arms, at the soft lips that twisted at some unknown thought or sensation, she whispered, "I've never felt better."

***

Ketch remained at Isabelle's bedside as she restlessly slept off and on during the remainder of the day, waking only to feed the baby. At her request, he had dragged the crib over to the bed so she could simply reach out to touch William whenever she desired. He fanned her as she slept and listened to her soft moans, her hand occasionally drifting to her belly, a belly that he thought was still far too distended for having expelled a baby.

In the evening, he answered a knock upon the front door to find Jack Mallory. Maria stood behind him with a basket of food, Helen at her side, fairly bouncing with a desire to enter. Ketch invited them in.

When Mallory offered his congratulations, the caution in his voice told Ketch that he was aware of the circumstances surrounding the birth. The young man, however, did his best to appear optimistic. "Is Isabelle feeling well enough for visitors?"

Isabelle called to Ketch, and he hurried back to her bedside.

"Is someone here? I thought I heard voices."

"'Tis the Captain come to see you and the babe. I can ask him to come back tomorrow if you—"

"No," she said near a whisper. "Let him come see William."

Jack Mallory, like James Logan before him, made it a practice to visit the families of any children born at Leighlin, and Ketch could tell this meant a great deal to Isabelle. Mallory's forehead wrinkled with concern when he saw her, but he quickly hid his alarm and bent over the crib. Upon seeing the squirming child, a genuine smile grew on his face. Ketch expected to see a certain amount of melancholy, but none seemed to exist. When the young man reached into the crib, William gripped his finger, drawing a chuckle. Helen hovered about, peering into the crib, barely able to keep her voice quiet.

Isabelle murmured, "You may pick him up if you'd like, Captain."

Mallory hesitated as if self-conscious but then succumbed to his desire with a glance at his smiling wife. As Mallory lifted him, William gave a small burp, which made Helen giggle. Thankfully, nothing spewed forth to spoil their master's jerkin. The young man appeared at ease with the baby in his arms, unwittingly shaming Ketch. Mallory grinned, his face close to William whose flailing arm bumped his chin. For a moment, Ketch thought he might kiss the child. He recalled Maria telling him about the siblings her husband had lost when he had been a mere boy, another similarity between the two men that now gave Ketch inexplicable comfort.

"You did a fine job, Isabelle. I'm sure your husband is very proud of you."

A spark of life flared in Isabelle's eyes as she whispered, "Thank you, Captain...for everything. My son is free thanks to you. We'll never forget your many kindnesses."

Mallory cleared his throat, obviously touched by her sincerity. "Well, we won't tire you out by staying." He returned William to the crib. "I hope you're feeling better soon."

Isabelle faintly smiled her gratitude and watched him leave, towing a reluctant Helen, who called good night to William. Maria lingered and stepped over to Isabelle's bedside.

"Would you like me to stay with you tonight?"

"That's very kind of you, Miss Maria, but I'm sure I'll be fine."

Maria touched her shoulder. "Very well. But if you change your mind, don't hesitate to send for me."

When night came, Ketch offered her the soup Maria had brought over, but Isabelle said she was not yet hungry. Instead, she spent her waking moments with William in her arms, trying her best to hide her discomfort. Ketch considered removing the dressing to check on the wound but decided to abide by Willis's instructions. Besides, it might be better to avoid seeing what lay beneath, for his sake as well as Isabelle's. In the candles' glow, he watched William nurse, listened to his grunts and suckles, his tiny fingers pressed against Isabelle's shining flesh. Impulsively, Ketch bent to kiss her breast then her lips.

Softly, she said, "You must come to bed."

"You'll be more comfortable sleepin' alone. I'll just set here in case you need somethin'."

"No. Please, come lie down with us."

As directed, he walked William until the child burped—a great, manly belch that made his eyes bulge and caused his father to chuckle. When Ketch went to place him in the crib, Isabelle insisted he return him to her. Stripping off his clothes, Ketch crept into bed with her, William between them, making his strange little noises of contentment.

"Izzy, he can't sleep with us," he said gently. "We might crush him."

"I know, but let him stay just a bit longer, then you can put him in the crib." She smiled at the child. "I can't wait for Mama to see him."

Her happy expression was the last thing Ketch remembered before drifting off and the first thing he remembered three hours later when he awoke to the baby's cries.

Through the darkness—the candles now extinguished, an oversight Ketch was too exhausted to rectify—he heard Isabelle's quieting voice, felt her move in bed, heard her stifled groan, followed by whispers to her son. The boy's hungry outcries died as his mouth found that which he sought.

Ketch dozed off again, and when next he awoke, the first traces of early morning light filtered through the windows, and the temperature of the room had become more comfortable. Isabelle lay asleep, looking almost peaceful for the first time since her ordeal had begun. Ketch had no memory of returning the boy to the crib, but there William lay, yawning, bright eyes following his father, who got out of bed and pulled on his breeches. Ketch paused at the crib. William squirmed and shoved a fist against his mouth.

"Yer not the only one hungry," he whispered before returning to Maria's basket in search of breakfast.

Isabelle ate a lukewarm gruel that he spooned to her after she fed William, though she still had no appetite and consumed barely half of it. Maria arrived and sent Ketch off to work. When he returned to check on Isabelle at midday, Maria was on the front porch, William in her arms, Helen next to her. They reported that Isabelle was asleep, so after he peeked in on his wife, Ketch returned to the kiln.

When he arrived home that evening, he found his wife restless in bed, Maria still there, wiping Isabelle's sweaty face.

He asked, "What's the matter?"

"She has a fever."

"Should I fetch Willis?"

"He just left."

"Ketch," Isabelle faintly called.

He crossed the room and sat next to her on the bed, grasped her hot hand. For the first time, he saw fear on her face.

Ketch looked to Maria. "What can be done?"

"Willis changed the dressing and bled her. He says he'll come by in the morning and do so again if she's not better."

Ketch's anger rose at the thought of Willis cutting Isabelle. And the fever...had Willis's incompetence caused it?

"Why don't you get something to eat?" Maria encouraged him. "I had Rose bring supper over for you. When you're finished, I'll go back to the house. I'll stop by again before you go to bed."

When Maria returned later, Isabelle was no better. Nor did she improve as the night dragged on with Ketch at her bedside. She struggled to feed William, and the baby seemed to sense her discomfort, crying for some time even after being fed, agitating Isabelle even more. At her urging, Ketch picked the infant up and tried to hush him while pacing through the warm house. The breeze had died completely, trapping the day's heat in the cabin, making William peevish. By morning, Isabelle's fever had worsened, and when Maria arrived, he sent her with almost a bark to find Willis.

Willis, uneasily shifting his weight, ordered Ketch from the bedchamber before he would bleed Isabelle. Having little faith in the procedure, Ketch petitioned Maria to have Isabelle dosed with laudanum.

Maria hesitated. "Perhaps Rose could nurse him. She still has milk from little Isaiah."

But Isabelle vehemently opposed the idea, not wanting another Leighlin woman to suckle her son, no matter how poorly she felt. Her determination in this matter gave her a surge of stubborn strength that nearly lifted her from her wet pillow.

"None of the womenfolk here have showed me any charity to speak of. Who's to say how they'd treat William?"

With her usual quick way of thinking, Maria offered to seek a nursemaid from David Archer's plantation, and only through Ketch's lengthy pleading did Isabelle finally agree, by then exhausted from the fight. Afterward, she sent Willis and Maria from the chamber and had Ketch bring William to her. She held the baby in her trembling hands and kissed him then offered her breast. Ketch sat with her as she fed the boy, then he returned the child to his crib. When he turned back to Isabelle, she began to softly sob.

***

The nursemaid arrived long after dark, a young African named Fanny. Though reluctant to leave her newly-weaned child behind, she had no choice—Ketch had insisted she come unencumbered.

While Ketch moved the crib into Isabelle's former bedchamber, Fanny held William with little tenderness. Alone together in the room, Ketch—lacking any scrap of patience or sympathy for the woman's plight—quietly warned her that if she failed to treat his wife's son with the utmost care, he would see to it that she regretted her negligence for the rest of her life. David Archer's slaves knew Ketch's reputation, so it took nothing further to acquire her assurance that her duty would be performed satisfactorily.

He spent the rest of the night at Isabelle's bedside and watched helplessly as her condition worsened. Even dosed with laudanum, she tossed about in bed, often waking and asking confused, sometimes incoherent questions of her husband, who attempted to soothe her. One time when she asked for William and saw neither the boy nor the crib, she remained agitated until Ketch fetched the boy to her. Ketch administered more laudanum, which pulled Isabelle away again. She trembled, her skin hot to touch one moment and chilled the next. Her breathing increased to ragged, rapid panting at times, and her pulse raced beneath Ketch's fingers. He was at a loss as to how to help her except to place wet compresses and talk calmingly to her, trying to keep his tone as worry free as possible as he stroked her hair. Several times she called for her mother through her semi-conscious state. He considered sending for the woman, but the thought of Louisa seeing her daughter so sickly and distraught—if Waterston even allowed her to come—squelched the idea.

When Maria returned in the morning, she tried to send Ketch to Leighlin House to get some sleep, but he refused.

"I was thinkin'," he said, voice strained and hoarse from his sleepless night, "mebbe you could talk to Rose. She knows somethin' 'bout plants an' all, the healin' kind, how to make simples. Mebbe she knows of somethin' what could help Izzy. And don't let that damn

317

Willis back in here, wantin' to cut her again like some God damned blood-sucking bat. It hasn't helped a lick, and she just keeps gettin' weaker."

Pokeroot, boneset, jimsom weed tea...nothing Rose provided made a difference. And as the hot day progressed, Isabelle slipped farther away, her chills worsening, racking her small frame even under multiple blankets. A violent storm roared through in the afternoon, but even its noise and fury failed to reach her senses except to elicit a few additional whimpers and fearful murmurings. Ketch maintained his post, not even leaving to make sure Fanny was properly caring for William. Maria brought the infant in a couple of times before she left that night, but William seemed to sense his mother's delirium and agitation and would fuss and start to cry, to which Isabelle often responded with even more distress, as if trying to return to consciousness and tend the baby.

During the night, Isabelle's breathing grew even more labored, rattling through the candlelit gloom. Ketch, too exhausted to even keep himself upright in a chair, sat on the floor, resting against the bed, his hand slowly stroking Isabelle's arm beneath the blankets. As he had for so many hours now, he talked to her, sometimes whispering, sometimes speaking in a regular conversational voice. Conversational... He had rarely been conversational before marrying Isabelle. How he missed the sound of her voice, ached to hear it again, to hear her laugh and tease him, to feel her fingers playfully trying to smooth the vertical furrows from between his eyes. He missed their simple routine every morning, every evening. At the thought of their lovemaking, he groaned and cursed himself for ever having taken her into his bed.

***

Isabelle heard William's plaintive cries but was helpless to find him, to console him. She rushed from cabin to cabin in the deserted slave settlement. The sky above was ash-gray, the air chilled, but she wore no shawl to ward off the wind. William would be cold without her. Perhaps that was why he was crying. Her search grew more frantic, but she found that she had no voice with which to call his name. She kept trying to call in the hopes that her voice might soothe William, tell him that she was coming for him.

The forlorn scene around her melted away, and she found herself in Leighlin House. It too was empty and without warmth. She had no time to wonder where the Mallorys and the servants were, for she could

318

hear William's cries here, too. Desperate, she raced from chamber to chamber, again trying to call his name but still unable to utter a sound. Tears flowed down her face.

Sunlight flashed through the stair hall windows, offered hope. She flung the front door open, for now William's cries seemed distant, no longer in the house. Her gaze flew over the grounds, the gardens empty of gardeners, the sward devoid of sheep. Then her attention reached the river and a skiff anchored mid-stream. She could just make out something upon one of the thwarts, something light-colored like William's blanket. With a cry, she raced down the steps and out across the sward. The sun had faded again.

Someone appeared before her, blocked her path. She cursed him and tried to push past, but he would not allow it.

"Leave him be, Izzy."

She stared up at Ketch. He had two arms now and he used them to restrain her.

"William's alone on the river. I must go to him."

"Leave him be, Izzy. He'll be fine."

"But he's crying. He needs me. Let me go!"

None of her fear reflected on Ketch's face. She realized he was clean-shaven, and neither the pockmarks nor the burn scar was present. He looked at her with mesmerizing calm, and her struggles stopped.

"I'll fetch him for you," he said. "But you must stay here."

She obeyed, though she had no idea why, and watched him head for the landing. He disappeared below the terraces, but to her dismay, he never reappeared farther along between the ornamental ponds. Yet, she remained there. He had promised that he would fetch William, that she needed to stay here. But where had he gotten to? When she looked to the river, she no longer saw the boat, no longer heard William crying. Had the anchor broken free?

"Izzy!"

She was in their cabin, seated at the empty table, a sweetgrass basket sitting before her, elegantly made, flawless, complete. Coil upon coil of sweetgrass and bulrush and palmetto, forming an intricate pattern. She could smell its sweetness. Somehow, she knew that it was she who had made the exquisite thing, but when had she gained such skill? How proud her mother would be.

"Izzy!" Ketch's voice again, calling from outside.

She moved toward the door, her frantic emotions of a moment ago now gone. She felt placid and light, happy for some unknown reason. The bright sun outside gave the cabin a cheerful glow, spilled its

319

warmth inward as she opened the front door and stepped onto the porch. She did not see him at first, but once she left the porch and shaded her eyes, she saw him walking along the lane toward her, unhurried. Ketch was smiling, and he had his right arm around a boy, one grown tall and strong, almost a man. How much he looked like his father. With a smile of her own and the sun growing warmer upon her skin, Isabelle started toward them.

CHAPTER 27

Ketch listened to the mournful rhythm of the shovels as they chuffed into the mound of fresh dirt, watched the soil fall back whence it had come, heard the initial dull thump of it upon the coffin below as the two slaves hurried to complete their task. He knew what they were thinking, what every slave at Leighlin thought—he had killed Isabelle, not with his hands but with his seed, that he had planned it this way. But he thought no more of their opinions or anyone else's. Instead, he focused on the falling earth, the smell of it, the sound of it upon the wood until the coffin was covered and then it was just earth upon earth, muted, closing the hole.

He had made the coffin yesterday after Isabelle had died, pressing Leighlin's carpenter to assist him, a begrudging order, for Ketch would have preferred to do that last thing for Isabelle himself. How she used to praise his craft, often spending time with him in the shed-row, steadying pieces of wood for him or handing him tools. As he had contemplated the coffin, he doubted he would create anything ever again.

Jack Mallory had found him in the shed-row. Ketch had neither heard nor seen his coming, for he was bent over his work, his hair— left loose without Isabelle to tie it for him—falling forward and acting as a curtain against peripheral vision. Ketch sensed the young man's presence only when the carpenter stepped away from the coffin to face his approaching master. Straightening his stiff back, Ketch paused in his task long enough to acknowledge Mallory. He was loath to show his master or anyone else the misery that filled him. He continued with his deliberate planing.

"I'm sorry about Isabelle," Mallory said in a quiet voice filled with genuine sympathy and sorrow. "If there's anything we…I can do…just let me know."

Ketch nodded.

"Take as much time as you need from work. I've already told Samuel."

He knew he should thank Mallory but had no desire to speak...to anyone. He wanted only to be left alone. Though he appreciated his master's sentiments—he was comforted by the emotions in the young man's voice, for it showed how Isabelle had touched her master—simply hearing those things, feeling them emanate from another, sharpened his already unbearable grief.

Mallory continued, "Would you like me to speak over her grave? Maria and Helen would like to be there as well, when she's laid to rest."

"No." The word came forth too bluntly. He tried to gauge Mallory's reaction and saw veiled concern. The young man would worry about what he might revert to now that Isabelle was gone. Ketch tried to smooth over his tone. "I'll just need a couple hands to dig the grave and fill it in when the time comes."

Mallory lingered as Ketch resumed his work. Undaunted, the young man said, "I must admit when you came to me to ask for Isabelle's hand in marriage, I thought it a ruse." He waited until Ketch looked up. "Maria told me at the time that you were in love with Isabelle. You can imagine how I responded." A small smile twitched the corners of Mallory's mouth. "I'm glad I was wrong." He paused. "I know Isabelle hoped that one day we'd put our differences aside. When I was cleared of those charges last year, I promised her that I would do my part." Mallory extended his hand. "I aim to keep that promise."

Surprised on more than one level, Ketch slowly straightened. He tried to hold the young man's gaze but succeeded for only the time it took to shake his master's hand. With an acknowledging nod, he turned back to his work, and Mallory left him.

As the slaves buried the coffin, rain threatened from the southwest—its scent mingled with the earthen smell. But just rain, no storm in the air. He stared at the gaping wound in the ground here behind his home, just at the edge of the clearing, and considered that Isabelle would no longer be tormented by Carolina's violent storms. At such times, she had clung to him in their bed, face pressed against his neck or chest to hide from the flashes, using his embrace as her only shelter. The memories made him wish again that he were alone, that he could have done all of this by himself, but his cursed missing arm prevented it, as it prevented so much, including dressing his wife for her burial in the green dress she had worn for their wedding. Maria had helped with that task, the two of them grim-faced and silent.

She had arrived that morning to find him prostrate at Isabelle's bedside. He had no idea if she had come of her own volition or if someone had fetched her, but she touched his shoulder and sat next to him on the floor. She seemed to understand his need for silence. Although aware of her tears, he remained focused on Isabelle's pallid, cold face. Distantly, he heard Fanny in the next chamber behind her closed door, trying to comfort the motherless baby. He had no idea how long he remained there after Maria's arrival, and he was quite certain if she had not come, he would have maintained that posture until death found him, but eventually the young woman went to collect fresh water and returned to help him with the body. When they were through, he clipped a lock of his wife's hair and folded it into a piece of cloth. Then he took her wedding ring from the box where she had preserved it during the last of her pregnancy.

"D'ye think she'd mind if I kept it?" he mumbled, staring at the simple thing in the palm of his hand.

Maria closed his fingers around the ring, and he remembered a time when he had recoiled from her touch or the touch of anyone. "I'm sure she would prefer it."

Now his hand drifted to the ring where it hung around his neck on a rawhide string, the metal warm against his skin.

With the grave filled in, the slaves left, shovels hefted over their shoulders. The breeze freshened, heralded the nearing rain. The light faded another few degrees. The pines swayed and whispered louder. From where he sat, he saw nothing but the mound of dirt.

"Mr. Ketch?"

Helen's voice seemed to originate from a dream or a memory, so he paid it no heed. Then he felt a familiar light touch upon his shoulder and heard her words close. The heady aroma of roses overpowered the earthen scent.

"Mr. Ketch?"

He turned to see the child, her face serious and sad, her teeth tugging at her lower lip as if afraid he would be displeased with her presence. She carried the sweetgrass basket that Isabelle had made for her birthday, a bouquet of roses within.

"I brought these for Izzy."

Ketch stared at the flowers and thought of the roses in the *Adventuress*'s aft cabin during his wedding, the perfume now bringing painful clarity to the memory.

"May I put them on her grave?"

He blinked away the moisture in his eyes and nodded, whispered, "Aye."

Helen placed the flowers with care, bunching them together to keep them from tumbling away. Ketch reflected upon how much grieving the child had already endured in her young life, of his part in causing some of it. The pain of his culpability, adding to his guilt over Isabelle, nearly crushed him.

"Thankee, Miss Helen."

She returned to his side, expressionless and sober. He wanted to say more to her, to tell the child how important she had been to Isabelle, how they had known the influence she had had over her brother when it came to both of them, how much they loved her. But all these things were beyond his capability to convey, so he said nothing more and stared at the flowers as the rising breeze tickled the petals.

Without a word, Helen kissed his cheek. Then she slipped her arms around his neck to embrace him, her golden hair soft against his cheek.

***

Alone, Ketch sat at the little table behind Malachi Waterston's house, a chair long-familiar now. He had arrived after Louisa and Mrs. Waterston had taken Robert and Elisha—now almost a year old—to visit Mrs. Waterston's sister-in-law on the other side of town, so he had to suffer a lengthy wait for their return. Malachi Waterston was gone to his business. When Molly had given Ketch excuses as to why he should be denied admittance to the house while Mr. Waterston was absent, Ketch's raw nerves propelled him to growl a curse at the girl and nearly shove her aside. He would curse Waterston himself if he dared show any displeasure at his unannounced presence. Ketch vowed to see this onerous duty through and as quickly as possible.

Hearing the women and children return, he tensed and got out of his chair to wait restlessly, toying with the wedding ring around his neck. Through the open back door, he heard Molly speaking distantly to her mistress. Ketch considered going into the house, but before he could gather such courage, he heard steps coming through the pantry. The muck sweat that had enveloped him now seemed like ice upon his skin.

When Louisa saw him, she smiled with tentative hope and regarded him almost warmly.

"The baby's come?" Her expression tempered when she saw the wedding ring. "What is it, Mr. Ketch? Is something wrong?"

When he was finally able to form words, they were hoarse with grief. "The baby came. He's fine... William. That's the name Izzy gave him."

"And Isabelle?" Her voice failed her.

"The boy was a breech birth. Izzy…she survived it somehow but…she took sick with fever."

Louisa seemed to shrink before him, her mouth opening, tears springing to her eyes, tears he knew he could not bear. He needed to get away.

"She died."

Louisa emitted no sound for a long moment, her mouth a shape of unspoken agony, hands coming up to her head as if to cover her ears and keep from hearing more of this horror. Then she let out a long wail that pierced his heart and brought Mrs. Waterston rushing through the pantry. As the woman reached the door, Louisa began to sink to the ground. Ketch tried to support her with his inadequate arm, but grief pressed her too heavily downward and it was Mrs. Waterston who caught her. The white woman stared at Ketch for an explanation, but he could say nothing. When Louisa began to sob, "My child, my child…" the realization seemed to strike Mrs. Waterston, and her pale skin grew even paler.

"I'm sorry," Ketch said.

Louisa covered her face with her hands, seemingly unaware of anyone now.

At a complete loss, Ketch looked to Mrs. Waterston, repeated, "I'm sorry," then fled back through the house.

***

Ketch remained away from Leighlin for several days; not that he was aware of the time lapse. Hours and days, morning and night, all rolled into one endless blur in Charles Town's taverns after he had visited Louisa. Surviving his own grief was torture enough but to have brought such sorrow to Isabelle's mother… Only a coward would have deserted her there behind the Waterstons' house, yet he could not subject himself to her tears and the sounds that she made, magnifying his desolation.

So he drank until he could not walk, and when he recovered enough to walk, he instigated fights with any sailor drunk enough to take no regard of his missing arm and some who were quite sober. Then he drank himself into unconsciousness again. When he finally awoke, four days after leaving Leighlin, he found himself aboard the *Nymph*, Josiah Smith scowling down at him after he had doused him with a bucket of water. But the tepid river water failed to fully revive Ketch, and he awoke only when he heard William crying from somewhere nearby.

He cracked his eyelids open. His bedchamber. He lay in the bed he had shared with Isabelle, the bed in which he had condemned her to death. His head throbbed like never before. Night was closing in. He was thankful for the room's dimness. When had he last eaten? He had no appetite, just a sour, unhappy belly. His parched tongue disclosed the passage of time since he had drunk anything other than alcohol. But he dragged himself out of bed with little regard for those necessities and went to the back door where he stood unsteadily and stared out at Isabelle's lonely grave. Rain had shrunk the mound. He turned from it and left the haunting house and the grave far behind, fled into the western forest, far beyond Leighlin's lands into pure wilderness.

Two days later, he wandered back out, dirty, haggard, chewed by insects, dehydrated, and close to delirium. He staggered through the stable-yard, past Jemmy and the blacksmith, who stared at his torn stockings, filthy breeches, gaping collar, and hair hanging in dark greasy strands around his face. But Ketch was only vaguely cognizant of them, had no regard for what they whispered to one another. He stumbled across the sward where sheep and cows fell away before him, calling concern to their young.

On the front porch of Ketch's cabin, Fanny sat with William, but for a brief, hallucinatory moment he saw Isabelle holding the baby and speaking lovingly to him. But he came to his senses enough to see only Fanny, and she was not speaking endearments to the child. In fact, he had little memory of her ever saying much to him beyond telling him to hush.

"Mr. Ketch." She stood. "They's been lookin' for you, wonderin' where you got off to. Miss Maria be frettin' somethin' powerful. An' Miss Helen, she—"

Ketch continued into the house, found a bottle of rum, and went to his bedchamber. He sat on the floor next to the cursed bed and drank the bottle dry. Fumbling across the room, he picked up a basket Isabelle had made before William's birth—a narrow basket with curled sides and a sturdy handle so he could easily carry William. Then, with dogged purpose, he went to the nursemaid's chamber where she now lay upon her bed in the afternoon swelter. Perhaps she was asleep; perhaps she merely pretended to be. Ketch unlatched the side of the crib and awkwardly scooped the sleeping baby into the basket, which Isabelle had lined with the softest of quilts, one her mother had made for the child. William stirred and yawned, a pink fist appearing from beneath the quilt, but his eyes remained closed, and he drifted off again.

Ketch followed the lane past the front of Leighlin House on a line that was by no means straight but at least determined. This was the hottest part of the day, a time when life at Leighlin ceased to move—no slaves tending to Ella Logan's gardens, no work beyond the terraces and ponds at the landing, no movement out near the flooded north rice field where the endless toil of the harvest would begin once the fields were drained. The distant memory of Isabelle suffering through last year's harvest briefly touched him, tightened his grip upon the basket.

Beyond the house, he turned left, following a course more by memory than by clarity of the present. Over the bridge, farther along the tree-lined lane, down to the river's edge.

His steps slowed and the alcohol seeping through his pores made the day's heat unbearable. He set the basket down and fell to his knees, unwittingly splashing the baby. William stirred in his dampened blanket and began to fuss. Agitation reached his limbs, and his twitching caused the basket to rock and nearly tip to the side. Ketch stared stupidly at him for some time, watched the little toothless face pinch and color with anger. He knew that anger all too well, knew its power and destructiveness, its unstoppable force, its violence, its isolation. In time, it would grow in the child, for Isabelle would not be here to discourage it, to offer a love that the boy would need to counteract his father's breeding.

Ketch could not yet do what he needed to do and instead sat there on his haunches in the water, the river taking some of the heat from his blood, soaking his shoes, stockings, and breeches, taunting his thirsty tongue with its brackishness.

At last, trembling, he edged over to the quivering basket. William's fussing had turned into full-fledged squalling, eyes pressed shut, dark hair wild. Ketch hesitated again, felt his chest tighten, his breath catch. Through blurred eyes, he stared at the baby, marveled at the strength of his cries. Then he struggled the infant from the basket and drew him to his chest to steady both of them. Instantly, William settled, and his wet eyes opened to look upon his father. But the calm was short-lived, and he began to squirm and quietly protest. Ketch looked beyond the infant to the water below, the darkness of it, the ugly brown muck beneath. His own ragged breathing reached his ears, and his sight clouded. Nonsensical mumblings fell from his lips. He started to lower the child, stopped, pulled him back against him, the trembling much worse now, his hold upon William precarious and growing more so with the baby's movements. The tight muscles in his neck pained him, and he forced himself to unclench his jaw. He bent forward, closer to the water, opened his arm, William's head cradled in his hand...so tiny and delicate, as easy to crush as a small ripe melon. Ketch closed his eyes, told himself this was best done and done quickly. The water lapped against his arm; William reacted to its touch.

A child's cries reached Ketch's ears, but it was not his son's voice. Instead, the cries were higher pitched, distant, muffled. His sister's cries there at the edge of the Thames...then nothing.

Ketch opened his eyes, saw William's anxious face beneath the water's surface, bubbles trailing from his nose. With a sudden jerk, he slipped from Ketch's tenuous hold, sinking to the riverbed. Gasping in horror, Ketch reached for him, struggled for a slippery hold with his single, awkward, cursed arm, pushed the baby against his leg for leverage and brought him out of the water.

"Ketch!"

Someone snatched the coughing babe from him, and in dazed confusion Ketch watched Maria rush the baby up the bank. She dropped to one knee and leaned the boy over her thigh, struck his back as he coughed, followed by a small flow of water from his mouth. She stared at Ketch with the same sense of betrayal displayed in the library that day they had discovered Ezekiel's murder.

"What in God's name were you doing—trying to kill him?"

Ketch struggled for words, looked down at the water, wondered how long William had been submerged—a second? a minute? Terrible clarity rushed at him, and he crawled onto the bank. Maria turned slightly to protect the baby with her body.

"Is he hurt?" he rasped.

William's coughs turned into strident crying, and Maria stood, the infant to her shoulder as she continued to pat his back. Ketch got to his knees, reached for the child, but Maria kept out of range. His head spun and his legs shook, making it impossible to stand.

"Are you out of your mind, Ketch? Surely you are. Where have you been?" Her attention went to the baby, her hand at the back of his wet head, her lips near his ear, murmuring words to soothe him. She took up the basket's quilt and wrapped him in it, taking another step away from Ketch, though he could tell she did not fear him, could see that he was in no shape to forcibly reclaim the child.

Ketch sank to the ground. "You have to take him; you have to keep him. I can't...I can't do this...not without Izzy."

Maria's suspicion turned to open amazement as she rocked William from side to side.

328

"Look how he's settlin'. He needs someone who knows what to do with him. You care for him. He feels safe with you."

"Ketch," she said, halting his desperate babble. "William is your son. He belongs with his father."

"For God's sake, you saw what I almost did."

"You're drunk. You're grief-stricken and distraught."

"I don't know the first thing about takin' care of a babe. You would know what to do with him. That cold fishwife Fanny, she's worth no more'n her tit can offer him. He needs a woman what cares about him. He shouldn't know nothin' about me, about what I've done…like this."

Hopeless, he covered his face with his hand. If he had been alone, he would have wept. William's cries and coughs trailed away to small, almost contented sounds, as if he had already forgotten the trauma of a moment ago. Maria sat, said nothing for a time, and all Ketch heard was the soft song of the breeze through the surrounding trees, the call of ducks passing above, and William's gentle grunts and chirps.

"How did you come to find me?"

"I saw you from Helen's chamber when you walked by. She's been worried about you; we all are."

William sucked on his tiny fingers, making Ketch remember Isabelle nursing him during those few peaceful moments she had with her child.

He groaned. "Izzy would never forgive me if she knew what I almost did."

"Grief has driven sense from your head." Maria paused, and her voice softened. "You look a fright. When's the last time you ate? Or slept?"

"I dunno."

She frowned and gently but with weight behind her words said, "Go back home now. I'll have Rose send some food over. You need to sleep. You'll think clearer then. I'll bring William and Fanny into the house for the rest of today and overnight, so you can rest."

She got to her feet and waited until he stood, too. It was difficult to accomplish, for now that the mania had passed, weakness caught up to him and nearly drove him back to the ground. Yet, somehow, he managed to remain upright and follow her back to the lane.

CHAPTER 28

Although Ketch managed to choke down a few bites of what Rose delivered to his table, he had no ability to sleep. Forsaking his own bed, he tossed about in Fanny's bed, but even there he could not escape Isabelle's memories. When he considered what he had almost done to their son, he feared Isabelle's absence had already allowed the poison to return. All too quickly. His heinous actions had given credence to the concern seen in Jack Mallory's eyes in the stable-yard those days ago. Would Maria tell her husband?

When evening drew nigh, Helen and Maria visited him with William, so he could say good night to the child. He felt so low that it was difficult to even look at his guests, let alone talk to them, especially William. But he knew Maria had a mission, a determination to shake him back to his senses. She refused to let him forget about William, whether he wanted to or not. Helen, however, seemed quite ignorant of his latest sin.

Maria forced him to hold the baby, and when he gathered enough courage to look at his son, William's innocent expression amazed him. To think the little thing would have the ability to form a judgment against him was foolish, yet Ketch was still struck by how oblivious and content the child appeared, how unconditional and forgiving. Such realizations increased Ketch's guilt, and he wished he could hand William back to Maria, but he knew by the look on his mistress's face that it was best if he made no such attempt.

Maria said nothing about her husband knowing what had occurred down by the river, though she must have said something to him in order to keep William in Leighlin House this night.

When it came time for them to leave, Helen said, "I'm so glad you're back, Mr. Ketch. You should come live in the house with us now. Won't you be lonely here? William could share my chamber with me. I could tell him a bedtime story every night."

Ketch managed a small smile for the girl as she took William from him. "William would like that, to be sure. But if he's to live with you,

you'd have to ask yer brother." He felt Maria's sharp glance but refused to acknowledge it.

"I will!"

"No, you won't, Helen." Maria touched her shoulder. "This is William's home, his and his father's."

Helen kissed William's nose, and the infant flashed an enchanted smile, squirming. "He missed his daddy. Look how happy he is now."

"He's happy 'cause a beautiful girl is holdin' him and kissin' him."

Helen giggled and said good night as Maria took William then guided her off the porch and into the twilight.

Ketch had never felt true loneliness before in his adult life, but as night closed in around him and the sounds from the nearby kitchen house and the distant slave settlement died with the breeze, he felt surrounded in a black, suffocating emptiness. The natural noises seemed deafening, disturbing, as if he had never heard the insects and night creatures before. Unblinking, he sat at the table with a single candle lit upon it, stupidly watching a glossy brown and black skink scurry across the floor and disappear behind a broom in the corner near the pantry. For what seemed an eternity he stared at the broom. Then, in vain, he searched the cabin for alcohol. When he considered crossing over to Leighlin House's lower level to see if he could acquire drink there, Maria's lecture on the trek back from the river about his dangerous, negligent drunkenness returned, and he knew no one at the house would oblige him. So, he extinguished the candle and went to Fanny's empty bed.

He thought of what Helen had said about them moving into Leighlin House. Such a thing did not matter to Ketch, but how he wished it for William. Surely Maria saw the logic and sense to what he had proposed. Any child would thrive in such an environment compared to living alone in a cabin with a crippled, incompetent father. He had to find a way of convincing her.

Then, remembering her words, "This is Williams's home," the solution suddenly came to him.

***

The raucous cries of crows awoke Ketch in the early dawn, a discordant crew that increased in numbers as he stirred. It took him a moment to realize where he was. Time slowly gained relevance, and he crawled out of bed, stiff and still tired. After a hurried mouthful of food left over from the previous day, he started for the stables where Samuel met him with an inquiring look. As they mounted the wagon's seat and the gang climbed into the back, Samuel refrained from pressing Ketch for details about his long absence. He seemed to sense his old shipmate's need for distraction, and so they headed into the forest, talking only of work.

The hour of restless sleep Ketch had garnered did not sustain him for long. He performed his tasks at the kiln mechanically. If only he could sleep, yet to sleep in that house, without Isabelle...it was impossible. And, after today, he would no longer have to be concerned with that.

By midday, enough barrels of tar had been filled to merit a delivery to the landing, a duty Ketch always performed. He waited while the slaves loaded the barrels, then he slapped the reins against the droopy-eared mules and started off down the narrow, crude lane. The large barrels behind him jostled noisily. It felt good to get away from the others and absorb the cool shade of the forest as he drove.

When he reached the perimeter of the stable-yard, he pulled the mules to a halt under the protection of a live oak. Their scant tails whisked frantically at flies. Ketch hesitated there, contemplated the idea he had conjured, reconsidered. At last, he dismounted and went into the barn to retrieve what he needed.

Once at the landing, he waited for the slaves to unload the barrels for the *Nymph*'s next journey downriver. From there, he drove to his home.

As he secured the mules, William's cries reached him. He found the child alone in the crib in Fanny's chamber. When he bellowed the wet nurse's name, she failed to appear. How long had William been crying, unattended? A grimace of fury clenched the baby's face—eyes tightly shut, soft skin suffused red, gums bared, lips quivering, limbs flailing. Ketch hesitated then unlatched the side to swing it down. Once the sound and vibration on the crib drew the baby's attention, the stridency of his cries diminished and his eyes opened.

"You don't like it here no more neither, do ye? Well, we're goin' to fix that." He bent down to lift the child. "You wonder why yer mama don't come pick you up, aye? Well, I may not be yer mama, but I'm afeared there's no help for that. You'll just have to settle for me."

The back door opened. Fanny appeared in the chamber doorway and flinched at the sight of Ketch and his glower.

"Where was you, wench?"

"I...I was in the privy, sir."

"You left him here a-cryin'?"

"He been a-cryin' most the time we been back here from the Big House, sir. My boy don't fuss like this 'un do. I fed 'im but he still a-squallin' like a bear cub. I reckon it the heat."

Ketch had a wild inclination to backhand the girl, but he remembered what he had come here for, so instead he handed William over to her. The child continued to fuss, seemingly disturbed by his father's hostility.

"Take him down to the river and set with him in the shade by the landing. There's a breeze comin' off the river. Mebbe it'll help him fall asleep."

His idea—or perhaps the fact that he even had an idea about how to comfort William—appeared to astound Fanny; she stood with her mouth slightly open until he barked at her to get moving. He followed her to the front door and waited until she was beyond sight past the garden's northern border. With a long breath, he gathered himself and refocused on the task before him now with William safely away.

From the wagon, he carried buckets of tar into the cabin and, grim-faced and determined, spread the black ooze liberally throughout the dwelling. Then he ignited each room. Afterwards, calmly, without hurry, he left, closing the front door behind him, taking nothing with him but the lock of Isabelle's hair.

***

By the time Ketch reached the kiln, Leighlin House's bell could be heard to the east, clanging the alarm. Black and gray smoke curled like a thick serpent over the distant treetops. Just as he pulled the mules to a halt, Samuel hurried up, his attention on the ominous cloud.

"Something's afire," he said in a rush, climbing next to Ketch on the seat. "I hope to God it isn't the house again. Let's go."

By the time they reached Leighlin House, flames had engulfed Ketch's home beyond saving. A bucket brigade of white workers and slaves worked feverishly to throw water upon the kitchen house in case the breeze shifted and sent cinders in that direction. Jack Mallory, in his shirt sleeves, assisted and directed the effort, shouting, his dark hair speckled with ash. Josiah Smith was there as well. Behind the kitchen house, Maria desperately worked the pump.

The roaring flames and smoke frightened the mules, so Ketch halted them near the rear portico where a knot of women from the kitchen staff and the main house clustered. Helen stood among them, restrained by Mary. Fanny was there, too, with William in her arms. Ketch and Samuel rushed toward the kitchen house. Maria saw him coming, and relief washed over her tired face; obviously, she had feared he had lit himself ablaze. When he took over her duties at the pump, she turned away without a word, bearing an unusual pallor, a vaguely familiar one. Her husband rushed over as if first seeing her and took her by the hand to pull her away from the kitchen house. His displeased glance told Ketch that he, unlike Maria, had known better than to think his wayward worker had torched himself.

"Go to Helen," Mallory urged his wife in a gentle but firm tone. "There's plenty of hands to help."

The quickness with which Maria obeyed struck Ketch and brought home the realization of what lay behind her poor color and unusual weakness. But he could think no more of her condition as he concentrated on filling the buckets others thrust under the spigot.

Once the kitchen house appeared no longer in danger, everyone stopped to watch the fire complete its destruction of Ketch's dwelling. The wooden fuel turned to charred ruin, the chimney a black pillar, the only thing left standing. Ketch, drenched in sweat from the day's heat as well as from the fire, felt a mixture of relief and sadness.

Finally free, Helen ran to him and took hold of his hand. "Oh, Mr. Ketch, your house! We was afeared you was inside."

"Don't fret, child. You can see I'm not roasted, can't you?"

His tone appeared to take her aback, and she studied him with curiosity and bemusement. Equally weighty was Jack Mallory's gaze from near the kitchen house. Ketch looked one last time at the skeletal, smoking remains of the cabin then returned to the mule team.

***

At the end of the workday, Ketch drove the wagon back to the stables, Samuel silent next to him, the small gang of slaves in the wagon bed also quiet. Ketch could imagine the stories that would be woven in both Leighlin House and the slave settlement about today's mysterious fire. Surely all were wagering that he had set the conflagration, that he had completely lost his faculties at last and would now return to his old ways.

In the stable-yard, Jemmy met them to attend to the mules. "Mr. Ketch, sir. Miss Maria said for you to come in for supper with Samuel and sleep in the Big House."

But Ketch had no intention of going to Leighlin House. As long as William was there, that was all that mattered. Staying among the other men would be uncomfortable for all involved, as well as dangerous, for if one of them dared speak a single indiscreet word about Isabelle or their child, Ketch knew he would irreparably injure the offender.

"Jump up to the house, boy," Ketch ordered. "Give Miss Maria my regrets and tell her I'll be sleepin' here in the tack room. And fetch me back some o' that supper I can smell, along with a tankard of ale, hear?"

"What about the mules, sir?"

"I reckon Samuel will let me have one o' his boys to see to 'em till you get back. Now shove off."

When Jemmy returned with a large bowl of beef stew and a tankard of ale, Ketch had already settled upon Jemmy's cot in the tack room. He said nothing to the boy, who eagerly left when waved out.

The food held little interest for Ketch, but he forced it down anyway, finding much more satisfaction in the ale. Both made him feel considerably better, and he lay back upon the cot and watched the orange light of the setting sun paint the pane of the room's single window. Slowly the colors faded to pink then gray, and eventually darkness swallowed the room where he lay on his back, breathing in the comforting aroma of well-oiled leather, listening to the quiet sounds of the horses eating hay in their stalls.

He had half-expected, half-hoped that Maria and Helen would bring William to him as they had last night, but by now it was far too late; William would be asleep in Leighlin House as would Helen. And with any luck, today's destructive display would ensure that the child would remain there, away from his unstable father.

***

That night and throughout the next workday, Ketch thought often of William, missed him in a subtle way. He did not worry about the boy, though, fully confident in Maria's care of him. Perhaps by now she had convinced her husband that William would indeed be better off living with them. Maybe the loss of her own babies would help forge a desire to keep the infant.

When he and Samuel arrived at Leighlin House's lower level that evening for supper, Thomas awaited with a message that summoned Ketch to the front portico after he had eaten.

After making sure to bolster his courage with the hearty meal and plenty of beer, Ketch reported to the portico. Mallory was there but not alone; Maria sat in a chair next to him, avoiding Ketch's gaze. Josiah Smith sat at the far end of the portico, puffing upon a pipe, staring out across the sward and the grazing sheep, never acknowledging Ketch. Ketch had a distinct feeling from Smith's unusual distance and the tension in the air that Mallory and his wife had recently quarreled, and that Smith had wisely sailed clear of the confrontation. Mallory had a harried look about him, and instead of the lemonade that Maria sipped, he drank brandy. But he offered neither to Ketch, nor even a chair. Ketch had hoped to see William here and wanted to ask of him but could tell by Mallory's clouded brow that he should hold his tongue until spoken to. Helen's absence foretold the gravity of the coming conversation.

"Maria told me what happened down by the river the other day," Mallory began. When Ketch's dismayed gaze went to Maria, the young man continued, "Don't be angry with her. She was only trying to help you. She told me what you asked for your son. Of course, I told her it was out of the question, especially considering that in another seven months or so she will have our own child to care for, God willing."

This confirmation of Ketch's suspicion, along with Mallory's uncharacteristic invocation of God, amazed him, but still Maria refused to look at him. At first, he thought her avoidance stemmed from what Mallory was about to say regarding William, but now he sensed that she was greatly disappointed in him…again, perhaps a disappointment deeper than any before. Considering her miscarriages, she probably thought him an ungrateful bastard for wanting to be rid of his son.

"However," Mallory continued after a swallow of brandy, "I have to agree with your belief that your son would be better off in the care of someone other than yourself."

Hearing another person say this, especially Jack Mallory, jarred Ketch, unsettled him, though he knew he should rejoice at the young man's realization.

"So," Mallory said, "when I was in Charles Town today, I met with Malachi Waterston and proposed on your behalf that William live with his grandmother. It took some convincing on my part to get him to agree to a possible contract. He fears, of course, that William will interfere too much with Louisa's duties to his own household. As you know, they have their second child now. But I told him the contract, should you agree to it, would be null and void if he finds that raising William is too much of a distraction for Louisa. The agreement would include you providing a monthly stipend for the boy's care. Waterston said he would agree under the condition that when William comes of age, he will be beholden to Waterston for a term of seven years, either as a servant or, if he shows an aptitude, as an apprentice in his business." Mallory's brown eyes darkened. "Maria is convinced your behavior lately is strictly because of Isabelle's death. That's understandable, of course, to an extent, so I'll give you the benefit of the doubt when it comes to grieving for your wife. By taking the responsibility of rearing your son from you, I will expect no further…distractions, or destruction. Do you understand?"

Ketch nodded shallowly, his mind spinning with all he had been presented. The terms were fair, yet the very thought of bartering over the future of Isabelle's child made him sick to his stomach and increased his shame. But he should be grateful, he told himself. William would be better off with Louisa, in a warm family home with other children. And perhaps apprenticing with someone of Waterston's standing would also promote William's interests later in life, would raise him to something more than a plantation hand or a carpenter, someone who could escape the violence of his heritage.

"Will you agree to Waterston's terms? Or do you need time to think about it?"

His cold expression caused Ketch to struggle to find his voice. He whispered, "I agree to 'em."

Maria emitted a small, exasperated sigh, and finally looked at Ketch. He realized she had wanted him to disagree with her husband, had wanted him to show some determination to overcome his flaws as a father. Frowning, he stared at his feet, felt lower than ever before. He had to clear his throat for his next words to come out in something other than a croak.

"When will William leave?"

"Maria and I will be visiting the Waterstons tomorrow; we'll take William with us, and I'll bring the documents back for you to sign, unless you wish to go with us."

Ketch rubbed his beard, could say nothing more for fear of losing his precarious resolve.

"When the harvest is over, you and Samuel will be in charge of rebuilding the cabin. Once finished, you and Samuel will live there. In the meantime, you may remain in the tack room, if you prefer."

Sharing the cabin was, he guessed, Maria's idea, to keep him from being alone.

"Good night, Ketch," Mallory dismissed him.

Ketch wanted to ask to see William but feared his request being rejected as much as he feared looking upon the child. He managed to mutter his hollow thanks before turning to leave the portico with heavy steps.

***

Although Ketch normally slept late on Sunday, especially prior to his marriage, he was awake at sunrise. He had gotten little rest, the remote tack room accentuating his singular existence. All night he had battled within himself over the predicament with William, with what he felt was best for the child versus what Isabelle would have wanted. Though he now had a solution, thanks to Jack Mallory, it failed to leave him with the peace of mind for which he had hoped. He felt cowardly yet reminded himself over and over that Charles Town would offer William many more viable opportunities than Leighlin, especially considering how much the community would have grown by the time William was a young man. And Louisa knew all about raising a child.

Ketch knew that he should accompany his son to Waterston's but feared Louisa's reaction to his decision. How well he remembered the doubts in her eyes the day he had met her. He had no desire to witness those doubts realized.

He questioned his decision to try to keep his paternity from his son, to offer only financial support. Would William start to ask questions in later years as to how he came to live in such an environment? Would Louisa be able to deny William's heritage as Ketch would insist so the boy would hold no hope that his father would reveal himself? And how would he feel about the boy when he saw him in town as he surely would on occasion? Would he have a driving urge to seek William out, to admit the truth and purge the guilt that would build over the years? And if so, what would William's reaction be? Certainly not warmth and affection, perhaps not even understanding. All too painfully, Ketch recalled his own experience seeking out his birth father. He could still hear the man's angry rejection, the foul names he had called his mother, blaming her and Ketch for wrecking his own marriage. Ketch had wanted to hate the man for his heartless irresponsibility but had instead felt empty and worthless.

The Mallorys, he surmised, would be leaving within the hour to catch the remainder of the tide down the Ashley, to take Isabelle's child away. Surely they would bring William by the tack room for farewells, but Ketch knew after the long, brutal night that he could not look upon his son, for he feared he would crumble. So he left the stables, crossed the sward far from the house, and headed past the burned cabin to his wife's grave, to be with her, to try to explain himself, to convince both of them.

But his effort to avoid detection fell short. Helen's voice startled him from his daze where he sat next to the shaded grave in the already warm, breezeless morning. When he turned toward her approach, his blood ran cold—she was carrying William. Far behind her, Maria and her husband stood as a singular figure on the lane, the young man's arm around his wife's waist. Fanny stood a few paces behind them with a valise. The couple's attention lay upon Helen and her purposeful march and perhaps upon the grave beyond, a grave that would signify much to them with a baby on the way. Ketch now understood Mallory's conflicting emotions after he had lost his first child and his implied reluctance to compel his wife to possibly undergo a second ordeal.

If Helen was cognizant of Ketch's aversion to having his son brought so close, she showed no concern, her expression set.

"I couldn't leave without bringing Izzy her flowers."

Disturbed by her cold attitude, he forced a smile and took the three roses from atop William's swaddling, the thorns removed from each stem. The baby's clean scent drifted to him above that of the flowers; Maria had apparently bathed him. His thick dark hair was already dry. The infant, bright and inquisitive, peeked from behind Helen's arm, twisting Ketch's empty stomach into a horrible knot. He wanted to curse. If it had been anyone but Helen, even Maria, he would have ordered them away, but he could not hurt the girl's feelings, especially because her gesture was innocent. Or was it? Perhaps Maria had purposefully sent them.

"William couldn't leave without saying good-bye." She looked at the baby instead of at him. "Didn't you want to say good-bye, Mr. Ketch?"

He cleared his throat, set the roses upon the grave. "Sometimes 'tis best not to say good-bye, Miss Helen."

When he sat back, cross-legged, Helen forced William upon him. He had no choice but to cradle the child against him lest he fall into his lap.

"He likes it when you hold him. See, look how he's squirming like a little mouse."

William's face opened in what passed for a smile, breaking Ketch's heart.

"Miss Helen, there's really no time. You'll miss the tide if you tarry, and yer brother will be vexed."

"I'm going to miss him. Aren't you?"

"Of course, I will, child."

In sudden, pent-up exasperation, she demanded, "Then why, why are you sending him away?"

"'Tis just best for him. Mebbe when yer older I can explain it better."

Anger overtook her. "Daddy used to say that to me when he would sail away, but then he died, and he never got to explain. So, explain it to me now." Her adult tone revealed that she recognized his cowardice and lack of bottom. When he avoided answering her demand, she continued, "Won't you please let him stay? I could take care of him for you."

For the first time, Ketch realized just how much his son meant to Helen. Perhaps she feared that William would be the only baby she would get to play with and pamper. He had taken so much from her; how could he deny her this as well? He feared she may even revile him for it.

"Why must you send him away?" Absently, she touched the baby's toes where they had snuck into view. "Did *your* daddy send *you* away?"

A sharp, unexpected pain flared deep within Ketch. He stared at her, and she stared back, her fine jaw tight and set with fortitude. From somewhere in his turbulent mind, Sophie's lost cries echoed anew, echoed until the Thames swallowed her, as the Ashley had almost swallowed William.

His son's face twitched into a smile again. But then he seemed to sense his father's unrest, and a tiny line marred his face between his eyes, reminiscent of the two vertical creases that were now nearly a permanent mark on Ketch's face.

Ketch looked toward Jack Mallory and his wife, at their closeness, considered their patience with the moment, then he looked back at Isabelle's grave, at the roses still with a touch of dew nearly hidden among their petals, catching the light that filtered through the trees. Looking back to his son, he knew that nothing—not even sending William away—would ever remove the pain of losing Isabelle and that William should not be made to pay for his weakness. If anything, he should be thankful that William could so remind him of everything good about his wife, truly the only goodness in his entire life. And perhaps he could provide William with the father figure he never had.

In his awkward, unbalanced way, he got to his feet, holding the boy securely against him. William made a contented gurgling sound, a hiccup almost like a tiny laugh. His left arm waved in the air, fingers curling and uncurling, as if wanting to touch his father's beard. Ketch put his lips to the baby's fingers, closed his eyes as William gave him a tweak.

Helen stood but said no more, watching closely. When Ketch took deliberate steps toward the Mallorys, his strides at first short and uneven then growing longer and more assured, Helen hurried to keep up, her eyes always upon him.

Ketch expected to see displeasure upon the Mallorys' faces, perhaps impatience. But Maria looked hopefully at him, seemingly holding her breath, fingers tightening upon her husband's arm. Mallory hid his emotions as he studied Ketch.

"I want for William to stay."

His declaration took a moment to reach master and mistress, but Helen reacted with a release of physical tension, hopping up and down with a cheer.

"I know what yer thinkin'," Ketch pressed onward, "and I don't blame you. And mebbe I won't be able to do right by him, but…I need to try. I want to try."

Maria breathed again, and a smile broke across her face.

"Please, John." Helen tugged on her brother's sleeve. "Let William stay. I promise to help with him. He won't cause any trouble. He's such a good boy, really. You even said so yourself last night, remember?"

The young man's face colored, and he cleared his throat.

Helen continued without a pause. "He and Mr. Ketch could stay in the chamber next to mine since they don't have a home of their own."

"Helen." Maria touched her shoulder, gently shushed her. Helen bit her lip, pressed her hands together as if this would help dam her flow of petitions.

Ketch waited for Mallory to speak. William watched his father with an odd intensity before the infant's tenuous focus shifted to Maria and her husband, and he wriggled a bit as if delighted over something, his legs kicking.

"Perhaps," Mallory started in a measured voice, "it would be cruel of me not to let him stay. That is, *if* you truly are committed to him."

Relief and hope spread through Ketch. "Aye. 'Tis what Izzy would want. 'Tis what I want. Leighlin is William's home…and mine. We should be together."

Maria's hand drifted down to take her husband's hand, and they exchanged a knowing look. Mallory's attention shifted to William, who had quieted his enthusiastic sounds. The young man smiled. At that moment, everything became clear to Ketch—his master's intentions to send William away had been a fabrication, a ruse to make William's father realize what needed to be done and to willingly embrace that responsibility, that blessing.

Pleasure in the success of his plan reflected in Mallory's grin as he said, "I fancy we should be on our way. Don't want to miss the tide, do we, Maria?" He reached for Helen's hand. "Perhaps you and William should come too, Ketch. I'm sure Louisa would love to meet her grandson."

AUTHOR'S NOTE

When I wrote my Jack Mallory trilogy, Ketch was always a favorite character of mine. He started out a bit one dimensional in the early drafts of *The Prodigal*, but a friend of mine encouraged me to flesh him out, reminding me that no one is all bad or all good. So, that's what I did, and his role in the trilogy grew and took on an importance I had never imagined at the beginning.

Once I had finished the trilogy, there was one nagging question that remained: Did Edward Ketch ever find love? That single question inspired me to write this novel. The poor guy had been through so much hell in his life, he deserved some happiness. I'm glad I could give him some, albeit still with a sprinkle of tragedy.

If you haven't visited the wonderful city of Charleston, South Carolina, I encourage you to do so. My research trips there were wonderful. Some readers will recognize Drayton Hall on the cover of this novel. That was a photo I took during one of those trips. Drayton Hall and Middleton Plantation were inspirations for various aspects of Leighlin Plantation, as well as the Archers' plantation, Wildwood, which is seen throughout my Jack Mallory trilogy.

A word about the slave dialect portrayed in this novel. Of course, we don't know exactly how slaves spoke in 17th century Carolina. Many slaves then were first generation Africans, so they wouldn't have known English except what they picked up from their enslavers. It makes sense that there would not have been the prevalence of English as a primary language until later generations. As a writer, I wanted to convey a flavor of dialect without making it a distraction to the reader. It's always a precarious balance for an author. So, hopefully, the linguists out there won't be too incensed.

Lastly, I would like to thank authors Tinney Heath and Kim Rendfeld for their help with this manuscript.

Made in the USA
Middletown, DE
15 November 2019

78735177R00203